Dead Edge

Jack Ford

ONE PLACE. MANY STORIES

HQ
An imprint of HarperCollins*Publishers* Ltd
1 London Bridge Street
London SE1 9GF

This paperback edition 2018

1

First published in Great Britain by
HQ, an imprint of HarperCollins*Publishers* Ltd 2018

ISBN: 978-0-00-820458-7

Printed and bound in Great Britain by
CPI Group (UK) Ltd, Croydon, CR0 4YY

In loving memory of my Mum and
Dad – always and forever.

'And ye shall know the truth, and the truth shall make you free' (John 8.32)

CENTRAL INTELLIGENCE AGENCY MOTTO

'It is estimated that between 26.4 million and 36 million people abuse opioids worldwide, with an estimated 2.5 million people in the United States abusing prescription opioids'

— US CENTERS FOR DISEASE CONTROL
AND PREVENTION

THE ENDGAME – The Endgame is the last stage of chess when only a few pieces are remaining. Not having the skills to turn the resulting endgame into a checkmate can cost you many wins, turning many otherwise easily won positions into draws or... even losses.

1

CHESS MOVE d4 Nf6

Heartburn, or whatever the hell it was, had a way of creeping up at the most inconvenient of times – at least that's what Huck Barrington Jnr. liked to tell himself the burning sensation and fluctuating pain was.

Letting his symptoms occupy such a bromidic term was certainly easier to digest than acknowledging the pre-cursor warning signs of the heart attack his cardiologist liked to tell him – on a depressingly regular basis – was waiting round some proverbial corner for him. And, if scaring the hell out him wasn't enough, his physician sanctimoniously backed it up by talking figures, like some smart-ass Wall Street statistician. Figures of the millions of Americans killed each year by ventricular fibrillation. The number one killer in the US. Jeez, the guy made it sound like a sniper was on the loose.

Aggravated, Huck sighed. Rubbed his chest.

Knew it only served as a purely psychological curative, and decided to convince himself for the third time in the same amount of minutes that it was just acid reflux, caused by the extra portion of eggs over easy and red sliced onion he'd had at the grill bar in the entrance of the airport. Despite being a married man – twelve long years married – Huck had to accept the pretty waitress with the honey blond hair, size eight waist, and showgirl bust had featured in his decision to stay to feed his unsatisfied hunger.

He burped.

Loudly.

Loud enough for the grey haired lady next to him in the check-in line to sniff the air and turn her head away in disgust.

Not apologising, Huck caught the eye of a girl who was stood a few feet away by the escalator, under the large American flag hanging down from the ceiling. She was staring at him. What the hell her problem was he didn't know. Well he'd go on ahead and stare right back. Ended up being the first to turn away.

With a dampened ego – never something Huck Barrington Jnr. took lightly – he chanced another side glance. Damn her, she was still staring. Can't have been more than fourteen. Wore an oversized thick blue jacket along with thick blue jeans. Small. Olive skinned. Plaits too tight. Skin blemish free, unburdened by the curse of adolescent acne which had plagued his own teenage years.

He sighed again. Turned away. Glanced around. And thanked God – though being an atheist he knew it was a very loose term – that he was catching a flight to Pittsburgh. The place was a sea. A heaving mass of overweight bodies dressed in white satin and frayed tassels as tourists descended on Memphis for the Elvis revival weekend. A deluge of stick-on sideburns walking through check in.

'It doesn't look like it, Mr Barrington. I'm sorry.'

Huck flushed red. 'You can't just cancel a flight and then tell me there isn't another one... There *must* be.'

'There is, sir, but like I say, the next one is full. The only available seat isn't until twenty-three, twenty.'

Huck cleared his throat. Raised his voice and spoke to the immaculately groomed airline service agent with as much disdain as he could muster. 'Perhaps I'm not making myself clear. So let me spell it out to you, *ma'am*. I don't care how you do it, but you *need* to get me onto the next Goddamn flight!'

Security stepped in. Big. Tall. Eyes dog mean.

'Is there a problem?'

Huck answered with the disdain still swirling in his mouth. 'Actually, yes there is. I want to get on my flight and get the hell out of here. That's not a crime is it?'

'Sir, there's no need to be aggressive.'

Agitated, Huck felt the prickle. The sweat. Seeping down and through his shirt.

Rubbed his chest again. Kneading. Caressing with the yellowed tips of his fingers. And over the security guy's off-white shirt shoulder, he gazed at the girl. Still staring. The look in her eyes making her seem older. Judging him, when her fledgling life gave her no room to judge.

Christ, it was getting hotter and he could hardly breathe. He scratched hurriedly at his collar as if hands held and throttled, and he pulled at and undid his top shirt button.

'Look, I just need to get my flight.'

'Sir, are you okay?'

'I'm fine.'

Huck didn't hear the agent's reply, as he felt the heat wrap round him like a snake constricting his prey. His panic rose as fast as his heart raced and the sweat rolled down. It was finally happening. This was it. This was the end. This was what his cardiologist had warned him would happen.

And as Huck waited for his heart to stop, to give up right there in the middle of the white-washed airport, his terror-filled eyes watched the girl undo her button. Undo her jacket. Mirroring his actions...

Then it suddenly hit him. Relief engulfing him as hard as terror had just done. *Goddamn* his doctor for fuelling his fears, because right then he understood what was happening. What his trouble *actually* was... He was just hot... *She* was hot. Quickly he looked around at the short sleeves and open collars. Everyone was just Goddamn hot. They were in Memphis, for God's sake.

Huck exhaled. Wiped the dripping sweat off his face. Laughed into his hands.

Loud.

'Something amusing you, sir?'

He'd forgotten about the security with the mean dog eyes. 'Far from it. I'm just hot, that's all. Hot!'

'Sir, have you been drinking?'

Ignoring the guard's question, Huck's stare flickered back to the girl. Decided to try a smile. Hell, she was only a kid after all.

He watched her continue to unfasten the buttons on her ugly, thick, blue jacket. Eyes dilated. Never blinked. Watched her mouth something to him. And Huck thought it was the darnedest of things; he was sure she just mouthed the word,

4

Sorry. He shook his head. Waved abashed and said, 'It's fine. Are you okay?'

The girl reached inside her shirt. Then with only the slightest of pauses, pressed.

The wave of the bomb mercilessly struck and tore. Showering and scattering flesh like an unlicensed slaughter-house. Smoke swelled and filled the airport as dozens of body parts lay unrecognisable in their shredded, dismembered, mutilated form. And by the blasted-out water fountain, the severed head of the 14-year-old bomber lay next to that of Huck Barrington Jnr.

2

c4 g6

The bomb went off at the same time.

Time difference two hours.

It struck with indifference. The youngest victim, a 6-month-old boy.

3

Nc3 Bg7

Jefferson County, Colorado. Taking the name of the great third President. A place where vast plains collide with the Rocky Mountains. A place of harsh, white-painted winters where summers are reminiscent of Steinbeck novels. A place where thunderstorms catch travelers off guard along the miles of trail ridge roads, curving and snaking along the skyward spans of landscapes with pine trees sweet smelling like candy stores. Jefferson County. A place where the detention center is conveniently situated by the combined court. The court where Thomas J Cooper found himself sitting in with a judge who was swathed with hell and grit-like determination to have his name chalked on a jail cell by the end of the day.

'You don't just get to ignore a court order, Mr Cooper, no matter what the reasons. It's clear you have no respect for any kind of authority, which frankly surprises me having read all about your distinguished career in the military... Mr Cooper, are you even listening to me?'

Cooper nodded. Said nothing. Thought it was best. Ninety milligrams of OxyContin and a hundred of Sertraline mixed with Valium had a way of making him not sound his best.

Cooper's lawyer stood up and cleared his throat. 'Your honor, I object to the insinuation that my client has no respect for authority. As the court knows he suffers from post-traumatic stress disorder as well as survivor guilt, in relation to the accident.'

Looking like he'd just sucked a slice of lime without the gin, the judge shook his head. 'I take it, counsel, you're referring to the accident which happened *seven, eight* years ago?'

'Yes, your honor, but… '

'*Eight* years ago, Mr Edwards. We're talking almost *eight* years.'

'What the hell has eight years got to do with it?' Cooper said.

The judge frowned. Tilted his head as if his hearing was playing tricks on him. 'Excuse me? Did you say something, Mr Cooper?'

'You're too damn right I did.'

So Cooper's old friend and attorney, Earl Edwards, the only person he knew in the county who was still willing to represent him, barked his orders. 'Coop…! Shut the hell up. I'll handle this.'

And Cooper did what he always did: whatever the hell he wanted. He stood up and then, like a game of Simon says, so did the court's bailiff, twitching and hovering his fingers over the gun in his holster, that he never got to use but practiced fast-drawing in the mirror every night. But it wasn't him Cooper was looking at. It was Earl. His deep-lined

8

face, reminding Cooper of the sand ridges along the North Carolina shores, stared into his.

Cooper watched the perspiration on Earl's forehead as he felt his own trickle of drug cold sweat trail down his neck.

'*Please*, Coop. I got this.'

'Is there a problem, counsel?' the judge asked.

Earl got there before Cooper did. Diving in like a peregrine falcon.

'No problem, your honor. No problem at all. I just need a minute to speak to my client.'

Earl dropped his voice. Real low. The kind of low saved for the movie theater.

'Coop, *please*. You're making this worse, if it can get any worse. Trust me, man, I'm in your corner, but you got to calm down and let me do my job.'

'I'm not stopping you doing your job, Earl.'

'Then sit the hell down! You know as well as I do you've messed up too many times. They're not interested anymore. Not about the accident, not about what happened to Ellie.'

Earl's words came right at Cooper. Shooting him down like a small-caliber pistol. And it was only after he felt the soft expensive silk between his fingers that he realized he was grabbing hold of Earl's suit.

'Don't you say her name! You hear me, Earl? Don't you say it!'

'Mr Edwards…! Mr Cooper! Can I remind you we're in court of law and not in some high school locker room! Any more behavior like that and you'll *both* find yourself in the cells tonight.'

Earl shot Cooper a stare.

Pushed him off.

Made sure he sat back down in the chair.

'Sorry, your honor. It's just important the court understands...'

'Mr Edwards, I hope you're not going to start lecturing the court.'

'No...No, it's just my client has been in Africa for the past few weeks and...

The judge brought the gavel down hard, prompting Cooper to think of the end of a record breaking bid at Christie's auction house. 'Sit down, counsellor, you can save the speech till after lunch.'

'But...'

With his waxy pallor further bleached by the rows of fluorescent lights which'd just been flicked on, and his Southern state voice sounding like each word was being played by an over tightened instrument from Manny's music store, Judge Saunders said, 'Mr Edwards, I advise you to listen to me, not least because my highly acidic stomach will not sit quietly through a long speech telling me how remorseful your client is for not turning up for his court-ordered psychological sessions, nor how contrite he is about the fact he's only done three hours of the fifty-two hours' community service he was sentenced to on June 9th. Whilst I'm sure your reasons will certainly try to appease the state of Colorado, at this moment in time, counsel, they certainly won't appease me. I therefore think it's wise to take a recess. However, let me warn you and Mr Cooper here: even when the irregularities of the body are once again in a state of contented realignment, I have to say that after hearing from the treating doctor on Mr Cooper's psychological and drug rehabilitation progress report earlier, I already feel inclined to revoke his formal probation.'

'Your honor, I...'

'Mr Edwards, cut it right there and save the surprised look for the junior judges; we've all been to law school... You and your client were warned this might happen when the court changed Mr Cooper's probation from summary to formal. And I'm sure I don't have to remind you that to get your client to attend court today, the sheriff's office had to pick him up from whatever hole he was hiding in. So it seems clear to me with no progression being made, even with the gift horse of prohibition, that a jail term, with sentencing in a couple of weeks, might be the only way to proceed. So if I were you, Mr Edwards, I'd think very carefully about what you're going to say to the court this afternoon when we return at two thirty.'

4

e4 d6

The call came as no surprise, nor what was said, nor how it was said. Rounded. Meticulous pronunciation intentionally concealing the foreign accent. 'We had a deal.'

'Not that deal. You know that was never on the table. It's impossible. I told you that before. I would never and *could* never agree to it. You know that.'

'What I know is you have to make this happen. However you do that is entirely up to you,' the caller said.

'I won't be put in this position.'

'You won't? Are you sure about that?'

'Abso-goddamn-lutely.'

There was a pause before the caller said. 'Then we carry on until you're persuaded otherwise. Though I am surprised. I would've thought the message of bombs and countless dead would be enough to make you realize there's only one way out of this… The toll of the dead is in your hands.'

'Goddamn you! I gave you all I could.'

The caller laughed mockingly. 'No, *we* gave you all we could. You got what you wanted and now we want something in return.'

'You had it already. There is no more. And you know nothing was ever one sided. What we had was a fair deal. We both know that and we both got what we needed… Look, even if I wanted to do this, what you're asking is an impossibility. I can't do it on my own. There are two people needed to make such an action happen. It isn't just me. It's not like before.'

'Then you find a way for the other person to see it your way. I don't think you want a war. I think you have enough of those already… But if it does come to that, it'll be like nothing you've seen before. Hell will be unleashed.'

'And you don't think there'd be a war, a massive fall-out if I did what you were asking? You do know who he is and what he stands for?'

The contempt from the caller was palpable. 'What *you* say he stands for.'

'What I *know* he stands for. What you're asking doesn't make sense! It's not in either of our best interests, because we'll end up coming after you… It can only end one way. Jesus Christ, you gotta see that this will cause a resurgence and reignite everything we've fought against for the past few years… I can't do it. The answer's no.'

The caller's tone was light but heavy with threat. 'I pride myself on my English but it seems you're not understanding me clearly. This is not a negotiation. We shall cast terror into the hearts of those who disbelieve. Their habitation is the fire and you will suffer in this life and go to hell in the next.'

'Listen to me and listen carefully…'

The caller interrupted. 'No, it's you who'll listen… Eventually you'll realize you need to sacrifice a pawn to continue with the game you started.'

'But it isn't a pawn, is it? We're not talking about a pawn.'

'That depends on how you look at it. And in case you think that this is just an empty threat, we have another reminder for you. Hopefully this one will help to persuade you to come to the right decision.'

'You bastard. You don't have to do this.'

'Look at it this way. At least you've got a warning this time… Next Wednesday, the government building. Eighteen forty-five hours. Chatham, Illinois… Do what you think's right.'

5

Nf3 O-O

'What the hell did you think you were doing in there?'

Earl Edwards slammed Cooper hard against the cool tiles of the court house restroom, reminding Cooper of the fact Earl had been the high school wrestling champion.

'Earl, listen...'

He slammed again. Only this time harder. High school state champion three years running.

'Don't. I don't want to hear any crap coming out of your mouth, Coop. But I do want to know why only one of us was trying back there? It's always the same with you, Coop. Destroy everything you got going for you. If it's jail you want to go to, carry on doing what you're doing.'

A bald guy on the wrong side of two hundred pounds walked in. Looked at them. Walked right out.

'What do you want me to do, Earl?'

'I want you to let me do my job! And let me tell you something, Coop, you're not making that easy. Look at you. We're here to try to convince the court you got it together. That you're willing to do the programs. But can you do that?

The hell you can. You come here so wired I'm surprised you can even hold your head up... Where did that tall, handsome, clean-living guy go to, Coop?'

This time Cooper slammed *Earl* hard. Reminding *him* of the fact he'd been the armed forces wrestling champion... *Four* years in a row. 'Don't pull that one on me, Earl. Not you. I'm trying, okay. Things have been a bit tough lately.'

'Coop, you're losing it, man. We all get what's going on. We all feel for you, but when's it going to stop? You've messed up your marriage. You're messing up your job. And it's starting all over again.'

'I don't know what you're talking about.'

'I'm talking about Ellie.'

There it was again. The shot. Only this time it wasn't done with a small-caliber pistol. This time Cooper felt the hit from a Remington pump.

His breathing was fast. Hard. Short. Shallow. Damn it, he could hardly get his breath.

'What did I say, Earl...? I told you, didn't I? I made myself real clear... I said, Earl, don't say her name. But what do you go and do...?'

Cooper punched his fist into one of the cubicle doors, swinging it wide open. Any other time a guy sitting on the john with his pants round his ankles and a face full of shock might've made him smile. Right now, there was nothing funny about anything.

'... You went and said her Goddamn name.'

Earl shook his head. His left cheek going into tiny pulsating spasms. Always did when he was under stress. Always

16

did when he was about to say something he knew Cooper wasn't going to like.

'You listen to me right now. You're freefalling, man. I don't know *exactly* what's happened in the past couple of weeks, but I do know you're going backwards. We all love you. I don't know another guy who's got a big a heart as you do, or is as loyal. But since you got back from the Congo, I don't recognize you.'

It was Cooper's turn to shake his head but he added his hand, interweaving fingers through his strawberry blonde hair. It needed a cut. Hell, when didn't it? 'You sound like my wife.'

'I would do if you even had one anymore. And that's my point. Why throw it away because of...'

Cooper's hands pounded into Earl's chest. He stumbled back. 'You really going to say her name again?'

'I don't have to because we both know who we're talking about. Judge Saunders is right. It's been almost eight years since the accident. *Eight.* And you know something, Coop? You're as dead as she is.'

Cooper's fist found Earl's mouth before he'd decided what he was going to do. It split open like the skins of the fried red tomatoes at Mama's diner on Main Street.

'What is it with you? What is it with any of you? You of all people, Earl. You really saying that I shouldn't at least have *tried* to find her? You think I was wasting my time looking for someone I loved? Do you, Earl? Is that what you think?'

Cooper watched Earl get up from the floor. Wiped his suit before his mouth. He said, 'What I think is you need to let it go.'

Cooper stepped in close. Real close. Close enough to smell the blood on Earl's lip. 'I don't care what you think I need to do, Earl. I don't care what the others think. But for your information, I have given up on it... on finding her, but the guilt... the guilt, Earl, it kills me. From the moment I open my eyes to the time I go to sleep.'

'Coop, listen...'

Earl stretched out his arms, with his six-foot frame three inches shorter than Cooper's. Giving Cooper that look which cut him down like a cotton plant at harvest back in Missouri. The look which told Cooper he was being unreasonable. The look Earl had given him when they'd had their first fight back in high school over twenty-five years ago. And like then, Cooper knew Earl was right. But like then, Cooper pushed those feelings away and looked right past him.

'Coop, come on. This is me. Earl. What you trying to do? Drive me away? Because that's never going to happen. Come on, dude. I'm your friend.'

'If you're my friend, you'll get off my back.' He opened the restroom door to go.

'Coop!'

It took five paces along the highly polished floor of the court house corridor before Cooper turned round. Five paces and one thought...

'Earl, I'm sorry... I don't know what's wrong with me. I appreciate what you're trying to do, but...'

Interrupting, Earl glanced at his inexpensive wristwatch. 'Shut the hell up and listen. We haven't got time. There's many a bar in town and many a beer we can do this over, but for now we gotta put everything aside and work out how we're going to keep you out of jail. You've given Judge Saunders all the ammo he needs. So we gotta have a plan when we go back in there… Coop…! Coop! What the hell are you doing?'

Cooper lurched forward and grabbed hold of the woman who'd just hurried past him in her tight cream suit and curls done up too high. 'Ma'am, what did you say to that man?'

She looked flustered and affronted all at once. 'What?'

'To that man back there… I heard you say something. I need you to repeat what you've just said.'

Maybe it was because she heard something in Cooper's voice, or it was the fact he was still holding onto her arm, but she answered. Real quickly. As quickly as Earl had done back in the courtroom to the judge.

'I… I heard on the news. There's been a bomb. Suicide bombers apparently. Several in fact. Also shootings. Lots of people dead. Memphis, Washington… Denver. Apparently they're saying the President was there.'

'Where? Where was he?'

'He was in Denver when one of the blasts went off. They said on the news he was visiting an elementary school…'

Cooper shook her as if trying to shake the words right out of her rouged mouth. He said. 'What else?'

'I… I… I don't know.'

'But is he okay?'

'I don't know… I guess.'

'But you don't know? You don't know for sure?'

'No… No… They didn't say.'

Cooper didn't even bother looking at Earl. Just ran. Heard him calling after him. Didn't stop. Didn't turn. He needed to go. And fast. Problem was he'd forgotten how fast his friend was.

Earl caught up with a heavy pant. Holding onto Cooper as they stood under the glass dome of the Jeffco court house.

'Coop, what's going on? What the hell are you doing? Where are you going?'

Cooper couldn't see for the sweat which ran down his face in rivulets. 'Let go of me, Earl. I gotta go.'

'Is this something to do with the President?'

'I'll call you. I swear.'

Earl's words followed Cooper. Landing on nothing but the still, dry heat of the afternoon.

'Don't bother… You hear me, Coop…? Don't you bother!'

6

Be2 e5

The hard concrete of Jefferson County Parkway pounded through Cooper's sneakers. Pounding through his head as he sprinted along the tree-lined sidewalk. Pulled down heavy from the drugs whilst the Colorado sun scorched a pattern of fire on his back. Parked car after parked car. Empty vehicle after empty vehicle fuelling his alarm.

He stumbled as he ran, looking for a cab in the deserted streets and not realizing the loud cry for help he'd heard had come from him, until the call of panic cut at the back of his throat. The only thought making sense to Cooper was somehow he had to make the twelve mile trip to Denver.

The sound of a car, an engine, had Cooper spinning round. He squinted. Shielded his eyes from the sun. And there on the other side of the road, driving down the public highway, like water to a thirsty coyote, was a rusting grey Honda.

Cooper exhaled. Long. Hard. Tasting every second of the relief because although the driver didn't know it yet, Cooper knew *that* car was going to be his one-way ticket to Denver.

Quickly he darted across the middle section. Scrabbling up and along as the Honda began to drive past him. Briefly Cooper thought about hailing, waving the guy down like he was summoning a yellow Checker taxi in NYC. But for once, sense kept his mouth shut and his hand firmly by his side. His mind was messed up, but even he wasn't going to bet on the driver stopping for a sweat drenched, wild-eyed guy.

Cooper dug for an energy he wasn't sure he had, trying to push himself forward, feeling the burn of his legs as he ran to get in front of the station wagon.

He dived.

Threw himself round in a one eighty.

Closed his eyes.

Heard the slamming of brakes accompanied by the noise of the horn which told him he was still alive.

He peeled his fingers off the burning hot metal of the hood, thumping his fist on top of the roof to counteract the pain, then watched as the driver's eyes welled with terror. Three hundred and twenty pounds of fear. His stunned deliberation – as to whether to risk driving off or not – costing him, giving Cooper the chance to fling open the door.

'Hey, sir, how's it goin'?'

The gaping mouth full of nachos and the remains of a cheese dip on his lap made Cooper feel bad for the guy.

'Here's the thing, sir. I need your help. I'm not going to hurt you but I need to borrow your car.'

The guy started choking. Real hard. Guacamole-colored saliva dripped from his mouth and onto his chin. He gave no words to Cooper, just nodded like a marionette on a string, his jowls wet with drool as he cowered from the hard pat on his back from Cooper.

'Look, it'll be okay... My name's Thomas J. Cooper. If you go inside the court, ask for an Earl Edwards. He's my attorney. He'll vouch for me... I *will* return your car, sir. But hey, you can always ride along with me if you're concerned that I won't bring it back. Or if you prefer, you can always get out here.'

Cooper didn't blame the guy. Heck, he didn't blame him at all, though he reckoned it was the fastest the Guacamole guy had run since high school.

7

O-O Nc6

Cooper put his foot down and drove. Over the mid-section of Weimer Street. Over the sidewalk of Johnson Road. Over anything that got in his path. Swerving. Weaving through traffic. Keeping his eyes out for the cops as he sped down the freeway towards Denver.

Sign read, 60.

Speedometer read, eighty-five.

Sign read, Do Not Pass.

Cooper undertook using the shoulder.

Whatever it took to get there.

Trickles of sweat bled between his fingers, causing his hand to slip as he jabbed at the radio buttons trying to listen to the news of the unfolding events. To anything which would tell him *where*. How. But as for *why*, he needed to leave that one for another day.

*

Fifteen minutes in and Cooper was gripping onto the Honda's steering wheel as if he had it in some kind of neck lock. Keeping it from running right out from under him. He was wired and if the drugs had worn off he couldn't tell. The adrenalin hitting him harder than any handful of OxyContin ever could.

A couple of hundred yards past the Denver health center at the top of Bannock street, the crowd worked better than any satnav could, showing Cooper he'd arrived at his destination. A phalanx of the bewildered, of the traumatized, of cops, of news anchors, formed and filled the street.

Not bothering for the car to stop fully, nor waiting to turn off the engine, Cooper opened the door. Jumped out and raced into the crowds, pushing through, ramming and wedging himself towards the front.

'Move it…! Move it…! Get the hell out of my way!'

He gave loan of his emotions to a stranger, turning and yelling in his face as if somehow it was he who'd caused this pain… Panic. Terror inside him.

'Did the bomb go off here…? Where's the President…? Is he still in the school…? Answer me, dammit.'

The dark-haired stranger's head lolled back and forth as Cooper held his shoulders. Tight. Shaking. Hell, he just wanted answers and he didn't care how he was going to get them.

'No…'

That was all he needed. Didn't need more. More would've cost time.

Frantically, Cooper ran back to the car, and without looking to see if anyone was in his way the Honda burnt up rubber as he reversed the car, taking it into a J-turn.

Clutch in.

Clutch out.

Shift to first.

Up and along the side walk, over the mound, banging the gears full throttle. Didn't know where he was going but wherever it was he knew he had to find it.

Within five minutes, Cooper had got himself back on the highway and beyond, forcing the rusting station wagon well outside its limits. Sun in his eyes. Pain behind them. A migraine screwing in. He pressed his palm against them to stop the throb. Took his hands off the wheel for only a moment. But he knew that's all it took.

The Honda swerved, running onto the grassland like a breakaway horse. Smashing and slamming the axle along the rock scattered terrain, dragging the steering off balance as the brakes began to lock.

Fighting to regain control, Cooper drove into a snaking skid whilst the mismatched tires ploughed up the prairies. And although it took less than a minute to pull up sharp, for the second time that day, he trembled as he exhaled. Real long. Real hard.

He rubbed his head, for all the good it did. Glanced at the sun. Knew he was looking due east. And then Cooper looked some more. But it wasn't the direction that interested him. It was what was on the crest of the hill.

Without hesitation, Cooper floored the accelerator, forcing the old '83 Honda's speedometer to touch and quiver at ninety. The engine was racing faster than the car seemed to be able to move. Smoke was billowing up and the smell of burn-out filled the car, but it could've blasted right in half for all Cooper cared. As long as it got him over that ditch he was headed for… He angled the car so he could hit it like a ramp. Fast. Forward. But most of all up. Cooper knew it needed to go up.

A dense cloud of smoke thickened in the car's interior, making it difficult to see, while the car juddered at maximum speed. 'Come on…! Come on…! Come on!'

Wheels hit the edge at well over a hundred. A brief sense of suspension followed by a bone-shattering impact.

Head flicked back.

Front teeth sunk deep into his tongue.

Blood filled his mouth.

The Honda nose-dived, crashing into the hard ground on the other side. The engine seized and the grey driver's door swung open. Fell right off.

Desperately, Cooper rolled out. Running. Scrabbling. Holding his shoulder at the same time as trying to pop it back into its socket. He ignored the pain and the cold sweat and the clothes sticking and the blood dripping down his chin like he was the Guacamole guy.

But none of it mattered to Cooper because now he could see the President's black motorcade in the distance. And as crazy as he knew it was, right there was where he was heading.

*

Cooper felt it before he knew what was happening and it took him clear off his feet. Sending him through the air. Heat and energy expanding, blast-waves of air rushing out from the Honda as it exploded into a fireball of orange flame. Black smoke storming up to fill the skies.

The explosion flung him down as unceremoniously as it'd picked him up. Thundering him into the ground. Pain shot through his ribs, ricocheting into his shoulder, whilst teeth once again found his tongue to sink deeply into.

Sucking up the pain Cooper crawled onto his knees. Pushed himself up onto his feet. He didn't turn but he could hear sirens. Cars breaking away from the motorcade. Drawn by the blast, racing towards him.

Instinct had him running but he was aware there was nowhere to run on the grass covered plain. They were closing in. Herding him up like the buffalo.

He could almost feel the heat from their engines as the Tannoyed words crashed across the quiet of the Colorado land.

'STOP! THIS IS THE FBI… GET ON THE GROUND… DO IT NOW…! I REPEAT, THIS IS THE FBI… GET ON THE GROUND OR WE WILL SHOOT!'

Then, like someone had reached into his body to tear out his muscles, a raw torture of fifty thousand volts surged through him, dropping Cooper hard onto his knee caps.

Neck snapping back.

Eyes rolling up to sockets…

… teeth through tongue.

8

d5 Ne7

It was the call he was expecting. Later than he thought. But with the same meticulous pronunciation. And once again there were no surprises. None.

The caller said, 'I congratulate you on your initiative. I must say I'm impressed. I did wonder how it'd play out because there's no doubt that you couldn't afford anyone to find out exactly what it is you're doing. Have done... Are about to do. Though next time there won't be any warning. There'll be casualties. Lots. Next time we'll let slip the dogs of war. Unleash hell. And make no mistake, there *will* be another 9/11.'

9

Nd2 a5

On any other day the boy would've wiped away the large droplets of sweat which sat and mixed with the dust on his sun scorched skin. But today was different. Today he needed to concentrate and finish off the present he'd been making for his mother. And although the brightly colored paper collage had been trickier and taken longer than he'd imagined, he was certain she'd be pleased.

His faded Mickey Mouse T-shirt, and bleached out jeans held up by a piece of string, gave him little cool. And the corrugated roof, like iron waves sitting on the brick house, painted in hues of summer barley, gave him no shade. But he smiled, his happiness as it always was; warm and strong like the winds which blew across the burnt yellow grasslands under the African skies.

Above the sound of the exciting buzzing of flies, a noise in the distance made the boy look up. He tilted his head, listening again. Not recognizing the sound. Frowning, he got up, only then wiping the sweat off his face, leaving the precious collage on the ground.

He walked forward to the wide dirt road, the dust like a haze making the sun seem darker than it should be and the afternoon seem later than it was. Beneath his feet a rumble. He looked down at them curiously, as if somehow they would speak and tell him of the mystery of shudder.

The tremble began to become harder and with it the noise greater. Roaring louder, reminding him of the stories of the animals which preyed and stalked in the forests. He shivered at the thought of such creatures but curiosity moved him forward. He was, after all, seven years old, and at seven years old, he knew he was almost a man.

With renewed vigor, the boy stood in the middle of the road, looking into the thick haze which swirled and churned. Then like his mother pulling back the tattered drapes each morning, the curtain of dust parted, sweeping aside to reveal a huge object which reminded him of the giant horned beetles.

His face smiled, delighted at whatever it was that was moving towards him. His face a spectacle of amazement, of wonder, as the mechanical insects trundled forwards.

'Run Bako… run!'

The boy whipped round at the cry of his name then watched as a vision of red burst up from the man's head like a sequencing fountain before it imploded, splitting apart into pieces.

Bako's scream seemed to freeze in the air, almost as if his anguished cry hung suspended, trapped between the visible heatwaves rising up from the road.

A loud explosion behind Bako triggered him to run as balls of flame fired from armored tanks burnt and blazed alongside him. He heard the cries of people, of neighbors, of friends as they fell, picked off, and pools of red became their final resting place.

Tears welled and ran down Bako's cheeks, causing his vision to become blurred. But he was glad. He didn't want to see the woman he knew dropping her baby as gleaming metal struck into her face, splitting it in half as if it were his grandfather cutting the cassava. And he didn't want to see the tiny brick church crumble as the monster tanks blew it into rubble. Nor did he want to see his mother's friend, filled with terror. Her top torn. Her skirt missing as two men dragged her inside a house. But he did want to cover his ears to drown out her screaming.

Through the machine gun fire and the grenades, Bako scrabbled along, tripping over the freshly dead. He turned the corner to see a man coming towards him holding a blood-soaked machete. Whites of eyes marbled, ruddy with rage yet laughing, opening his arms as if to embrace Bako like his uncle had done this morning.

Bako backed away, running again, now through the smell of the kill and the screams which cut through the air as violently as the parangs did.

Quickly, he headed round the back of the small brick houses, making his way home, the thought of it spurring him on to run faster, helping him to push through the pain of his torn feet.

In front of his house Bako could see his mother. Searching.

Calling his name as smoke filled the skies. She cried out. Waving as he ran into her arms.

'This way, Bako, we'll be okay if we go into the bushes. But quickly... quickly.'

They began to run, but without warning, Bako slipped his hand from his mother's, heading back towards the house.

'Bako, no! Bako! Stop!'

He could hear his mother calling but he didn't turn. He wanted to make her happy. Wanted her tears to stop falling and he thought he knew how.

Quickly Bako grabbed the collage before speeding back towards his mother.

'Bako...! Come...! Bako.'

He reached out to take her hand but it was his mother's hand which now suddenly slipped away from his, as she began to sink to the ground. Her yellow dress turning red, her eyes holding Bako's stare one last time before rolling. Closing.

This time Bako's cry splintered the air. He pulled at his mother's arm.

'Get up, mama, get up! Please get up... Look, mama, look what I made you.'

He pushed the collage to her as she lay in the tributary of blood which flowed and bubbled, stemming from the countless dead.

'See what I made for you... See, mama, see.'

He stood up, stumbling backwards, tilting his head to the sun. Blinking. And just for a moment he didn't know what it was he was feeling. A sudden warmth. Then cold. Such cold.

Glancing down, Bako touched his Mickey Mouse top. A hole where the face once was. Red. Wet.

And then slowly. So slowly. Bako dropped to the ground. His head lolling back as his body snaked, winding as it fell on top of his mother with his blood oozing, coloring the brightly painted collage red, whilst the chill of death rose and mixed with the warm winds of the ensanguined African plains.

10

Rb1 Nd7

'Get your ass up!"

Cooper could hear a voice but he wasn't sure where it was coming from. He didn't bother trying to open his eyes to find out. Hell, he'd already attempted that one. And the way he saw it, no man was born to suffer a pain like that. And as for any attempt to move, from the position he was lying in, it wasn't even an option. And so if that meant staying here forever, wherever *here* was, well, Cooper reckoned, all things considered, that was fine by him.

'You listening to me...? Give me that water, Officer.'

'Jesus Christ!'

Cooper scrabbled up as the water hit him. The sudden movement caused jolts of pain to tear through parts of his body he'd forgotten he owned. His limbs cried out in agony, along with his swollen, dried tongue which shrieked in searing, primal pain.

'Okay, now we have blast off. That's more like it... You look like shit, by the way.'

Cooper stared at Earl through paint-peeled bars whilst cold water trickled, dripping off from split ends to channel down the side of his nose and balance on his philtrum like a circus act.

Cooper cleared his throat, imagining his hands round his long term buddy's neck. 'You're enjoying this, aren't you, Earl?'

'Too damn right I am. At least in jail, you can't go and run off on me.'

'Where am I anyway?'

'Where they brought you after your cannonball run, over a *week* ago. You were lucky they didn't throw you in the county jail. Someone must've called in a favor.'

Cooper wiped his lips. Big mistake. Felt like he'd just been kicked in the mouth. 'Don't play games, Earl, tell me where I am. I haven't got time for this.'

'Oh, I think you've got plenty of time, Coop. In fact, with the list of things they want to charge you with, time seems to be all you'll have. So off the top of my head, it goes something like this. Grand theft auto, aggravated motor vehicle theft in the first degree, reckless driving, exhibition of speed, vagrancy...'

'Vagrancy?'

Earl nodded, his over-gelled, jet-black hair staying perfectly in place. 'Take that one on the chin, Coop; something tells me that charge is going to be the least of your worries. Oh, and just in case you didn't realize, this is before you add on skipping Judge Saunders' afternoon court session, and everything he wanted to throw at you. Want me to carry on?'

'Nope. I get it... How did you know I was here?'

'Officer Monroe called me. He recognized your sorry butt. He was the officer who picked you up the last few times. Anyway, once the Feds realized you weren't a significant threat to the president, and once you'd been checked out by the doc, they placed you in the custody of the Jefferson County Sheriff's Department... Jeez, Coop, you got a big problem if you can't remember any of this.'

And he was right. Not remembering was a problem because right then it led on to him remembering. The dam of amnesia crumbled, the flood of memory came crashing in, bringing an anxious tide of tight, strangling breath. 'Is he... is he okay?'

Earl looked puzzled. 'Who?'

Cooper gripped onto the cell bars as if a drowning man. He spilled his words as quietly as he could. 'The President. Is he okay? Was he hurt...? Just answer me, Earl.'

'Coop?'

Banging on the steel bars blasted an agony through Cooper's shoulder. 'Just answer me! *Please!*'

'What's going on?'

'Earl, Goddamn it!'

Puzzlement drilled into Earl's words and if Cooper hadn't known him so well, it might've sounded like scorn. 'Yeah... yeah, of course. He's fine. Coop, what's this about? What's the President got to do with anything? I...'

Cooper didn't hear the rest of Earl's words. He just vomited. Right there. Retching up his relief. His fear from the pit of his stomach.

'Christ, Coop. You okay? I'll go and get someone.'

Cooper slumped hard on the iron contraption they called a bed. 'No, it's okay. Wait, look. I just need you to get me out of here. How much bail are they asking for?'

Earl's feet shuffled. 'Here's the thing Coop, I can't.'

'Can't what?'

'Can't get you out. Rather, I'm not going to do that.'

'I love you, Earl, and I'm sorry about everything. Truly. But let's put it right on the table; your jokes have never been funny, and right now, they're even worse than usual.'

Earl's expression became pitiful. 'I'm sorry, Coop, this isn't a joke. I promised I wouldn't help to get you out, not this time. But I still wanted to come down to see if you were alright.'

Cooper stood up. Too fast. Pain ripped through. 'What the hell are you talking about?'

'I promised I wouldn't. Look, I'd better go, I'll get one of the officers to come and clean that up for you. And I am sorry... I'll see you soon. Okay?'

'Earl...! Earl! Don't you leave me here...! Promised who...? I'm talking to you, Earl. Come back here—'

'Hello, Cooper.'

That voice which sang the backdrop of his childhood. Screamed the setting of his youth. Cried the resentment of his military days and the chant of sorrow. That voice, it explained everything.

Cooper stared at his Uncle. Captain Beau Neill. Commandant and kin. One-time martinet, these days a monk.

With as much hostility as he could muster, Cooper said, 'I take it this is your idea, Beau, not to get me out of here.'

Beau chewed on his unlit cigar. Dug his fingers into the top of his throbbing sciatic nerve, something he often told Cooper was his *test of suffering*. With disappointment dripping from his voice, Beau pulled a disappointed face. 'What the hell did you think you were doing, Cooper? You never change do you? But no, for your information, keeping you here wasn't my idea.'

Cooper gritted his teeth. Regretted it straight away. 'Just get me the hell out.'

'Sorry, no can do. There's a person who thinks keeping you here just for a little while longer might help you think about what you've done, and I have to agree.'

'I'm not a kid, Beau.'

'No you're not, Coop, but you sure as hell act like one.'

'Is this what they teach you in the monastery, Beau? How to be compassionate?'

'Oh don't worry about me, Coop. I've got a lot to learn and a hell of a lot of sins to repent, so I'll just go on and add this one to the list. And hey, I can live with that.'

'Is this funny to you?' Cooper said.

'Not one Goddamn bit...Tell me something, Coop, because I need to know if you've lost your mind completely... Enlighten me as to what made you think it was a good idea to follow the President's motorcade? Because I'm guessing that's what you were doing. But here's the really big question... Why?'

'I dunno... maybe it wasn't the smartest of things to do.'

The shaking of the head in cold disapproval was the epitome of disdain. Something Cooper knew Beau was well versed at. 'You got that damn right.'

Cooper took a deep breath. Tried to hold onto his temper. Gave up trying. 'What the hell was I supposed to do? Come on, tell me, seeing as you've got all the answers.'

'What the rest of us did. Keep our damn heads and find out the facts first. If I'd had a knee jerk reaction and acted like that when I was a Captain in the US Navy, just because I'd heard something, what kind of Captain would that have made me? Or when I was serving in...'

Cooper cut Beau down. 'You don't have to give me a history of your military career, Beau. I served under you and I know exactly the kind of Captain you were.'

Beau stepped closer to the bars. Hissed his words. 'Are we going to go through this again? Cooper, I was *not* responsible for the accident, and you know that.'

Hurt bobbed off Cooper's words. 'I never said you were, Beau. Problem is, when I'm stuck on one side of the bars – the wrong side – and you're on the other and you won't help me out, well, I can't help but feel resentful... Reminds me of that day.'

Beau came back with hostility. 'You can't help yourself, can you?'

'You were not only my Captain, you were my Uncle, and when I asked you... *begged* you to *help*, you turned your back and you walked away...'

'Now you listen here, Coop, I don't know how many times over the years I've had to say it, but it was too damn late. Now let it go.'

Quietly Cooper said, 'You make it out like it's a bad thing to love someone.'

'You puzzle me, Coop. I don't understand you, because

40

the only relationship you seem to have or *want* is with a dead woman. What about with all the other people who care about you? You push them away. You don't give a damn about them or how they feel. That's why I don't get this crazy car chase you did. The majority of the time you don't want to know. But yet, you do a mad dash. Was it the drugs? Turn your mind?'

Cooper wanted to smash something. Anything. Anything which would give him some breathing space from his Uncle Beau. 'No, it wasn't the Goddamn drugs. I just... I just...'

'Don't say you care, Coop, because we both know you don't.'

'That's bullshit. It's just...'

It was Beau's laugh which cut in this time. Harsh. Bitter. And Cooper wanted to grab right hold of him until he shut his mouth.

'You were going to say, *It's complicated*, weren't you, Coop?'

Flatlined by Beau, Cooper appealed. 'Just let me out of here. *Please*.'

'Oh no, like I say, there's someone here who thinks a few more hours locked up might do you good. Put some sense back into that head of yours.'

'I don't know what you're playing at Beau, but I...'

'Hello, Tom..'

Mid-sentence Cooper stopped. Left his mouth wide open.

'You look like shit by the way.'

He stared at his wife. Rather, his estranged wife. Rather, his almost ex-wife and mother of his only child. He said, 'So people like to keep telling me, but hey, it's good to see you too, Maddie.'

41

WASHINGTON, D.C.
USA

11

a3 f5

'I don't get it. What the hell have you guys been doing?'

President John Woods sat chewing the top of his pen. He watched the grainy CCTV recording of the latest bombing attack on home soil as he sat in the over-air conditioned situation room whilst ignoring the tight cramps in his stomach – a direct and unwelcome result of last night's state dinner held for the Prime Minister of Canada, where he'd consumed in enthusiastic abundance the Appalachian cheese. Today, however, he was sure as hell paying for it. He said, 'You're telling me there was no warning?'

Charles 'Chuck' Harrison, acting chief of the CIA Counter Terrorism Center took a sip of the iced water in front of him.

Slowly.

Shuffled his papers.

Slowly.

Sniffed and then inhaled.

Slowly.

Making damn sure the dozen or so gathered in the 'sit'

room knew he was going to make the President wait. Because he didn't appreciate it. Woods' tone. Not one Goddamn tiny bit.

He could have understood, if he was some nappy-ass kid fresh out of college, or even one of Woods' sycophants – who to his mind filled every inch of the White house. But then he guessed that was Democrats for you. Brownnosers talking about tolerance.

Heck, George W. Bush had had his faults, but at least he hadn't held back when it came to getting the job done with air strikes and boots on the ground, or when enhanced interrogation was needed – as it so often was – for some fundamentalist full of warped ideology, who was less than forthcoming with vital intel. And contrary to what the 2014 Senate report had said about EI, it *did* make a difference. A hell of a difference. A few days of walling, waterboarding, electrodes to the genitalia, along with sleep deprivation music made the most brainwashed of men begin to talk.

To his mind, the FBI had sold their souls, reporting to the Senate that it'd been *them*, not the CIA, who'd gotten most of the information from the alleged mastermind of the 9/11 attack, Khalid Sheikh Mohammed – or KSH, as he was usually referred to. And as a consequence of their perfidy there'd been a public outcry with emotions running high and liberalists bandying about the word *torture*. Hell, he just called it *getting answers*.

Then Obama had come into his administration with so much fanfare. The black man had crawled out and celebrated in the streets as if they'd just been emancipated. It was a Goddamn joke, with the irony being that Obama had become a puppet to the white man anyway, worried about not learning from Afghanistan or Iraq, and not wanting another war. But they were at war. Had been for a long time now. The war on terror. And the sooner everyone realized they were in the midst of world war three, the better. Though Chuck wasn't certain realization was going to help matters, because now of all times America needed a Republican as Commander-in-Chief, and what they'd been landed with was Goddamn John Woods.

John Woods stared at Chuck, knowing exactly what he was doing. He'd never like the guy, and he wasn't sure why but instinct told him the man was a sadist and a racist one at that. And hell, it wasn't *just* because he'd read the classified CIA reports on the enhanced interrogation in the black sites where Chuck had been in charge – though those had certainly added to his theory. Savage, and in excess of what was already excessive. No, there was just something about the guy. The same something he'd had about the guys in the college football team who strutted around fanning their tails. Peacocks. And the same something he'd had when he'd first met his ex-wife, but had pushed aside. Shoot, he should've listened to his gut on that one.

But then, Chuck wasn't about personal and liking him was beside the point. Maybe it was better that way so lines never blurred. He was real good at what he did. Damn good. Experienced. He'd been a military man first, before changing direction to join the CIA, Counter Terrorism Centre. Worked hard. Eventually became Chief of Station in Khartoum, Sudan in the nineties, moving to Tehran, before getting the top agency post in Baghdad at the height of the Iraq war.

And now he was acting Chief of CTC, since Brent Miller's debilitating stroke last month. The stroke hadn't come as a surprise, only that Brent hadn't had one earlier.

Brent had lived at the job. Sustaining himself on sixty cigarettes a day and very little else. He'd even had an aluminum fold-up bed in the office, as if on summer camp. And folklore had it that when his wife had picked up her stuff and left him, Brent hadn't even noticed, even when he'd returned home on a few occasions for a change of clothes. It'd taken an email from his wife's attorney a couple of months later for him to realise she'd gone and had filed for divorce.

Chief of CTC was one of the most pressurized jobs there was. No doubt about it. Even more so than his, Woods figured.

So for now Chuck was acting Chief. The only man at the moment who was really up to it. Whether or not relations between them would withstand the position becoming permanent, only time would tell.

Clenching tight and refusing to excuse himself for the call of the bathroom, Woods said, 'Chuck?'

'Mr President?'

'You need me to repeat the question?'

'With due respect, Mr President, it didn't feel much like a question. More of an accusation with the finger of blame pointing directly towards the CTC. Something I take exception to.'

Shifting his weight onto his other elbow, to try to ease the build-up of gas and excess cheese, and trying to curb his temper, Woods shook his head. 'For Christ's sake, accountability goes hand in hand with the job.'

'I agree, and I'd be happy to hold my hands up, but as the bomb was on Homeland, I'd say it was the FBI who needed to answer your question.'

'I'm asking you.'

'I know you are. But may I remind you, Mr President, the CIA doesn't work on home soil. It's not our jurisdiction.'

'Oh come on, Chuck, cut the crap, who do you think you're talking to? Officially that's what you like to put out there, but both you and I know that's far from the truth.'

'All I know is without procedure there's chaos, and I run my department by the book.'

'Like I say, Chuck. Cut the crap. This is the CIA we're talking about, not the New York public library. Don't ever try to bullshit me. People are dying and getting hurt out there. America is on red alert.'

'I repeat, Homeland is not our jurisdiction.'

'If that were the case, why do you have this guy, David Thorpe, in your custody?'

Drily, Chuck answered. 'Because he's there on the CCTV footage. It's obvious to anyone he's our bomber.'

'Don't get smart with me, you know exactly what I mean... I want to know why, when this is an FBI issue, you took him off American soil to Turkmenistan to question him almost immediately after his arrest? I've had the director of the FBI on the phone as well as the Attorney General. And let me tell you. They're not happy. And hey, what do you know, neither am I, Chuck.'

'Mr President, if you've got a problem with the way I'm managing the CTC, I feel I'd have no other option but to step aside so a more suitable candidate could take over the role. My duty to this country and the security of the American people is paramount. I won't hesitate on doing what's needed.'

Woods rolled his tongue in the back of his mouth. Tried not to be goaded by the glint in Chuck's eye – nor by the fact Chuck knew he was the best man or woman for the job, so he had him by the balls... Failed on both counts. 'Start explaining, because I need to tell the FBI what the hell is going on.'

Chuck looked around the room. Made a sweep count of the number of pens in the pot-holder. Began to count the number of files on the table. Forced himself to break away. It was a habit. A tiring one. Surveying everything including the most banal of stuff. A direct consequence of working too long in intel. There was no switch off button. Ever. Not when you were on vacation. Not even when you were making love.

Drawing his eyes away, Chuck said, 'Mr President, not everyone here is privy to the level of classified information we need to discuss. Perhaps we can convene with just the necessary?'

Woods nodded. Slightly afraid to make a sudden movement. Watched most of the assembled men and women walk out. Envied the fact they could use the restroom.

12

b4Kh8

Maddie drove. Hard. Fast. Making sure Cooper felt every moment of it. Every bump. Every Goddamn pot hole on the road back home. To the home they'd once shared before life with him had become too complicated. To the home their six-year-old daughter, Cora, had loved.

To the home where she'd packed her bags, taking too long about it, just in case he'd come back home and begged her to stay.

That had been last year. And she wished she could say she'd never looked back. But she had. Damn, had she. She'd looked back so many times her neck hurt. She didn't even bother trying to deny to herself how much she still loved him. But loving someone wasn't enough if they were hell bent on destroying themselves. And Cooper was. And like a maelstrom she knew he'd pull and draw everyone who was near enough down with him.

'You want to slow down a bit, Maddie?'

Maddie side-glanced Cooper, as they sped along Colorado's dirt track roads in the heat of the afternoon sun. The dial hit eighty-five miles per hour, and the dust blew from underneath the wheels as if on fire, and the wind billowed in through the open Chevy windows, and she brushed away spiraling curls from her eyes and shouted over the sound of the engine. 'No, actually I don't, Tom. You know what I actually want to do? I want to go faster...'

She put her foot down.

Hard.

Harder.

Pushing the engine. Swerving those holes in the road. And not giving a damn.

'Remind you of anyone, Tom? Do I? Bring back memories from your cannonball run?'

'Jesus, slow down, Maddie! What the hell's got into you? I know you're mad at me, but wasn't leaving me in a cell punishment enough?'

'Mad at you? Oh you haven't seen mad, Tom. You wanna see mad, Tom? 'Cos I can show you that.'

Maddie pushed down on the accelerator, touching the worn out brown carpet of the Chevy floor with her equally worn out cowboy boot.

'Whatever it is you're pissed about, killing us both won't solve things.'

'Won't it? Isn't this what you want, Tom? Isn't living on the edge what you want to do?'

'I won't tell you again Maddie... *slow down*.'

'No, Tom, because this is the only way you feel isn't it? Fast. Dangerous. To hell with anything else. With *anybody* else.'

'Maddie...'

'You feeling this, Tom? You feeling it? Doesn't it feel good…? Or are you feeling scared? Desperate? Out of control? How about powerless? You feel that one? Powerless. That one's good. Eats your soul. Like there's nothing you can do to stop, and any moment you're going to watch a car crash and feel the pain that goes with it.'

Cooper brushed the sand out of his mouth. 'I'm sorry… Okay. I'm sorry!'

The car hit ninety-five and Maddie glanced over at Cooper. 'Not good enough, Tom! Everything's just a big-ass sorry with you… Do you know how hard we've all tried to stop loving you? Because we would, you know, if we could. We've all been through hell, thinking that we're going to lose you. And then just as things start to quieten down you go and do it all again like the last time, and the time before Goddamn that.'

'Maddie…'

'No, you promised, and you just couldn't keep your promise could you? And before you ask, these aren't tears in my eyes, it's the Goddamn wind.'

Cooper let go of the seat he'd been holding onto. Tightly. Still shouting. Still not quite sure what had brought this on. 'I don't get it, Maddie, because remember, it was *you* who walked away. You walked out on me. You didn't want *us* anymore.'

Maddie screamed at the top of her voice. Shrill and high, reminding herself of the bobcats which roamed and hunted the Sonoran Desert at night. 'How dare you, Tom!? God, I always wanted us. I always loved you. But you? Most of our marriage you weren't even present. And when you were, you never even noticed I was there.'

'That's not true.'

Maddie swerved the car. Had Cooper holding back onto his seat. 'It is true, Tom, and you know it.'

'You're acting crazy, just stop the Goddamn car and we'll talk.'

'I thought crazy was where it was at.'

Maddie slammed her foot on the brakes. The '54 Chevy churning up the earth like a cyclone.

Cooper flew forward.

Banged his head.

Sense told him it was best not to look for sympathy.

Pushing open the door, Maddie marched round to the trunk. Banged it. Sprung right open. Pulled out a Beretta 87. Marched right on back to Cooper.

'There you go, Tom. Take it.'

Cooper cocked his head. Hadn't a hell clue what she was talking about. But then women and sense weren't always an equal equation in his experience. 'What? I don't know what all this is about.'

Deep brown eyes stared at Cooper. Pain filled them. Love filled them. But most of all anger lounged and simmered in them.

'You're right, Tom. It wouldn't have made any sense at all if we'd crashed back then. Both of us dying. Now that wouldn't be good. So as this is about *you*... here you go.'

Cooper's strawberry blonde hair blew over and covered his eyes. One blue. One green. He didn't need to look at her to know the woman had lost all sense. 'I don't know what's got into you.'

'Don't you, Tom?'

Maddie pulled back the hammer on the single shot nine-inch pistol. Span round a one eighty. Faced and aimed towards the bottom of a flowering cactus. Two shots. Two dead shovel-nosed cobras.

She turned back to Cooper and said, 'No, you probably don't. You don't even have a clue... Now your turn.'

Cooper gave a half smile to Maddie. She was one of the best shots he knew. Hands down there was no competition. And many a time her steady hand had gotten him out of scrapes.

'Can I pass on this?'

Maddie shook her head. Spun the gun. Pushed the pistol grip towards Cooper.

'Hell, no.'

Cooper held onto his sigh. Then couldn't hold it in any longer. He let it out. Hard and loud. Irritation began to seep up and over Cooper. Patience wasn't always his strongest point. And right now, after almost a week in a cell and his tongue feeling like he'd caught it in a vice, his patience had just gone and run out. 'Maddie, just give me the Goddamn keys, I want to go home.'

'Do it.'

'Do what? For Christ sake woman, I love you. You hear that. I love you. But this... This, what we're doing right here, can we do it another time? Because I'm beat.'

Maddie didn't take away her gaze. 'If you're so hell bent on killing yourself, why don't you just go on right ahead and do it? Put the gun against your head and pull the trigger. Go on... Save us all the time and heartache, Tom. Then we can lay you to rest on the top of a hill somewhere. I could pick some daisies from the ranch and Cora and I – remember her, Tom? Your daughter? Well, we could make the grave look real pretty. And we'd give you a big old stone with your name on. Here lies, Thomas J Cooper, he lived as he died; quickly, selfishly and it was over in a shot... So what do you say?'

Cooper bent his six-foot-three frame down. His handsome, tired face towards Maddie's brown freckled one. Inches away. Smelling the perfume he'd bought her from Paris. 'I say, this time... this time you've finally lost it.'

'No, Tom, you have. All the pills and...'

Cooper jumped in. 'Those pills are legit, Maddie. Prescribed from my shrink. They help me sleep, okay?'

'Don't kid yourself, Tom. You can't do without them or...' She trailed off and Cooper looked at her curiously.

'Or what?'

'... Or without the memory of her.'

Cooper rubbed his head. 'Jesus, has this all been about Ell... about... you know...'

'Oh my God. You can't say it, can you? You can't even say her name.'

'Of course I can.'

'Then say it, Tom... I need to hear you say her name.'

'Why?'

'Why? You don't think it's strange that after all this time, after *eight* years you can't say it? You've made her almost sacrosanct.'

'That's a dumb thing to say.'

'Is it? Because God knows when we were together all you did was worship her. It was like living with a ghost, haunting every moment of what we did. How did you think it made me feel when I listened to you call her name in your sleep instead of mine? Or when I saw her things neatly boxed in the attic, like you were waiting for her to return.'

'It's all I had left.'

'No it wasn't, Tom, you had me but you never thought about that. You never thought about *me*.'

'Jesus, this is crazy.'

'It's not, and God help me, I hate her more now that she's dead than when she was alive.'

'Maddie, what's the matter with you?'

'I just want you to say her name…*Say it*.'

'You're not thinking straight.'

'Just say it.'

'Look, what's the big deal?'

'Then say her *fucking* name.'

Cooper kicked the car. Felt the pain. 'I can't. Okay. I can't…You happy now?'

Maddie blinked. Then blinked some more. This time it wasn't the wind. Nor the dust. Nor the scorch of the sun in her eyes. This time they were tears. Tears which seemed to come straight from her heart. And as she watched the heatwaves rise up from the road ahead she took a deep breath and quietly said, 'Come on, I'll drive you home…'

13

f3 Ng8

The corpses burnt. Piled up high. Women on top of men and men on top of women and the bodies of the children blistered and charred as the greed of the fire reached them, devouring the flesh as they lay at the highest point, like a peak on a mountaintop, forming a summit built of the dead.

And the fire spat out its smells and sent up black smoke which twisted and clouded, warping the sky of its light.

The young soldier standing nearby yawned, then smiled as he finally managed to work out it was a picture of Mickey Mouse on the boy's T-shirt. With his curiosity now satisfied, he threw the lifeless body into the burning flames. This was the last village. At least for now. The area had been cleared. All the houses, buildings and churches were nothing but ash, and now all that was needed was to wait for more instructions.

14

Qc2 Ngf6

The usual sound and visual recording in the 'sit' room was turned off. The only people left were Chuck Harrison, and Woods' Chief of Staff and long-term trusted friend, Edward 'Teddy' Adleman as well as Lyndon Clark, Secretary of State, a tall, poised straight-talking black man.

Clearing his throat, Woods said, 'This better be good, Chuck. You better have a damn good reason for having the bomber in your custody so I can appease, or at least *try* to appease, the FBI.'

Chuck, also clearing his throat – a side effect of the intense vigor of the air-con – said, 'Before I start, Mr President, can I just confirm our prisoner transfer meeting is still going ahead on Friday? I think I'm probably correct in thinking it'll be a ghost meeting so I won't be able to get my staff to confirm it via the presidential memoranda. As I said last week, it is a matter of urgency that we look at the current approaches to prisoners like Abdul-Aziz bin Hamad.'

'Chuck, we need to get on with this, but to answer your

question, yes it is going ahead, though and as *I said* last week to you, prisoner transfer and release of terrorists – particularly terrorists such as Bin Hamad – is no longer this administration's policy. We do not negotiate with Al Qaeda or their off-shoots. Now, if you don't mind, we're on the clock...'

With just a single blink, and not – and never – giving away his feelings unless there were deliberate and strategic motives, Chuck nodded. 'Okay, well as we know, Boko Haram, whose official Arabic name is...

Lyndon Clark interrupted: 'Jama'atu Ahlis Sunna Lidda'awati wal-Jihad.'

Chuck cut Lyndon a hard stare. 'Exactly. Which loosely translates to...'

'People Committed to the Propagation of the Prophet's Teachings and Jihad.'

'Lyndon, would you like to take this meet?'

'If you like.'

Chuck, not for the first time, wondered what Woods had been trying to prove putting another colored man in such a high-ranking role. First it was Teddy and now Lyndon. It was bullshit, because there'd also be an agenda. Lyndon would always be running round needing to prove something. Proving he was as up to the job as the white man. Proving he wasn't selling the African-Americans out with his policies. Proving above and beyond anything else – including and *especially* being a colored man – he was first and foremost a citizen of the United States who loved his country like the founding fathers had.

Chuck smiled. Didn't reach his eyes. Didn't reach any part of him. 'There's nothing to prove here, Lyndon.'

Lyndon Clark touched his small goatee beard. Sneered. Which met his eyes. Which met every damn part of him. 'I'm not following you, Chuck. Care to expand?'

'What I mean is. It won't make any difference to the way I feel about you or how you're doing your job.'

Woods looked at Chuck. Then Lyndon. Eyes fixed on each other. Bolted together. Felt like he could go right on and cut the air in two with a scythe. 'Chuck, continue with what we're here for.'

'Certainly, Mr President, and just to refresh, Boko Haram – as we all know – were founded in 2002, though they didn't really launch military operations until 2009. They're a rebel group and self-professed Islamist movement, based mainly in northeast Nigeria, though there are offshoots in Chad, Niger and Cameroon. Recently they've stepped up the wave of suicide bombings, mass attacks on villages, including looting and killing, forcibly conscripting men and boys, and of course there's also the abduction of women and children. Especially girls. I'm sure everyone remembers the international outrage and the campaign in 2014 when they abducted more than two hundred schoolgirls from Chibok town in Borno state.'

Woods nodded. 'Bring back our girls.'

'Yeah and as yet we're still waiting – though all here present will appreciate that's probably not going to happen. They've either been forced to become slaves, married off or used as suicide bombers... The main objective for Boko Haram? To overthrow the government and create a caliphate state. Most tellingly, and a growing concern, is they've also pledged their allegiance to ISIL. The US designated them a terrorist group in 2013.'

Woods looked at his watch. 'How does this all fit in?'

'Well, what we've been doing is working on fresh information in regards to the movements of Boko Haram. Human intelligence tells us the bomber, David Thorpe, who we now have in our custody, and are questioning in one of our sites in Turkmenistan, has direct links with a group we've been following in Nigeria.'

'How reliable is your HI?' Woods asked.

'Very. And that's why it's important *we* question him rather than the FBI. So our operation isn't at all compromised.'

'Ok, so here's my questions. Do you think he's linked to the suicide bomber at Memphis airport, as well as the bombers in the other states last week? You think they were in a cell, or could it be a case of a wave of copycat lone wolves, who were perversely inspired by one another?'

'I think it's the former, Mr President. The suicide bombings were definitely coordinated attacks and it's a likely supposition, well, more than likely according to HI, that this attack from this particular bomber was spaced a week apart from the others to create an even greater impact on the country. As in, we had the first spate of bombings, then over the following two or three days everything was on code red, the American people were *afraid*. Then, like a mass movement, there was a sense of a *united front* amongst everybody. A determination to carry on with life regardless. Stats show cancelled flights throughout the country were re-booked. A surge in people going to the movie-theater. Showing the terrorists they won't win. And then, bang. Right out of nowhere, another bomb. Only this time bigger. Much bigger. Everybody's worst nightmare. Causing maximum psychological impact to the American people.'

Woods glanced over at the black and white security tape. Un-paused it. Watched it again. The bomber, David Thorpe, had walked into a coffee shop, hence the *Washington Post* – much to his irritation – naming the guy 'the coffee shop bomber' and even going on to report how the guy took his coffee.

Non-fat.

No whipped cream.

Eggnog Latte complete with cinnamon sprinkle.

Afterwards David Thorpe had sauntered over to the truck he'd driven. Locked it then walked away, only for it to explode twenty minutes later, taking down half a government building in Chatham, Illinois. It seemed almost miraculous that there hadn't been fatalities. A lot of the area had been closed down, after reports of a chemical spill had forced evacuations across three to four blocks. However, there'd been a hell of a lot of destruction

Thorpe's face had been clear on the CCTV, and the FBI had picked him up easily from a small place near Willowbrook, just off state 55. A two-and-a-half-hour drive from where the bomb had exploded. Reports said, the guy had just been getting on with it. Getting on with his business like everyday folk did. Like nothing had happened.

'I don't agree,' Lyndon said.

Chuck leant forward. Tilted his head. 'Excuse me?'

'I don't agree. This bomb that Thorpe used was sophisticated. The others weren't. Far from it.'

'I don't see what difference that makes, *Lyndon*.'

'Oh come on, it's elementary, there's no way a cell group jumps from the most basic of basic suicide vests made with common household products to a highly complex and powerful bomb. You don't go down to the local drug store for that. I say this is something different. Not connected.'

'Everyone's a counter terrorism expert.'

Lyndon strained to hear. 'Did you say something, Chuck?'

'No... No, I just think you're wrong. So wrong it's untrue. Boko Haram, who we think all these recent bomb attacks are linked to, have also developed connections and taken on philosophies of other militant groups, such as Al-Qaeda and, as I say, ISIL. Therefore, using such an elaborate bomb isn't so far removed as you think.'

Woods said, 'What do we know about David Thorpe personally?'

'Born 1966. Nigerian descent. He's single. Newly divorced, though he separated from his wife five years ago. One child aged ten, but apparently he doesn't see them much if at all. He works full time at a local car showroom. After his wife left him, he rediscovered his religion, though it wasn't long before he began to study Wahhabism – a form of Islam widely practiced in Saudi Arabia. Wahhabism is seen as an ultra-conservative branch of Islam and is often referred to as the revolutionary branch. It also forms the fundamental ideology of ISIS, Boko Haram and Al-Shabaab, as well as several other jihadist groups. And what they say is the reason behind all their actions is to form a caliphate.'

Woods nodded. 'And the problem with a caliphate is that it's the model of Medina, all about expansionism.'

Chuck said, 'Give me a government and a foreign policy which isn't all about that and I'll give you Switzerland.'

Against his better judgement, Woods smiled and Lyndon shook his head, speaking thoughtfully. 'Boko Haram just don't travel though, Mr President. I don't buy it.'

Woods looked at Lyndon. 'Think about it, though. When Al Qaeda first started out, AQ wasn't an operational organization like it is now, but only an idea. There was only Bin Laden and Abdullah Azzam. But unlike his counterparts, Bin Laden decided on the idea of fighting the *far enemy* instead of the *near enemy* which had previously been targeted, and over time his idea became a franchise. Jihadists from all over the world came to him based on his philosophy of the far enemy. He trained them in guerilla techniques and warfare – basically how our CIA had trained him during Afghanistan's war against Russia. He is also funded these franchise associated groups, and lone wolf operators, who were deadly and driven on by Bin Laden's philosophy. So maybe these bombers, although linked to Boko Haram, have taken on the philosophy of the far enemy... Us. America.'

Taking a sip of water, Chuck looked at the President. '*Dar al-harb*. Land of war. That's what's happening here. Terrorist groups feel they can validate what they do, attacking the far enemy, because they feel they're fighting a holy war. And that's my guess on what was driving David Thorpe.'

Woods, feeling the first tingle of pins and needles in his fingers, stretched his hand out. 'I mean, I understand you'd want your own land and county. Right now in the world there isn't an official Islamic state. That can only happen when there's a Caliph and Caliphate, and apart from the problem with expansionism, there's nothing wrong with a Caliphate in its purest form. People don't get that Islam isn't just a religion, it's a way of life for an individual and a society as a whole. It's a system; a ruling, economic, administrational, social, penal and personal one. But what's happening here with all the jihadist movements, well, that's about terror and our job is to stop it. But the damn problem is the whole thing has created such a divide, not only within the Muslim community, but within the world as a whole.'

Chuck agreed. 'Which goes back to our bomber, David Thorpe. He became very vocal about his allegiance to such groups, but in particular to Boko Haram. Hate preaching. Speaking of violence. And eventually he drew the attention of the authorities. A few years ago Thorpe was put on the federal No-Fly List.'

'He's still on it, I take it,' Woods said.

Chuck shook his head. Contemplated taking a sip of water. Changed his mind before stifling a yawn. 'Nope.'

'Jesus, Chuck, you kidding me? What happened?'

'What I can see from the data he was taken off about a year ago.'

'You need to bury that one.'

'Well, someone along the line clearly thought Thorpe was no longer a danger.'

'Until he blows up a building. And why Chatham? What's there? It's just a pretty village south of Springfield.'

Deciding he needed to let the yawn out and not bothering to cover his mouth, Chuck shrugged. 'Excuse me, I was up late… Sorry, what was I saying? Oh yeah, it's a real tragedy, sir.'

Woods peered at Chuck from above his rimless glasses.

The man was cold. Didn't even try to hide it. But then, it took a certain sort of someone to work in CTC and, over time, desensitization took over.

'And as for the question, Mr President, of why Chatham? Who knows? He might have just put a pin in the map. But we're looking into that.'

John Woods turned to Teddy Adleman, who'd been uncharacteristically quiet. He suspected the reason Teddy had said nothing was that his feelings towards Chuck Harrison were the same as Woods'. The least time having to converse with him the better.

'What do you think, Teddy?'

Teddy nodded to Woods. Nodded at Lyndon. Didn't bother looking at Chuck. He spoke in a hushed voice. 'So if we're saying Thorpe isn't a lone wolf, and he's linked with the other bombers, my question is why didn't he kill himself too? Like the others. I see the profile and I get it. But Lyndon's right, something just doesn't fit...'

Woods was curious. 'Go on.'

'The fact is, Boko Haram is a domestic terror group. Focused on their country. This, as far as I know, will be the first time they've come outside the immediate vicinity of Nigeria and the neighboring countries.'

'Chuck, you want to pick that up?'

'Mr President, there's a first time for everything. There's a metamorphosis in terrorism. What was once is not necessarily any longer.'

'And apart from the No-Fly List, and a couple of interviews with the FBI, there was never any other eyes or ears on David Thorpe?' Woods asked.

'None.'

'Is he talking?'

'Nothing, but hey, we can easily remedy that. It'll be like the good old days. Show him we mean business.'

'For God's sake, Chuck, are you seriously talking about EI? And just for the record, wherever it's carried out, it's not okay. Torture is *never* okay.'

Chuck shrugged again and took another sip of water and leant back on his chair and winked at Lyndon and pulled at the hair in his ears and said, 'Hey, whatever happened to having a sense of humor? But for *my* record, I disagree, and when it comes down to it, I don't care what any of the liberalists say. I know for a fact every citizen, senator and even you, Mr President, would be calling on a guy like me to get the information from a prisoner, if that prisoner had taken and kidnapped a loved one. They'd be begging me to use enhanced interrogation; water board the hell out of that son-of-a-bitch like there's no tomorrow. And it wouldn't matter to them what I did as long as I brought their kid or whoever it was back home safely. I know you'd want me to get the information from a person who took your son, wouldn't you, Mr President? No matter *what* it took.'

Woods said nothing.

'Think about it, Mr President, and tell me I'm wrong... You can't, can you? And that's the point. What's the difference between getting information about a loved one in danger, or getting information about this country which is also in danger? Because that's how I see America. As something I love, will protect and keep safe. Which means if I know that there's someone with information about attacking this great nation and hurting her, then I *will do* all I can to make sure that threat isn't carried out. We need to stop all this sentimental bullshit and outright hypocrisy, because otherwise we will keep having attacks on Homeland. Whatever it takes to protect and serve... By any means necessary.'

Lyndon P Clarke smiled. Wide. It hit his eyes so hard they sparkled. 'One of your heroes?'

'What?'

'Just that it's good to hear you quoting Malcolm X, Chuck. Who would've thought?'

Woods, not even attempting to hide his own smile, said, 'Lyndon, are you still going out to Turkmenistan?'

'I am.'

'I can't see any need for that,' Chuck said.

To which Lyndon answered, 'No, I'm sure you can't. But I'll see you there.'

A hush. A breeze of tension settled in the air before Woods asked, 'Have we got anything on the other bombers yet, Chuck?

'We got nothing, Mr President, but the odds are they didn't come from the US. No doubt smuggled in just for this purpose. It'll take longer to find out who they are – or rather who they *were* – because they're only kids. Terrorist kids, but kids nevertheless.'

'They were somebody's children, Chuck. They didn't wake up one day and decide to get involved with this on their own. Take their life. Someone, somewhere got them to do this. But the point is they're dead when they should be in high school or college. They were somebody's babies. I'd say they were as much a victim as everyone else.'

Chuck Harrison clenched his teeth. Hard. It was bullshit. And hell, he was going tell Woods just that. 'Bullshit.'

'Excuse me?'

'Bullshit, Mr President. Those kids. Those *victims* as you call them, well, let me tell you, a lot of them are more radicalized than any adult. Not a day goes by when somewhere in the world, there isn't a kid strapping on his or her suicide vest to cause the most damage and the most casualties. Why? Because they believe they're going to get the pleasures and blessings of paradise. They'll leave behind their crippling poverty and a life less lived with one push of a button. That's all it takes. One push for them to reap their rewards in paradise.'

Woods said nothing.

'And the problem you have, Mr President, is that you can't give a definitive answer and say their beliefs aren't true. And because you can't, you will always have the threat of suicide bombers happy to go to paradise, no matter what the age.'

'But you must see they start off as victims, even if it's a victim to their environment.'

Chuck gave a small smile. 'No, what I see is terrorists.'

'Chuck...' Woods paused.

Tried again.

'Chuck...'

Winced.

Then said, 'Excuse me, everyone, I just need to use the bathroom.'

15

Nb5 ab4

Chuck Harrison took the call in his car on the way back to Langley, where the HQ for the CIA was based. He listened. Turned up the radio and simply said, 'Meet me at my house.'

*

Forty-five minutes later, Chuck stood by his large, newly installed glass and steel water fountain. He hated the damn thing. God knows what the designer thought he was doing. But then, he supposed his instructions had been more than just a little ambiguous.

Tall.

Wide.

Don't care if it's round.

Don't care if it's square.

His only specification: it needs to produce jets of water. *Lots* of jets. As noisy and as vigorous as possible.

So after a dozen men and two weeks of work, and several complaints from neighbors in the private gated community, and a visit from a balding noise control officer to come and measure the output of sound, and a big-ass bill, he'd got what he'd wanted… *Needed*.

He'd never taken chances. Didn't trust anyone. Went hand in hand with the job. Nobody trusted anybody. They said they did, but he knew damn well that wasn't the truth. Truth didn't play a part. That was the title of the game.

It often played out that it was the most principled of colleagues who would turn and end up working for the other side. Then, sometimes, it was just the mundane, insider politics of the CIA who ordered the eyes and ears. But that's what made them good. That's what kept the field agent alive. Because you never knew. Never knew who wanted to bring you down.

The secret was to believe everything and to believe nothing. So if it meant getting a Goddamn water feature the size of which even the White House would be proud of, to stop ears listing to conversations by distorting the pick-up on their listening devices with the sound of the water, then that was something he just had to live with.

And it was here, in front of this monstrosity of a garden feature, where he had every conversation which was longer than a *hello*.

Chuck sipped his glass of iced tea as he watched his housekeeper bring Arnold Willis, an ambitious thirty-something CTC case worker with thick blond hair and eyes as green as the trees of Wisconsin.

Waiting an appropriate time for his non-English speaking Peruvian housekeeper to go back inside the house, Chuck snarled, 'Take your clothes off.'

Arnold Willis stepped backwards. Hit the side of his leg against the fountain wall. Almost fell right in. 'Sorry, sir?'

'I said, take your clothes off, Willis.'

'Sir, I don't understand.'

'What the hell is there to understand, Oklahoma boy? The point is I like to cover all eventuality. No ears, no wires and no possibility of them. And before you ask, no I don't trust you. But don't take it personally; I don't trust anyone. So take off your clothes and put them over there by the bench.'

*

Arnold Willis tried and failed horribly to stop himself feeling self-conscious as he stood in front of Chuck in the mid-afternoon on what was clearly a chilly day.

'What I want to know, Willis, is who the hell okayed the polygraph test on the bomber?'

'On David Thorpe?'

Rubbing the side of his head, and throwing the rest of the iced-tea away on the lawn, Chuck snapped, 'Yes, of course, David Thorpe, who the hell do you think I meant?'

'Sir, it was the President, sir.'

'When? Because I was with him just this morning and he didn't mention anything then.'

'The call came through around mid-day. We did try to get hold of you.'

'And when you didn't, you thought it was just okay to send orders through to Turkmenistan for them to go ahead and do it?'

'Sir, I wasn't anything to do with it. It was the deputy

director who took the decision. The President's office wanted to get it done as quickly as possible. Marked urgent.'

'You got the results?'

Willis nodded. Wanted to scratch his chin. Decided against it if it meant revealing his modesty.

'I have sir, they're in my jacket.'

'Have you shown them to anyone else?'

'No, sir. Absolutely not.'

Guardedly, Chuck enquired. 'Anything out of the usual show up on the test?'

'Yes, sir. The strange thing is although David Thorpe is clearly shown on the CCTV footage driving the lorry before parking it and walking away, as well as the coffee staff IDing him, along with the fact that he had traces of ammonium nitrate on his clothes and hands, the polygraph test isn't clear cut at all. It was rendered inconclusive. All the tests were.'

'What do you mean?'

'Well, after the first test was inconclusive they redid it two more times. It's odd because when he says it wasn't him who built the bomb or drove the truck or even went for an Eggnog latte, even though he's clearly there on the tape footage, the test results are still reading inconclusive rather than pointing to him lying, which you would've thought it would. The only thing he does admit, is that it was him on the tape and the test shows a pass for that.'

'Even he couldn't deny that one.'

'I realize that, sir, but off the record the guys in Turkmenistan say he does sound very convincing when he says he doesn't know anything about the bomb. And don't forget, sir, only 5 to 10 percent of people's tests are found to be inconclusive.'

Chuck took a step towards Willis. Narrowed eyes. Mouth held tight. 'What are you trying to say?'

'Nothing... I... I just mean it sounds like he's telling the truth.'

Fingers jabbed into Willis' bare chest. 'You ever say that again and you'll be sorry. You understand me? That kind of talk, there's no place for. The guy's a terrorist. Simple. I don't want you repeating that crap to anyone.'

'Yes, sir, it was just... it was...'

'Just what? You think polygraph tests are infallible just because the CIA use them all the time?'

'No.'

'Didn't you read the National Academy of Science report on them? Casting doubt? Reasons why you may get an inconclusive test include inadequate question formulation, based on bad case facts. Questions that are compound or ambiguous. The absence of care by the examinee of getting caught in a lie. The matter of not giving a damn about the consequences. It's the job of the examiner to determine the proper psychological set for the polygraph examination. Did you know all that?'

'No, sir, I didn't.'

'Then maybe you should. And apart from anything else, if he didn't know anything about it, tell me why the hell he was driving a truck with false plates which were registered to a vehicle that'd been crushed six months ago... Now put your clothes on... And Willis?'

'Yes, sir?'

'Like I say, I don't want you mention the results to anyone else.'

'What about the President? Shouldn't I get them to his office?'

'I don't think you're listening. I said, no-one else. I'll sort out the President's office, okay? So now we're all good... But Arnold.'

'Yes, sir?'

'Just one other thing. If you want to continue working for the CIA, don't ever let me hear you refer to this again...'

16

ab4 Nh5

Cooper sat in his '54 Chevy watching the heatwaves rise up from the engine, mixing with the heatwaves of the day. He'd parked on the cactus-lined dusty road where he could see the small airstrip belonging to Onyx Asset Recovery. A company which specialized in tracking down high value boats and planes, mostly for banks, leasing companies and on occasion governments.

This was where he worked. Onyx. The remote office he'd been operating out of for the past six years. It was built in the middle of four hundred acres of wilderness. Hot desert land based just outside North Scottsdale, Arizona, with God-given views.

He hadn't stepped foot in the actual office in a while. Last year he'd returned from a job in the Democratic Republic of the Congo, and he'd come back messed up. More messed up than when he'd gone.

The breakdown of his marriage hadn't helped, but in

truth, when it had been up and running, it hadn't helped him either.

His marriage reminded him of the infamous Ford Pinto. On the outside it looked okay, but the issues were there long before it'd even clocked up any mileage. A flawed design, a lack of reinforcement, and all held together by substandard bolts which quickly came loose, eventually piercing into the heart of the tank, causing it to erupt into flames.

On his return from the DRC, Maddie and Beau had insisted on him going back to see his shrink at the VA Medical Center. But he struggled. Struggled not to feel ashamed. Yes, he'd served *and* fought for his country, he'd been proud to do so, but his problems weren't directly linked with combat, nor what he'd seen during his time as a Navy SEAL. His problems were linked to a woman. A woman he'd loved. His childhood sweetheart who he hadn't been able to keep safe. But the shrink at the Veterans' Affairs Center liked to bandy the letters *PTSD* around. And at that point, he always took his exit. Because how could he sit next to his military brothers, whose problems *were* a direct result of war, and hold his head up high when it hadn't been a battle which had caused his torment?

Okay, the accident eight years ago had been in part caused by the approach and attack of their yacht by Somalian pirates, but that certainly wasn't a reason to go to the VA Medical Center, cryin' and hollerin', no matter what the psychiatrists liked to try to tell him.

This was his doing. Period. And he had to deal with it. Consequently, instead of feeling like he was discrediting what it meant to be a veteran, a hero, he'd found a private shrink… Quite a few, actually. And so when things got really bad and he couldn't sleep and the nightmares came and he just felt like he was on the edge and he wanted to end it all but didn't know how, well then, they'd be there waiting. The quacks. With their prescription pads, giving him anything he needed. Anything. At a price… A heavier price than he ever realized.

Cooper sighed as he opened the bottle of pills. Shook two out. His body was still in pain from the Taser. Shook another one out. Just to be on the safe side.

In the distance he saw Maddie, who also worked at Onyx as a recovery operative. He hadn't seen or spoken to her since she'd dropped him off at his ranch back in Colorado a couple of days ago. And if he was honest, he would be happy to leave seeing her for another couple of days. It'd been fine working together when they were still in a marriage. Well as fine as it ever could be.

He knew he needed to be man enough to work with her without a problem. After all, she was great at what she did.

He held her in the upmost respect.

He admired her.

He trusted her.

He valued her opinion…

But Goddamn, he didn't know a man alive who wouldn't want to run for the hills if they had to work with their estranged wife.

His job was his life and his life was job, so he couldn't quit. Not that he didn't think about it. A lot… Every day. And he couldn't exactly ask Maddie to quit. Ultimately he knew it wasn't really about her. And besides, it'd actually been Maddie who'd got him to come on board and get his investigator's license to join the small but successful firm.

Maddie had worked at Onyx for just over seven years, since her commission in the Navy had ended, having heard of them and their reputation, and knowing it was a place her specialized skills could come into play. Though she hadn't been the only one to hear of it. Cooper had heard of Onyx long before he'd known Maddie, and he'd known her for years – since the first day of Aviation Officer Candidate School, at the beginning of his military career, when they'd become good friends.

His knowledge of Onyx came from the fact it was run by Dax Granger... Ellie's father. His almost-father-in-law. If he'd only got round to asking her. And he *had* been planning to. When his tour of duty in Kenya came to an end. But then... Then the accident had happened, and everything became too late.

Working with Dax was difficult. And it had never gotten any easier. If anything, as the years went by, it'd gotten worse.

At first Dax had been too busy in his own grief to bother with Cooper, but as the fog had lifted, Dax's anger towards him arrived. The blame. The culpability. The pain. It had all been sent his way. And there was nothing Cooper could do about it... Because he *was* to blame. So he had to accept it. Accept that son-of-a-bitch guilt like it was ten men beating up on him in a bar. Because it hurt. Crippled him. Weighed so heavy at times he thought he couldn't breathe.

He'd often wondered, why Onyx? Why not get a job somewhere else? Maybe having to see Dax was part of some kind of penance. A painful reminder of what he'd done. Or perhaps being around Dax Granger was what he needed, because when he saw him, he could see Ellie.

And if he did leave, where the hell would he go? He'd drifted before. And it hadn't ended up pretty.

So he'd taken any assignments which came through in recovering assets from Africa. And that had just been perfect for him. Because it gave him the ability to travel, the reason and permission to go and search; but then he'd got lost in himself, believing Ellie was somewhere out there in Africa. Never once accepting she'd drowned that day.

Sometimes, he'd extended his stays up to a couple of months at a time. Just drifting. Just looking. It hadn't mattered where. Who cares where? It'd just made him feel better and everyone else feel worse.

From Kenya to the Congo to Chad to the Sudan. Getting stuck in hell holes. Getting stuck in jails… Getting stuck in drugs. And each time it was Maddie, his beautiful, loving, undeserving Maddie, and his friend, Levi Walker, who'd come and gotten him out.

And somehow, and somewhere along the line, he'd got together with Maddie. Details hazy. Timeline hazier. But she'd been good to him. Always. That he did remember. That he would never forget. Then like an entry out of a hillbilly's diary, she'd gotten pregnant and when he was wired enough, he'd proposed in a drug-induced rush of emotion whilst sitting waiting to see his therapist. For that he was ashamed. She deserved so much better.

He couldn't even remember their wedding day. Only photos proved they had.

But even after they'd got married he'd carried on searching for Ellie, and Maddie had carried on begging him not to, and it was only after their daughter, Cora, was born did he come to a full stop. Resigned himself to the fact it was over. So he tried to clean himself up. And he tried real hard. Tried to be a good Daddy. Tried to be a loving husband. Tried to forget the past.

But then, last year, after seven long years, Ellie's death certificate had come through. Officially confirming her passing. And it'd sent him spiraling. Spiraling towards Africa. Towards the nightmares. Towards the pills. And towards the edge he was about to fall off. And no matter how hard he tried, he couldn't seem to find his way back.

He thought the love for his daughter would stop it. Act like a clasp. Fastening him to where he had to be. But it hadn't. Didn't. Because he couldn't feel it anymore. Not himself. Not the people around him. And although he knew it was crazy the only thing he felt was Ellie, and the need. The need for her to still be alive so he could wash away his guilt, because if he could do that, if he could somehow know he hadn't killed her, then he might be able to find his way back. To feel again. To feel life again. Knowing he had the permission to live and love again.

'Hey, Coop, what's happening?'

Cooper's thoughts came to an abrupt halt, screeching to a stop like a car in a pit stop. He waved at Levi Walker, watching him pat down his neatly cornrowed afro.

Like Maddie, he'd known Levi since his military days. And like Maddie, he could trust Levi with his life.

'What you doing hiding your sorry butt out here? Granger's got a job for you. If you want it. But he's on the warpath.'

Cooper smiled, happy to see Levi. 'Hell, when isn't that man complaining about something?'

'Yeah, but that something always seems to be you. Don't know how you do it, Coop.'

Not wanting to think about Granger anymore, Cooper changed the subject. 'How's Mrs Walker, by the way?'

Levi kissed his teeth. 'Dorothy. She'll be the death of me. Can't a man have a drink without being cussed and moaned at? She makes Granger seem carefree. I don't know what you're smiling at 'cos she's not best pleased with you. You promised to take her to church, remember? Man, you should've heard her when you didn't show up, she bitched all day. Couldn't even slip out to go fishing, made me clean out the yard. You owe me.'

Cooper laughed. 'Shoot, Levi, tell her I'm sorry.'

'Tell her yourself. Take the heat off me a bit. But perhaps you should wait a few days; she won't be happy to see you looking like that. You know you look like shit, right?'

Cooper stepped out of his truck. His six-foot-three frame towering over Levi. Touched his pocket to make sure his blister of pills was there. Put a cigarette in his mouth and gave a rueful smile. 'Would it surprise you to know, you're not the first one who's said that... Come on, let's go and see what Granger's got in store for us.'

17

g3Ndf6

Teddy Adleman walked into the Oval Office with a cup of green tea which Joan, Wood's secretary, had enthusiastically made him. It smelt bad and it tasted worse. 'Mr President. You okay? You look a bit peaky,' Teddy said.

'I'm fine.'

'The Appalachian cheese still bothering you?'

'Yep. Everything going through me like a Goddamn sieve. You?'

Teddy winked and patted down his growing afro. 'Yep. There's fire below deck. Joan got me drinking this green tea. Don't think it'll do a damn lot of good though.'

Woods' secretary knocked before putting her head round the door. 'Mr President? Naomi Tyler is here.'

Woods sat on the cream, flower-patterned sofa. A new and welcome addition to the office. The last couch had felt like somebody had just taken it out of a dumpster, with its springs driving into you like you were lying on a corkscrew.

Craning his neck to look behind him at Joan, Woods

said, 'Show her in... and Joan, you think you could make me one of those green teas? Oh, and I like your hair by the way. Short cut suits you.'

'Mr President, I've had it like this for the past six months, but I appreciate the compliment.'

*

Naomi Tyler, an honors graduate and a former communications director of the Vice President, and one of the newest of John Woods' senior advisors, clutched her phone. 'Good morning, Mr President. Good morning, Teddy. Just to run down your out of towners for this afternoon. Shall I start?'

Flicking a large crumb of toast on the floor, which had inexplicably got caught on the ankle of his sock, Woods nodded. 'Sure. But if I'm not happy with it, Naomi, I'll be canceling and heading up towards Martha's Vineyard. I could do with some downtime.'

'Mr President, I'm afraid we wouldn't be able to cancel anything at this short notice. I'd go as far to say it'd be impossible. Unless of course you're taken ill, then...'

'Naomi. Naomi. I'm joking.'

Naomi Tyler, in a tone which could have been mistaken for the sound of a heartbeat monitor flatlining, replied, 'Oh yes. I see. Very funny, Mr President. Very funny.'

Woods raised his eyebrows, thinking the following:

Naomi was brilliant.

Sharp.

Intelligent.

Astute as hell.

Could organize better than any military personnel he'd ever met.

But as for a sense of humor? It was positively lacking. Nothing. Not one bone of funny.

Teddy's lips twitched at each side. 'Don't humor him, Naomi, we both know his jokes aren't funny. But he likes to think it's everybody else who can't see the funny. Isn't that right, Mr President?'

'I know I'm funny,' Woods said.

'Not according to the *Washington Post* you're not. What did they say about your jokes at the White House Correspondents' Dinner? Oh yeah, and I quote, *Perhaps the President should leave the jokes to his professional speech writers, but if his politics ever become as bad as his sense of humor, America's in trouble when it comes to next year's NATO summit.*'

'Hey listen, Teddy, if people don't get my jokes, I'd say that's their problem, not mine. Anyway, sorry, Naomi, please carry on.'

'Well, you've got the ceremony for the families of the servicemen and women in Delaware at fourteen hundred, and then there's only a really tight window before you need to be in Baltimore for the start of the Wounded Warrior Ride to help raise awareness of our nation's heroes.'

'I need to see my speech for that, there's a couple of things I want to change. Go on.'

'Ok, then your sixteen hundred bilateral meeting with the VP and Prime Minister of Albania is cancelled because of the current code red situation. The VP will be doing that alone and he'll bring you up to speed during your twenty-one hundred call with him. Instead of the meeting you'll convene with the National Security Council at CIA Headquarters, Langley, no later than sixteen thirty. And of course it's closed press then at eighteen hundred – I know it's later than usual, and apologies for that – you'll give the usual statement to the pooled press. Then at…'

Woods put up his hand. Cut in. 'Naomi. Don't do this to me. I quit.'

Touching her immaculate, slightly too-tight weave, Naomi frowned and, looking flustered, glanced down at her cell, then at Woods, then back down at her cell, then thought about glancing at Teddy but in the end said, 'That's a joke isn't it, Mr President? That's one of your funny jokes.'

'Well, it was until you killed it.'

Teddy Adleman grinned. 'Naomi, can you excuse us? I need to run something by the President.'

Naomi glanced at her watch. 'But…'

'Breathe, Naomi. I promise I won't make him late. Give me five minutes and whilst you're at it have some of Joan's green tea.'

Naomi said, 'That's funny.'

'No, it isn't.'

'It's not a joke, is it?'

'Absolutely not.'

*

Woods stretched his arms above his head. Got a nasty twinge in his back as he did so. Gave a yelp of pain and decided he was getting old. 'What's up, Teddy?'

'Something interesting. I wanted to run it past you.'

Getting himself in a better position, Woods kneaded his back. 'Go on.'

'I had a call from an old colleague last night who works in the police department in Chatham. He's been a cop longer than most people have stayed married. An all-round good type. Anyway, a couple of days after the coffee shop bomber – '

'You have to call him that?'

'Nope. Not if it offends.'

'I'd rather we stick to calling him by his name. Plain old David Thorpe. It just feels like the press are making it into a media circus by giving him a nickname – a kind of celebrity status. Takes away from the heinousness of the act, and helps to fuel the massive advertising campaigns terror groups like Daesh have. He'll be on the cover of their magazine, *Dabiq*, before you know it, hailed as a Goddamn hero... I don't know, maybe it's just me.'

'No, I'm with you there, John.'

'Tell me something, Teddy. When did terror groups start to have such a slick propaganda machine? Have you seen that magazine? It's like a glossy periodical, makes *People Magazine* look outdated.'

'It's just another piece of the jigsaw in their mass-radicalization drive. Make it look like anyone who joins will be part of some blockbuster Hollywood movie.'

Woods picked up his green tea. Smelled it. Put it right back down on the walnut table.

'You know they named the magazine after a small town in Syria, because according to Islamic prophecies that's where they'll have their last battle, before the end of the world occurs.'

'Got to give it to them, they know a great marketing angle when they see it. Makes it all sound appealing... Sorry, John, I've just become aware of the time – and aware Naomi's probably on the other side of that door having some kind of panic attack, so let me get to the point. My guy got a call from this kid – well, when I say kid, the man's in his twenties. Apparently he tried to tell the FBI that he had some information which might be of interest to them, but nobody would listen. He's a bit of a loner, got some kind of learning difficulties, and has a history of calling up the police department telling them things like he's seen a UFO, he knows who really killed JFK, the world is about to be taken over by an invading alien life force.'

'Sounds like a movie tagline.'

'Well, exactly, the kid's clearly a bit of a conspiracy theorist. He's been marked down as a timewaster by the Feds, and newspapers got wise to him a long time ago – one media outlet had to get a civil restraining order against him because he was making up to two hundred calls a day. He's spent time in the slammer for breaking other orders against him. Spends most of his time hauled up in his apartment surrounded by all this equipment which tracks and monitors hurricanes, earthquakes and stuff, no doubt trying to track down aliens as well. Like this is his hobby. But here's the thing, his place is located only a few blocks away from where David Thorpe's truck exploded. Anyway, he's got this junk set out all the time. Apparently you can't move for it.'

'I take it from the word junk, you mean equipment.'

'Exactly... So one of the things he had was a seismograph. Go figure. But basically, I guess you know, a seismograph records earth tremors and the propagation of electric waves and the like. Says he never turned this thing off, and this is where it gets interesting: kid swears blind there were two unusual recorded tremors that evening.'

'What do you mean?'

'Well, his seismograph picked up the tremor of the bomb, but a split second later, it also picked up another tremor. He's convinced there were two blasts.'

Woods shrugged, slightly distracted by Teddy's moustache, a new but not necessarily flattering addition to his face. 'Yeah, one would be the bomb, the other tremor would be when part of the building came down.'

'That's exactly what the FBI said to him, brushed him away like he was some kind of bug, they're not interested. But he kept calling the station where my friend's based, almost got himself arrested *again*. That's when my guy went to see him just to check he's okay. Like I say, the kid's got issues.'

'And?'

'The kid's adamant there were two bomb blasts and the actual building coming down is recorded on a different seismic wave. This buddy of mine, the one who's been a cop forever, who's had to listen throughout his working life to that *gut* that cops have, he feels the kid's genuine.'

'Not that I'm taking this seriously, but it's easy enough to prove. Get an expert to study the readouts.'

'Well it would be easy, if he had them.'

'I'm not following.'

'The night before my buddy decided to go and see what this kid was all about, turns out his apartment was broken into. And you can guess the rest. The seismograph along with all the recordings were taken.'

'What? Oh come on, Teddy, like you say this kid clearly has issues. He's a fantasist. I can't believe – in the nicest possible way – you're taking up my time telling me this. I mean, who in Chatham is going to break into his place for seismograph readings? You said yourself he's got a history of calling up the police department with all kind of crazy stuff. It's sad. He probably didn't even have a seismograph. Did he report the break in?'

'No, didn't bother.'

'There you go. It's obvious. He didn't have anything to report, but had to make something up when your friend went to see him, because how else was he going to explain why he didn't have a seismograph in his apartment? He probably never thought anybody would ever visit and when they did, he had to lie to cover up the fact he didn't have one. I get that.'

'Not necessarily. Maybe he didn't report it because he really did figure no-one would believe him.'

'Is he saying anything else was taken?'

'No. Place wasn't even trashed and the lock wasn't even busted.'

Woods raised his eyebrows. 'So how did they get in?'

'Well, and hear me on this, if anyone really did get in, it must have been an expert job, not some bum breaking in and looking for a few bucks. It was a straight in and out job.'

Woods rubbed his face and absentmindedly reached for the cold cup of green tea, and immediately regretted it and pulled a face and put it down and said, 'This all sounds like a load of baloney. I wouldn't give it a second thought… but I'm picking up you're giving it some credence.'

'I trust my buddy and he seems to trust the kid, even with his history.'

'You're not making this easy for me, because if what he's saying is true then…'

'Then we've got a problem.'

'And you really believe it?'

'Part of me says, this kid is just looking for some kind of attention and the whole thing is bull. That's the rational, reasoning side of me but the other part of me – and it's speaking loudly – says to go along with my buddy's instinct; this kid is for real.'

'Did your friend tell anyone else about this?'

Teddy shook his head and stood up and spoke all at the same time. 'No, and he told the kid not to say anything either until he got back to him.'

'So, if we go for a minute with the idea he's telling the truth – and that's a big if – the next question is, do we know who else apart from the FBI this kid called about the recordings on his seismograph?'

'That's the problem. There were a lot of people, I think. He was obviously pretty determined to get somebody to listen. But the main people were the FBI, Chatham police department and, oh yeah, get this: the CIA. Counter terrorism. Chuck's department. But not only his department, Chuck himself.'

18

c5 Bd7

'Who drank all the Mountain Dew? You never heard of restocking? What is it with this place?'

Levi sat in the kitchen of Onyx. Feet up and grinning. 'Don't look at me, Coop. Never liked the stuff myself. Too gassy.'

'Is that a fact?'

'Sure is.'

'Straight up?'

'Straight up, Coop.'

Cooper grinned. 'Let me tell you some...'

'Well if it isn't Thomas J Cooper, returning from the dead – though to look at you the jury's still out on that one.' With Levi's conversation cut short, Cooper turned towards the sound of the thunderous voice. Not that he had to look. This was Austin Rosedale Young. 'I heard you were back. But I say, for how long? How long till you run off this time, boy? Come on, Thomas, why don't you save us all the trouble and turn your sorry ass round and go back to wherever and whatever you've been doing? What do ya say, sugar?'

His strong Texan accent filled the small room but Cooper said nothing. Just stared. Stared at the figure dressed head to toe in denim, refusing to let Rosedale get to him like he'd let him get to him before.

'You lost your tongue, boy? Come on, Thomas, I'll pack your bags for you now.'

Since his military days, Rosedale had always been Cooper's nemesis, though in fairness to Rosedale when they'd been in the chaos of the DRC last year, in the depths of the rain-soaked forests amongst pain, murder and witchcraft, Rosedale had come through for him. Stopped him falling off that edge he was so often on. They'd found an understanding. A friendship? Perhaps… Maybe then. But now? Never.

He'd seen Rosedale a few times since the DRC investigation. They'd been fishing. The three of them. Levi, Rosedale and Cooper, putting the world to rights amongst the lakes of Michigan. But he'd been struggling to hold it together. And Rosedale had struggled not to be his obnoxious self. But that had been then. And now? Welcome home.

Standing his six-foot-five frame, with an additional two inches of cowboy boot, in the kitchen doorway and chewing on the oversized, unlit cigar in his mouth, with a delighted look in his eyes and a wind-tanned face and his previously dyed black hair now brown, Rosedale winked.

'Get off my back. And if it's alright with you, I'd like to pass…' Cooper said.

'Pass on what, sugar?'

Cooper blew out his cheeks. Felt the packet of pills in his pocket. Felt his temper rise. Felt his fists tighten. Untighten. 'Just get out of my way. What's your problem?'

Austin Rosedale Young, a one-time American sniper, a one-time fellow SEAL, a one-time CIA clandestine agent and now a fellow employee of Onyx, leant towards Cooper. 'My problem, Thomas, is that despite your promises to stop doing crazy, you're still doing the pills – and don't try to deny it, you're a campaign boy for opioids. A pharmaceutical company's dream and, as such, you're a liability to us and this job.'

'I told you before. I'm clean.'

'I know you did, and I told you before… *bullshit*. But I tell you what, why don't we put this baby to rest once and for all? You turn out those pants pockets of yours and prove me wrong, 'cos we all know you'd like to do that… Well?'

'Go to hell.'

'What's the problem, Thomas? You got something to hide?'

'When I have to answer to you, let me know.'

'Maybe not me, but what about to your daughter? Don't you think you should be answering to Cora? Telling her why Daddy is never around?'

Cooper stood back. Two steps. Made it three. Tilted his head. Straightened it up. Shook it a little. Shook it again. 'What the hell has my daughter got to do with you?'

'Well, someone has to look out for her.'

Cooper opened his arms. Wide. Bemused. Hell, no, he was pissed. And big time. 'Am I missing something here? Have I suddenly stepped into the wrong life? The life which has you in it. Which has Austin Rosedale Young telling *me* about my own kid. Now *that* is crazy. And if I didn't know better I'd say you had a dog in the fight.'

Rosedale flicked up his cowboy hat and leant to the side and crossed one foot over the other and smiled and winked and said, 'No dog, Thomas. Just telling it how it is. Let's call it concern.'

'What's going on?'

Maddie stood behind Rosedale, who immediately stepped aside for her to pass. Her brown hair tumbled over her brown face which held her brown freckles and hid her brown eyes.

'Well? Levi, you want to tell me what's going on?'

'Can a man not sit here and have a Mountain Dew without interruption?'

In his ear, Cooper said, 'I knew it.'

Throwing her Tiger Anderson rifle on the table, Maddie turned to Cooper. 'Is this funny to you, Tom? Because I don't think there's anything funny about you and Rosedale at each other's throats. We're supposed to be a team.'

He sniffed. Irritated. Trying to hold onto the last drops of patience. 'Rosedale thinks it's okay for him to tell me about Cora.'

Maddie gave a small smile to Rosedale. 'Well, somebody needs to tell you. Our daughter needs better, and the thing is, you know it.'

Cooper didn't have to look in a mirror to know he'd turned red. Red like the desert paintbrush plants which grew high up in the Colorado Mountains by Little Bear Rock.

'Maddie, I don't think this is appropriate to do this here.'

'Don't you? And why would that be, Tom?'

'I know you're pissed with me and I'm sorry I've hurt you, but doing this is not okay. So I'm asking you to stop because everyone in this Goddamn place seems to have lost their minds – but especially you, Maddison.'

'Don't speak to her like that.'

Cooper whipped round quick. 'Rosedale, keep out of it.'

'The hell I will, Thomas.'

The touch on Rosedale's arm from Maddie didn't go unnoticed by Cooper.

'It's okay, Rosedale.'

'You sure?'

Cooper said, 'Yeah, she's sure. My *wife* is sure.'

At which point, Dax Granger prowled past the open doorway like the solitary lynx, not bothering to turn to look, not bothering to stop, just growling his orders as he disappeared down the hallway. 'All of you. In my office… *Now*. And that means you too, Levi.'

19

Rb3 Ng3

The four of them stood in Granger's office, reminding Cooper of the times he'd stood in front of the principal back in high school when trouble had followed him like the winter followed fall.

Through the side of his mouth, Cooper whispered to Maddie. 'When the hell did you and Rosedale get so cozy?'

Whispering back but determined to turn it into a hiss, Maddie replied, 'Shut up, Tom.'

'I think we need to talk.'

'There's nothing to talk *about*. So just drop it.'

Leaning back on his brown leather chair, Granger hard-stared Maddie and Cooper. Glanced down in disgust at the salad his wife had made him. Let out an annoyed grunt, irritated by the fact it was ultimately a pile of Goddamn leafy lettuce and *not* the Pastrami double white crusty sub with the added delights of onion, cheese, and yellow beer mustard that he'd asked for.

Transferring his culinary disappointment towards his

employees, Granger said, 'You two finished your conversation? Finished your gassin'? Because maybe it's escaped your notice but I've got a business to run.'

With transference clearly the order of the day, Cooper, still pissed and ruminating heavily over Rosedale, snapped at his boss. 'We're not kids, Granger, and my days of standing to attention finished when I left the military.'

Granger sat up. Leaned forward. Picked up his fork just so he could shake it at Cooper.

'Here's the deal. I don't want to get into any conversation with you. You're lucky you're even here after the stunts you pulled this year. If it wasn't for Maddie pleading your case, this place would be a no entry sign to you. You understand what I'm saying?'

'Oh, I understand alright, Granger, but it may surprise you to know that the only thing I want to do is my job. Nothing else. No fights. Nothing. So no conversation suits me just fine.'

Granger pushed his glasses up his nose and raised his eyebrows. 'The job is all you better do, and I'll be watching.'

Cooper said nothing.

'Okay, so this job came through last week. They came to us because Onyx has a worldwide reputation of being the best in the business.'

Taking a long, drawn-out pull of his cigar and letting the smoke slowly twist and rise over his face to hit the brim of his cowboy hat, Rosedale winked, 'So you like to say.'

'Put that out, or at least open the window. And you can give me one whilst you're at it. And don't say anything about *I shouldn't be smoking*, I'll look after my own Goddamn health if it's all the same with you. Plus, for your information, I don't just *like* to say. It's a fact. We *are* the best, *No job is too big or...*'

'*... too much trouble.*'

The fork was pointed at Rosedale. 'Is my business a joke to you, Rosedale? Because if it is, you can get the hell out too... Now, this job. It's sensitive. So no questions. No straying from the objective. And yes, that's directed at you, Cooper. What we have is a missing ship. A small general cargo ship, owned by a Turkish company.'

Maddie said, 'What's their business?'

'Import and export. Shipping everything from olives to live stock.'

'That's what you call sensitive?' Maddie asked.

'Look, to tell you the truth, I don't care if it's olives, meatloaf or Goddamn waffles they're into. If I say you treat this job as sensitive, that's exactly what you do... It's not the usual kind of job where the bank is owed, or a private firm wants their money. Nobody owes anything. Probably the first time we've ever had that, but as our success rate in locating high value assets from all over the world is markedly greater than those of our competitors, it makes sense for a company to contact us, for tracing purposes only... The ship's believed to be at a location just off the coast of Tubruq, Libya. In fact they've given me the ship's coordinates.'

'If they've got the coordinates then how can it be lost?'

Granger banged his fist down on his walnut desk and wasn't too perturbed to see his lunch box, along with wilted salad, knocked onto the floor. There and then he decided there'd be nothing else for it, he'd have to go and get a crusty sub. 'Jesus Christ, Cooper, I told you *not* to ask questions.'

'Come on, Granger, there's asking questions and then there's common sense. Why don't they go and see themselves?'

'Enough, okay... This is the deal: the coordinates show the ship is roughly twenty miles off the coast of Libya, but the shipping company can't be one hundred percent sure it's there.'

'They've never heard of tracking? AIS tracking? LRIT equipment? The crew must have radioed in vessel data position at least every six hours?' Maddie mused.

'What is it with you people? *No* questions. This is what they want.'

'Come on, Granger, you're asking us to go and fetch a ship off the coast of Libya and do a job without knowing details.'

'Actually, Maddie, I'm not asking you to take back the ship to them. I'm asking you to go and see if it's there.'

'But then you want us to take it back to port, right?'

'No. The specific orders are not to board the ship.'

'What?'

Granger, red faced now, shook his head. 'The brief is, go and speak to the owner. Then go to the location. See if it's there. Report back to the owner. Period.'

'But...'

'No Maddie, no more. But for your information – and this is only so you'll shut the hell up – all the tracking and long range radios are turned off. That's all I know myself.'

'I don't get it. They can't. There are regulations.'

'They can and they did, and it's not for you to get. It's for you to do your Goddamn job.'

Maddie pushed some more. 'But what about the crew?'

'What about them?'

'Well, what happened to them?'

Granger shuffled in his seat, and shuffled the papers on his desk, though Maddie suspected his uncomfortable look was less to do with his positioning and more to do with what he was holding back on.

'Broadly speaking, Maddison, they got into trouble.'

'What kind of trouble? And why didn't they radio coast guards for help? Or failing that at least send out a signal? Someone would've come. To quote the UN Maritime Convention on the Law of the Sea...'

As quickly as possible, because he certainly wasn't in any kind of mood to listen to Maddie quote anything, much less maritime law, Granger cut in. 'Spare us on that one.'

'Well, my point is if they'd signaled for help the other boats and ships around would've proceeded to render assistance.'

Granger got up from his chair and walked across the room to the door and with something like relief, opened it and signaled for them to leave. 'Unlike you, Maddison, they listened to orders. Now if you wouldn't mind, I need to make a phone call.'

'I'm not following.'

'Maddison, the crew's orders were not to radio for help under *any* circumstances... Now look, I've told you everything I can. You, Rosedale and Cooper will be leaving on Thursday, you'll get all the other details later today. Levi, you'll be doing the usual administration and base support stuff here at home. I'm flying to New York tonight so I won't see you till you all get back. But let me say this. You three, I'm warning you. God knows I am. Locate the boat, then just come back here. That's it. That's the objective. Nothing else. *Just do your job.*'

20

hg3 Nh5

Chuck wasn't sure what it was about the White House coffee but it always tasted as if it'd been made with a splash of resentment. A spoonful of democratic antipathy towards anybody who wasn't a liberal sympathizer.

Putting his cup down, he faced President Woods. Crossed his mind how well the man looked, compared to the last time he'd seen him when he'd looked positively ill. Not that the President's health was his concern, nor problem. His problem was Woods' policies, which hindered, restricted, curtailing his ability to protect the country he'd spent his life trying to protect.

Frustrated, Chuck snapped the top onto the silver fountain pen he never used. Faded away from his own thoughts and faded back up into the conversation, to hear – for what must have been the eighth, ninth time, in less than half an hour – the words 'no way' from the supposed people's President.

'No way, Chuck. Abdul-Aziz bin Hamad? He's affiliated

with Al Qaeda. No. We discussed it a few weeks ago at length and my same reply stands; it's not even on the table.'

'So you keep saying, Mr President, but I don't understand your stance on this. Prisoner swaps, prisoner release, lifting sanctions and negotiation. These are nothing new. I don't have to give you a history lesson but it's been going on since the time of George Washington.'

'And in some kind of shape and form it'll continue, but prisoners who the United States government deem to be terrorists, will no longer be used as high value negotiation chips.'

Chuck looked around at those present. Woods, Lyndon, who thankfully was keeping quiet and Teddy, Chief of Staff. 'You know what keeps me awake at night, Mr President? It's how to keep America safe. I ask myself the question, am I missing anything? Is there something more, however unorthodox, which I and the CIA should be doing? And it's the unorthodox which helps keep my department one step ahead. What is detrimental to us is, as Donald Rumsfeld said, our failure of the imagination on what is likely.'

Woods, not wholly without flippancy, replied, 'I prefer to work on factual.'

'To work solely on the basis of factual would be to fail in my duty, Mr President. It would be an impossibility to do so. Most times my field agents only have the luxury of factual when our imagination has worked out what is likely. Rumsfeld was right when he talked about how when we have the likely, the likely takes us down the road of risk and uncertainty, and only at the end of it, likely *may* turn into an actuality. It is after all about the known unknowns.'

'But that's *exactly* why we have you and the CTC. To find out those things, whether through human intelligence, data or visual technology.'

'And it's still HI which gives us the most intel, but that's only because the CIA are able to negotiate with countries and governments who sympathize with the ideology of the terror groups. And as you know, Mr President, prisoner release using high value detainees, such as Bin Hamad, are essential to that negotiation for the CIA.'

'There are other ways, Chuck, and I know other administrations have been more open to this course of action, but not this one…' Woods paused, finally succumbing to the plate of chocolate cookies in front of him, then added, 'I'm not changing my stance on this, Chuck.'

Watching crumbs from the chocolate cookie flake off, at the point of entering Woods' mouth, and float down onto the highly polished table to form a circular pattern, Chuck, irritated by what he saw as dangerous liberal thinking, shook his head. 'You're making a big mistake, Mr President.'

Woods took a large gulp of the simple black coffee Joan had made him. He didn't know what it was but there was something about the White House coffee; it always tasted pretty damn good. 'I won't go against the American people. As we speak, America's afraid. We're on code red. We've had bombs and suicide bombs and people are afraid out there. So we need to stand as a nation. That's the only way we're going to win the war on terror. To stand as one.'

As was Chuck Harrison's practice, he said, 'Bullshit…! This isn't a union address speech, or some campaign trail to pick up votes. This is real, Mr President, and I know what we're up against. The only people who stand as one out there is *us*. The CIA. We're in the field. On the ground. We go in *way before* you bring any of the red team analysts to weigh up the odds of collateral damage, *before* you sit around this table watching in real time the military offensive, and *before* any hi-tech drone strike. And the only reason why any of those guys *can* do their job is because we've paved the way. Alone. Without back up. Without assurances that what we're getting into is really what it seems. So, with respect, the idea that somehow the nation stands at one, is complete *bullshit.*'

Woods thought.

Contemplated.

Weighed up.

Wondered if.

Then decided *not* to haul up Chuck for the way he'd spoken. Passion often induced the versing of tongues towards the expletive. 'I'm sorry, Chuck, but I made an oath to serve the American people, and I *won't*, when they're not looking, release the terrorists who've waged war against and masterminded attacks on our nation.'

Chuck, in a tone which did not rise or did not fall, said, 'You really don't know what you're doing, and a lot more people will get hurt unless you act now. You're putting lives at risk.'

Woods, using his tongue to dislodge a piece of cookie from one of his back molars, which needed fixing, pointed at Chuck. 'I think you're on dangerous territory, here. I don't appreciate at all what you've just said, and I certainly don't appreciate the way you're saying it.'

'You may not, but it's a fact. A hard fact. Like it's a fact that you want me to go into battle, but you're sending me into the ring with my hands tied behind my back. I don't have to tell you that war is not just played out on the fields. It's behind the scenes. The communication. The *negotiation*... The deals we are compelled to do whether we like them or not. There's been many a possible conflict which has been prevented by all of the above. And that's what I'm saying is: to help us fight terror, Mr President, I need to be able to make deals. I need a way to find out about the whens, the wheres and the hows.'

'Chuck, I have to call a close on this meeting soon, but to put it straight on the table, I don't want the CIA being what it was. It's a new dawn. More transparent. More ethical. The reputation needs to be rebuilt.'

'I don't know what you think we're running here, Mr President, but trying to turn the CIA into a political PR stunt just isn't going to work. All the politicians on either side love to holler about making America great again. But I'd settle for making it safe again right now.'

Losing his temper, slightly – a lot – Woods growled. 'And how the hell are we supposed to do that when you want us to release prisoners like white doves at a wedding?'

'Nobody's saying that. What's important is the selected few. We need to keep friends with some of these countries. Sometimes we have to realize the prize is bigger than the stake. To release a prisoner, to transfer him back to his own country – even if that prisoner is a major league terrorist – in exchange of vital intel from unusual, uncooperative or even hostile governments is *worth* it. I know it may stick in our throats, but let it stick. Let it choke, compared to having to stand and watch another 9/11 because we weren't willing to play the game.'

'This government won't be blackmailed.'

'Not blackmail, Mr President, just how things need to be done. This is a new era. The Middle East is a complicated animal, and sometimes you need to feed it. Countries such as Qatar, where Bin Hamad is from; as you know, it's paramount we're able to maintain good relations so we're able to keep our military base there. We all know that without it, things would be so much more difficult to monitor. We couldn't keep an eye on the Gulf, or Iraq and Iran, or the terror groups within them. Not only that, Mr President, but we rely on them to mediate between us and groups like the Taliban. Mr President, I'm advising you as the acting head of the CTC that you shouldn't rule out the necessity of prisoner release and transfer.'

'Chuck, I respect your knowledge on these matters. But this administration won't be part of what I see as being complicit in this chess game. We do things properly around here.'

'There's no such thing as properly when it comes to this country being attacked. Whether it's from lone suicide bombers, or from more sophisticated assaults... If it were me, Mr President, I'd tear up and throw out all those legislations that go back and forth between you and Congress. There is no rule book anymore. No laws are going to protect you from what's out there. And believe me, if you don't, you're going to regret this.'

'If I didn't know better, Chuck, that sounds like a threat.'

'A threat? You kidding me? I'm not the one you need to

be worrying about. The threats are when everyday folk ride on the subway. When they take their kids to school. When they step onto a plane or train, go to work, or even wait in line to buy groceries. It's waiting for them. And mainly because it's getting harder for us to stop it. The explosion of the internet. Encrypted communication, which as a nation we are *so* behind with; even the terrorists are more advanced than us. And when you add to that the reluctance of a number of Middle Eastern governments to assist, we've got a major problem. What it cuts down to is we're trying to follow leads, prevent and foil attacks, and all without help from your administration. You're costing lives.'

'You're talking bull, Chuck.'

'Am I? Am I really? I don't think so. You know what my idea of bull is? It's when you won't release prisoners the CIA are asking you to, *because they're terrorists*, yet your administration will sell advanced weaponry to the same countries that these terrorists come from – and not just come from, some of them are even transparently affiliated to the governments of their kingdoms.'

Woods clenched his teeth, regretted it immediately as his back molar sent out a warning shot.

He said, 'That is a *different* issue.'

Chuck shook his head. 'Try telling that to the solider who's being shot at by terrorists with an advanced weapon. The same advanced weapon sold by the United States government.'

'For God's sake, Chuck, we don't sell to terrorists.'

'Agreed. But we do sell to governments who we know sympathize, donate money and weapons to the groups that want to see the West destroyed. And if we're talking about Qatar, weren't they the ones who gave Khalid Sheikh Mohammed sanctuary? A hiding place? Mr President, the scars from 9/11 are still healing, still unresolved, yet we deal, negotiate and do business with countries who are known terrorist sympathizers, as if we're inviting them to the Minnesota state fair... Everything is connected, Mr President. Everything! And one day, it'll come back and bite America on its ass... Let me tell you something. You put me in the post because you knew I was the best at what I did. There is *nobody* better for the job, yet you continually block me and question my judgment. We have to jump through *Goddamn* hoops so the country can sleep well in their beds and people can get up and go to work without fear.'

For the first time in the meeting, Lyndon Clarke added to the discussion. 'Chuck, I think now would be an appropriate point for you to calm down.'

Chuck glared at Lyndon. Stood up. Walked round towards him. 'Not too long ago in this country you could never speak to me like that. You understand what I'm saying, Lyndon?'

'Are you kidding me, Chuck? Are you really saying what I think you're saying?'

The coldness hit Chuck's eyes. Words. Whole demeanor. 'I don't know Lyndon, you tell me. What am I saying?'

'Chuck, I'd say that's enough. Don't go there,' Woods said.

Chuck, pouring himself a glass of water, shrugged. 'Understood, Mr President, I know when to stop. Isn't that right, Lyndon?'

Calm, quiet and tense, Woods said, 'We've got to close now, but there is just one other point, Chuck... What do you know about a kid who had this theory that there were two impact tremors on the day of the bomb?'

Calm, quiet and tense, Chuck replied, 'I have no idea what you're talking about, Mr President. Should I?'

'Some information came to me via one of my staff that this kid was making a lot of noise about a seismograph reading he'd taken on the evening of the bomb. He was desperate to get someone to listen. Called up every agency there was, apparently.'

'There's always someone with some kind of conspiracy theory.'

'That's true, but according to this source, he got in contact not only with the CTC, but you actually spoke to him.'

Chuck shook his head. Locked eyes with the President. 'Not wanting to sound disrespectful, but it hardly sounds likely does it? I mean, if I met up with or spoke to every crazy oddball who called up the CTC, I wouldn't have time to do my job... So, *no*, Mr President, I certainly didn't meet up with some mixed up kid from Chatham with some mixed up theory. But I'm curious, how did this *source* of yours know I'd *supposedly* spoken to him? Did the kid tell them that we'd met up...? Seriously, Mr President, I'm surprised you even asked me.'

'Why did you say Chatham?'

'Excuse me?'

'You said, the kid was from Chatham. I never told you that.'

With as much ice as Chuck could muster, he said, 'I know you didn't, but I don't think I'd be much use as a counter terrorism expert if I couldn't figure out the simplest of things.

You told me he'd taken a seismograph reading on the evening of the bomb, so it's pretty basic to guess he comes from the area, seeing as all the other bombs went off in the afternoon. I don't know what you're trying to insinuate, but whatever it is, I don't like it. Now, if you'll excuse me, Mr President, I have a country to try to protect.'

21

f4 ef4

The heat of the day made the air feel heavier, denser than it really was, and the miles of clearing where villages had once stood stretched out into the distance, where the distance met the edge of the earth and the edge of the earth met with the unforgiving sun.

Shots fired out from guns, and the sound drifted and disappeared far into the beyond.

'Hold the gun firmly... that's it. Against your shoulder. Hold it steady. Have you got your aim?'

'Yes.'

The cudgel was carved from the locust bean tree, and the strike to the side of the head ruptured and split the skin of the soldier's temple as they fell, toppling down into the burnt-out grasslands which no longer gave shelter to the lizards and snakes that darted and weaved, seeking refuge from the African sun.

'Comment t'appelles-tu? What's your name?'

'Amira.'

'Bonjour, Amira. Welcome… But I think you're forgetting your manners… How should you address me?'

Through pain filled tears, Amira cried. '*Commandant.* Commandant.'

'Yes, Amira: Commandant. Do not forget it.'

'No, Commandant.'

'We cannot always oblige; but we can always speak obligingly…Voltaire. He was a French poet, but he was a man who spoke out against Islam. And what does that make him, Amira?'

The blood ran into Amira's mouth as she shook and began to talk. 'A Kafir, Commandant.'

'Good, Amira. You're learning.'

'And what is a Kafir?'

'An infidel. A non-believer, Commandant.'

'Excellent. And what does it say to do with non-believers, Amira?'

'It says, when you encounter the Kafirs on the battlefield, *cut off their heads until you have defeated them. Seize them and kill them wherever they are*… Commandant.'

'That's right. A Kafir will always be our enemy and we shall always treat them as such. Now get up.'

Pushing herself back up onto her feet, Amira picked up her gun, listening to the graveled voice of the Commandant. 'When I tell you, fire your weapon.'

'Yes, Commandant.'

The Commandant signaled, shouting to a nearby solider who stood attentively a short distance away.

'Our newest soldier, Amira is ready…'

Turning back to Amira, whose-dirt covered face was

streaked with blood, the Commandant said, 'Hold your aim... Fire.'

The gun discharged a round of bullets which hit the sand, spraying and plunging into the hot dry earth.

'Try again, Amira.'

'Yes, Commandant.'

She aimed once more.

'Now wait...Wait... Fire...'

A smile spread across the Commandant's face. 'Amira, look, a hit. You did well. God is great.'

In the distance a woman staggered. Trying to run. Trying to push through the pain as the bullet embedded deep into her calf. Tearing it open to expose the tissue. She stumbled over the dead bodies of those who had gone before. Her screams merging as one with the cries of the others. The men and women. The children. Who stood, lined up and ready, waiting for their turn to become the target.

'Again, Amira, you need to get it right. Finish it off. But this time, aim for her head.'

A shot.

A thud.

As the woman fell to the ground in the distance, where the distance met the edge of the earth and the edge of the earth met with the unforgiving sun.

22

c6 bc6

It wouldn't have been a house he would ever have chosen to live in. Not under any circumstances. But as Cooper dried his face in the cream and gold secocnd floor bathroom, he couldn't deny that 1600 Pennsylvania Avenue felt real homely. Which was strange, considering.

Cooper didn't bother to look in the mirror. What was there to look at? He knew his hair was on the top of his head. He knew his face held his nose. He knew he ought to get a shave. Anything else, he didn't need to know. Not the bloodshot eyes. Not the fading red and yellow bruises which made his skin look like the setting of the sun.

He let out a long sigh. He slipped his hand deep into the pocket of the well-worn jeans he'd gotten out from the back of his closet, and then like a high voltage shockwave, it hit him. Jolted. Sending him spinning. He'd forgotten it was there. The pills... The pills... The OxyContin he was trying to part ways with, but which never seemed to want to part ways with him.

Caressing the roundness. The smooth hard shape. Cooper twirled it over, over and through, between the gaps of his fingers. Welcoming it like an old friend. And then he stopped. Stared at himself in the mirror. Seeing but not feeling.

He watched this stranger in the mirror, the way their mouth blew out their breath. The way they quickly sucked back the air.

Chest out.

Chest in.

Then he watched their hand slowly pull the pills out of their pocket and heard them say, 'So what do you say, Cooper? What's it going to be? Which way you going to choose this time?'

He turned away before he heard the reply, popping the pill into his mouth as he exited the bathroom to walk along the hallway, forcing his mind to think of nothing but the idea of having nothing to think of.

'Dude! Seriously! How long does it take a guy to use the bathroom? *Black Ops* waits for no man.' Jackson Woods grinned, gesturing Cooper to hurry back to the private sitting room and the abandoned game.

He winked at Jackson, saying nothing as he tried to ignore – as he always did – the thick, raised scar running down Jackson's forehead. The result, as well a constant reminder, of what had happened that day on the yacht all those years ago.

'Coop! Hey!'

Hearing the voice behind him, Cooper span round on the heel of his boot, feeling it sink into the cream, deep-pile carpet.

'Hey, John, how's it going?'

President Woods tilted his head. 'Maybe it's going better than it is with you.'

Half smile. Almost. Cooper said, 'You think?'

'Can we talk, Coop?'

'I thought that's what we were doing.'

Woods stepped in. Head still tilted. 'Jackson, can you give us a minute?'

Hating the tension but desperate to break it, Jackson tried to make light. 'Oh come on, Dad, not now! I'm about to totally annihilate Coop. I'm on a kill-streak and I'm feeling lucky.'

Woods, not taking his eyes off Cooper, spoke to his son with an inflexibility. 'Jackson, I said I need a minute.'

Without another word, Jackson slipped back into the sitting room, gently closing the door behind him, leaving the two men facing off in the hallway.

'Why do you make it so difficult all the time, Coop?'

Wanting to feel the buzz of the pill begin – desperate to – Cooper pulled back. Away from the smell of expensive cologne. Away from the perfectly smooth-shaven face only inches away. 'Listen, John, I don't know what you're talking about.'

'That's why we need to talk.'

'No. That's why *you* need to talk. I'm fine.'

'Really? You don't look it.'

'I know, I look like shit. Now tell me something I don't know.'

Woods wiped his hand down his chin. Keeping his temper. Keeping his mouth from saying anything he'd later regret.

Didn't work. 'Cut the crap, Coop. I heard about everything that went down. You could've been looking at a long time in a jailhouse.'

'And how's that?'

Woods' voice had raised. Pulled himself together. Spoke in a pissed hush. 'How's that? Am I missing something here? You need me to jog your memory?'

'No.'

'Grand theft auto, aggravated motor vehicle theft in the first degree...'

'Be my guest, why don't you? I mean, who am I to say no?'

'...Reckless driving, exhibition of speed, vagrancy...'

'Leave vagrancy out of it... Have you finished now, John? Because I hear an Xbox calling my name.'

'Where the hell do you get off being so casual about it?'

'I don't mean to be rude here, but I'm trying to figure out *quite* what it has to do with you, John.'

Woods felt the pulse in his molar begin to throb. 'You wouldn't be standing here if it wasn't for me. I called in some favors.'

'You?'

'Well, not *me* exactly, but I got someone I know to call in some favors.'

'Wouldn't want to leave a trail.'

'Goddam it, Coop, why do you have to make everything a fight? Even when someone's trying to help you.'

'I didn't ask you to help me.'

Infuriated, Woods gripped hold of his temper. 'No, you didn't, but stupid me, thinking you'd prefer your freedom to sitting on your stubborn ass in a cell. No need to thank me, hey Coop. Anytime.'

'Have you finished? Can I go now? Because I'm here to see your son.'

Woods stared and shook his head and closed his eyes and said, 'Why, Coop? Why does it have to be like this?'

'It doesn't. Here's the thing, John, I could just say *hey*, and you could just do the same. But the problem is, *you* want to talk when there's nothing to say.'

Quietly. 'What were you doing?'

'I'm not following.'

Woods touched his slightly dry lips. Felt the speck of peeled skin. Didn't pull.

'What were you doing? Why did you drive towards the motorcade?'

As excuses went, Cooper knew it sounded like a bad one. 'I just needed to get my head clear after the court.'

'So you hijacked some guy's car? Went like a bat out of hell down the highway? Off-roaded, then crashed, before running away from the FBI? All that just so you could clear your head?'

Cooper shrugged. Finally felt the buzz of the pill beginning to work. 'Yeah, well if you put it like that... anyway, as nice as this chat is, John, I'll be damned if I'm going to let Jackson beat me.'

Woods grabbed Cooper's arm. Hard. Tight. Wasn't letting go. 'No, I want to know.'

'Let go of my arm, John.'

'Just tell me.'

It was Cooper's turn to step forward. 'What do you want

118

me to say? That it was crazy? Or do you want me to say something else? Is that it? You want me to say I was worried? There. There you go, I said it. *I was worried something had happened to you.*'

Woods was taken aback. The unexpected words anaesthetized his anger like a tranquilizer dart. 'For real?'

'Listen, John, don't read anything into it. I was full up and brimming over with every pill there was. I was wired. Crazy ass. Things got on top of me. Now if you want to go and find something which isn't there. Go ahead. But you'll be wasting your time. I was high. Period.'

'I don't want to hear that, Coop. I thought you were off them.'

'I am. I was. I wasn't then. I am now. These things happen.'

'Coop... I know what happens when you take those pills, and I know you say the doc prescribed them to you, but...'

'The doc *you* recommended, don't forget.'

'You wanna blame me? You wanna blame me? Is that it? Because I'll take it, Coop. You can send anything my way as long as it helps keep you away from all that crap... I'm concerned about you.'

Cooper's mind began to haze. Mouth dry. Cold sweat ran down his back. He was wired, and thought it was best to make an effort not to slur his words. Carefully, he answered. 'I told you, I'm off them. So no need to be concerned... Now drop it, okay?'

After a few seconds of silence, Woods, pulling himself back on track, took a deep breath, changing the subject to something more palatable. 'How's Cora?'

Cooper shrugged. Tried to look nonchalant, didn't really

know how the hell she was himself. And for that, along with a list of other things, he felt ashamed. 'She's good. Real good.'

'It would've been nice for you to have brought her.'

'It's complicated.'

'Why.'

Cooper sighed. Again. Agitated now. Wanting to get away. 'She's getting older, and last time I brought her, she began to tell Maddie she'd been in a big white house.'

'That's cute.'

'No, it's not. I don't want her to say anything and I'm not going to start asking her to keep a secret. There are too many secrets round here already, don't you think, John...? Anyway, listen, I'm going to get back to Jackson.'

'Okay, sure... and Coop, you are being straight with me about the pills, aren't you? You wouldn't lie to me?'

And in a tone Woods couldn't work out, but knew he didn't like, Cooper said, 'No more than you'd lie to me, John.'

23

dc6 Ng3

The reverberating sound of the distressed, screaming baby filled – jammed, packed – every corner of the darkened room.

Shrill.

Shrilly.

Shrilled.

And deafening.

Ear splitting agitation.

And even Chuck Harrison couldn't concentrate on his thoughts as he swaggered across to the three by three box standing in the middle of the room.

He gave a nod towards the one-way interrogation mirrors which walled every side of the room, and directly the sound of the crying stopped. Ceased. A welcome hush descended, lifting the palpable angst from the tense jowls of the military officers, who gave a long exhalation of relief.

Chuck said, 'You should try the real thing, gentlemen! That's a recording of my friend's baby. Looked after the thing one night, damn near sent me mad.'

He winked. Then opened the box lid and, like a magician performing his trade, he pulled up a man. David Thorpe. The coffee shop bomber.

Aggressively, Chuck dragged him out and over the steel side of the container, which was too small to do anything in but crouch and contort and twist up in the stifling confinement.

Thorpe tried to stand but his sweat-drenched legs and weakened muscles wedged in spasms. Stiff with cramps. Crying out with pain. Fear. Terror. Blindfolded. Chuck watched, emotionless, turning his nose up from the stench of urine and drying feces which covered and flaked from Thorpe's body and matted in his unkempt Afro.

Again Chuck nodded, but this time to the uniformed soldier, who went across to Thorpe and implemented the silent order with a kick from his steel-toe boot. A dragging of the arm. A throwing. A sliding of the naked Thorpe across the room, to come to a halt by the feet of Chuck.

'Hey David, how the hell are you doing? Care for a seat?'

Trembling. Crying. Handcuffed. Thorpe nodded.

'Well that's a darn shame because there's only one chair.'

Chuck sat down, bending forward and lifting up Thorpe's blindfold. Small, terrified brown eyes, which hid under heavy lids, stared up at him.

'Well hi there, David. Good to see you. Not doing too well by the looks of things. Now, I want you to show you something. Okay...? David, I can't hear you. I said, *okay*?'

'Okay.'

'Good. Now watch.'

Thorpe, shivering naked, viewed the grainy pictures of the

CCTV footage playing on the large TV screen. Showing him driving up in a large Scania truck. Showing him parking. Showing him drinking the infamous coffee the press would write about. Before showing him walking away down the block.

'Now let's get to the important bit shall we, David?'

Chuck forwarded the security video until the digits in the top right of the screen read 18.45.

'Now watch the truck, David. Watch it real carefully.'

The black and white footage stayed focused on the vehicle as the digits on the screen climbed up in seconds until it read 18.47 then instantaneously the truck exploded. Blowing out and up into a colossal cloud of smoke before the screen went black as the CCTV camera was destroyed by the blast.

'So you want to go over it again with me? Why did you do it, David?'

Licking his dry, parched, deeply cracked lips, Thorpe said, 'I didn't.'

'You didn't? That wasn't you driving and leaving the truck?'

Weakly. A struggle beyond struggles, Thorpe managed an exhausted reply. 'Yes, but I don't understand.'

Chuck smiled. Roughly pulled down the blindfold over Thorpe's eyes again.

'What don't you understand, David? Because the fact that you don't understand is the part *I* don't understand.'

'It wasn't me.'

'It wasn't you?'

'No.'

'That wasn't you on the CCTV footage?'

123

'It was, but…'

Chuck flicked through a file on the desk in front of him. Inside it were photos. Paperwork. Print outs.

'Shucks, call myself the head of CTC? I've gone and got myself the wrong person. There's me thinking you're David John Thorpe, born 22nd November 1966. The same David Thorpe in the footage and the same David Thorpe who had ammonium nitrate traces on his clothing and hands. Have I got that all wrong?'

'No…'

'Let me ask you this, do you have affiliations with Wilāyat Gharb Ifrīqīyyah? Boko Haram?'

A pause. A hesitation. A glance round as if he could see through his blindfold and through the mirrors. Unsteadily, Thorpe answered. 'I did.'

Chuck banged his fist on the table. 'Did or do?'

'I was messed up.'

'Messed up. Is that why you planted the bomb, because you were messed up?'

'I didn't.'

In a controlled and quick movement, Chuck grabbed Thorpe. His hands on either side of his face, drawing him in towards his own. 'David, shall we start again? Was that you on the CCTV?'

'Yes.'

'Was that you driving then leaving the truck?'

'Yes.'

'Okay, so are we going to stop going round in circles?'
Thorpe trembled. Said nothing.

Flicking through the files again, Chuck continued. 'You

were interviewed by the FBI six years ago and you were also investigated in 2016 after being linked to a man who became a suicide bomber in North-East Nigeria, killing thirty-five people... And you were also put on the No-Fly List. Seems to me you were a bit more than messed up.'

'I was lost.'

'Lost, now? You know what I do when I'm lost, David? I look at a map. I turn on my GPS. I might even ask some passing folk which way to turn. What I don't do, David, is blow up a building.'

With his head down and his tears dropping into his stark-naked lap, Thorpe wept. 'No, I mean I was lost when I was interested in Boko Haram. When I was posting those messages, the terror, hate... it was only because I was trying to get my life back together.'

'Is this what you call getting your life back together?'

'No. I...'

'What happened to you, David? Had a rough childhood? Hated your middle school teacher? You Goddamn scum.'

With great strength, great effort, Chuck grabbed the hand-cuffed David Thorpe, taking him and sending him reeling towards a tank full of iced water. Dunking him below the surface. Pushing him down with his foot as he struggled and flailed.

'I want answers.'

Spluttering, quivering, David Thorpe scrambled, draping his body over the side of the tank, trying to get his breath back before inadvertently tumbling out onto the hard floor, reminding Chuck of a wet fish falling out of a fisherman's net.

Then, using the handcuffs to drag him, Chuck hauled Thorpe along the floor. Heaving him up onto his feet. Then brought the chair up, close. Sitting down and looking up at him.

'Keep your hands up.'

Slowly, nervously, Thorpe put his hands up into the air.

'Don't drop them.'

Feebly, Thorpe nodded, standing humiliated and naked in the middle of the room. Handcuffed arms above him.

'You got it easy. Some folk here were held in pitch dark, windowless lockups for months at a time. Deprived of sleep and made to stand up for days at a time, and I mean days. If their legs gave way they were made to hang by their arms instead. One detainee I know was forced to stay awake for eight solid days in a row. So you see, you have got it easy with me, but it'd be a hell of a lot easier if you gave me a full confession, so the American people will feel satisfied. There's a lot of fear back home and I've got to bring to justice those responsible. So, what are you waiting for?'

'I can't.'

'You want to go back in the box, David?'

'No... No!'

'So you'll give me a confession? Because the problem I have is your polygraph test was rendered inconclusive. Now that won't do, will it? There can't be any room for doubt. Besides, we both know you did it, don't we?'

Thorpe, without thinking, dropped his arms down. And without a moment's hesitation, Chuck stood up, brought back his fist, slammed it hard into Thorpe's stomach. Sent him down to the floor. Curled in a ball. Coughing out phlegm and remorse.

'I said don't drop your hands, boy! Now get up!'

Slowly and unsteadily, and with the blindfold cutting in and his tears unable to soothe his eyes, Thorpe stood.

'Do you acknowledge that was you on the tape?'

'Yes, that's me, but I can't remember…'

'Why did you do it? Keep those hands up.'

'I don't know.'

'You want to go back into the box, David?'

He shook his head.

'Then you need to start talking.'

'I don't know…'

'The *box*, David… How long were you in there last time? Thirty-six hours wasn't it? And they put insects in the last time, didn't they? And you don't like insects, do you? No. And we'll do that again if we have to, but you can stop it. Make it all go away if you answer me, and give me that confession… Shall I help you, David? Was it to do with Boko Haram? Were you acting in their name?'

'No. I…'

'The box, David… The insects, David… Was it the Boko Haram?'

Hysterically sobbing, Thorpe nodded his head, 'Yes.'

'Good. Good. So tell me, why did you do it? Think carefully! Think about the box, David, before you answer me… Was it because you hate America and what the West stands for…?'

'Yes.'

'Good. Now we're getting somewhere. See it's not difficult, is it? Here's another one. David, are we, the American people, are we what you would call *the infidels*?'

Thorpe shook his head. Dropped his arms. A blow to the stomach sent him reeling back on the floor. Chuck stood over him. 'Are we the enemy to you?'

'Yes. Yes...Yes... No more, please.'

'And is that why you did it? Is this your confession?'– Chuck picked up a piece of paper from the file and began to read. *'I vowed to bring black days to the supporters of nations that have associated themselves with the bombing and persecution of Islam and in reply to their hostility I wreaked revenge. And what you can expect will be more severe and much more powerful than you have done. I did this by the permission of Allah and in the name of the Wilāyat Gharb Ifrīqīyyah*...We found it in your house, David.'

From the floor Thorpe lifted his head. Shook it. Said, 'I didn't write that.'

Chuck took back his foot. Brought it in hard, then dragged Thorpe towards the box. He began to scream as he was bundled in. 'I think you did write it, David.'

'Okay! Okay! Please...! Please! Whatever you say. I wrote it. I wrote it! Please, no! No more!'

Chuck stood back whilst the two US soldiers pushed Thorpe down, shutting the lid of the box as the shrill, deafening sound of a baby crying filled the room once more.

The door of the room opened and a tall, sinewy man dressed in military uniform walked in, shouting over the sounds of the screaming child, 'Excuse me, sir, but you're wanted in the other room.'

Chuck nodded. Walked out. Threw his red cable sweater over his shoulder as if about to go on a stroll on West Hampton beach.

In the next room Chuck sneered a greeting to Lyndon P. Clarke, Secretary of State. 'Mr Secretary, it's good to see you.'

Lyndon paced. Angry. Pointed finger. 'What the hell did you think you were doing in there?'

Chuck smiled. 'Questioning the prisoner.'

'That's not questioning and it certainly isn't authorized. You know that.'

'You're damn right Lyndon, I do, but we got his confession, didn't we?'

'We didn't need it. He's there on the CCTV.'

'No, you're wrong. There needs to be an explanation, a sentiment so we can tell the American people the right person is now detained. One less terrorist on our streets. They need to have an understanding, some kind of statement, and now he's confessed we've got exactly that.'

'What kind of confession? The kind he agrees to whatever you say because he's terrified. The kind that he denies leaving but then under duress and fear he agrees he wrote it? That's the problem with torture, Chuck. It's morally wrong.' Lyndon stopped. Wiped the back of his neck. It was damn hot.

'Torture? Hey what can I say, Lyndon? You say *to-mayto*, I say tomato. You say torture, I say enhanced interrogation… Plus I'd say it's pretty hypocritical of you to try to give me a lecture on morality. You're part of all of this as much as I am.'

'How d'you work that one out?'

'You're here, aren't you? You're part of the administration which keeps places like this open. So just because you don't get blood on your own hands, Lyndon, it doesn't mean you didn't throw one of the punches.'

'Bullshit. You've dehumanized that man in there, and whatever he says now you'll never know if he's saying it because it's the truth, or he's saying it because he's in fear... You need to get him medical attention.'

Chuck cut a cold stare. 'When it's time.'

'No, *now*.'

'This is *not* your jurisdiction. You are no longer on US soil, Lyndon. I do as I see fit.'

'I'll be reporting this back to the President.'

'I'm sure you will, Lyndon, but then that's what you do, isn't it? God, what is it with nigg– ' Chuck stopped. Then an exaggerated cough.

'What the hell did you just say? What were you going to call me?'

A smile. Wide and goading. Chuck looked amused. 'Call you...? I wasn't going to call you anything, Lyndon. I was just going to say, what is it with niggly coughs? They just come out of nowhere. Can't seem to get rid of it. Why, Lyndon, what did you think I was going to say?'

Lyndon P Clarke stepped up into Chuck's face. His whole body tense, hovering.

'I'll get you, Chuck. Mark my words, I'm going to get you out. I'll be on your back. I'll be up your ass, until you make a mistake and when you do, then I'll be there, waiting. I'll make sure you get what's coming to you. Whatever it takes. *By any means necessary.*'

24

Rg3 fg3

It was a simple phone call made in the leafy green quiet of a side road in the Potomac Hills, Virginia, three miles outside Langley.

'It's me. I need you to shut down a problem.'

25

cd7 g2

'Cora, do you have to do that?'

'Yes.'

'When I say *do you have to do that*, what I mean is, Cora, *please* don't do that, honey.'

'But Mommy, Daddy likes me to collect them.'

'Are you sure about that?'

'Yes. I'm getting them ready for him when he comes. Is he coming soon? Is he coming today? Can he come now? Can you call him? *Please*, Mommy.'

Maddie looked at her daughter, and wondered where the five years had gone to. Though it was almost six years, as Cora liked to remind her on a daily basis. And just for a moment – a split, fleeting moment – all she wanted to do was put Cora in the back of the car and drive her to wherever Tom was so she wouldn't have to see her little girl pining, wishing, hoping her Daddy would come and play with her in the way only Daddies could… The other thing she wanted to do. Just for a moment – a split, fleeting moment – was to wring Tom's neck. And preferably slowly. Real slowly.

Walking across her bedroom to where her daughter was sitting, Maddie decided neither thought was very helpful.

Going to happen.

Really a serious proposition.

Or conducive to moving forward.

But she had to admit the latter thought was often a delightful fantasy when Tom was being obnoxious. Unbearable. Offensive. Disappointing. Frustrating… Right there she broke off her thoughts. Not healthy. Not beneficial. Focus. Yes, she had to focus on the positive. Nothing else. And breathe.

Exhaling to the point of feeling slightly dizzy, Maddie crouched down, leaning her body on the apple white chest of drawers that she'd made and painted herself, to look at Cora's new obsession. In that aspect her daughter very much reminded her of Tom. No… No, she wasn't going there. Breathe. Focus on the positive.

'Let me see, honey.'

'You like them?'

Maddie stared at the pile of worms and other unpleasant crawling insects Cora had painstakingly collected from their back fields.

'Cora, can't you put them in a jar? Or at least a box? I don't think I really want them crawling on my wooden floors.'

'You don't like them?'

Covering a large fat lie, Maddie smiled. 'Yes, honey. I think they're cute, but I think they'd be even cuter if you put them somewhere safe.'

'That's why I keep them in my pocket. They all go in there.'

'They must get squashed in there, Cora.'

'No they don't. Ask them.'

Cora scooped up three worms from the floor and pushed them straight onto Maddie's ear.

'Ask them, Mommy.'

Maddie, trying not to be ridiculous, squeamish, grossed out by the fact there were *three* earthworms making out with her ear, and trying to tell herself she wasn't going to fall into some stereotype of female neurosis – because after all she was not only a highly decorated ex-Navy officer but also a skilled pilot, an expert in close hand combat, and not forgetting an excellent gunwoman – said, 'My Cora, you've put them very close to my ear.'

Cora looked at Maddie very seriously and wondered if her Mommy really did know about *everything* there was to know in the whole wide world, because if she *did,* then how come she didn't know about this?

With a really long, puzzled sigh. The kind of sigh she often heard her Daddy do, Cora said, '*Yes*, because how else are you going to hear them?'

'Ok, well, Mr Worm, I'm Cora's mom. And I'm just wondering, when she puts you in her pocket, do you get squashed?'

Cora's face gleamed. Eyes shone bright. 'What did they say?'

'They said that they liked it in your pocket but they'd like it better in a box, outside near the stables.'

Cora quickly pulled the worms away from Maddie's ear. Angry. Hurt. 'They did not say that... Can we go now?'

Knowing she'd called it wrong, Maddie beat up on herself. 'Sweetie, I'm sorry. Look, you're right, I probably didn't hear them properly. They probably said that your pocket was the perfect place.'

Cora gazed up from underneath her tumbling blonde curls. 'You think?'

'I know.'

'You want to take one with you?'

'*No*... I mean, I can't take it to Turkey, can I?'

'Yes.'

'I don't think that's such a good idea. It really might get squashed then... Cora, can I ask you, are you really alright about me going away again? Because I don't have to go, you know. And now you're getting older you might want me to stay at home like a regular Mommy. I could still work at Onyx, but just in the office. I'd help Granger, and oh what fun that would be... But my point is, honey, I can always stay here instead if you need me.'

Cora's face answered the question before her words did. 'No way! Grandpappy always lets me have double chocolate chip, *and* he lets me go riding way longer than you do, and even longer than Daddy.'

'Is somebody ready?'

Maddie looked up at her father. It was stupid. Real stupid. But all of a sudden she felt like a little girl again. There was something about this tall, strong, Afro American man. Proud of his roots. Proud of his country – though she knew at times the two didn't always make a perfect match – which made her feel inadequate. She couldn't remember a time when she hadn't felt that way. And she was damned if she knew why. But she *did* know she'd spent most of her life proving to him she was capable of being her own woman.

'Yes, we're ready. All packed. Run out to the car, Cora, and I'll come in a minute... Oh, Cora, aren't you forgetting something?'

Cora grinned. Scooped up the worms and insects. Pushed them hard into her pocket. Skipped right out.

Maddie turned and spoke to her father. 'Everything's the same as usual. Granger or Levi can contact me if there's a problem, or even if Cora just wants to speak to me and she can't get through on my cell or by Skype. Like I say, it shouldn't be more than a week. From what Granger says all we're basically doing is going there and back. I really appreciate it. Thanks, Daddy.'

Marvin scowled. Cut his eye. Stared in the way only middle school teachers knew how to.

'Don't thank me, Maddie, we love having her. She's my granddaughter. But I tell you something, I'm not happy.'

Lowering her tone, Maddie stared hard. 'I know, Daddy. So you keep saying. Every time.'

'I wouldn't have to say it every time if you just came to your damn senses. What sort of job is it for a woman, let alone for a mother?'

'Not this again... I enjoy my job. Just like I've enjoyed all the other jobs.'

'No, you *think* you enjoy it. But the fact is, ever since you were little you've wanted to show me how much you don't need me or your Momma, but home is where you belong.'

Maddie looked incredulous. 'To Mississippi?'

'Yes, to Mississippi. You could settle down, get yourself

a nice job in town. Who knows, you might find yourself a good man. A proper father to Cora.'

'Stop. I don't want any of those things; the only thing I want is for you to accept me for who I am. I'm happy, Daddy.'

Marvin kissed his teeth. 'I don't know how you can be. Your Momma and I are so disappointed. Only yesterday we were asking ourselves, how did you go so wrong?'

Resigned, Maddie asked. 'Have you finished, Daddy?'

'Actually, I haven't, because whilst the Good Lord is blessing me with the truth, let me tell you something else that's been playing on our minds...'

'Don't let me stop you.'

'Your Momma and I think the amount of guns you have isn't normal. It isn't healthy. Whenever I walk into that room where you keep them all, I'm looking for the saloon doors – think I've stepped into the Wild West.'

'Don't exaggerate.'

'Cooper has a lot to answer for. I think he's led you astray. He's a mess, and won't be happy until you are too.'

'I wondered when we'd get onto him. And you know full well, we're over.'

'Until you decide to take him back... How you ever got together with a white man, I'll never know.'

'Stop right there. Have you heard yourself? And anyway, as I say *every* time you say this to me, I say, *look at Momma*. She's white. So I'll never understand the problem.'

'Your momma is very different. She embraced who I was and didn't try to change any of my views.'

'You mean she had no choice, otherwise she'd find herself on the other side of your anger, Daddy.'

Marvin scowled. 'I want you to take that back. That's simply not true… You know, I don't like this side of you, Maddison. You can get real mean. Spiteful. But however nasty you want to be, I won't change my mind about that man. I warned you about him. White folk are different to us.'

'Well *that* man – that *white* man – is Cora's Daddy. Cora *is* her Daddy and Tom *is* Cora. So whether you like it or not, he's here to stay. I don't want to hear you say another word about him. You keep your opinions to yourself, and keep them away from Cora. I'm warning you, Daddy, don't make me choose… Now, I'd appreciate if you could wait here so I can go and say goodbye to my daughter in peace.'

26

Rf3 Qd7

Cooper wasn't feeling any better than Maddie, who wasn't feeling any better than Rosedale, who wasn't feeling well at all and had been unusually quiet during the long, relentless eight hour drive which only served to fuel his ever-growing resentment of the administrative error made by a certain Levi Walker, who'd inadvertently caused their three hour stopover in Lisbon, to turn into three whole days.

But they were here. And at that moment *here*, to Thomas J Cooper, felt like sweet relief.

Stepping out of the large grey SUV, surrounded by the kaleidoscope of sights and smells of the pine forests and the olive and citrus groves, which sat peaceably in the dusty ground, Cooper stretched out his back and listened to the first words Rosedale had said in the last couple of hours.

'Just wait till I see him.'

'Who?'

'Who do you think, Thomas? Levi, that's who.'

'Jesus, just drop it now, that's all we've heard from you in the last three days.'

'Well the damn fool never seems to get anything right. How hard is it to sort out connections? We're supposed to be professional. Now if you'd done the bookings, Maddie, there wouldn't have been a problem.'

'Don't be so hard on him. Mistakes happen,' Maddie said.

In the balminess of the Mediterranean day, she smiled at Rosedale, who tipped his cowboy hat. 'Yes, ma'am, they do. Maybe Rosedale Young needs to take a leaf out of your book and find the good grace of patience.'

Irritated by what he saw as a sickly display of newfound friendship, but more irritated by the fact that Rosedale had bizarrely begun to refer to himself in the third person, Cooper ground his back teeth, ruminating on the fact that the three day delay meant the secret stash of pills tucked and hidden in the cut-out sole of his boots would be finished in exactly two days' time. He scowled at his partners. 'Look, when you guys have finished your Burns and Allen routine, can we focus? We need to be out of here in two days, *max*, okay? And Rosedale, is it too much to ask, on this assignment, that you don't try to make us live in planet Rosedale? I mean, what is it with speaking about yourself in the third person all of a sudden?'

'Illeism.'

'What?'

'Illeism. The art of speaking in third.'

'I never asked you *what* it is… I just want you to quit it, okay? I'm not in the mood. Oh, and for your information, it's not a Goddamn art.'

'Rosedale thinks a certain person should lighten up, Thomas.'

Cooper threw down his blue jean jacket. 'Are you kidding me, Rosedale? Are you seriously wanting to press all my buttons?'

Stepping in quickly and not wanting the atmosphere to turn into what occasionally, sometimes, did happen when they worked together, Maddie asked. 'Why two days, Tom? I'm up for it, but just curious as to why.'

Cooper tried to keep the paranoia away. Tried to ignore the feeling of Maddie being able to read exactly what was on his mind and, leaning against the hot metal of the SUV and unable to hold Maddie's gaze, he shrugged. 'No reason. Should there be? I just think if all we're doing is speaking to these shipping guys and then sorting out a seek and observe, how long can it really take? And besides, it's been a while since I've seen Cora. It'd be neat to spend some time with her.'

He turned away, feeling guilty for using his daughter as an excuse. Then, needing to distract himself, he looked around at the private port which was tucked away, set below the Turkish mountains which swept down towards an irregular coastline of stony capes and hidden bays abutting the glistening, turquoise sea, where bouncing sunlight leapt and pirouetted off the lapping waves. A large white building stood next to a windowless brick construction on the empty harbor. The whole place seemed deserted.

Behind them a sudden fierce noise of tires and engines roared, dust and dirt whirling and clouding to the point of distorting their visibility, whilst cars raced round. Revving engines. Circling. Trapping them in like animals.

Rosedale bellowed over the voracious sound. 'Maddie, get in the car! Maddie!'

He pulled at the vehicle's door.

Shut.

Locked.

'Where's the key? The key! Maddie!'

Frantically, Maddie dug into her front right pocket.

Left pocket.

Back pocket.

'I haven't got them! Tom, the keys! Quick!'

Cooper backed towards where Rosedale and Maddie stood, eyes not shifting from the speeding vehicles, encircling them ever tighter. 'They're over there in my jacket... *Shit...*'

'Just put up your hands. Go on. Put them up, Tom. Rosedale, go on. Whoever they are maybe if they see we're not looking for trouble...'

Maddie trailed off as car doors were flung open. Heavy boots thudded on the ground, along with the unmistakable jangle of guns as dozens of men dressed in canvas camouflage stampeded towards them.

Hands in the air, Cooper shouted. 'Barış için geldik! We come in peace! Barış için geldik!'

The gun smashed into Cooper's face, staggering him backwards. Pain and blood poured from his nose.

'Tom! Tom!'

Maddie's voice was lost under the rage of the man's scream as he bore down on Cooper.

'*Yere yat! Yere yat! Yere yat!*'

With reddened anger, vicious fury, the man kneed Cooper hard in his groin, sending him twisting to the floor. Hitting the ground and writing in pain. Coughing. Spluttering. Struggling under the weight of the man's foot pressing his head into the ground.

'Yere yat! Yere yat! Yere yat!'

He stayed groaning on the floor whilst the shouting continued and a well-aimed fist brutally punched Maddie in her stomach, before she was kicked to the ground to the sound of Rosedale shouting her name. Seconds later, Rosedale's blood splattered over her from a fierce blow to the side of his head.

A few feet away, Cooper tried to shift position, but the pain and the weight of the man made it impossible. Then, without warning, a searing agony drove through his shoulders as his arms were violently pulled back behind him. Tape around hands. Tape around feet. Bound. Unable to move, whilst powerless, helpless anger flooded over him as he watched Maddie's and Rosedale's heads being lifted up by the hair, tight tape forced onto their mouths, before boots pushed both their faces back down, and their cheeks cut and ground into the stony earth, the metal muzzle of a rifle jabbing against each of their temples.

Moments later the three of them were dragged by their feet. And then with three cruel, hard blows, one to the back of each head, they blacked out. They were then unceremoniously thrown into the back of separate cars, which sped away in a new cloud of dust.

27

Bb2 fe4

'Teddy, I need a word.' Woods put his head round the northeast door of the Oval Office, where Teddy was in a heated discussion with his secretary. He added, 'That's if you can spare the time.'

Teddy grinned, his black skin shining from an over-enthusiastic application of cocoa butter and said, 'Sorry, Mr President, I'm just trying to convince Joan the green tea she brings in for us is already too near healthy for me; but now, God forbid, she wants to introduce nettle tea to the office.'

'I'm glad to see you got your priorities right, Teddy. Who needs to work on next Sunday's weekly address on opioid addiction when our coffee could be under threat? But seriously, Joan, I hate to break it to you, but I'm with Teddy on this one. Now if you'll excuse us...'

Woods walked back into the Oval Office, followed directly by Teddy.

'What I'm going to say might sound strange but I can't get it off my mind. You know we were going to go over the failing VA appeals process for veteran benefits this Saturday?'

Teddy nodded. Said nothing.

'Well, I think you've been working too hard recently. I really think you could do with a vacation.'

'A vacation? I'm completely lost here, Mr President.'

'I think you should get out to the countryside. Go see a friend. In fact, why don't you take a flight to see your police buddy across in Chatham? Go on Friday, you can be back by Saturday night.'

Teddy said, 'No problem, Mr President, and whilst I'm there, who knows who else I might bump into.'

28

Rf8 Rf8

The large metal door, slightly rusting from the ocean salt, creaked open, letting in the dazzling sunlight, abruptly rousing Maddie, Cooper and Rosedale. Hunched together, still tied, still gagged, whilst the pain of burning muscles, caused by the abnormal position their bodies were secured in, ran through them like fire.

As quickly as the light had appeared it went, blocked by an unshapely silhouette. Broad and wide and six-foot tall, with a strong voice and a firm command. 'Bring them outside.'

Two men scurried into the small, damp, room. Untying with resolved efficiency the Onyx team before roughly pushing them outside into the bright day, causing Maddie, Rosedale and Cooper to squint as they shuffled barefoot onto the hot, stony ground.

The man who'd appeared in silhouette now stood with his back to the sea, as the sunlight emphasized his weather-worn, dark olive skin, and the flecks of grey that sat like snowflakes in his coal black hair, whilst his stomach hung below his belt like a melting ice-cream..

He said, 'Let me introduce myself, and apologies if my English isn't as good as it should be. My name is Ismet. And you must be...'

He paused, looking at Rosedale then down at the American passports he held in his bulbous hands.

'... Mr Austin Rosedale Young.'

Ismet stepped forward ripping the gag off Rosedale's face. 'It's good to meet you, Mr Young.'

With the blow to his head still making him feel nauseous, and aware caution was needed and anger best put aside, Rosedale said, 'Actually, people call me Rosedale, and now we're finished with the formalities, I'd appreciate it if you could tell me what the *hell* you want from us.'

The man, ignoring Rosedale, looked down at the other two passports. Flipped them open. Glanced up and smiled. 'Hello, Mr Cooper, it's good to meet you, though your passport photo doesn't do you justice.'

Cooper winced slightly as his gag was ripped off. 'Like my friend here said, I want to know what this is about. You hear me?'

'Oh I hear you, but one thing at a time.'

'You bastard...'

'You're either brave or foolish, Mr Cooper. Look around you.'

Behind Cooper, five other men appeared, heavily armed, with expressions saying they were looking for trouble.

'And you must be Maddison. Maddison Cooper... I take it somehow you two are related,' Ismet said.

Through clenched teeth and anger, Cooper growled. 'She's my wife and I want to know what you're playing at.'

Ignoring him, Ismet directed his conversation to Maddie. 'Well, it's nice to meet you, Mrs Cooper. And apologies for your unexpected welcome. Your husband is quite right to be annoyed.'

Ripping off her gag, Ismet looked at the trio. Gave a wide smile. 'You must understand, we can't be too careful.'

'What are you talking about?' Rosedale said.

'I'm sure you've noticed that we're situated not too far from neighbors who aren't always particularly friendly towards us. The border of Syria is only a few miles away, and then further up we also have Iraq and Iran. So you see, when you arrived it was about precautions.'

Cooper snarled. 'Precautions? You beat us. Tie us up. Keep us prisoner. And you call them precautions? I call them a Goddamn liberty!'

Ismet gave a sickly smile, not sounding the least sincere. 'As I say, Mr Cooper, I can only apologize again; a misunderstanding. My men weren't sure who you were. After all, we were expecting you three days ago.'

Maddie, rubbing her wrist, stopped. Looked up at Ismet in shock. 'What? You mean to tell us, you're the person we're here to see?'

'Exactly.'

Cooper lurched forward but Rosedale held him back. 'You son-of-a-bitch, what makes you think you can get away with this?'

With a chuckle, Ismet opened his arms, gesturing to the men standing on the harbor, guns ready and waiting. 'Mr Cooper, don't make this harder. If it's any consolation,

I… how do you say it? I squared it with Granger. You'll be compensated well.'

Maddie turned to Cooper. 'I can't believe Granger's okay with this.'

'Oh I can, honey, that man's got a dollar sign where his heart should be.'

Ismet continued. 'There are shower facilities in the building and I had my men take your bags up. I'm sure you'll want to change. And, afterwards, we can talk through the details of the job.'

The three of them stood in the heat of the sun and with blood, dirt and sweat-stained clothes they looked incredulously at Ismet. Rosedale said, 'You think after what you've done, we'd still do your job?'

'Yes, Mr Young, I do. Isn't that your motto? *No job is too big or too much trouble*?'

'This one's the exception. I don't like your attitude. Go figure.' Rosedale paused. Touched his head and added, 'Where the hell's my hat? And my boots for that matter.'

'With your bags. And hopefully after your shower, once you've refreshed, you'll reconsider. I'm sure we can sort this out… Now if you'll follow my men, they'll take you up to the bathrooms. I'll see you in my office shortly.'

As the trio followed, resentful but grateful at the idea of a hot shower, angry but relieved that the situation wasn't a lot worse – as it certainly could've been – Ismet pulled Cooper back, waiting to speak until the other two had disappeared inside.

He went into his pocket.

'I think these are yours, Mr Cooper. My men found them when they searched you.'

Ismet passed Cooper a cellophane wrap of pills. 'You should be very careful, Mr Cooper. Smuggling drugs in or out of Turkey carries a very heavy prison sentence. And our prisons aren't what American ones are.' He winked, adding, 'I'm sure you've seen *Midnight Express*.'

'They're not drugs. Well, not like you think they are.'

'No?'

'No.'

'Then maybe it would be better to store them in your wash bag rather than in the heel of your shoe. Seems an odd place to put them if there's nothing to hide.'

Cooper's manner stiffened. He looked down. He looked up. 'They're not all there.'

'No? Is that a problem?'

Cooper stepped forward, smelling the deep, rich aroma of coffee on Ismet's breath.

'Where are they?'

'Mr Cooper, I have no idea. Perhaps my men dropped some when they removed them from your boot.'

'And you think it's okay to go around searching a person when they're knocked out cold?'

'They were being vigilant. As I say, you can't be too careful. Who knows what a person might be hiding. I hope this doesn't cause *too* much of a problem to you.'

Cooper exhaled. Hands on hips. Eyes down. 'No problem.'

With perception having led him already to this point, Ismet smiled. 'Mr Cooper, I'm no doctor, but I think there might be.'

'And I think you don't know what the hell you're talking about.'

'Are you sure about that? Because if there *was* a problem, perhaps I could help.'

As if somebody else was controlling his mind and his voice, but more importantly his integrity, Cooper found himself saying, 'How?'

'If you and your friends stay and do my job, Mr Cooper, I'll make sure *whatever* it is you need, you'll get. And of course if you prefer we can keep our arrangement between ourselves.'

Cooper looked down at the pills in his hand. Worked out there was less than a day's worth remaining. Then tried to swallow the panic as he looked up at the hundreds of acres of blue sky and across to the cerulean sea as a memory of Ellie came into his head and visions of the person he'd once been, once liked, who'd once been full of honor, danced about in his mind. He looked at Ismet. 'I can't do it. It's impossible.'

'Impossible? What's impossible, Mr Cooper? Because all I'm asking you to do is a seek and observe of my ship. Nothing else. The same job you came here to do. No harm.'

'I'll have to lie to them.'

'Not really. All you're doing is getting them to do what was agreed, and for that *you* get what you need to stay well, which is probably something the others don't understand.'

Slowly, as if he was dragging himself through quicksand, Cooper nodded. 'Okay. Fine. But I can't promise the others will go for it.'

'Mr Cooper, I have no doubt your powers of persuasion will find a way. Now come with me, so I can show you something.'

29

Bg7 Qg7

Ismet's office, at the top of the white building, jutted out over the sea, giving Cooper a slight sense of floating on air. Though he had to concede that his feeling of light-headedness could be in part down to the heavy blow to the bridge of his nose.

Scrapping off some dried blood which itched and irritated his face, Cooper looked about. 'It's a bit out of the way here, isn't it?'

'It's perfect for our small family business.'

'And all those men you have around you, are they part of this *small* family business?'

'I hear a tone of skepticism, Mr Cooper.'

'Just reckon, it must be expensive hiring all those henchmen to be on a twenty-four-hour guard.'

'Jobs around here are scarce, especially out of the fishing season, and although we don't pay a lot, we pay fairly. So we recruit the locals to protect our land and help out with the business.'

'And they have to do that with a Heckler & Koch submachine gun?'

A wry smile twitched on the corners of Ismet's mouth. 'You know your weapons, Mr Cooper.'

'I was in the US Navy. And I find it a bit of a surprise to see weapons which are used by the United States Special Forces in rural Turkey.'

'They're just a deterrent.'

'Tell that to my Goddamn nose.'

'I understand how you feel, and I can only hope eventually you'll accept my apologies, but we have to be vigilant. We have to look after ourselves.'

'Why not work out of a commercial port then? Wouldn't that be safer?'

'I only have two boats, that's enough to import and export all our products. We don't need the facilities at a huge port, and we like it here. You see, I was brought up in a small fishing village, Mr Cooper, and I have happy memories of those days.'

Cooper looked around the office as he talked, taking in the glossy posters of Turkish food products covering the walls. 'So you thought you'd recreate your childhood. A shrink would have a lot to say about that... Where?'

'Where what?'

'Where was the village?'

'In Qatar.'

Cooper studied Ismet's face. 'You're Qatari?'

'Yes, Mr Cooper... Now here, take this. It's a photo of the boat.'

Staring at the photo, Cooper took a few stunned seconds before he spoke. 'This is the boat? Seriously?'

'Yes.'

'I don't get it.'

Coldly, Ismet said, 'There's nothing *to* get.'

'But I assumed…'

'You assume too much, Mr Cooper. Like you clearly assumed I was Turkish because I'm based here. Assumption is a dangerous pastime…As I say, all I need you to do is locate the boat. You have the coordinates which are probably accurate down to a twenty square mile radius. I can't be more precise because the boat's radars are turned off, but it's what the crew gave me.'

'Where are they now?'

'They were taken ill and now they're back home in Libya. It's very unfortunate but sometimes, things aren't in our control… Now once you locate the boat, it's just a question of a quick external assessment. That's it. Very simple.'

'It seems too simple.'

'Maybe in a complex world, but life doesn't always have to be complicated.'

Cooper looked at him suspiciously 'You know, for someone who said their English wasn't great, it's pretty damn good. Surely it'd be easier just to get another crew to go and get it rather than leave it out there?'

A look flickered over Ismet's face which Cooper read as impatience.

'You're assuming again, Mr Cooper. Assuming getting a trustworthy crew is easy when costs and reliability have to come into it. It takes time to recruit, so in the meantime all I want is to make sure my boat is safe and it's anchored where they say it is because, at the moment, I'm just taking their word for it.'

'But why not get us to bring it back for you? Seems odd you wouldn't.'

'You talk too much and ask too many questions. Not everybody sees the world like you do. Now do we have a deal or not?'

30

Qe4 Qf6

With wet hair dripping down his back and sitting with a thick towel wrapped around his muscular waist, Cooper kept his voice low as he spoke to Maddie and Rosedale. 'Come on! The guy wanted to make a deal with me, he's desperate for us to do the job. And the thing about desperate is that it makes me curious.'

Rosedale, dressed in a clean pair of khaki pants, a lurid orange linen shirt – as was his usual fashion – and happily back in possession of his cowboy hat, kicked at the legs of the chair Cooper was sitting on. 'What kind of deal, Thomas?'

With a big sigh along with a hesitation, Cooper shrugged evasively. 'A deal where he thought he was being smart, where he thought he could buy me for a price. I persuade you guys to do the job and he makes it worth my while.'

Rosedale said nothing, instead he stared at Cooper strangely and with his Texan drawl sounding like a summer's day, he gave a crooked smile as he pulled heavily on his cigar. 'And nobody could ever accuse you of agreeing to a Faustian bargain, could they, Thomas?'

Cooper stared back at Rosedale ice cold, but directed the rest of his conversation to Maddie. 'What Ismet said about the Syrian border is true; we could've been anybody. No-one's going to wait and see if we were wearing suicide vests, or about to pull a bomb. Act first and ask questions later. I understand that. But there's definitely more to it all. Take a look at this photo... This is the boat. The boat which supposedly imports and exports *products*... See that expression on your face, Maddie, that's exactly how I felt when I saw it.'

'Where did you get this?' Maddie said as she stared at the photo.

'Ismet gave it me when I was talking to him. Right from the beginning this job seemed odd, but more so now.'

'So, what do you want us to do?'

Cooper smiled at Maddie warmly. She looked fresh and flushed from the hot shower.

'I want us to find out what's going on. It might be nothing, but my gut tells me something different... All we have to do is go see the boat.'

'I don't know.'

'Come on, Maddie, what harm can it do? We're here now. Don't tell me you're not interested.'

'I am, but...'

'So why the but? We'll go along the coast, find a fisherman to take us out there. They'll not only know the sea around that area, but because we'll be travelling in a trawler boat nobody can find out or be suspicious. All we're doing is looking.'

'And Granger? What do we say to him?' Maddie asked.

'He'll be on our case if he knows we're staying out here unofficially.'

'We tell him what we always tell him; a bit of bull… Flights delayed. Anything. We can get Levi to back up our story, it's the least he can do.'

Rosedale said, 'You're damn right it is.'

'So what do you say? Maddie? Rosedale?'

Maddie looked at Rosedale who looked right on back. And, being drawn by what her Daddy always told her got the better of her, curiosity had her. 'Okay, I'm in… Rosedale?'

'Looks like I'm in too.'

31

Nf3 Qf4

Ten minutes later they were throwing their bags in the back and climbing into the grey SUV. Maddic sat in the front, Rosedale at the back, watching as Ismet, with a look of puzzlement underlined with steely anger, walked up to Cooper.

'Where are you going, Mr Cooper? What about our deal?'

'Stick your deal and go to hell.'

Cooper, lighting a welcome cigarette, got in the car. Put his foot down hard on the gas. Sent a cloud of dust spinning up in the air as he took the tight bends of the dirt track roads at speed, driving away from the small, private harbor, leaving Ismet covered in a haze of dust.

WASHINGTON, D.C.
USA

32

Qe7 Rf7

Walking from the executive residence back to the West Wing, to have a meeting with his VP, John Woods slowed down his pace. Real slow. Because this walk, however short, in the open-columned walkway which looked across the Rose Garden, filled with a multitude of blossoming flowers, trees and plants, was his moment of clarity. His moment to take in the enormity of what was before him, what was behind him and what was the here and now. But more importantly his moment to give himself the pep talk he sometimes needed when the doubts seeped in, responsibilities overwhelmed, and decisions needed making which meant that lives would be lost.

So it was here, at this spot, before he stepped inside the Oval Office that, he told himself he could do it. And although he might at times, sometimes – *often* – not feel like the President of the United States, but like the small-town boy from Hannibal, Missouri, who dreamt of one day helping change the world, he had to tell himself he could still do

160

what was needed. He could still do his job. Holding onto the integrity of the young man he once was.

'Good morning, Mr President. You okay? That's a pretty serious expression on your face. What's on your mind? Need to share?'

Woods looked up at Teddy Adleman. Friend. Chief of Staff… But that damn moustache. Wondered how he was going to break it that there was a very definite similarity between his moustache and what Sean Connery was sporting on his face in the 1974 movie, *Zardoz*. He smiled gratefully but was unwilling to share. 'I'm not thinking anything really…Nothing.'

Teddy grinned and winked and touched his moustache proudly. 'Maybe that's something we better keep from the American people. I'm not sure knowing the mind of their President is filled up with *nothing* will be good for your Gallup poll rating… Anyhow, I know you're about to do a meet with the VP, but I really wanted to catch you as soon as possible, tell you about the kid from Chatham. If that's ok?'

'Sure. Funnily enough I've been having doubts about the wisdom of asking you to go. Damn well woke me up in the night. I felt I'd somehow overstepped my position. I really should've spoken to the proper channels but sometimes, Teddy, you hear something that nags at you and it just won't leave you. You want to find out quietly, but you're not quite sure who you should trust. As much as this job I'm in ought to make me one of the most powerful people on the planet, at times, Teddy, I've never felt so powerless in my life.'

'Mr President, right now, can we put aside our roles and just stand here as two old friends with no agendas, because as your buddy and nothing else, I'm worried about you… Is everything alright, John? And you know anything you tell me goes no further.'

'I know, and thank you. You've helped me through a lot over the years, both personal and professional, but there's nothing here to worry about. It's just been a rough couple of weeks and I'm feeling the weight of everything at the moment.'

'Yeah?'

'Absolutely… And on top of that I feel guilty.'

'Guilty?'

'Well, look around you. This place is like a fortress. Snipers on the roof, surface-to-air missiles, armed agents and emergency response teams, all to keep me safe in my bubble. But out there, Teddy, folk are terrified. The country is still on code red and although there haven't been any more bombs lately, it's only a matter of time. What the hell kind of world is it when you're frightened to go to work or school in the morning, or even when you go to watch a ball game there's a sense something might happen. It's bullshit, Teddy. And I feel guilty that I'm wrapped up in cotton wool, *especially* as I don't feel like this administration is anywhere near winning the war on terror… Anyway, tell me how your friend was in Chatham. Was he able to tell you anything more? Is the kid still insisting that he took a seismograph reading?'

'Well maybe he would, if he could. I didn't even get to go to see my friend.'

'Why?'

'My friend Shane called me, told me not to bother… The kid's dead, John.'

'Jesus, what happened? Was it an accident?'

'No. He was murdered.'

'What? How? When?'

'My buddy Shane had tried calling him several times over a few days, but he'd got no answer, so he took a drive to the kid's apartment. Found the door open. He was lying in his bathroom. Single bullet to his head. And the long and short of it is, nobody knows anything.'

'No-one saw *anything* at all?'

'Nope. Not a thing. No witnesses. No CCTV. No plate recognition. Nothing. Nobody heard or saw anything. And get this. No prints anywhere in the apartment either. Apparently there's been a few violent robberies in the area and they want to put it down to a break-in gone wrong.'

'I don't know what to say... or think.'

Teddy said, 'Me neither. And I know I'm no cop, John, but I do know this doesn't smell right at all.'

33

Qe6 Rf6

With the sun slowly setting, leaving a blood-red and crimson sky in its wake, Cooper rested his weight on the stone wall which ran along the edge of the tiny fishing village down by the sea. He suspected it was probably a popular *time out* smoking spot for errant husbands wanting a few hours' peace from nagging tongues, because although he was only on his sixth cigarette the number of butt ends was at least ten times that amount.

He was tired. They'd driven two hours along the coast and tomorrow they'd have to find a fishing boat to take them out to the ship, but for now they were booked into a small Turkish tavern which smelt of clean sheets and homemade food. And it was there he'd last seen Maddie and Rosedale, in the bar enjoying the local musical entertainment.

The place was the stuff of vacation brochures. Real pretty. He closed his eyes. He breathed deeply. Feeling the cold sweat run down his back and hoping the cramps and shakes weren't about to set in. He'd taken his last pill just after they'd left the port.

The sound of a car made him bolt up straight. He stared, fixing his eyes on the vehicle as it slowly drove towards him.

'How did you persuade them, Mr Cooper?'

'By telling them we were doing the job without you knowing.'

Ismet, sitting, leaning his sizable body out of a dark black car, wearing dark black shades along with a dark black shirt, smiled. 'I'm impressed. For a while back then, I was worried, but when I got your call I realized some things in life *are* as predictable as one thinks… here, this is what you want.'

Cooper strode up to the car, snatched the large bag of pills out of Ismet's hand, stuffing them quickly in his jacket pocket. 'Are they the right ones?'

Ismet answered with a smirk. 'Exactly what you asked me to prescribe.'

Feeling ashamed, Cooper kicked at the sandy colored ground. 'When I've located the ship, I'll come back on my own and let you know what the situation is.'

'What about the others?'

'Let me worry about that.'

'And Mr Granger?'

'As far as he goes, we're not doing the job.'

'Whatever you say.'

'I'll be in touch… And just so you know, I hate myself for doing this.'

Driving off, Ismet said, 'Clearly not enough, Mr Cooper. Clearly not enough.'

34

Qe8 Rf8

Acres of blue beyond acres of blue. Deep, wide and powerful. Explored, yet eternally unconquerable. Explored yet a mystery holding secrets. That's the way Cooper remembered it. And that's exactly how it still was to him. The sea. The ocean. A place he'd been drawn to from the first time his Uncle Beau had driven him fifteen hours from the plains of Missouri to Emerald Isle, North Carolina, as a frightened eight-year-old boy. Where they'd stood, bare feet on the cold white sand, whilst the wind and the rain besieged them and he'd kissed and said his last goodbye to his Momma before releasing her ashes into the ocean, to hold them safe until the day he'd meet her again.

His love affair with the ocean had started that storm-filled spring day but it'd ended on the day of Ellie's accident. And this was the first time since his discharge from the Navy, not long after he'd watched her reach out to him and call his name.

'What the hell's wrong with you? You look like you're in a state of grace. That's some kind of stupor.' Rosedale kicked the base of Cooper's boot, jarring his whole body.

Wiping his mouth with his sleeve, Cooper sat up. 'Do you have to do that?'

'I do if I think you're dead.'

'Shut up, Rosedale, I'm just seasick.'

'Don't give me that, Thomas. You've spent a good part of your life in the Navy. A SEAL, no less, but now I find you lying on the wet wooden deck of a fishing trawler, saying you've got seasickness. What's going on?'

'Out of practice. What can I say? Give me a hand up.'

'Get up yourself.'

Without Rosedale's assistance, Cooper got up. Unsteadily. And leant over the boat's rail, watching the white surf racing with the bow.

Over the loud, shuddering noise of the engine, Rosedale put his fingers under Cooper's chin, turning his face towards him. 'Is that the new word for it, Thomas? Look at you. You're high. Wired.'

'The hell I am.'

'Oh, I think you are. Shall I call Maddie over and ask her? I'm sure she'll know. What do you say?'

Cooper flicked Rosedale's hand away. Rolled his tongue in his mouth to try to get some saliva. 'Leave Maddie alone, and leave me alone whilst you're at it for that matter.'

'Where did you get them?'

'Jesus, Rosedale, go and be a jackass to somebody else.'

Rosedale grabbed hold of Cooper's shirt. Shaking him about. A bit. A lot. 'You brought them with you, didn't you? Didn't you! Look at you, you're a mess. Can't even fight back, can you?'

'I'm just ill, I told you. Thirteen hours chugging along on

167

this old boat would make most people sick. Now get your hands off me.'

'Have you thought what would've happened if you'd been caught? Because I know. Maddie and I would've been in the frame too. This is Turkey. You don't mess about with that crap here.'

'What? Have you seen *Midnight Express* too?'

A tight, close upper cut burst open Cooper's bottom lip. Crashing him down to hit the deck hard. Slipped back into a cold pool of stinking water and fish entrails.

'And don't ask me what that was for, because you know damn well. What you should be asking is how you're going to explain this to Maddie.'

He wasn't going to feel it. No way. No damn way was he going to allow Rosedale to get to him. He swallowed down the lump in the back of his throat. Covered his face and with a voice he didn't recognize, which broke and cracked, he shook his head. 'There's nothing to explain.'

'Oh my God, Tom, what's happened?'

Maddie crouched down, pulling Cooper's hands away from his wet, bloody face. 'Jesus Christ, are you crying? What's happened?'

Using the bottom of his shirt to wipe his whole face, Cooper, red-eyed, tried to smile. 'No, of course not, I'm fine.'

Gently, touching his lip, Maddie turned to Rosedale accusingly. 'What the hell do you think you're playing at? Answer me.'

Rosedale opened his mouth but his sentence was beaten and replaced by Cooper's one word.

'Don't!'

'Don't what?' Maddie said.

Tasting the salt from the sea mixed with the salty blood on his lips, Cooper for the second time in a short few minutes slowly got up, listening to Maddie go after Rosedale like the dog with that bone.

'I asked you a question. And now I'm going to ask you again, Rosedale. What are you playing at?'

'Leave it, Maddie.' Cooper said.

'No I won't, because I want to know what happened to having each other's backs? We're here to do a job, not beat the crap out of each other. So go on, what are you playing at?'

Rosedale shrugged as he glanced at Cooper. 'Yeah, that's right, what am *I* playing at? I guess it's just Rosedale being a jackass.'

Maddie scowled. 'That's it? That's the explanation? You know you can be such a jerk sometimes... Oh, and Rosedale, by the way, it's true what Tom says, you speaking in third person just irritates the hell out of us all.'

A quick flash of hurt crossed through Rosedale's eyes. He nodded his head and before turning away. 'Message understood... Loud and clear.'

35

Qe7 Rf7

The old trawler began to slow down as the dark-haired, black-bearded captain, with his wind-leathered face, waved his hand to gesture that the boat the Onyx team had come out to see was right there in front of them.

Maddie acknowledged the captain, returning his wave as she walked across to the starboard bow to where Rosedale and Cooper, who weren't speaking to each other, stood already looking at the ship.

She hesitated to decide which one to address. And not really wanting to speak to, or favor, either of them, Maddie left it slightly ambiguous. 'Well at least the crew was telling the truth. The co-ordinates they gave are almost bang on. What do you think? I must say that's one hell of a ship just to import and export olives, or whatever Granger said.'

Neither men answered, just continued to marvel at the boat. Millions of dollars' worth of marvel. But then you get what you pay for. And a *stealth* ship was certainly something to behold.

By the time she'd come to the end of her naval career,

the US had several ships with advanced stealth technology, though the industry evolved so rapidly that today's science very quickly became yesterday's news. But even with the most cutting edge, almost futuristic development, the basic principles were the same. The primary objective with any stealth technology was simple: not to be seen or heard.

The standard ways were to reduce the acoustic, thermal and wake signatures of any ship. The acoustics were dealt with by getting rid of the smooth, metallic surfaces, changing them to carbon composite materials which absorb and soak up the radar waves, along with replacing the rounded, hydrodynamic body with the construction of flat surfaces and sharp angles to deflect the radar's cross section, scattering and preventing the signals from bouncing back to the source. In this way the ship's detection range was reduced by up to ninety-nine percent.

Stealth manufacturers were also continually developing the best ways of minimizing the temperature of the boat, so that the ships could not be located by the enemy's infrared detection equipment. But one of the biggest problems, and a flag of a giveaway, was the wake of the ship, acting like a trail, exposing the route and ultimately the position of the vessel. Although it was certainly trickier to get round this problem, one of the ways they lessened the wake was by shaping the hull and revolutionizing the way the vessel sailed through the water, to distort and vary the usual pick up patterns. And then there was the one bit of stealth technology which remained ageless, and was perhaps her favorite one of them all. The good old fashioned camouflage paint. Maybe it was silly, but it never ceased to amaze her how a bit of careful shading and shadowing allowed a massive, state-of-the-art craft to fade and become one with the horizon.

Managing to take her eyes off the high-tech, matt grey and black ship, Maddie asked, 'Okay, now what?'

The men said nothing.

'Are you kidding me? Rosedale? Tom? What? Now all of a sudden I'm the bad guy? Okay, fine, have it your way… But just so you know, Cora behaves better than you two at the moment.'

And with that, Maddie walked across to her oversized Rothco Military cargo bag and backpack. Rummaged. Searched. Shook her head at the thought of Cooper and Rosedale. Pulled out a variety of steel-strength but light-weight Kevlar climbing ropes, along with other apparatus.

'What the hell are you doing? Maddie, you stop right there.'

'Oh, *now* you want to speak to me, Rosedale?'

'Thomas, come and see what she's doing.'

Almost snorting with the derision she felt, Maddie's words were scornful. 'This really is something else. All of a sudden not only are you speaking to me, you're speaking to each other, and all because you want to tell me what to do. But the thing is, Rosedale, right now, I'm not interested in speaking to you or Tom.'

She turned her back on Rosedale and proceeded to expertly attach a grappling hook with a skilfully tied bowknot to one of the ropes. Concentrating. Fixed. Focusing. With a serious look and her tongue sticking out, she connected the six-part, streamlined, custom made, pneumatically powered plummet gun. This was a baby version, made by the same people behind the Tactical Air Initiated Launch system used by the Navy SEALs, which would shoot the hooked rope high into the air and reach the deck of the ship. Batman gun it was not, but highly developed device it was.

Cooper, slightly unsteadily, walked across to Maddie. 'No way.'

Maddie said nothing. Latched the rope carefully through and onto the gun.

'Hell, woman, I'm talking to you. I said, no way.'

Maddie stepped into her harness, pulling the straps around her waist and over her shoulders.

'Maddison! Listen to me!'

Making another loop with one of the ropes, Maddie didn't even bother to look up at Cooper. 'Save it, Tom. Not interested.'

'There's no way, you're going on board. No Goddamn way. We're here to see the ship. That's it. Now we have, we're going. Tell her, Rosedale.'

'You know how much I'm going to hate to say this Maddie, but Thomas is right. Crap. See, I said it. But he is.'

Ignoring them both, Maddie signaled to the captain. 'Nearer. Can you take us nearer to the ship?'

Cooper, also gesturing shouted to the skipper. 'No! No! Don't.'

With a large smile and her big brown eyes twinkling and with a little wave to the old sea captain, along with a fluttering wink, Maddie said, '*Please.*'

They began to move, and with the fishing boat bobbing and drawing up to the side of the stealth ship, Maddie looked at Rosedale and Cooper, amused by their synchronized hostile glares.

'Like it or not boys, I'm going on board... Now, stand back.'

Feet slightly apart.

Knees bent.

Grounded stance and the plummet gun pushed firmly against her shoulder, Maddie calculated the distance between her and the stealth ship's deck. Then, squinting up through the glare of the sun, she pulled back the trigger. And released. Felt the kick. Watched the spinning hook lift and take the ropes into the air before landing with a hollow thud.

Quickly pulling back and down on the ropes, Maddie heard the hook trail and drag back to latch onto the ship's rails. Exactly where she wanted it. A further sharp tug locked the hook securely into place.

She grinned. 'Cat got your tongue, boys?'

'No actually, I'm just lost for words,' Rosedale said,

'Why? Because it's me?'

'No.'

'Because I'm a woman?'

Rosedale thought, *yes*, said, 'No, of course not. It's because you're usually the sensible one, Maddie. The one that keeps us together. So let's just turn right on back.'

Maddie regarded the men with a look of surprise. 'I thought that's why we were here. What's wrong with you guys? When have we ever *just turned right on back*? That's not who we are.'

'No, but it's who we should be. We should use Levi as our prototype. The man doesn't do more than breathe. Never goes beyond anything but second helpings.'

'Rosedale, you know perfectly well Levi has your back

as much as I have. Tom, come on, if it wasn't for you, I'd be on a plane back home. You were the one who encouraged us and suddenly all you want to do is look.'

Cooper knew under usual circumstances he wouldn't have thought twice. Not even once. And whether it was because the pills Ismet had given him were slightly different to what he usually took, or whether it was the numbness of life which came hand in hand with painkillers, or even perhaps the persistent thoughts of Ellie which had entered his mind the moment he'd stepped on board, but from the minute they'd set off, he'd never had any intention of going on board. Never. All he wanted to do was turn back round. Let Ismet know the job was done and he'd upheld his side of the bargain. And then... Then fly the hell home and hide out at his ranch where no-one could tell him how he should feel. How he should be. And how he should get his life to resemble something that looked like life.

'I never mentioned *going* on it. Christ, Maddie, this is just crazy...' Pausing, and not quite knowing what else to say, Cooper looked at Maddie with hazy eyes adding, 'Honey, listen...'

He stopped.

Closed his eyes.

Felt the rush of sweetness arrive in his mouth.

Didn't manage to get to the side of the boat in time.

Wiping his mouth and chin of the watery vomit, sheepishly, Cooper gave a half smile.

'Sorry about that. Seasick. Who would've thought?'

Rosedale said, 'No-one.'

With the rubber-coated grappling hook held by the rails,

Maddie talked as she fitted two mechanical ascending devices. With one attached to her harness, and one attached to the line with a loop for her foot, she stepped up onto the side, using Rosedale's involuntary shoulder as a balance.

'You do realize if you go up there, then that means I do too. Forget him, he's in no fit state. But me, I'll have to join you, and Miss Maddison, you know how I hate climbing almost as much as I hate admitting that Thomas is right on anything. This is *exactly* why I left the Navy to join the CIA. This, and the incident with the raccoon of course.'

Not wanting to get embroiled in any of Rosedale's elaborate stories, Maddie spoke firmly. 'I'm not asking you to come on board. I'll be fine, and the climb is easy. The way the boat is shaped. The flat surfaces. It's a cinch.'

'I don't like it.'

'Rosedale, I'm not sure if you've noticed but I'm not asking you to like it. There's nothing to think about for me. We're here and I'm as curious as hell... See you on the other side.'

And with a giant step, Maddie soared off the fishing boat, swinging across to the ship. Moving up the rope towards the deck with diligence and expertise.

Rosedale turned to Cooper. 'So come on then, drugstore cowboy, what's it going to be?'

'Doesn't look really look like Maddie has given us much choice, does it? We can hardly let her explore the ship on her own... And Rosedale, whilst I think about it, hit me again, seasick or not, next time you can be damn sure I'll fight back.'

36

Qe6 Rf6

Once on deck, the ship looked like any other ship the three of them had been on over the years during their esteemed careers. Though, as vessels went, compared to the majority of the colossal US Navy ships Maddie had served on, this was somewhat diminutive.

'You know guys, I'm not real comfortable looking around without a weapon,' Cooper said.

Striding purposefully along the deck, Rosedale came to an abrupt halt by a large grey door, which neither Maddie nor Cooper had noticed.

'You'd think they might lock this,' said Rosedale as it swung open to reveal a wall-mounted gun rack containing an arsenal of automatic weapons. 'You never know who might come along.' He unlatched a Colt M4 carbine and threw it at Cooper. Hard. 'Happy now?'

Making sure the gun was loaded, Cooper nodded. 'I think you already know the answer to that one... Okay, Maddie, seeing as this was your idea. What are you calling?'

'Split up. Take a look around. It's pretty small so it

shouldn't take long. Rosedale, do you want to take the pilothouse and bridges? Tom, why don't you take the engine and store rooms and anything else which looks interesting on the lower decks?'

'Great, just how I wanted to spend a sunny afternoon; down in a dark basement.'

'I'd say you were already there, Thomas, wouldn't you?'

'Rosedale. Tom. Can you guys quit? Right, I'll take the deck, galley and the different quarters. We'll sync watches and meet back here in twenty minutes. And seeing as you're handing them out, throw me one of those guns, Rosedale. Preferably that Smith and Wesson M & P15.'

Rosedale raised his eyebrows, smiling warmly. 'You like your semi-automatics, don't you, Maddie? Remind me never to give you reason to come after me.'

'Rosedale, if I ever came after you, you wouldn't even see me coming.'

37

Qb3 g5

Slumped at the entrance of a large canvas tent, legs wide
apart to ease the straining trousers around his heavy thighs,
the Commandant sat on a hot metal chair, surrounded by a
number of gathered soldiers, swatting away the flies which
landed with noisy anticipation on the seeping sweat that
trickled leisurely from between the fat rolls of his neck.

A foot away from where he sat, slightly away from the
others, a single soldier, cross-legged on the floor, stared
motionlessly down at the grains of sand, watching as they
began to whirl in the warm African winds which were
starting to pick up.

'Who? Who amongst you... Amira, will you? Or how
about you?' the Commandant said. He pointed to a rangy
male, his white eyes sketched with fine red lines, looking
out from sunburnt skin.

'Stand up. Go on...'

The soldier stood. Fearful. Hesitant. Glancing towards the
cross-legged soldier.

179

'Go on.'

'I can't, Commandant.'

Slowly – very, very slowly – the Commandant got up, his thick body moving surprisingly gracefully towards the source of his displeasure. 'Can't?'

Hot painful tears, as if edged by fire, burnt down onto the soldier's face. He shook his head fervently and his tiny voice filled with the cry of torment. 'Yes, Commandant, I can't… I can't… He's my brother.'

'Shoot him.'

'I can't. *Please*. I can't.'

As slowly as he'd moved before, the Commandant raised his arm, pointing his gun at the soldier. Grinding the muzzle against his head. 'Shoot him!'

'I'm begging you, Commandant. Don't make me! Please!'

'Je dis maintenant! Shoot him!'

Quaking with fear, the soldier struggled to hold still his gun. Then, like the Commandant had done, he too raised his arm, pointing it at the head of his brother, whose violent trembles convulsed his body.

'Shoot.'

The soldier closed his eyes, hearing his brother's pleas for mercy.

'I said shoot! Shoot! Shoot!'

The bellowing from the Commandant merged into the bellowing blast of the gun into the bellowing cries of the soldier, *'I'm sorry. I'm sorry. I'm sorry…'*

And his brother fell to one side and the grains of sand promptly became visible through the wide gaping hole in his head, whilst the perimeter of flesh flapped soundlessly in the warm African winds and the terrified soldier shook uncontrollably as a patch of urine oozed out across his pants, as his brother's blood oozed out across his.

'Bien.'

Then with a smile and a tap of his finger, the Commandant pulled the trigger, blasting a bullet into the remaining brother's head.

The Commandant looked at his hands then crouched down, using the dead soldier's hair to wipe them clean from the splattering of blood. Turning. Addressing the terror-frozen group of soldiers who watched, fixed with fear, the Commandant said, 'Now, Amira, you choose. Who are you going to pick next?'

38

Nc7 g4

Eighteen minutes later, Cooper had walked through the hot, dark and echoing walkways of the ship. The place was empty. Devoid of anything *including* smells and dirt. It was certainly the cleanest ship he'd ever been on. Like a sanitized, high-tech version of the *Mary Celeste*. Everything seemed wrong. To his mind the reinforced store rooms were too small to resemble a suitable space for shipping crates. And hell, who even had reinforced store rooms?

To the side of him, he saw a small object. He bent down, picking it up, before a sudden bout of dizziness suddenly engulfed him. Blocked his thoughts. Stopped him right in his tracks.

His stomach ached. His mouth was dry. And a cold ripple of sweat swathed his body.

He leant his arm against the wall. Steadied himself. Breathing. Exhaling. Deep and long puffs out. Then letting himself glide down the wall gently, he dropped his head between his legs, feeling his body rock back and forth, sensing the sea's waves adding to his discomfort as tighter cramps began to set in.

Remembering he'd passed a bathroom not too far back, Cooper decided to see if he could manage to cajole himself to get up and move, and make his way back there.

With excessive force, Cooper, almost falling into the metal bathroom door, pushed against it with his body, causing it to bang violently open, bouncing off the wall several times before it waned into a slow rhythmic swing.

His legs felt weak and he found himself having to prop himself up against the large steel storage cupboard by the lidless silver john.

Fumbling in his pocket and with shaking hands, Cooper hurriedly pulled out the bag of pills. Took out two. Greedily guzzled them down.

Maybe it was because he'd been sick on the boat and he'd retched the pills back up, but they weren't working. Not helping. Not strong enough to fight off this feeling which attacked his body and his mind with overwhelming intensity, because whatever it was that Ismet had given him they certainly weren't his usual poison.

Running the cold water faucet, Cooper put his head under the flowing water. Left it there. Letting the water rush over his face, down his nose and gush in and over his mouth.

Dripping hair glued to his head as he pulled himself up, supporting his weight against the stainless steel sink. His stomach tightened. Again. Cramping. Again. Lurching contractions forcing his stomach to expel what little content was in there through his mouth, through his nose.

Exhausted. Resting his forehead against the mirror above the sink, he spoke out loud.

'Come on, Cooper, we've been here before. Come on…'

Breathing hard. Heavily. Trying to calm the shaking, the cold, the sweat, the increased heart rate which battered inside his chest, he pulled back to standing from the stooped position he found himself in. Continued to stare with disgust at himself in the mirror.

Behind him he saw the double doors of the storage cupboard fly open.

A body fell out. Fell forward. Tumbling hard onto the ground and for one split second Cooper wasn't sure if this was real or if he was hallucinating.

'Jesus Christ! Oh, Jesus!'

Spinning round, he knelt down, frantically turning over the tiny body. It was a child. No more than ten. His eyes half open. And his fragile frame swamped in a bright yellow T-shirt and ragged shorts.

Instantly, Cooper felt for a pulse. Something. Faintly. Well he thought so anyway. Hoped so. But he couldn't be sure as his hands were shaking from the pills. He pushed his head against the boy's chest. Listening. Yes, he could hear something. Just.

'Shit. Come on!' As he lost balance for the second time, he cursed out loud at his pathetic, fumbling attempts at trying to scoop the boy up from the floor. He bent over, resting his hands on his knees. 'Come on!'

A deep breath.

A fast exhale.

Baring teeth and digging deep, driving himself on with a loud incoherent yell. Forcing himself to be able to do what was needed.

As he scooped up the boy, he caught a glimpse of the

inside of the cupboard. Where the back wall of it should've been, in its place a second door, leading down into blackness.

'Quick! Help! Help!

Cooper stumbled out into the ship's walkway, banging into the walls, taking heavy gasps of air as his heart raced away and his head span. Halfway along, he slid down the wall, his legs giving up once more.

'Come on! Rosedale! Maddie! Help!'

He heard his roar echoing and rumbling along the empty corridor as he pushed himself back up the smooth metal pillar. His cold sweat dripped over the boy's face, and as Cooper continued to carry him, the child's head lolled to the side and his eyes showed only the whites as his pupils rolled back into his head.

'No! Don't, don't… He's dying! Rosedale! He's dying!'

At the stairs leading up to the deck, Cooper attempted to drag himself up.

'What the hell?'

He heard the sweet sound of Rosedale's voice. 'Rosedale, here! I'm here.'

The door flung open and the sunlight shone in.

'Jesus, Thomas.'

Rosedale sprinted down the stairs, taking the boy with ease from Cooper's arms.

'He was in a cupboard.'

'What?'

'I'll explain later. Where's Maddie? I got to check to see if anyone else is in there.'

'Tom! Rosedale! Listen, I…'

At the top of the stairs, Maddie appeared, cutting short

what she was about to say. She rushed down towards the men, her eyes fixed on the boy as she listened to Cooper talk.

'I found him, Maddie, and I'm going to see if there are any others down there but I need you to lower the ladder if it's there, but if not, or if it's easier, just harness him to you and take him down to the boat.'

'That's what I was going to tell you, Tom. He's gone! The boat's gone!'

'Oh Jesus. Okay, look, Rosedale you'll have to take him up on deck and try some CPR, whatever it takes, just keep him alive...'

As Rosedale rushed up the stairs with the boy, Cooper turned to Maddie.

'We need to get some help, Mads. Go to the pilothouse and radio in and...'

He trailed off. A memory hijacking his present. A recollection like he was there. Living, seeing it and smelling it. The day of the accident. He'd radioed in on the day of the accident.

'Tom...! Tom!'

He could see it now. Ellie. They were in the water. Desperate for help. The boats. The pirates coming towards them.

'Tom!'

He could hear the helicopters. He could hear her calling his name as the masked pirates approached, firing their weapons. He could see the three skiffs bouncing off the surface of the waves. And he could feel the cold water.

'Tom! What the hell's wrong with you? Tom!'

He could see Jackson floating face down. Sea of red blood. He couldn't see Ellie. Where was Ellie...

'Tom! For God's sake!'

Cooper wiped away the trickling sweat on his face, using the moment to reorient himself. 'What, Maddie? What's the matter?'

Maddie stared at him. 'What are you doing?'

'Nothing... Sorry. Nothing. Look, I'm going to go and search for anyone else.'

And without looking back, Cooper staggered back towards the bathroom, leaving Maddie to radio for help.

39

Nd5 Qc1

'No, no, no. This isn't happening,' Maddie muttered to herself as she desperately tried to figure out any of the controls in the pilot room. It was like nothing she'd seen before. Even if her life depended on naming any of the equipment on the Navigation Bridge she probably couldn't. The irony of her thoughts hit her painfully hard. It may not be her life which depended on it, but it was certainly the boy's. And the way it was looking... She stopped her thoughts from heading down that road. Concentrated on what she was doing.

The vessel monitoring system. The dynamic positioning control station. The echo sounder. In fact, the whole of the integrated bridge system. So usually familiar and recognizable on any ship. Any ship but this one. And right now she didn't know what the hell she was going to do.

Metal security screens covered the computer equipment and were inaccessible behind a large sliding steel grille, locked with finger print technology. The usual dials and buttons and controls weren't even there. Only a multitude of glass panels with no discernible controls. Essentially, though, the one thing which was truly vital was for her to work out how to use the radio… If she could only find it.

Running out of the pilot house and down the stairs to where Rosedale was still performing CPR, Maddie listened to the words she didn't want to hear.

'We're losing him…'

'Rosedale, where's the small bag we keep the cell phones and iPad in?'

Coming up from giving mouth to mouth, Rosedale shook his head at the same time as placing both his hands, one on top of the other over the middle of the boy's chest. Counting. Pressing down hard enough to make the child's chest move inward before relaxing to let it rebound back out. Immediately he began the process again but quickly said, 'It's on the fishing boat. Unless Thomas has it.'

For a moment Maddie didn't say anything. Couldn't. And wished she could ignore the panic rising inside her. The first rule the three of them had was: whatever else happens, whatever else they leave, whatever they did no matter how long or short – never leave the bag.

'Rosedale, I'm going to find Tom. I think we're in trouble…'

*

Heading for the stairs, Cooper emerged before Maddie got there. He was panting. Pale. Sweating. Waxy pallor wiping away his handsome looks.

'There's nobody else down there, Maddie. Not that I can see. Is help coming?'

Quickly pushing to the back of her mind how ill Cooper looked, and not trusting how her voice might sound, Maddie slowly said, 'Tom, where's the bag? The bag with the cell phones in?'

'Haven't you or Rosedale got it? How's the boy?'

'He's not good, and no *we* haven't got it, you were in charge of it. Damn it. It must be on the boat... I can't unlock any of the navigation equipment, it's impossible to work out and I can't even find the radio.'

Not as fast as usual, Cooper ran to the pilot house, consciously not looking at Rosedale and the boy.

He stopped in the doorway. Glancing around with total dismay at the set up.

'Oh my God.'

Coming up behind him, Maddie asked, 'What are we going to do, Tom?'

Cooper said nothing.

A moment later he turned and ran.

40

Qd1 Qd1

A hard yet calculated tap with the butt of Cooper's gun to each corner, cracked but didn't shatter the mirror. Not wanting to waste any more time, Cooper, knowing it was his only option, hooked his fingers underneath the edge of glass. Pulling it carefully. Desperate for it not to break.

'Damn...Damn it.' The mirror was too firmly stuck down to lever any of it off.

Using his gun again, Cooper quickly tapped along one side of it to produce a jagged edge in the hope of making it easier to ease it off the backboard. With an unwavering determination, he placed his fingers on the broken edge. Then pulled.

The pain shot into his fingers as the glass pushed and embedded into them, ripping through flesh and tissue. Brutally shredding. Violently cutting.

And the blood streamed down. Painting his hands red. Covering his arms as it trickled down. And the torture he experienced, making his eyes roll back as he managed to extract the large piece of mirror he needed.

Dropping to the floor with a cry, he curled into a ball as he tucked his hands underneath his armpits to try to alleviate some of the bleeding. Some of the agony.

With the piece of mirrored glass under his arm and with the pain trying to hold him back, Cooper staggered along the corridor.

Up the stairs.

Onto the deck.

'Maddie… Maddie, take over from Rosedale…Rosedale, I need you over here.'

Maddie turned to look at Cooper. And just for a second she froze.

'Tom!' Snapping herself out of her momentary trance, she ran towards him, unable to process quite what she was seeing.

Cooper's face was smeared with blood and his clothes looked like they'd been freshly dip-dyed. Streaks and large clots of jelled blood dried and coagulated on his arms whilst the flesh on the tips of his fingers hung down shredded as a stream of blood ran from them.

Before she could say anything else, Cooper hollered., 'Maddie, just do it. Take over from Rosedale.'

She nodded and answered in a voice stripped of conviction. 'Okay. Okay.'

Leaving Maddie in charge of the CPR, Rosedale ran over to Cooper and, only allowing the tiniest flicker of emotion to show on his face when he saw the state Cooper was in, he asked, 'What's your plan, Thomas?'

'I need you to help me up onto the roof of the pilothouse.'

Rosedale nodded, racing up the stairs with Cooper following closely behind.

Immediately, Rosedale clasped his hands together, creating a step for Cooper to climb on.

Cooper put one foot on Rosedale's hands, and leant his knee against the big cowboy's shoulder.

'Push me up,' Cooper said.

With incredible strength, Rosedale raised his cupped hands slowly up, lifting Cooper higher and enabling him to use his elbows to wriggle his body onto the top of the flat roof.

'Pass me that piece of mirror.'

Rosedale quickly stretched and passed it up to Cooper who took it and hurriedly wiped off the blood. Looking out to the ocean, he glanced around. Then stared into the distance. Focusing on the West horizon.

Standing Westwards, Cooper grimaced with pain as he held the mirror with one hand and picked up the rays of sun on it, working out the angle of the reflection. Stretching out his arm he made a V shape with his torn fingers, making sure the light bouncing off the mirror pointed at the center of the V in the direction he was facing.

Satisfied at the angle of the sun on the blood stained piece of mirror, Cooper, with an uneasy sigh began to send out a distress signal.

Flashed three dots.

Tilting the mirror quickly in and out of the sun.

Flashed three dashes.

Letting the mirror stay and reflect the rays for longer to generate a lengthier burst of light

Flashed three dots again. Hoping the rays of sun would project off the mirror and cross the miles of ocean to be seen by a passing boat.

Minutes passed by and the sun still beat down with cruel intensity as Cooper continued to send out the international Morse code distress signal. He felt weak. Battling to focus as the pain in his fingers crushed him, and waves of nausea came and went.

And then in the distance, he saw what he was beginning to fear he would never see. A boat. A helicopter... Help.

He called down to Rosedale and Maddie as he stood in a pool of his own blood. Relief cracking his voice. 'They're coming. Someone's coming.'

41

Bd1 Rf5

It felt like an hour. It'd been eight by the time they'd been taken back to shore by a NATO helicopter. The boy with no name had been flown to a Cypriot hospital and although no-one had said it, Cooper knew it was very unlikely he was going to pull through. The initial diagnosis had been heat exposure along with dehydration, and the coma he was in, it looked like he was staying in.

With his hands bandaged, Cooper clumsily tried to smoke his cigarette as he leant against a tree in the dark of night directly opposite a small bar.

Watching.

Waiting.

Something he was good at. Like a wolf watching his prey.

Maddie and Rosedale had driven directly to the airport, full of shock and without answers as to who the boy was. Full of anger at how events had quickly turned into a tragedy.

And he was shocked.

And he was angry.

But the difference was, he wasn't going anywhere. The

difference was, he was going to get answers. One way or another.

Maddie had been pissed with him that he'd decided to stay. Worried and anxious. Although he'd tried to assure her there was nothing to be worried and anxious about… Well, not for him anyway. And Rosedale had just stared. Shaking his head at him. Mouth tight with disapproval. Saying more than a thousand words could ever say.

An hour later. Still standing. Still watching, Cooper finally saw what he'd been waiting for.

The hunter was about to get his prey.

Throwing his cigarette down and grinding it hard into the soft ground, Cooper pulled up his blue jean jacket collar. Strode with purpose towards the bar.

Inside the air was thick with smoke and the smell of alcohol mixed with the sizzling meats on the grill mangal cooking over a charcoal fire. And the chattering voices rose up, serenading the night.

Cooper glanced round. Feeling his jaw tighten. Feeling the anger burn into his soul.

He headed for the far corner where a group of old men sat chatting. He stopped. Smiled. Then without warning slammed his foot against the legs of one of the wooden stools sending the man who was sitting on it sprawling across the wooden floor. The group of old men shouted at him in Turkish.

Ignoring them, Cooper grabbed the guy by his coat, using the shooting pain running through his hands and down through his fingers as the driving force to spur himself on.

Picked up the man. Threw him hard against the wall,

sending one bottle of wine and six glasses and two tables and four chairs skidding across the floor.

'Remember me? Remember me?'

The man, wide-eyed with terror, nodded as Cooper pressed down with his boot against the man's chest. He pulled him back up, to the sound of the guy's leather coat tearing. With his broken English and his hands up in surrender, the fisherman stammered.

'Please… please, you no understand.'

Through clenched teeth, Cooper snarled. '*I* don't understand? What don't *I* understand, *sir*? That you drove off and left us on the ship in the middle of the sea? That you stole all our bags and belongings? Is *that* what I don't understand?'

'Sorry… I… please. No hurt.'

With the blood coming through the bandages on his hand, Cooper shook the man hard. Flipping back his head. Flipping it forward.

'No hurt? Really? Is that what you think, no hurt? Well let me tell you something, captain, it's too late for no hurt.'

Proving his point. He slammed his forearm across the captain's mouth. Burst his bottom lip in two.

'You see I'm holding you responsible for the boy that was on the ship.'

Confusion creased the captain's forehead as blood trickled down from his lips. 'Boy? Please. What boy?'

'You see it doesn't matter what boy. Not anymore. That's another thing that's too late. He's probably not going to live, because of you. You see if you hadn't left us and taken our bags we might have been able to save him. But because you did, he's in hospital and it doesn't look like he's coming out. So the question is, captain, what am I going to do with you?'

'Please.'

Cooper threw the man against the wall. Again. 'Stop saying please. Gets me right here. Makes me real mad.'

'Sorry... Sorry.'

'Don't like sorry either. You see the problem is, you should never take on a crazy guy who's got nothing else to lose.'

Then quickly but with controlled, deliberate rage, Cooper clutched the captain's torn coat collar, dragging him along the floor to the entrance of the bar.

Kicked him right outside.

Dragged him back on his feet.

Swung his fist clean against his chin.

Put him back down on the dusty ground.

'Tell me about Ismet, captain.'

Shielding his face, the captain shook. 'I don't know.'

'You don't know what?'

'Ismet. I no know him.'

'So he didn't put you up to leaving us on the ship? You've never spoken to him? He's not part of it?'

'No. No.'

'Is that the truth?'

'Yes... Yes.'

'Because if I find out you're lying to me, I'm going to kill you. You understand that?'

The captain's face drained of color. Said nothing. Could only nod.

'Now I haven't fully decided what I'm going to do to you, but I'm coming back. Tomorrow. I want my bags and all my belongings. I don't want any of it missing. So whatever you've done with it, you better undo it. You understand?'

'Yes.'

'Oh, and captain. If the boy dies, don't worry, I'll make sure you'll get a maritime burial.'

42

Ne3 Rf4

Back at the private port set below the Turkish mountains, Cooper stood on the craggy hill staring down at the glitzy turquoise sea, looking like a precious stone twinkling under a jeweler's light.

He took a long, deep drag of his cigarette, leaving it to hang at the side of his mouth. Wiped away the cold sweat gathering in his sternal notch before getting back into the SUV, heading down to the large white building on the empty harbor.

'Mr Cooper, it's good to see you. I'm glad you called. I was beginning to wonder.'

Sauntering across to Ismet's desk, Cooper ripped one of the large posters off the wall, tearing it up as he walked. 'This is how it's going to go, you son-of-a-bitch. I ask you the question and then you give me the right answer.'

'What are you doing?'

'Wrong answer, because I'm the one asking the questions.'

Cooper walked around the desk to where Ismet sat. He span the chair round to face him and straddling his legs either side of it, grabbed Ismet's hair and forced a piece of the torn poster into his mouth with his bandaged fingers.

Like a stoplight hanging over a highway, Ismet's face turned bright red as he struggled to push Cooper away, but his strength was no match and, after a few seconds, panting heavily with fear shining out of his eyes, he abandoned his fight, sitting frozen looking up at Cooper.

'That's better. Now shall we begin? Who was the boy on the ship?'

Furiously, Ismet spat the poster out. 'My men will kill you for this.'

'Wrong answer again, Ismet.'

Cooper jammed a handful of poster deep into the back of Ismet's mouth. He began to choke, mucus bubbling out of his nose.

Cooper pulled the saliva-drenched pieces out of Ismet's mouth.

'I'll ask you again. Who was the boy?'

Ismet, dark-eyed and with a cutting stare, glared at Cooper. 'Go to hell!'

With rapid speed, Cooper tipped Ismet backwards on his chair, ramming the rest of the torn pieces hard into his mouth. Pushing it. Stuffing it. Shoving it in until there wasn't room for any more. Watching as his eyes bulged, his face ballooned and his panic caused his body to writhe as Cooper held his nose shut.

'You going to answer the question, Ismet?'

Squirming from the lack of oxygen and the force of Cooper's weight, Ismet gurgled a noise. And with a taunting smile, and a mocking tone, Cooper said, 'What was that? I can't hear you... Are you trying to tell me you're going to answer...? Is that a nod?'

He let go. Leaving a coughing, spluttering, gasping and spitting Ismet to get his breath back.

Handing him a tissue, Cooper asked again. 'Who was the boy?'

Rasping, Ismet tried to answer. 'What boy, where?'

With a dull, dense ache beginning to attack his stomach, and a chill in his body like the long dark winters of Alaska, Cooper, agitated, wiped the cold perspiration away. He'd thought there was enough OxyContin running through his blood stream, but now realized he might have been wrong.

'Ismet, you need to believe something, even if it's the only thing you ever believe in your sorry life... I want to kill somebody. Don't matter who. Don't matter how. But it so happens you're the only one here. So do the math.'

'Mr Cooper...'

'And before you think I won't. Look at me... Do I look like a man that has time to play games? Between you and me, Ismet, I'm one helluva a mess right now. And at this moment, I don't care. I don't care what happens to me. And I certainly don't care what happens to you. So, I'll ask you again, *who was the boy on the ship?*'

Tense, strained, Ismet rasped, 'Mr Cooper, even if you threaten to kill me.'

'*Promise* to.'

'Even if you *promise* to kill me. I still won't be able to tell you. I have no idea what you're talking about.'

'The boy. We found him almost dead on your ship.'

Ismet clenched his jaw. Unease spreading through him

like a forest fire. 'I told you not to go on board, Mr Cooper. For every action there is a consequence. There are people I have to answer to who won't be happy with your decision.'

'Like I give a damn about that. All I care about is the boy and why he was on your ship.'

'Clearly you've already made up your mind that I've got something to do with it, and therefore you won't believe me when I say that I'm sorry such a tragedy has happened. It's not uncommon to hear such stories, but nevertheless each time it happens, it's no less tragic… I'm assuming you took him to hospital?'

Cradling his stomach with his arm as the acute withdrawal cramps intensified, Cooper nodded. 'A NATO helicopter took him.'

A short silence. A soulless stare along with a supercilious smile. 'NATO… you should congratulate yourself. Who knows what would've happened to the boy if you'd followed my instructions… Perhaps this is a reason for celebration rather than accusation.'

The fear of the impending withdrawals distracted Cooper from being able to think clearly. To hold on to the certainty he'd had before. To be able trust that instinct which told him what felt right. What felt wrong.

Staggering back, to rest on the desk, Cooper said, 'Don't mess with me.'

Ismet smiled. Stood up. Strolled with confidence towards Cooper. 'I'm not. And sadly, there are some desperate people needing to do desperate things to escape from totalitarian regimes. Their lives and their families are under threat. Or they're simply just looking for a better life, to be able to live without fear. We forget how lucky we are, Mr Cooper, not to have to resort to hiding between the wheels of a lorry, underneath a train, stowing away on a ship, or even putting your children in a dinghy to sail across the sea, never knowing if you'll see them again. You just read about it in your papers, but we see it. Daily. And it never gets easier. Especially when it comes to children. We try to be vigilant when it comes to checking our ships before they sail, specifically for this reason, because as you know, Syria is only a few miles from here. I don't blame them. If I was in the same position, and saw an opportunity to flee my persecutors, I'd take it. Wouldn't you, Mr Cooper?'

Slipping slightly on the edge of the desk, Cooper muttered, 'I'm asking the questions.'

A twitch of a smile. A glint. 'So I see.'

'And the ship. Why was it...'

Ismet interrupted. 'A stealth ship...? These are unsafe waters, and this is my business. This is all I have for myself and my family. I don't know if you've ever had nothing, but I have, and it's not a pleasant place to be. I'm a simple olive exporter. Out there on the ocean I can't protect myself. Aside from it being hard to pick up on the radar, my ship acts as a deterrent. People think twice. It's a jungle out there. Piracy. Kidnapping. Robbery. Dangerous waters... Are you alright, Mr Cooper? I could get my men...'

'No. No. You don't go anywhere.' Cooper put his hand out in a gesture of authority, but finally lost his balance and slipped, sliding to the floor.

Standing above a sweating, shaking, trembling Cooper, Ismet grinned. 'Okay. Whatever you say. You're in charge.'

With a fading whisper, with eyes rolling, with his body going into spasms, Cooper said, 'So, the boy...'

'... Is clearly part of this tragic scrabble for survival. And it won't be the last time this happens. I'm just sorry you were caught up in it. But to think I had anything to do with it is, how do you say it? Absurd. Frankly absurd... Mr Cooper, can you hear me...? Mr Cooper...'

43

Ne1 Rb4

In the bedroom of Levi's small ranch just outside Phoenix, Cooper lay in bed. He listened as Dorothy gave him a piece of her mind.

'It's no good tryin' to give me all that sweet talk. You might as well save it. You ain't got the good sense God gave a rock. Don't bother giving me a *but*, either. I'll tell you when you're fine. And don't try to get out of bed otherwise I'll be all over you like white on rice. You hear me?'

'I can get out of bed. My legs aren't broke.'

'You heard what the doctor said.'

Cooper gave a wry smile at exactly what the doctor had said. Or rather what he had done. Which was little more than getting out his fancy pen and written with his fancy swirls another prescription for another lot of pills. Welcome to hell.

'Dorothy, he never said I couldn't walk. I've got things to do. Got people to see...' Cooper trailed off as a memory of Maddie came into his head. He didn't remember much after he'd collapsed. Not really sure he wanted to. Maybe if he really thought hard there was a slight, vague recollection of Ismet's men taking him to the airport. How long after he'd passed out they'd taken him, he didn't know. Hadn't bothered to find out. It was all a blur. The journey home. Even being tucked up into bed in the Walkers' house. There was nothing there. All of it nothing but a fog. All of it apart from the way Maddie had looked at him when they'd sat on the private plane Granger had sent for him. Disappointment didn't even come close.

'I appreciate everything you've done, but really I got to go. I need to see Maddie.'

'That woman's a saint, Thomas. You know that? If it was me, I wouldn't have bothered flying all that way just to bring you back, I'd have left that sorry butt of yours in Turkey.'

Cooper managed a smile. Warm and loving. 'We both know that's not true.'

She kissed her teeth at him. 'All this foolishness. All this wanting to get up and break bad. Wanting to carry on. Well, let me tell you, Thomas Cooper, you couldn't carry anything right now, not even a tune in a bucket. And if it wasn't for my back, I'd have a hankerin' to give you a whoopin' for all the worry you've caused. How you thought this was okay, I'll never know.'

'Woman, why don't you leave him alone?'

Dorothy Walker pursed her lips. 'Levi, in all the time we've been married I've never wanted your opinion and I'm not going to start wanting it now. You hear me?'

Levi, rested on the smooth-sanded wooden door frame Cooper had put in last fall. He shrugged, watching his wife tucking the sheets tightly under the mattress of the bed Cooper was lying in. 'At least this way it's your ass she's bugging and not mine.'

Shooing him away, Dorothy said, 'Don't stand there like a tick on a dog, go and make yourself useful, Levi Walker.'

'I need to speak to Coop.'

'Go on then, but don't make it an excuse not to go and fix that fence. Always looking for your behind,' Dorothy said.

Cooper winked at Levi. 'What's up, man?'

'It's Granger, and it's not good.'

'How did I guess you were going to say that?'

Levi's expression was awkward. 'He had a call. I don't know how to say this.'

Dorothy rejoined in the conversation. 'It's never stopped you talking your rubbish before. As for Granger. That man thinks the sun comes up just to hear him crow. The way he talks, going around barking orders, telling folk what to do. Snaps at everybody. If I had my druthers, neither you nor Levi would be at that job.'

'Woman, please, stop your noise… Coop, they know what you did. Getting the pills from Ismet.'

'I have to go and speak to them. Try to explain.'

'Don't think that will do much good.'

Cooper said nothing. Played with the hem of the bed sheet until Dorothy slapped his wrist away and sat down heavily on the bed, pulling down and straightening her rose pink cotton skirt. 'I heard about it too, Thomas. I spoke to Maddie earlier. Made me madder than a wet hen when she told me, I can tell you. But then I know that's not really you. Not the Thomas I know.'

Cooper gave a long sigh. 'I don't know where people get this idea from. Maybe it's easier to make excuses than see what I am. But it is me.'

Leaning in, almost nose to nose, Dorothy put her hand on Cooper's heart and quietly spoke to him.,

'No it ain't. Not in here. That's what counts. Not the stuff in your mind where crazy happens. It's in there. And in there beats the heart of a good man. A man of integrity. Courage. Strength. A man who loves little Cora, and loves his friends with the same passion he loves his family. But right there's the catch. Because you love so hard. It's like being in the eye of a storm. Calm and quiet at the center but when it goes wrong like it did with Ellie, then all around you those strong winds which have been circling and forming, knock everything out of their way, leaving behind a trail of destruction. It's not the heart of you which is the problem, it's what comes with you. But I'll always be here for you no matter what, and so will Levi, for all the use he'll be. Let the faith in yourself be bigger than your fear. Which also means getting off those damn pills! I told the doctor as much, sent him away with a flea in his ear.'

'Dorothy, you know you're my tonic.'

Dorothy Walker pulled her green cardigan tight around her. 'You find me as you see me.' She stopped and shook her head then smiled and said, 'Thomas, I can see you have to go. See it in your eyes. I ain't going to stop you, I understand sometimes a man has to go and tend to his field.'

Planting a kiss on Dorothy's head, Cooper said, 'I love you, Dorothy, thank you.'

44

Bg4 h5

Chuck wondered as he often wondered, why the hell it was he ended up dealing with the lowest forms of life just to get things done. His days at the moment seemed to consist of dealing with governmental issues on policy, legislation, and the constant re-alignment of ideas and procedures when it came to dealing with terrorism – with Woods and Secretary of State Lyndon P Clark looking about as frightening and as threatening to the enemy as Touché turtle and Dum Dum.

To Chuck's mind, his life was further hindered by the circus of the liberal left advocating a confusing mix of inter- nationalism and isolationism. America shouldn't have to ask permission to invade an enemy nation alongside another country whose own agenda, by definition, wouldn't be the same as that of the US. The tactics should always be of offensive strategies; rapid, decisive operations, together with baiting and bleeding; to induce rival factions to engage in a protracted war against each other, *so that they bleed each other white*, whilst the USA, the baiter, lingers on the side-lines, watching. Waiting. Maintaining its military strength, until the time was right for going in and destroying the already battle-fatigued parties. But as Woods seemed inept, and determined to keep America in a precarious position when it came to the enemy, Chuck, as the head of the CTC, had a duty to the citizens of this great nation to do something about its safety. And that's how, day after day, he had to deal with the low-lives, the sewer rats. Harry Gibson was a case in point.

'So you know exactly what you're supposed to do?' Chuck said.

Harry, trailing his hand in the cool water of Chuck's flamboyant fountain nodded, and with an air of effeminacy, an exaggerated campness, and a suggestive tone nodded. 'When have I ever not known what to do? That's why you want me, isn't it? I know exactly what you require. When have you ever been disappointed with any of my performances?'

Chuck tossed a white envelope to Harry who sniffed it. 'Perfumed, I hope?'

Chuck said nothing. But that sure as hell didn't mean he didn't want to.

Harry, opening up the envelope, whistled. 'I was never paid this well in the CIA. What was I doing for all those years?'

'That's exactly why they got rid of you.'

'*Meow*. I see that tongue of yours hasn't got any less catty over the years, Chuck.'

'Harry, listen to me. It gives me no pleasure to work with the likes of you. You should've made the best kind of agent, willing to go to go as far as it's necessary for your country.

But I guess no one looks favorably on a grown man caught in the Middle East with young boys, do they?'

Harry's face darkened as he replied. 'We both know the accusations weren't true. Not my style. Quite the opposite in fact.'

'Not according to the authorities.'

'I'd say it was just an excuse to get rid of me, wouldn't you, Chuck? How does it go? Always shoot the man who knows too much. Strip him of his reputation so no-one will work with him or trust him gain... Apart from you. You work with me because you knew it was bull. I was the most trustworthy agent out there, which meant people would listen when I voiced my concerns about what was going on in some of the black sites over there. And that just didn't suit you, did it? Not even close.'

'Hey, Harry, you know there's nothing more tedious than a guy with a conspiracy, apart from an unemployed guy with one.'

'Chuck, you robbed me of my life. Have you any idea what it was like in Al-Ha'ir Prison?'

'Saudi Arabia has never been known for its soft approach to punishment.'

Harry leaned forward, grabbing Chuck by his white, crisp linen shirt. 'You think it's funny being raped? Tortured? Beaten on a daily basis?'

'If it wasn't that prison it would've been here. As a whistle-blower. They would've locked you up and you'd be still sitting looking at four walls. You can't go round telling tales about other agents.'

'You mean you.'

'It would've been a violation of the Intelligence Identities Protection Act. It's a good job that journalist you contacted let me know. I did you a favor. No-one takes too kindly to whistle-blowers. Ask Edward Snowden.'

'A favor?'

'Yes, you're out, aren't you? I paid your blood money, to get you out. Couldn't have done that here. You should be thanking me, Harry.'

Eyes wide with memory and a soul full of pain, Harry's voice was full of scorn. 'Blood money! Christ almighty, I was innocent, you know that. I lost my family. I lost it all. Everything and anything that meant anything to me, I lost. I haven't seen my kids in years and I never will. And it's all down to you.'

A cold calculated tone. A voice uncaring. 'The only thing I had to do with it was helping you out. Giving you a chance. Where would you be without me, Harry?'

'With my family. With my job.'

'You might not want to admit what you did, but you're kidding yourself. Or is it a question of still wanting to blame the alcohol...?'

'Is that what you're calling it? Is that what David Thorpe the coffee shop bomber would call it? Would he call it alcohol? Is that what he's going to blame it on?'

Pushing Harry's hands off his shirt, Chuck stared with disgust. 'If you were wise, you'd stop right there. You and he have nothing in common.'

'Really? Are you sure about that? Because I'd beg to differ.'

'Harry, there were photos of you. Remember? The Saudi

police took them in the morning when they raided your apartment. You and them. Those boys... So stop deluding yourself and think yourself lucky I'm willing to work with you.'

Raw bitterness and steaming anger was ladled onto Harry Gibson's words.

'You've made damn sure of that, haven't you? Made sure you're the only one who'll give me the time of day. Made me need you... I have to give it to you, Chuck. You're good. But then it takes someone this good to be in your position.'

Not wanting to get drawn further into the conversation they seemed to have on a frequent basis, Chuck pulled something else out of his pocket. A small wrap of foil tightly sealed and taped up in a transparent grip-seal plastic bag. He handed it to Harry.

'Here. Take it. Though don't do anything until I give you the go-ahead. Understand me? You do *nothing* until you get my call, but it's exactly the same as it was before.'

Taking off his jacket to reveal a Desert Eagle 44 tucked in his shoulder holster, Harry held the grip-seal bag whilst looking at its contents. 'Not quite. We're not talking your average guy here, are we?'

'What's your point?'

'The money's good – but it could be better.'

'Don't push it, Harry.'

'I think all things considered that's exactly what I should do. Isn't that what you taught us when we were stationed in Khartoum? Push for more and never take the first offer. Negotiation is the key.'

Standing up, Chuck glanced through the fountain of

water and across to his immaculately kept gardens, some-thing his gardener made him pay through the nose for, and something he couldn't care less about one way or another. Drew his eyes back to Harry. Followed the lines around his deeply pockmarked skin. Put one foot on the small stone wall.

'Negotiation only works if one side has something the other one wants more.'

'And I'd say that was you.'

'Not really. I can find guys, ex-CIA or ex-military, who'll do the job just as well. Maybe better. I'd say you were just a convenience, rather a necessity. *You* however, like you say, you need me *and* this money, much, much more than I need you.'

'That might be true, Chuck, but what if I was to say you also need me to keep my mouth shut and that will cost you.'

Sniffing the air and feeling the sun on his skin, Chuck laughed. Hard. Loud. Looked at Harry and said, 'If you were to say that, I'd reply by saying, you're not even supposed to be in this country, Harry. Authorities think you're locked up abroad for life. No-one knows I paid your blood money. No-one knows you're here except for me... So then I'd say, remember the prison in Saudi? The one you hate so much. Well, all it'd take was one phone call from me to have you taken back there... So if I were you, Harry, I'd be real careful with what I was saying.'

45

Bf3 d5

'Think about this. If we'd just gone right ahead and flown back home we would never have gone to the ship, which means we would've never been able to help the boy.'

Maddie walked up close to Cooper. Inches away. Letting him feel every part of her scorn. Letting him smell every part of her disdain.

'Don't you dare. Don't you dare use that boy's plight to justify what you did.'

Stepping away from the onslaught of intensity, Cooper, guilty and angry and filled with self-loathing, snapped. 'What the hell *did* I do, *Maddison*? I never put *you* in danger. I never sold *you* out. Not really. It was *myself* I sold out.'

A hard, bitter laugh. Cutting scorn. 'That's crap, Tom. Bottom line is, you made a deal with Ismet and lied to us, pretending you were curious about what was going on.'

'I was... And my gut was right.'

Maddie's face was red now. As red as Earl's had been, as red as Granger's had been and as red as Ismet's had been.

'Stop, Tom! Can you hear yourself? That's not why you did it.'

'It's part of it.'

'Quit with the excuses. You sold us out right down the line for a pocket full of pills. We trusted you.'

'Yeah, well I trusted you.'

Maddie's finger came up sharp. She pointed. Wagged. 'Oh no you don't. You're not going to turn this round on us like you always do.'

'I'm not trying to do that. Why do you always think everything I do is a manipulation?'

'I wonder.'

'Maddie, look, I'm just saying I trusted you not to judge me. Not to make up your mind about what happened till you heard me out. I screwed up. Big time. I know. But isn't that what people do?'

'They do, but not on your scale. With you it's a constant merry go round of broken promises, and secrets and lies. Telling us you're clean. Telling us it's only a blip. Well, I'll tell you what it really is, it's bullshit. Complete and utter bullshit.'

Cooper knew he had no right to feel pissed, but he was, and he was going to say as much. His handsome face veiled in a mixture of pain and hurt. 'The holier-than-thou outlook on life, according to Maddison Cooper. Has anyone told you how Goddamn sanctimonious you can be? You know, I'm sorry if we're not all as doggone perfect as you, Maddie. But do you really think it's so easy to get off this stuff? Click my fingers and suddenly I'm clean? I've tried and you know it.'

'Then try harder.'

'Good job you never chose counselling as your career, your bedside manner isn't really up to much… Shall I tell you something, Maddie? When I go to the doctors to get help, you know what they do, they give me some more? It's hard… And if it wasn't hard, why in this country did drug overdoses kill more Americans than car crashes or guns last year? *Forty-seven thousand* people died in the US because of drugs. That's on average a hundred and thirty a day and most of those involved some kind of opioids, and at least half of those deaths are from overdoses of *prescription drugs*.'

'Yeah, but you still have a choice.'

Cooper stared at Maddie, looking into her beautiful brown face. Wanting her to understand when he didn't really understand himself how it'd come to this.

'You have it your hand. Whether it's the pills or the prescription from the doc, but it burns a damn hole in it. Like acid. You try to throw it out in the trash can. But you end up retrieving it. Then you decide to get rid of it further away. A block down. Throw it in the garbage at the nearby diner, but you end up sitting on your front porch thinking about it. Thinking about it lying there covered in trash. And that's all you can think about, like it's some kind of Goddess. And then the pain starts. The sweats. The cramps. The nausea. The sickness. And you try to crawl to the bathroom but you end up retching up on your expensive handmade rug. Unable to move. And as you lie in your own vomit all you can think about is that Goddess lying under a mound of vegetable skins, the scraped off food from the diner's plates, the soiled diapers and dirty rags. But it doesn't matter because you know that at 3 a.m. you'll find yourself waist deep in garbage. And you don't care if anyone sees you either, because all you care about are those pills. And that's how it is minute by minute. Hour by hour. Day by day. So no, Maddie, I wouldn't say at this stage it's a choice. Not one I would choose anyway... But I am sorry. Sorry I did this to you. To Cora. Just don't stop believing in me. *Please.*'

Before Maddie could reply, a roar like the Rocky Mountain cougar came from the Onyx hallway, crescendo-ing to a bellow until Dax Granger appeared. Ruffled shirt. Immaculately pressed pants. He stood in the doorway of the main office. Face like a crumpled dollar bill.

'Get out!'

'Granger, listen...'

'I said get out, Cooper, or I'll throw you out. Failing that, I'll go and get Rosedale to do it for me.'

'Hear me out, okay?'

'Hear you out? That stuff has rotted your brain more than I thought. I don't want to listen to another word you've got to say. You're full of crap, Cooper. You're finished. You understand? Now go.'

'Not till you listen to me. You owe me that.' Cooper said.

'I owe you jack shit. This is my business! My reputation! And you want to ruin it like you ruin everything. And God it's a long list. Your marriage. Your kid. Any relationship you've ever had you ruin. If Ellie had stayed away from you she would've been alive today. She would've been here with me and her Momma.'

Staggering back, Cooper shook his head. 'That's not fair. I loved her. She was my everything.'

Maddie flinched at Cooper's words as Granger shouted back.

'She wasn't yours, Cooper! She wasn't yours to take from me!'

The blow to Cooper's chin from Granger's clenched fist, he accepted gratefully and without a fight. Wanting the pain to be anywhere but in his heart or in his head.

'Now get out, Cooper.'

Scrambling up, Cooper spat the mouthful of blood onto the sand tiled floor.

'Okay, I'll go, but answer me one question… What was sensitive, Granger?'

'What?'

'You said this job was sensitive. What aren't you telling us? Because something just doesn't cut it.'

'It's you who doesn't cut it. You're a mess!' Granger said.

'That I know. I don't deny that. But you. I know you, Granger, and I know when something feels wrong.'

'I said get out, Cooper, and I won't tell you again.'

Granger began to drag a submissive Cooper by his jean jacket. Pushing him. Shoving him. Thrusting him towards the door.

'Granger, don't.'

'Keep the hell out of it, Maddie.'

Rosedale, who'd just stepped into the Onyx kitchen, turned to his boss. 'Watch your mouth, Granger.'

Granger whipped round to stare at Rosedale. 'I don't mind if you follow him too. And you, Maddie. You want to go? Because right now I'd be happy to see none of you again. Because at the end of the day, no matter how much you point the finger at Cooper, you both played a part in it too. You went along with it. Behind my back. Giving me some bull about not wanting to do the job, about flights being delayed.'

Maddie nodded in agreement. 'You're right, we did. And if you really want us to go, we will, Granger, but you haven't answered Tom's question. What *was* so sensitive about Ismet's job?'

Raging to almost the point of combustion, Granger snarled. 'This is all down to you, Cooper. Always wanting to stir up things which aren't even there to mix, and now you've got Maddison joining in the madness.'

'And me.' Rosedale said.

Granger eyeballed him hard. 'Who are you all of a sudden, Goddamn Fletcher Christian?'

Calmly, Rosedale replied, 'I'm just someone who'd be interested in hearing what you have to say.'

Cooper said, 'What are you hiding, Granger? Why won't you answer?'

'I'm not hiding anything. The fact is there's simply nothing to answer.'

'You don't think it's odd there was a boy on board?'

'No, I don't. Ismet explained to both of us how the situation is along that coast. You only have to turn on the TV and every news channel carries the story of migrants trying to board ships and stowaway.'

'Come on, Granger, the guy had a stealth boat.'

'I don't care. You hear that? I don't care if he had the Goddamn Flintmobile to ship his stuff. The fact is that's *his* business. Not yours. Not mine.'

'But it is. It's all of our business if he's doing something he shouldn't.'

'Like what? Come on, Cooper. What are you suggesting?'

'I don't know, but I do know in my gut it feels all wrong. Maybe I should do some digging on this guy.'

'You do no such thing. No-one here is going to do any digging. You got that? This is *my* company, and you follow *my* rules. So you leave well alone. Everything we do is based on confidentiality. Privacy and discretion are paramount for sustaining the reputation of Onyx. And let me tell you something: good reputations are hard to come by, but I guess you wouldn't know about that. So you digging about in affairs of my clients is a non-starter. It just isn't going to happen. Now, I've got a phone call to make and when I come back here in ten minutes, I want you gone.'

Granger turned on his heel and walked out, leaving Cooper, Maddie and Rosedale in the large, airy office. Not saying anything. Not looking at each other.

It was Cooper who broke the silence. 'I appreciate what you guys did. Having my back with Granger. Thank you.'

Rosedale said, 'Don't think this changes anything, Thomas. Not one Goddamn thing.'

46

N3g2 h4

It was quiet. Real quiet. But not the kind of quiet Cooper liked to relax in. It was the uncomfortable kind. The seat shifting kind. The kind which made every ticking clock seem louder. And the kind that had him brushing a fleck of dirt off his pants when there wasn't any dirt to be had.

With tight smiles, Beau and Woods sat on the couch in the private sitting room opposite Cooper, like some kind of tag team. Both raising their eyebrows. Both nodding their heads. Staring hypnotically like the snake in *The Jungle Book*, using mesmeric eyes to encourage him to be the first one to break.

Wouldn't do it. Goddamn it, he wouldn't do it. Not this time.

'This is nice.' Damn it. He broke.

Woods said, 'Yep.'

'Though I have to tell you, I've been at livelier wakes. What's going on?' Cooper said.

'Nothing.'

Trying to get a conversation out of Beau, Cooper turned

to him. 'So how's your day been? How's monkhood? Is that even a word?'

'Same as it always is. Which isn't a bad thing. There's something strangely reassuring about predictability.'

'You never tire of the quiet life, Beau?' Cooper asked.

'You never tire of asking me that?'

'Touché.'

'But to answer your question, *again*. No, I had too many years in the Navy. Too many tours of duty. But don't get me wrong, I'm proud to have served my country and I have absolutely no regrets.'

A dark accusatory tone. A sudden anger. Cooper said, 'None?'

Understanding exactly what his nephew was getting at, Beau kept his tenor sunny, smiled. 'Not really, I'm where I should be. It's not where I should always have been, but it feels right and that's all I could ask for.'

Draining the bottom of his cup and continuing to be mildly impressed – much to Teddy's disgust – with Joan's nettle tea, Woods remarked, 'It's just good to see you, Coop. And of course, Jackson loves you coming by. He misses you. Always appreciate you dropping in.'

Beau nodded in agreement. 'You shouldn't leave it so long, last time I saw you… ' He trailed off, realizing what he was about to say *maybe* wasn't the most sensible, the most tactful of things to come out with given the circumstances.

'Oh you mean when you left me in the jailhouse to have an extra think. That last time.'

Stern faced, tight lipped, Beau nodded. 'Yeah.'

There was that silence again. Damn it, it was pointless

even trying; he'd break first anyway. 'Have you had any more letters, John?' Cooper said.

Woods looked at Cooper, a strange expression passing over his face. A guarded stare and a closed reply. 'Why do you ask?'

Cooper, rather disconcerted by John's reaction, shrugged. 'Conversation. Concern. Take your pick.'

'Concern?'

Cooper opened his hands. Darted his eyes from Woods to Beau. And Beau to Woods.

'Yeah. Problem?' Cooper asked.

Not wanting any more tension, Beau muttered to his nephew, 'Leave it, Coop.'

Cooper looked at them intently. 'I'm missing something here, aren't I?'

Silence. Strained and uneasy. But this time, Cooper really wasn't going to say anything first. Instead he tried to work out what the problem was. The letters to John, albeit via Beau at the monastery, had started early last year. Anonymous letters. Saying they knew. Knew about the accident eight years ago. Knew what *really* happened on the yacht that day. But they couldn't. No-one could. The only people privy to such information were Jackson, John and Beau... That was it. All sworn to secrecy. *The pact*.

Contrary to what they'd told the authorities at the time of the accident, and unlike the rest of the world had been led to believe, it hadn't actually been *him* who'd sailed the boat into dangerous waters. It'd been Jackson, who'd been high on life and alcohol. Though he didn't blame Jackson, he blamed himself because he should've known better.

He'd been the one in the Navy's Special Task Force, helping to set up an anti-piracy directive in the area. Him. Not Jackson. And, after all it was because of him that Ellie and Jackson were there. They'd flown out to visit whilst he was based in Lamu, and the three of them had rented a yacht, sailing it up the Kenyan coast. Anchoring and having a picnic in the heat of the midday sun, before he and Ellie had taken a nap below decks. And when he'd woken up, he'd seen the shadows, heard the lapping waves, and he'd known they were in trouble.

Whilst they'd been asleep, Jackson had sailed the yacht into pirate-heavy waters. On top of which he'd been drinking. Heavily. But Jackson had been young and foolish and hadn't realized what he'd done. What he was sailing them into. But Cooper had known, hell had he just, and he'd radioed in for help. To the ship he was serving on. To his Uncle Beau. His Captain.

After the accident, the authorities needed to know what had happened. And right then, right there he'd made a decision, telling John – who'd also flown out to see him – that he was going to take responsibility. There hadn't been any doubt in his own mind that he was doing the right thing, because, after all, Ellie was missing – to the authorities, missing presumed dead. So they wanted answers. And if they'd known that Jackson had been at the wheel, drunk in charge of a vessel, they'd have hauled his ass into prison. A *Kenyan* prison. And Jackson couldn't have coped with that. And Cooper couldn't have coped with sending Jackson there.

So the official report stated it'd been an accident, caused and exacerbated by the pirate attack, with the vessel being sailed by him, an experienced Navy Lieutenant with an exemplary record. In other words, no repercussions, with no-one needing to know the truth.

That was the pact. And John had gone along with it. Uncomfortable to begin with, but knowing it was the best choice for his son, Jackson... *and* for his political career.

At the time of the accident, John had been Governor of Illinois, so the incident had became newsworthy. John, had done television interviews, and with them came an outpouring of public sympathy and support. Well wishers across America were rooting for Jackson to pull through after the horrific neurological injuries. It had been close – not many people survive a gunshot to the head – but ultimately he'd got through. Survived – even if he was eventually left with trauma-based depression. But America had been behind him. And although it hadn't been intentional, the public support had certainly helped John secure his party's nomination for presidential candidate.

Then on election day the supporters came in their tens of millions. Strangers who somehow felt an infinity with John, having gone through the journey of Jackson's recovery with him, put their check in the box by John's name... John James Woods. The People's President.

And over time the four of them had put the truth away, locked, chained and tightly sealed, until some of them started to believe the lies themselves...

Until last year that was when the first of the letters came. Telling John that they knew. They knew it hadn't been Jackson sailing the yacht that day.

Then another one had come, telling him he should do the

honorable thing and step down as President. And if he didn't. They – whoever they were – would make damn sure he did.

So yes, Cooper wanted to know if there'd been more letters. And he thought it was damn obvious why. He cared. Not because he was worried he'd get into trouble, hell, he couldn't give less of a damn if he tried. No, it was John, and it was Jackson he cared about.

'What's the big deal about me asking?'

Woods said, 'How about we change the subject, Coop?'

'I don't get it, John? Beau? Has something else happened? You got more letters?'

As tight as he could without actually keeping his mouth shut, Woods replied, 'Can we just change the subject?'

Cooper pulled a face. 'Fine... How's Jackson?'

'He's good, but then you should know that, seeing as you speak to him most nights.'

'I do, but that doesn't mean he always tells me how it really is. He hides his depression.'

With an exasperated sigh, Woods snapped, 'Coop, let's cut the crap.'

'Excuse me?'

Woods sat forward. A habit he had when he wanted to emphasize his point. 'I spoke to Granger.'

Dog-like, the back of his neck seemed to bristle with hairs he didn't even know he had. He snarled, 'And?'

'And, he told me exactly what had happened in Turkey.'

'About the boy?'

'No... Yes, but more about what you did.'

'What I did?'

'The pills. The ship.'

228

Cooper stood up, walking across to the window. Didn't like where this was going. Not one bit. He stared out at his favorite view from the White House; across the south lawn to the Ellipse. With his back turned to John, he spoke slowly. 'Don't give me any lectures. I've heard them all before.'

'Shame you didn't bother listening.'

'Who the hell do you think you are? I've told you, stay out of my business.'

'Granger and I go right back, so it is my business.'

'Not when you're trying to tell me what to do. You got that?' Cooper said.

Angry, snapping, Beau joined the conversation. 'You damn well listen to your father when he's speaking to you.'

Cooper whipped round to look at them both. 'Don't you Goddamn dare use that emotive crap on me.'

Woods tried and failed not to sound hurt. 'I'm sorry that it's such a pain in the ass to be my son.'

Cooper stared at John. Hard. 'Don't give me that, I hate it because it's just another one of your secrets. But hey, that's us all over. Secrets and lies. And before you think it, no, I'm not for a second suggesting we tell Jackson. Because God knows he carries enough on his shoulders without this. I can manage to be his brother *and* love him as I do whether he knows or not.'

'I don't know where you get your coldness from, Coop. Your mom was the sweetest...'

Blood-red anger filled Cooper. 'You leave her out of it. And now we've finished playing happy families, I'd like to see Jackson.'

Woods, steaming now, said, 'You listen to what I have

to say. I'm not going to give you a lecture on the perils of self-medication, but you know how I feel. And God knows we all went through it last year with you going crazy, and Jackson taking an overdose, so no, I'm not looking for that kind of year again.'

'I'm glad we got that sorted out.'

'Don't be so damn flippant, Coop. But I'll cut straight to the point. I need you to stay away.'

'What?'

'This job. Leave well alone. So any ideas you have about digging around. Don't. You understand?'

Just as mad, just as angry as Woods, Cooper looked amazed. 'What the hell are you talking about?'

'I spoke to Granger.'

'You're certainly his puppet, aren't you?'

'I had a chat with him, yes... But it was me who instigated it. These people who you're dealing with. It's... ' Woods trailed off.

Standing nose to nose. Six-foot-three to six-foot-three, Cooper asked with contemptuous curiosity, 'It's what, John? Because now – *now* – I'm real curious.'

A pulse throbbed in Woods' jaw. 'Just don't push it like you do everything else.'

'What's it to you...? Come on. Is this about Ismet? Is that what you're telling me?'

'I'm just telling you to *leave* it. I told Granger the same. It's not personal.'

'And if I don't, John?'

'Coop, I'm warning you. This is bigger than you.'

'Warning me? Seriously? Is that a threat, John?'

With his temper almost blinding him, his finger poking Cooper's chest, Woods spat his reply. 'Take it how you will, Coop. But if you don't stay away, let's just say you might regret it. Do you understand me?'

Pushing past John, Cooper headed towards the door. 'Go to hell.'

'Cooper! I'm warning you! Stay away!'

47

Nd3 Ra4

With the television on mute and his feet up on the Colorado blue spruce table he'd made last year with Levi, Cooper pulled a face as he knocked back the bottle of bourbon. He rarely touched the stuff, usually left it on the shelf in the pantry just waiting for moments like this. Moments like today. Moments like earlier. Moments like the past few weeks.

He stared at the TV, looking through rather than at the images flashing up on the screen, whilst unsteadily reaching along the couch to grab the newly acquired blister pack of OxyContin. Quickly popping them out. Shaking them around on his hand.

Looked down. Looked up. Looked around. Seeing the map of Africa with pins and strings and felt-tip markings depicting all the places he'd gone, partly for Onyx jobs and partly in the crazy-ass hope of maybe finding Ellie alive... if she had, as he'd once thought, been kidnapped by the Somalian pirates, rather than drowned. But that was then. All hope now was lost. Dumbed or numbed down. But it still haunted him. In his dreams. In every waking hour and in the whispering wind as he heard her call his name.

He smiled as he looked at the photo of Cora, which sat pride of place on the windowsill. Beautiful, clever Cora. That was the day he'd flown her and Maddie across to Nevada and, much to Cora's delight, he'd taken part in the Reno Rodeo. Coming last, but coming first in his daughter's eyes. He glanced at the clay pot she'd made at pre-school for him, which looked nothing like a pot at all. And then he looked back down at the pills in his hand. Feeling that burn as he spoke out loud.

'Hell no. Hell no. No you don't. You don't take me.'

With a quick, hard, determined throw, Cooper flung them across the room, scattering them over the wooden floor, and followed it up by hurling the bourbon against the wall. To hit. To shatter. To slide down. Leaving a trail of golden whiskey behind.

'Damn you, John!'

Wiping his face and feeling the spikes of his stubble scratching against his palm, he rushed into the kitchen. Scrambling up onto one of the chairs and bringing down a box from on top of the whitewashed cabinet.

Cooper threw off the lid and inside were dozens of small plastic bags. His collecting bags. The ones he began to obsessively amass eight years ago. Things from investigations. Things from Cora. From Maddie. Things Jackson had given him. Neatly in place. Collected and held. Keeping everything safe. Keeping everything in its place so nothing got lost. So nothing could go missing, *ever* again.

From the bottom of the box he dragged out a bag full of

leaflets. Hurriedly pulled one out. Reading it. Turning it over, before rushing to the phone.

Punched in a number.

Waited.

A click.

A voice.

'This is the twenty-four hour drug helpline, I'm sorry there's no-one here at the moment but... '

Slammed down the phone. Ran his eyes down the leaflet again.

Punched in a number.

... Again.

And waited... Again.

'Hello, this is the Colorado drug helpline, I'm sorry there's no-one here... '

And another number.

'This helpline and center is now closed, your nearest center...'

Pacing back into the front room, Cooper leant on the back of the chair. Breathing deeply. He could do this. Hell, how hard could it be? Maybe he'd been a bit hasty smashing that bourbon. Come on. He couldn't let it beat him...Again.

Glancing up, he stared at the TV. Then stared harder, trying to process exactly what he was looking at.

Jumping over the back of the couch and hurriedly shoving his hand down behind the cushions, Cooper searched for the controls, wanting to catch the last part of the report.

'...coast of Algeria, up to eighty children.'

Aghast he watched the full horror of the story unfold. On a small cove of beach were the bodies of children. Strewn like discarded rubbish. Washed up. Lifeless. Bloated. Mottled and discolored from the water. And then a thought. Through his blurry recollection. A hazy realization becoming clearer until he suddenly understood what he was thinking.

'Oh my God.' He heard his voice out loud. Hearing the fear. Hearing the panic.

Pulling out his cell, he punched a quick dial number.

Waited.

A click.

A voice.

'Hi this is Maddie and *Cora*, I'm sorry we're not here to take your…'

Cooper cut off the call. Rushed to his desk and grabbed up his car keys, picking up some of the scattered pills, before running out into the night.

48

Ngf4 Kg7

'Tom, what's wrong? God, you look terrible. You know it's almost 3 a.m? If this is about yesterday I don't want to talk about it.'

'It's not.'

Maddie wrapped her pale blue cotton robe tightly around her. The days of Arizona might be hot but the night-time air certainly chilled. She stepped outside onto the wisteria-covered porch, letting the door swing behind her.

Her corkscrew brown hair fell like waves over her freckled brown face. 'Then what is it?'

Cooper's words poured out to match the pouring sweat which seemed to seep out of every pore. 'Remember the boy on the boat?'

'Are you serious? Of course.'

'Well, do you remember what he was wearing?'

'No... I dunno, maybe.'

'Think Maddie, *think*.'

'Ok... he was wearing short pants and a T-shirt.'

'Yeah, but what color was the top?'

'Yellow, I think.'

Cooper, nodded frantically. 'Exactly. That's what I thought but I had to double check with you. But it *was* a yellow top… Have you seen the news tonight?'

'Tom, look, I'm tired…'

'Wait. Just give me a minute. I was watching NBC and there was a news report about some kids being washed up on the Algerian coast. And when they showed the bodies all over the shore line, guess what, Mads? They were all wearing yellow T-shirts. So it means our boy has something to do with these kids. Which also means *Ismet* has something to do with these kids.'

'Just because somebody's wearing the same color T-shirt…'

'It wasn't just yellow though, was it?'

Maddie thought for a second. 'No, it also had that large logo on it.'

'Like the kids on the beach.'

Watching Cooper's hand shake as he lit a cigarette, Maddie said, 'But we located the boat off the coast of Libya, not Algeria. It doesn't prove anything.'

'You're right, it doesn't, but it does prove there's more to it. Plus…'

Cooper stopped, realizing he was about to mention Woods' warning about leaving well alone. But he couldn't. Wasn't even a possibility. Maddie had no idea of his relationship with John and Jackson. Granger did. Rosedale did. So did Levi and Dorothy. Not the full story but part of the secret nonetheless. Even Cora was more in the know than Maddie, and that's how it was going to stay. Not because of anything other than it was easier that way.

Even the accident; she didn't realize it was the same yacht that Jackson had been on that day, mainly because of the way John and the powers that be had controlled the reporting of it. With the Navy helping to keep both his and Ellie's identity out of the news. Making it look like they were entirely separate incidents. And nobody was going to tell her otherwise. Not Granger. Not Rosedale. No-one.

'Plus what, Tom?'

'Nothing.'

'Tom, listen, you heard what Granger said, you gotta leave it. If you go digging around, you'll never get your job back. Let him cool down for a few days and then call him, but if you start doing this...'

Agitated, Cooper walked up and down the porch. 'You think I care about my job when this has happened? Up to eighty kids, Maddie. Eighty. How can you even compare it?'

'Of course I'm not. You know I wouldn't do that. What I'm saying is there's no proof. There's nothing concrete to connect those kids to that boy, so what you're doing is putting your job in jeopardy. For what? So there's the T-shirt, but then what? What exactly are you saying?'

'I'm saying the kids were on *Ismet's* boat. They have to have been.'

'But why? It doesn't make sense. How can the kids have got from Ismet's ship all the way to Algeria? The ship was anchored *down* the coast, off Libya. And you know as well as I do the Mediterranean doesn't have a tide.'

'I know something's not right. I just need you to trust me on this.'

'Tom, I know you care, but feeling something isn't proof. You need facts and there aren't any.'

'Why do you always go by your head, Maddie? What about in here?' His fist pounded his chest, his heart. 'Tell me you don't think there's something too.'

'I don't. What's more likely is a dinghy capsized which was trying to carry the kids across to Europe. Over-loaded, or just not a suitable vessel for crossing the Med.'

'That's exactly what they were saying on the news.'

Warmly, Maddie looked at Cooper. 'Well, there you go then. Tom, go home. Go to bed and call me in the morning. You need to get some rest.'

'Don't patronize me, I'm not crazy.'

'I never said you were. I'm just saying maybe you're not thinking straight. Get some sleep… and get some help… Goodnight, Tom.'

Cooper walked down the wooden steps of Maddie's house. He stopped and turned and pointed and said, 'Are those Rosedale's cowboy boots?'

Maddie glanced to the pair of boots by the front door, then she looked back down at Cooper. And in a quiet voice she said, 'Tom, go home. Don't do this to yourself.'

49

Kg2 Kf6

'Tom, it's Maddie. Call me.'

Maddie put the phone down, looking around the Onyx office. The whole place had been trashed, but oddly it didn't look like much had been taken. If anything.

She'd arrived as she always did at the weekend, in the early hours, knowing there'd be no-one here to disturb her, hoping to finish off the dull but necessary administration, dotting the I's and crossing the T's for the various banks and insurance companies, which, once completed, allowed her to get back and spend the day with Cora who she'd left with Rosedale.

Though when she'd arrived today, against the background of the rising Arizona sun, even before she'd pulled up she could see the place had been broken into. Inexplicably, neither the Onyx alarm, nor the alarm which was linked to a system at her house, had been triggered.

'So, what's the damage?' Granger growled, strolling up heavy-eyed behind Maddie. He sighed. Tired. Irritated.

And the clock on the wall mockingly striking 6 a.m. on a Saturday morning certainly didn't enhance his mood.

'Nothing much.'

'You call this nothing much? I'd hate to see what it looked like when it really was something. Have you called the cops?'

'Yeah, but they said it might be a couple of hours before they could send anyone.'

'I've got a good mind to stop paying my Goddamn taxes. What sort of country is this when it takes a few hours to come to the scene of the crime?'

Maddie, not bothering getting embroiled in Granger's morning mood, continued to look around. 'I guess they think it's not an emergency. They did ask me if I thought it might be kids.'

Still growling, Granger snapped. 'Look around. We're in the middle of nowhere. What kind of kids are going to come all this way just to mess up this place? Let alone get past all the security.'

'Obviously it's not kids, but I can see why they don't think it's an emergency.'

'I might point out that's exactly why we have such a problem in the United States right now, because people like you go around calling this kind of crime nothing.'

'I didn't say it was nothing.'

'No, but you might as well have done.'

Without replying, and not wanting to be caught up in another one of his rants, Maddie walked out on Granger, heading down the hallway towards the far end of the building where Granger's office was, immediately making a beeline for the CCTV equipment.

Logging in and accessing the Onyx security files, it didn't take her a moment to figure out all the camera footage had been wiped, and the hard-drive folders tampered with.

'Stop touching everything, Maddie, the cops will need to take fingerprints.'

'Seriously, Granger, I don't think they're going to bother for a few upturned chairs. I wanted to see if there was anything on the CCTV.'

'Well?'

Continuing to focus on the computer, Maddie replied slightly off-hand. 'Nothing. All gone.'

'What are you talking about? Have you any idea how much I spend on security? How can it be so easily wiped out?'

Maddie said nothing.

'Maddie, are you listening?'

'Yes, Granger, I am listening, and I know this is a really sophisticated system, so for them to be able to access it without locking themselves out of it and the alarms going off, they'd have to know what they're doing. But who would or, more to the point, who *could* do that?'

'I'll tell you who.'

'Go on then.'

'It's obvious.'

'Oh for God's sake, Granger, can you just tell me?'

'Maddison, I don't appreciate your tone.'

Hands on hips, Maddie looked at Granger exasperated. 'Granger! Just tell me.'

'Okay. Cooper, that's who.'

'Tom? No way! Don't even think that. I don't want to hear that.'

Granger stepped in Maddie's eye view. 'Why? Come on, is it so far removed from reality that he could've done something like this? The guy's got a screw loose. He's on some kind of destruction derby. This is his doing, mark my words.'

'He wouldn't do something like this. He loves his job and he sees everyone here as his family. You know that as well as I do.'

'Is that why he betrayed you for that crap he puts down his throat? Lied to us all? Pretended it was in the best interest of you and Rosedale?'

Weakly, with not much certainty, Maddie said, 'That's different.'

'No, it's not. Tell me how.'

'Well, for a start...'

She trailed off, unable to come up with something solid. Not wanting to catch Granger's eyes, to let him see her wavering belief in Cooper, she turned away.

'It's clear why he did it. Revenge. Because he's angry with me.'

'Don't be ridiculous, Granger.'

'Money, then. So he could go shopping for more doctors to give him that stuff he likes to take.'

'You're talking crazy. Tom has a lot of money.'

'Really? Well, I'm clearly paying him too much. So what then? Because there's got to be something. Aren't you worried about the way he's been behaving?'

Maddie paused for a moment before saying. 'Well, he did come to see me late last night... He was agitated, and even more so when...'

Interrupting, and unwittingly saving her from having to

tell Granger about Rosedale, Granger slammed his hand on the table. 'So he wasn't so far away? He was in the area. It all makes sense.'

'No, it doesn't. He needed to see me.'

'What about?'

Taking a deep breath, which gave her chance to figure out whether to edit the truth or not, Maddie answered as vaguely as she could. 'Things. You know. Cora... and stuff he'd seen on TV?'

'You're trying to tell me he came to see you in the middle of the night so he could talk re-runs of *Bonanza* with you?'

'No, of course not. It was something he saw on the news made him think... It probably sounds worse than it is, but it made him think about Ismet's company and what might be really going on.'

'I knew it. *Goddamn* him.'

Maddie, fading out from what Granger was saying, stared at the computer. A heavy, sinking feeling hitting her. 'Oh Christ...'

'What is it?'

'Just wait.'

'Maddison, can I remind you who the boss around here is.'

'Be quiet, Granger.'

Resentfully, Granger stopped talking.

After a few minutes of muttering and mumbling and tapping and side glancing Maddie, with as much hostility he could muster, she turned to look at him.

Her face was solemn. 'I've just had a quick look at the files. Don't worry, they all seem fine... apart from one.'

'And?'

'It looks like the only file which has been hacked and compromised is Ismet's one... The Turkish file.'

Enraged, Granger pushed the few remaining things off his desk. 'That son-of-a-bitch.'

'You can't jump to conclusions.'

'Can't I? Oh look, I just have... Come on Maddie, you're not really going to say it wasn't Cooper, are you? Who else? He was dead set on digging up something. Well, let's hope he included his Goddamn grave in that... I'm calling the cops.'

Maddie grabbed the cell out of Granger's hand. He exploded, firing his words as loud as she'd ever heard him.

'What the hell do you think you're doing? Give me that back. I said, *give* it me.'

'No. For a start you can't bring the cops in on this. What happened to sensitive and highly confidential, hey? There's one thing them coming for a small break in; it's another thing letting on our computer and security systems have been compromised. Not exactly great for that reputation of yours. And besides, both of us know you don't want to do that to Tom. Not really.'

'Oh, I do.'

'No you *don't*. Look, we don't even know he had anything to do with it. You wait here for the cops, and I'll take the helicopter and fly over to the ranch to see what he has to say for himself.'

'Okay, fine. But Maddie, you may not want to see him in trouble again, but right now I'd be happy if they locked him up and threw away the Goddamn key.'

50

Bd5 Ra5

'Don't do this to yourself... Don't do this to my Goddamn self?' Cooper ranted out loud, as he had done for the past few hours on the drive back from Maddie's. Her words inflaming every part of him. Burning across his brain like they'd been branded with a hot iron.

Sighing loudly, exasperated, he parked up at the ranch by the white picket fence. Hit the steering wheel hard with both fists. Imagining it to be the face of one Austin *Rosedale* Young.

So Maddie had left him. So he was a dead beat husband and a dead beat Daddy. He knew that. He knew he'd made mistakes and he sure as hell was paying for them. And he deserved to. Deserved not to have his family, after all the pain he'd caused them. He got that. But did that make it alright? Did that make it alright for the woman he still loved to jump into bed with that snake Rosedale?

'No it Goddamn didn't!' The bellow of his voice in the quiet of the Colorado early morning gave even him a fright.

Christ. He needed to hold it together. He'd try to focus on something else.

'Shit! Shit!' Easier said than Goddamn done.

Trying to calm himself down again, Cooper stepped out of his Chevrolet. Muttering. Cursing. Kicking any stone. Kicking any blade of grass in his path. But then a sudden exhaustion. A weight. A feeling like he was carrying a 55 gallon drum of Georgian corn on his shoulders.

Wearily he staggered up to the front door.

But stopped.

Short.

Dead in his tracks.

Listening.

Looking.

Listening some more.

Slowly. Real slowly, he put his hand down the back of his pants, pulling out a loaded Glock. Stepped sideward. Edged along the front of the house. Dipping down under the windows. Crawling along. Glancing inside. Glancing along. Still listening. Still watching. Straining his ears for something. Looking around for anything. Anything which would give him the sign that told him for certain something wasn't right.

Cautiously he opened the door, sliding his body inside, with the gun held tight against his chest. He stopped to look round. The room was a mess.

The broken bottle of Bourbon.

The scattered pills.

The cushions thrown off the couch.

The leaflets on the floor.

Phone off the hook… But then that was him, wasn't it?

Frowning. Searching his memory, Cooper began to recall

the night's events. He'd been feeling damn sorry for himself then… Yeah, he remembered trying to call the helpline and getting no answer, dashing his stuff on the floor. Watching the news before he'd gone to Maddie's. Rushing out and clearly, as evidence seemed to show, he'd left one helluva mess.

Breathing a sigh of relief, and pissed with himself at how paranoid, how jumpy he was becoming, Cooper put his gun back in his holster. Walked into the kitchen. Attempted not to think about Maddie and Rosedale. Attempted not to think about the two of them naked in –

A violent cruel blow to the back of Cooper's head knocked him unconscious, sinking him to the floor.

51

Bc6Ra6

'Are these the ballistic results on the kid from Chatham? I hope your friend was discreet when he got the copy.'

'Absolutely. You don't have to worry about that.'

Woods stretched out his hand to take a thin green file from Teddy. With feet up on the Resolute Desk used by the good folk such as JFK, Carter and Obama, he opened it. Flicked through. Scanning with speed *and* diligence – an essential quality he suspected anyone in office had to have – he frowned.

'No bullet?'

Teddy shook his head, absentmindedly helping himself to a chocolate and nut cookie from the plate in front of Woods.

'No, but before I carry on, remember the whole thing about the seismograph?'

Woods, unable to resist joining Teddy in a chocolate cookie, with his mouth slightly too full to reply politely, nodded.

'Okay, well the police department pulled a blank on the

kid's death. Although officially there's an ongoing investigation, *unofficially* it's been basically filed away in a drawer. Like I said before, there's been a spate of violent robberies in the area and they're blocking it in with that... But my friend, he's like a damn Rottweiler when he's got something between his teeth. He did some digging in connection with the whole seismograph thing. Mainly because something bugged him about the whole episode. It just didn't feel right to him. I mean it seems so obvious now, but he looked into the kid's bank statements and online ordering. Turns out every month this kid ordered a whole heap of paper rolls for his seismograph and the particular paper for it only fits on a few models. Real basic ones.'

'Too basic to pick up shockwaves?'

'No, apparently not. Even if you don't have a high tech electronic system you can still get accurate readings. They're pretty effective. Apparently kids in middle school make their own in science class.'

Woods, not quite sure where his thoughts were taking him, ventured. 'So it was all true. The kid really did have one. And then someone, for reasons we don't know, took it. You got any thoughts, Teddy? Or are we just reading into something which isn't there?'

The intercom of Wood's desk buzzed. He nodded to Teddy. 'Sorry, just give me a minute... Hey, Joan, you need me?'

'Mr President, Lyndon Clarke is on line two. He's apologising for the unscheduled call but would like to speak to you as a matter of urgency.'

'Put him through... '

'Mr President, huge apologies for this interruption,' Lyndon said.

Even though his Secretary of State wasn't in the room, Woods smiled. 'Hey, Lyndon, no problem, but don't let Naomi know you've barged a window without her knowing.'

Lyndon laughed, a fondness for both Naomi and the President reflecting in it.

Woods said, 'Teddy's here by the way.'

'Hey, Lyndon, you still owe me a dollar from the other day, don't think I've forgotten.'

'Hey, Teddy, you're such a cheapskate, you know that? If I added up how many Pepsis I've paid for from that damn drinks machine over the years, it'd add up to a hell of a lot more than a dollar... Anyway, I can hear Naomi's voice in my head telling me to get on with it. So here it is. Mr President, I got another call from the Qatari ambassador. They're not happy at all. Far from it, in fact. If I said they were furious about the situation that would be an understatement. I just need to know what your thoughts are and how you'd like me to proceed.'

'Truthfully, Lyndon, I thought we sorted this out the other day.'

'So did I sir, but they're threatening all sorts. I don't want to be presumptuous, but I think it might be wise for you to make a scheduled call as soon as possible, better still a meeting with Ambassador Shaheen. Just for appeasement's sake. It might be the way to go.'

Woods rubbed his head, as he felt the first bubbling of stress.

There were a number of reasons why the last thing anyone

wanted, or could afford, was a falling out with the Qataris. Top of this list was certainly the tight military relationship, along with the intelligence sharing they had established; in addition there were the billions of dollars the Qataris spent each year buying advanced weapons, helping to top up the very depleted US treasury – caused to some extent by the global economic downturn, with screens turning red in trading rooms around the world, as well as by the ongoing military expenditure and the fallout of the cost of Bush's and Obama's wars. In Woods' experience such relationships could quickly turn from good to precarious to difficult – very, very, difficult – in a matter of days, even hours. But the overriding fact was that when Chuck said, *America needed Qatar* – and other countries within the Middle East – as bosom allies, he was right. No question. The fight against terror relied heavily on the CIA being able to keep a watch on events over there.

There was the American base in Qatar, Al Udeid Air Base, providing the US with exceptional military access to the region. As of last year 10,000 US troops were stationed there. The largest US base in the Middle East.

'Yeah, I think so too. I'll get Joan to brief Naomi and then they can liaise with one of your secretaries to find a window for us both. A call would be easier and I could fit it in on the way to an out of towner but, I suspect, Majdi Shaheen would want a face to face.'

'I agree.'

'Okay, stay on the line and speak to Joan and I'll see you later for the fundraising dinner.'

Woods turned back to look at Teddy. Raised his eyebrows.

Shook his head and it was Teddy who said, 'I take it that was about what happened with the ship off the coast of Libya?'

'You got it in one. It doesn't look like they're going to let it lie as easily as I thought. Sometimes, I know how Chuck feels.'

'You're kidding?'

Woods grinned. Wide and warm. 'Okay, strike that. What I mean is sometimes I feel my hands are tied because, believe you me, sitting down with ambassador Shaheen and apologizing, *again*, is something I'd really rather not have to do... Anyway, sorry. Continue with what you were saying about the ballistics results.'

'Okay, so listen to this. The reason why there isn't a bullet was because it was taken clean out.'

Running his fingers through his freshly washed hair, Woods said, 'What do you mean?'

'Well, the kid was killed with a single shot. One bullet hole. No messing about. But *after* he was shot, the bullet was removed at the scene.'

'Jesus.'

'One reason could be that, as bullets can work like a finger print and can be cross-matched via forensics, whoever did this wanted to remove any link back to them. Also, wounds can offer an astonishing amount of information about the distance, speed, caliber of the gun and even bullet make and type, so maybe they removed the bullet first and foremost to disrupt the evidence... I'm stating the obvious here, but there's no doubt in my mind that we're looking at a professional.'

Annoyance beginning to seep through him, Woods

absentmindedly looked around the Oval Office, resting his eyes on the large portrait of Abraham Lincoln, the 16th serving President of the United States. 'And the cops are doing exactly what?'

'Like I say, John, they're bunching it together with the other robberies. It's the same problem all over. Lack of resources. Lack of man power, and when it's a crime like this with a kid like this, then it just goes on to a pile with all the other cases marked, *of no consequence*.'

'I want to say you're being harsh, but I get it, Teddy. Though this is different.'

'Not really, not at this stage anyway. We'd have to ask the correct channels to look into it before it got any legs. You want me to start the ball rolling?'

Woods paused for a moment. Glanced again at the lined, craggy, bearded face of Lincoln, then with his eyes flickering up at the ceiling medallion, which incorporated the Seal of the President of the United States, he spoke with a pained expression on his face. 'No, I want to sleep on this one. I've got to think this through. Because what if the kid was right, Teddy? What if there were *two* bomb blasts that day?'

52

Bb7 Ra3

'Look what you've done to yourself. What's wrong with you, Tom? Don't you ever learn? What if I'd been with Cora? How do you think she would've reacted?' Maddie stood over Cooper as he lay on the kitchen floor before dragging himself up by the door frame into a sitting position.

He touched the back of his head. Felt the sticky clump of hair, matted together with blood. Shit, it hurt like hell. Then a croak. A groggy reply. 'It's good to know what you think of me.'

'Do you know how hard you make it for me? How am I supposed to defend you when I find you like this?'

'Don't bother.'

Maddie squatted down to Cooper's eye level, shaking her head. 'But I do. Always… How could you do it?'

The headache, which a moment earlier had been throbbing in the background, was now beginning to take hold. Keeping his head in a vice like grip. Squeezing it to the point of painful distraction.

Conceding, to save any form of conversation, Cooper

muttered, 'Whatever you're talking about, I'm sorry, okay. Whatever it is, I shouldn't have done it. Now please, I don't feel so great, so can we leave it at that?'

Uncertain if she was bemused or bewildered, Maddie settled on fixing Cooper with a look of contempt. 'I came here hoping it wouldn't be true.'

'I guess you've had a wasted trip.'

She stared at Cooper, looking into his eyes. His eyes which she'd once thought so cute. One green. One blue. His eyes which had once been so full of life when Ellie had been alive. Now haunted. Now troubled beyond anyplace she could reach out her hand to grab him back from. His face, so handsome, but as if she was staring into a stranger's.

Slowly, she reached and drew her fingers along his cheek. Soft. Sensual. And forgiving.

'Why, Tom? Why did you do it? Onyx of all places? Help me understand. Were you so mad at Granger you wanted to hurt him? Or do you really still think your gut's right about Ismet? Or maybe it was because of Rosedale and I?'

Swiftly, verging on aggressively, Cooper pushed Maddie's hand off his face. 'Good thing about concussion is it often makes folk forget things. Not now though. Thanks for that, Maddison. I just love having that image of you two in my brain.' He stopped. Grimaced. Squinted at the pain as a slow realization began to creep over him.

'What did you say?'

'I didn't,' Maddie said.

'No, I mean about me letting you down. Something about Onyx.'

Hostile, Maddie snapped. 'You know exactly what.'

'That's the point, I don't.'

'But you said…'

'I know what I said, but that was just to shut you up… *Sorry.*'

'Let me get this straight, you're saying you never actually had anything to do with the break-in at Onyx?'

Cooper, shocked and rolling his words in a hell of a lot of surprise, said, 'No, of course not. When did it happen? And how? Granger has enough security to compete with the Pentagon. Jesus, Maddie… Why would you think I'd done it? I don't know what to say.'

Slightly ashamed, Maddie looked away. 'What was I supposed to think?'

'Not that.'

'But when you said…'

Cooper interrupted. Repeated. 'Not that.'

'Tom, give me a break here. Let me off. I'm sorry. And I can't even say it was only Granger. I believed it as well, *especially* when I realized it was only the Turkish file which had been compromised. I didn't want to…'

'Maddie, stop. I don't blame you. I haven't exactly given you reason to trust me. Granger, however, that does not surprise me in the least. I'm surprised he didn't call the cops.'

Maddie smiled and shrugged. 'He wanted to.'

Cooper smiled right back. 'But you stopped him… thank you.'

'So what happened here, Tom?'

'Someone jumped me.'

She pointed through to the front room, 'And they trashed the place as well.'

'No. That was me… Don't look so upset.'

Forcing herself not to reproach or query, Maddie asked, 'So, what do you think?'

Cooper attempted to get up. 'I think probably what happened to me will be why Onyx was broken into. I've got a few ideas… Here help me up… Shit.' He winced, ducking his head down as if bobbing under a low ceiling, as his movement triggered the pain to erupt again.

Reaching out her hand to help, Maddie frowned. 'You need to get that seen to.'

'No, we need to go to speak to Granger and find out once and for all what exactly he's keeping from us. I take it you've got the helicopter?'

'Yeah.'

Cooper began to walk towards the front door. Picked up a bottle of pills. Caught a glimpse of Maddie opening her mouth to say something. 'Not now, Maddie. Don't say anything… *please.*'

She nodded, trying to ignore the sense of complicity which began to creep over her. Cooper smiled. A real, loving smile. 'Come on, you can tell me everything on the way.'

53

Be4 Ra4

'So let's have it, Granger... Come on. There's no getting out of it this time.'

'You've lost your mind. You know that. Flipped out and flown away.'

Maddie gently touched Cooper's arm. Stepped between, distancing the two baiting men. Glancing at Granger, whose face was now as red as the cactus calico flower, she began to become slightly concerned. 'Granger, calm down, okay. This won't do your blood pressure any good.'

'Who made you Dr Quinn, medicine woman?'

'Sometimes, you can be really impossible. Look, we just want to know the truth. We asked you before, and you didn't answer, but this time, Granger, we need you to tell us everything you know about the Turkish file.'

There was a long pause before Granger quietly answered.

'Qatari file.'

'Excuse me?'

Granger rubbed his chest. Sighed. And, like a petulant

child, sullenly pushed away the flask of decaffeinated coffee his wife had lovingly made and insisted on him drinking. What the hell ever happened to a double strength, Colombian blend double espresso?

He uttered a discontented growl as he sat back on his desk in the now-tidy office. The cops, as Maddie had expected, had done little to nothing, apart from nodding, scribbling down the fewest of notes before using the bathroom and leaving. Rubbing his tongue hard against a fine set of teeth, he repeated, '*Qatari*. The ships are actually Qatari owned. That's all I know.'

'And you didn't care to share this information?' Maddie said.

'There are some things between myself and the client that stay in Vegas. That's the way they wanted it.'

'And what is it Ismet *actually* does? Does he even have an import-export business?'

Granger shrugged. 'Look, I've told you, I don't know anything else. All I know is they didn't want anyone to realize the ships were Qatari owned. Period.'

'Why though?' asked Cooper. 'And who exactly? Who's *they*? What's the name of this person, or even the company who owns them? I know there's Ismet, but who's behind him? There are so many unanswered questions.'

Granger simmered with anger. 'You know we often don't have that kind of information, due to the nature of the business. Often clients want discretion and anonymity. Fifty percent or more of our jobs come through third parties – though in this case it didn't. It came straight from Ismet's office.'

Cooper pushed it some more. 'But why use our company?'

'I keep telling you, it goes full circle. We're discreet. You only have to look at our work record. Governments, banks, high ranking dignitaries. Ismet knew he could trust us.'

'There's something more... *Much* more.'

Maddie said, 'Tom, Ismet was Qatari, wasn't he? I remember you telling us.'

'So?'

'So maybe it does make sense. Ismet's a Qatari national and he uses ships which are Qatari owned. Hardly a big deal.'

'But why say he owned them if he doesn't?'

'I don't know, Tom. Maybe he only leases the ships, and *that's* why he needed to find out where the ship was without letting the company know he'd lost one of their expensive vessels. I can see that. It hardly looks good for him, does it? Who knows, they might have thought twice about continuing his contract with them, and obviously the ships are fundamental to his business. Perhaps he couldn't afford that to happen, and needed to keep as quiet as possible about it.'

Vehemently, Cooper shook his head. 'No, I don't buy it. Ismet's story is too perfect. That's why it fits so well, don't you see?'

'But the truth does fit well. It fits perfectly. Of course it does. There are loads of reasons why they might not want to disclose they're Qatari owned, or just leasing Qatari ships.'

'Such as?'

'Tax reasons, perhaps. There are lots of companies who are registered in another country. It's probably inconsequential... It could even be to do with the precarious political climate we're in right now. As in, maybe it's better to have everyone think you're a Turkish company, rather than a Qatari one. I don't know, but Granger's viewpoint about it not being our business, well, he's right. They can do and say anything they like; they don't have to answer to us.'

'Finally someone's making sense round here.'

Maddie cut her eye. 'Be quiet, Granger... Hey, Cora!'

Cora Cooper ran into the room. Ignored Maddie. Ignored Granger. Ran straight into her Daddy's arms. She clung to him, gave a delighted smile as he picked her up. Nuzzled into Cooper's neck.

'Daddy!'

It cut. It stuck. The words strangled by his emotions. He just about managed to speak.

'Hey baby, I've missed you.'

'Missed you too, Daddy.'

'Did Grandpappy bring you, honey?'

'No, Rosedale did.'

It was like a blinding light hitting his eyes. Focus disappearing. And there it was again, the image of Maddie and Rosedale together. And now the image of his daughter playing happy families with that son-of-a-bitch.

It cut. It stuck. The words strangled by his emotions. He just about said, 'That's nice, baby. Is he here?'

'I sure as hell am, Thomas, how ya doin?'

Rosedale tipped his hat. Winked at Cora. Sent Cooper into a silent rage, but he said, 'I've been better. God knows I have... See you've got your boots on this time.'

Granger, usually one to let folk just get on with things, felt the tension like it was a rubber band striking his face, turned the conversation back. 'Anyway, Coop, that's the situation. Pretty damn nothing.'

'And that's why this place was broken into and I was jumped on, was it?'

'They're separate issues.'

'What about being warned off? Is that separate? Is that nothing? And you know who and what I'm talking about. I think you're still hiding something.'

Maddie looked from Granger to Cooper. 'Fill me in here. Tom?'

'Leave it, you hear me?' said Granger quietly.

'No, Granger, I want to know what's going on. We're all supposed to be a team... Tom, come on.'

Granger growled. 'I'm warning you, Coop, learn when to keep your mouth shut.'

Turning his back on Granger, Cooper ignored the advice as he talked to Maddie. 'I was warned a few days ago to back off. I can't say by who, but Granger knows all about it, don't you? You think they did this? That they were part of it?'

'I don't know, but I doubt it.'

'But that's not to say it couldn't be them,' Cooper said.

Granger seethed and Maddie, knowing better than to push Cooper on something he didn't want to reveal, spoke with disappointment.

'Why didn't you say about this before? Either of you? I love you, Granger, you know that, but if you don't give us answers, I'll join Tom in his digging and see what turns up. And for someone who values their reputation, I don't think you'll like it, because it'll hardly be discreet. I'll make sure of it. So would you care to explain what the hell is going on?'

He didn't. He didn't at all. And he didn't appreciate Maddie's bold-ass stance either. Not one Goddamn little bit, but Granger said, 'Okay, and this really is everything. And Maddison, you and me need a talk later… I had a call from a couple of people recently. One of them had connections with NATO. In the military commission. He basically told me we had to forget everything. The boat. The boy. Ismet. Pretend like it never happened.'

'What did you say?' Rosedale asked.

'What any sensible person would do. I agreed. Because that's *exactly* what *we're* going to do… Forget it all. *All* of us.'

'What about this place, and what happened to Thomas? We can't forget that.'

A mixture of exasperation and concern fed into Granger's words as he answered Rosedale. 'Look, being perfectly honest with you, I did think it was Cooper who broke in… It had all the hallmarks of him. Expertly overriding the security system. Hacking into the Turkish – albeit Qatari – file. I honestly thought it was him because he kept pushing to know more… and of course, he's crazy.'

Cooper said nothing. Granger continued.

'But as it wasn't him, it does get me thinking and it *does* worry me. And you know I'm not one to hyperbolize a situation but I do agree with Cooper – it could be somebody warning us off. I don't know who though.'

'Oh come on! You know as well as I do who's behind this,' Cooper said.

'*No, I don't know*, but I do know it's worked. We are officially warned off. You hear me? And whether it's the North Atlantic Treaty Organization or the Qataris, or who Cooper thinks it is, it makes no odds… I've deleted the file and all record of the job.'

Maddie said, 'Why? We might've needed to keep some of those details.'

'No, we won't. There are some people in this world you just don't want to mess with. And you three better listen because otherwise, to quote Dorothy Walker, if you don't, *then you ain't got the good sense God gave a rock.* And to quote me, if you don't, you may well be unleashing hell.'

54

Bd5 Ra5

Keeping his eyes on Cora playing with a number of bugs, both dead and alive, amongst the dry dusty desert ground, Cooper lit a cigarette, grateful he had his daughter to channel his energy into, rather than have to look at Rosedale who stood a foot away and had his stare locked and fixed on him. Son-of-a-bitch.

'Tom, what are you thinking?' Maddie asked.

'You mean about what Granger said, or about something closer to home?'

She sighed loud enough for Cooper to hear. 'What Granger said, of course. All this stuff about it being a warning, though I can't see it coming from NATO, can you?'

'Why not, stranger things have happened, hey Rosedale?'

Rosedale said nothing. Held his stare as Maddie continued to talk, as they sat by their cars in the middle of four hundred acres of wilderness. Hot desert land owned by Onyx.

'It's hardly a warning though, is it?'

Cooper frowned from under his strawberry blonde hair. 'What do you mean?'

'Well *whoever* it was, it was less like a warning and more like they were looking for something. I know you were jumped on, Tom, but that was just circumstance. Wrong place, wrong time. It wasn't like they were waiting for you, rather you got in their way. They were clearly looking for something… It's the only reason they hacked into the files. But what? I mean, there isn't anything.'

Cooper began to rummage in his well-worn green canvas bag. 'Apart from this.'

Cooper held up a small, black memory stick. Maddie looked at him curiously.

'I forgot all about it, what with the boy, and then with what happened between Ismet and I, and me getting sick… I'm not making excuses, I should've remembered…I'm sorry.'

Snatching it out of his hands, Rosedale gave Cooper no leeway. 'Damn right you should. I've said it before, but you're becoming a Goddamn liability. Those pills have turned your brains into mush.'

Working hard, real hard, not to get into a fight with Rosedale, Cooper focused his attention on the objective. 'I took it from the ship. I found it just before I went into that bathroom, where I found the boy. It just slipped my mind, I swear. But this is what they must've been looking for at the ranch, and maybe they thought we'd uploaded it onto the computers at Onyx.'

'What's on it?'

'That's the thing. I don't know. Like I say, I'd forgotten all about it. Rosedale's right, it was a stupid thing for me to do, but maybe there are the answers we're looking for on it.'

Maddie nodded. 'Tom, you said earlier someone warned you off. Who was it?'

267

Cooper blew out his cheeks. Watched Cora with love. 'Honey, trust me when I say, I can't tell you... But don't worry, I'm going to go and see that person as soon as I can... And believe me, I'll get some answers... one way or another.'

55

Bc6 Ra6

Dust from the tires drifted up and into the truck as Cooper sped over Arizona's state line into New Mexico, heading for Texas, and from there a flight from Rick Husband Amarillo Airport.

He needed to drive. And there was something about interstate 40, with its long-stretching roads which went on and on and on and on through the wilderness, through the cactus-filled desert past mountain ranges, where the Native Americans once roamed freely. Where man was second to nature. A place where he could get his head together. Just him and the road...

'Daddy?'

...And Cora.

'Yes, honey?'

'This is fun.'

He glanced; a smile, a grin and a nod. 'It sure is, baby. We should do this more often.'

They fell silent again as the warm wind blew through the '54 Chevy, blowing hair across eyes.

His cell on the dash began to vibrate, jumping around like a cat on a hot tin roof.

Quickly pulling off the road and onto the dry, bumpy grassland, Cooper reached over.

He answered, 'Cooper.'

'Mr Cooper?'

'Yes?'

The line was bad.

'It's Dr Panayiotou from the hospital... ' He trailed off, waiting to hear the acknowledgement.

Winking at Cora as he stepped out of the Chevy, it took Cooper a moment to realize who the caller was. 'Yes, yes. Hey, sorry... How are you doing?'

'You asked me to keep you informed about the young boy.'

'Sure, that's right. How is he?'

'I'm sorry, Mr Cooper, but he died last night...

'... Mr Cooper?

'Mr Cooper...?'

'I'm here.'

'I'm sorry but he didn't really have a chance. When he was brought in he was suffering from advanced dehydration as well as heat stroke. His brain had been starved of oxygen and his organs had already started to shut down... I am sorry.'

'Yeah, so am I... Did you find out who he is?' Cooper asked flatly.

'No, but we called him Andreas. It means brave. Strong. He was a fighter, I'll give him that. I'm surprised he made it as long as he did.'

Another pause. Cooper held back his emotions. 'But what about his parents? Someone must know who he is.'

'Mr Cooper, this is a situation we see all the time. There are thousands upon thousands of refugees. Separated from their families, or their families having been killed. A generation of displaced people, and nobody's really doing anything about it. This hospital is overwhelmed.'

'Thank you for letting me know, Dr Panayiotou. I appreciate you taking time out.'

'There was one other thing, Mr Cooper... Seemed very strange, given the circumstances, but a person came in here asking about the boy.'

'What? Who?'

'I'm not sure. He wouldn't leave his name. But he was very insistent on knowing the situation.'

'Do you know where he was from?'

'Again, I couldn't tell you, though he did have a very strong Middle Eastern accent if that's any help. I'm sorry I don't know any more.'

'No, that's fine... thank you... Dr Panayiotou, what about his funeral?'

'Mr Cooper, death is all around here. This is the island of the drowned. There's no room to bury him. He's been despatched in a refrigerated shipping container along with dozens of other bodies to the mainland, in order to be buried in a field of unmarked graves.'

Cooper clicked off his cell. Lit a cigarette. Walked away from the Chevy. Far enough away for Cora not to hear him cry out, nor see him drop to his knees.

'No! No! Not okay! Not okay!'

'Daddy? What are you doing? Are you looking for something? Are you looking for a bug?'

Cora stood above Cooper, the sunlight behind her, obscuring his vision as he squinted up, wiping and leaving streaks of dust on his face. 'That's exactly what I'm doing, honey, I'm looking for a bug. Just can't seem to find it… Come on, let's go.'

Cooper, stood up, dusting down his pants. Took Cora's hand.

Walked to the truck.

A deep breath. Turned on the ignition.

'Daddy, you weren't really looking for a bug were you? You were crying.'

Cooper glanced at his daughter as she sat on the sun-faded leather seats of the Chevy.

'Cora, I love you.'

'I know.'

'Do you? Do you really?'

'Yeah.'

'Well then that's all that matters.'

Clutch in. Clutch out. Foot down. Dust under tires… And almost a smile.

56

Bf3 Kg5

'It's great you brought Cora... I really appreciate that, Coop. Shame I can't stay longer but I've only got a window of ten. But it's great to see you. Both of you. Especially considering how we parted last time.'

'You bastard.'

'Excuse me?'

'Oh you heard alright, but if you want me to repeat it, I will... You *bastard*.'

Woods gestured his hands in the air as they stood in the middle of one of the newly yellow-painted master bedrooms of the Executive Residence of the White House. Walked up to Cooper. Right up. His face hard. Matching his stare. 'What the hell are you talking about?'

'I'm talking about what you did. But if you think for a minute you've warned me off, think again, John. I don't scare that easily. I'm only just beginning.'

Woods exhaled heavily. Flared his nostrils. Rubbed his chin as if wiping a drop of Lobster bisque off.

'What did you think I was going to do, John? Me of all people. You should know me well enough to realize that I wasn't going to take it lying down. Wasn't a warning enough? You had to send someone to my house...'

Woods interrupted. Quickly. Hell on leather. 'Hold on there. Hold on right there. I have no idea what you're talking about.'

'Bullshit.'

Anger sat on Woods' face. Sitting tightly in every muscle. 'What the hell do you think of me? Yes, I warned you and Granger off, but you don't understand.'

'What part don't I understand? I know they're Qatari.'

'He told you?'

'Yeah, he told me. Was this another one of the little secrets you love to have?'

'Don't be a jackass, Coop. I didn't think Granger was going to tell you, that's all. What else did he say?'

'Oh he didn't, which is why you'd better start talking.'

'I don't like your tone, Coop. Rein it in.'

'You're not supposed to like it, John. And as for reining it in, go to hell.'

'Watch your mouth and think about who you're talking to.'

'What? Are you going to start pulling rank on me now, John? Going to call for protection to have me removed? Look around you. There's no secret servicemen up here.'

Woods clenched his teeth. Worked hard not to clench his fist as well. 'I don't mean it like that, but show a bit of respect.'

Curling his mouth up in disgust, Cooper said, 'You want

respect? Then you earn it and you earn it by telling me exactly *who* it was who attacked me.'

'What?'

Slightly thrown by what looked like genuine surprise on Woods' face, Cooper quickly focused on what he'd come to say. 'Or wasn't that part of the plan? Were they just supposed to come in and out?'

Matter of factly, firmly, whatever it took to get through, Woods shook his head. 'Coop, listen. This is nothing to do with me.'

'Stop lying!'

'You're acting real crazy, Coop. You really need to calm down.'

Woods watched Cooper beginning to pace. Observed the sweat running down his face. The agitated demeanor. The hurried movements. The darting eyes. 'Are you high, Coop? Is that what this is all about?'

Cooper spun round. Voice loud. Angry frustration. 'High? Is that what you put everything down to? Well, sadly for you John, I'm not... Now, I'm going to ask you again. Start telling me what this is all about.'

'Coop...'

'The boy from the ship's dead, but then you probably knew that already. Going to bury him in an unmarked grave.'

'What? Please, Coop. I'm struggling to follow you. Help me out here.'

Like an exothermic reaction, Cooper exploded into a hot ball of anger. 'Help you? You want me to help you after everything you've done? All I want are answers, John. I just want to know the truth.'

Tired and short tempered already, it was Woods' turn to blow up. 'Truth? You want to talk about the truth? You have the audacity to talk about truth?'

'What's that supposed to mean?'

'The game's up, Coop. Enough! We know you wrote the anonymous letters.'

'What?'

Woods grabbed hold of Cooper's jacket. 'Oh now it's *what*, is it? All this time you made me think someone else knew about the accident. I was so worried I couldn't sleep at night. I thought any moment I'd have to tell the American people what I'd done. About the pact we'd made together. I'd have to expose all the lies we told. And do you know what that would've meant? It would've meant all the changes and all the policies and all the hard work I'd done for this country and fought for would mean nothing. Jack shit. Oh, and not to mention Jackson. What would've happened to him? The guilt he would've felt if I'd stepped down. God, I don't even want to think about it. But then all that doesn't matter now, does it? Because all along it was *you*.'

Cooper barged Woods into the chest of drawers. Knocked him sideward. Wanted to put his hands round John's neck – somehow didn't. 'Me? I wrote the letters? You've lost your mind. I was the one who covered up for Jackson. Made sure he was in the clear. I lost everything. *Me*. Yet you have the balls to think I wrote those letters.'

Woods spat his words. 'Maybe you couldn't handle it, was that it? Tired of everybody pointing the finger at you? Were you sick of the blame, Coop?'

Cooper pointed to himself. 'I blamed me, John. Every

second of every moment. I can taste it in my mouth, at the back of my throat. But does that mean I wrote the letters? Like hell.'

'Your prints were on the letter.'

'What?'

'Your prints. Beau took the latest letter to someone he knew. Someone discreet. Mine. His and yours.'

Cooper's face crumpled up into a snarl. 'So what did you do? Get Beau to take along something of mine with my fingerprints on? Because I'm telling you right now, they're wrong.'

'Of course not, because no-one ever thought it was you. But your prints cross-matched when they did a search. Came up from your stored prints on the military database...'

Wide-eyed, the hostility poured out of Cooper. 'You got it wrong.'

'I don't think so, Coop... Beau and I weren't going to say anything, not now anyway. Realized you must be pretty sick to do something like this. Thought it was part of your illness, you not being yourself because of your Goddamn addiction. Thought that one day you'd get help... God knows what we thought.' Woods stopped. Looked Cooper right up, right down and then said, 'Or maybe it's just because you hate me. Is that it?'

Cooper glared. Glowered. Shook his head. Rage flicking through him like tremors in an earthquake.

'I don't know how to express what I'm feeling right now. But maybe that's the way it should be because right now, John, I want to kill you, and I'm afraid of what I might do or say.'

'Then that makes two of us.'

Cooper leapt at John. Clasping him. Grasping him. Shaking him. 'Are you serious? You've just accused me of something I can never forgive you for. Look me in the eye, John, and say it was me. That you know *unequivocally* it was me who sent you those letters.'

'Get your hands off me.'

'Not till you tell me. Come on!'

Woods locked eyes. Locked stares. Blinked. Once. Twice. 'Then why were your prints there? There isn't anybody else. The only other...'

Woods stopped dead.

'The only other what, John?'

'... Only other print... There was another print. Inconclusive. It wasn't a complete print, and it'd also been compromised in some way so they ruled it out. It could've been Beau's or mine, they can't tell.'

'But you still think it's me who wrote those letters, even though there's evidence of someone else's prints?'

'What else am I supposed to think, Coop? Put yourself in my position. There is *nobody* else who knew about Jackson driving the yacht that day, apart from...'

Once again Woods trailed off. Cooper, still holding him tight, said, 'Apart from? Go on, say it.'

'There was Ellie.'

Cooper reeled. Directly dropped hold of John's blue shirt. 'Ellie? What the hell are you talking about?'

'Forget it. It's stupid.'

'No, John. I want to know why you would say Ellie? You of all people. So determined she drowned that day. Wouldn't listen to anything else. Both you and Beau. So why would you think even for a split, microscopic, minuscule Goddamn second it might've been Ellie!'

'I don't know.'

Cooper, hell-bent with rage, pushed Woods against the wall.

'Yes, you do! You know something.'

'Not really… Look, last year when I knew Granger was about to apply for Ellie's death certificate, I wanted to make sure nothing could be dug up or said about Jackson in the documents when the authorities read them to determine the death. I was only protecting him. So I made sure I got to see the records they held first. And it was like we told them – nothing had changed. It was all there. All our statements. The only thing different…'

'Go on.'

'The only thing different was the helicopter pilot and what he'd said. He'd contradicted one of the officer's statements. He said there was actually three skiffs. He saw three. But it doesn't change a thing. It's just a technical detail. As hard as it is, Coop, there was no way Ellie was getting out of there alive that day. She couldn't swim and she was way out in the ocean in the midst of a pirate attack and if drowning, hypothermia or exhaustion didn't get her, then you can be damn sure the sharks or bullets from the attack did. Face it, Coop, no pirate carried her off. I wish there was, but there is no happy ever after… She's dead, son. Dead.'

The room span. Legs became weak. A nausea rose as he staggered towards Woods' en suite bathroom. Holding onto the wall. Holding onto the door.

Then retching.

Vomiting.

Mucus and spit.

Sweet spit and mucus.

Wave upon wave of vomit and bile...

'Hey, Coop, are you okay? Coop? Open the door.'

Cooper closed his eyes for a moment, trying to steady himself as Woods continued to knock.

Rinsed out his mouth. Threw cold water onto his face. Headed back into the bedroom where Woods stood looking worried.

'I didn't know it would affect you like this, Coop. I'm sorry.'

A fast, sharp right hook sent Woods stumbling backwards. Smashing into the expensive coffee table. Hard.

'You made me think I was crazy. And over time I thought I was. The doctors. The pills. Trying to convince me I was wrong about seeing three skiffs. I tried to get it out of my head. But it wouldn't go and the more I tried to deny it the bigger it got and the crazier people thought I was. It tortured me, John, and you *knew* that. You knew how much it haunted me. I lost myself because of it. Because I knew I was right, John, and the guilt of knowing the truth but not doing anything about it has slowly killed me... Do you know how desperate I was that day for Beau to send out more help to try to find the third skiff, and see if she was on it? I begged him. Pleaded with him. But you know what he did? He looked me in the eye then walked away. I was his nephew, John, but I was also a damn good Lieutenant. I knew what I was talking about when I said there were three skiffs. I wasn't hysterical or irrational. I knew. But instead Beau insisted on believing the officers, who said there were only two skiffs… Do you know how I felt, John? Do you?'

'No, I don't.'

Cooper bellowed his words. 'Liar! Because you saw me that day and saw how afraid I was for her. I loved her. God, how I loved her. All I wanted to do was save her. And all you wanted to do was tell me how I should let her go because it was too late. And over the years I've talked about that third skiff, and over the years you've talked about how crazy I was. But it's all been a lie, like everything else. All a Goddamn lie.'

'No, it's not like that. I didn't know till last year.'

'But you didn't care to tell me when you'd found out… Does Granger know about this?'

'No, only Beau and I, and he wanted to tell you but Coop, last year you were in no fit state to deal with this. You were already spinning from the issuing of Ellie's death certificate. I was only looking out for you.'

Introspectively, Cooper asked, 'What happened to the report, John? The pilot's statement?'

Touching his bloody lip, Woods said, 'I got rid of it.'

Cooper wiped away the tears he hadn't known were even running. 'If it wasn't for Jackson, I'd have a good mind to tell the American people what we did that day. What their President is really like. You know I wish to God it *had* been me who'd written those letters. All this time I've wasted when I should've been out there looking for her and now it's too late… This is your fault, John.'

'What the hell's going on? Jesus, Coop are you alright?'

Jackson came into the room with Cora, who ran to Cooper, hugging onto his leg.

'Come on, honey, Daddy's got a bad taste in his mouth.'

Jackson looked at Woods and reached out to Cooper as he passed him. 'Coop, don't go. *Please*. What's going on?'

'Sorry, I can't be here right now. I'll call you later.'

'Tell me what's going on.'

Cooper said, 'I tell you what, why don't you ask *Dad*.'

57

Bb7 Ra1

Woods sat opposite Ambassador Shaheen, not feeling at all comfortable with the meeting. Not feeling at all well. And right now he was doing something he swore he'd never do. Because right now his mind was more on his personal life than on his professional one. On Cooper. On the big almighty fight. And no matter how much he tried to shift the focus from what had happened with Coop, to the discussion with the ambassador about the perceived failure of the US to stop NATO intervening, his thoughts were running all over the place like a little league soccer match.

And the sense of allowing his self-control – his self-discipline and resolve – to collapse, and therefore interfere with him doing the job the American people had entrusted him to do, felt like an overwhelming failure. The idea that he was only human and the idea that any father would feel the same way and the idea that this distraction was temporary just didn't cut it… Or help.

'It isn't a satisfactory position that we found ourselves in, and we certainly want not only answers, but also reas-surances.'

Woods was in no mood to try to placate. 'We gave you answers already, Ambassador. But out of respect for the relationship our two countries have, I thought it was best to partake in this conversation with you. But if I'm really straight here, your view on this occasion is difficult to comprehend. Preferring that NATO and the US Navy, along with the Combined Task Force 150, hadn't intervened in a search and rescue operation?'

Ambassador Shaheen. Olive skin. Hair boot polish black. Beard groomed into sharp angles. He took a sip of the dark roast coffee, spiced with cardamom. 'Mr President. Qatar, as always, appreciates the United States' cooperation, but this isn't about whether a refugee child was helped, it's about the security of the country which has been compromised. And besides, I understand the boy died.'

Woods raised his eyebrows at the apparent coldness of Shaheen, before looking across at Lyndon P Clarke and Teddy. Two proud, Afro-American men who sat professionally impassive with their backs towards the Oval Office fireplace. A favorite spot for press photo-call for visiting VIPs.

Noticing the ambassador's overly large hands, exaggerated by Shaheen's diminutive stature, Woods said, 'I wouldn't say it's been compromised in any way. They responded to an SOS signal. That's all.'

'Is that what you call it? As I understand it, it was a crude signal flashed out with a broken piece of mirror. This isn't the boy scouts of America, Mr President, this is international relations.'

'No harm was done, ambassador. It's hardly the Cuban missile crisis.'

'That's where you're wrong. A breach of agreement occurred. They had orders not to intervene, on *any* account. Even if it'd been the ship's own crew in distress, there was to be strictly no intervention. And they knew that. I wonder if you'd take such a laid back approach if the situation involved Qataris boarding a US Navy vessel.'

Pushing an image of Cooper out of his head, Woods tried to stifle his exasperated sigh with a cough. Didn't work. 'Ambassador, it was NATO, not us.'

'From where I'm sitting it's hard to see where one stops and the other one begins.'

Woods took a deep, patient breath. 'The US allows Qatar to ship around the arms which we've sold you without interference. Mainly because of the agreement we made with you, and we continue to give you our blessing. However, that does not mean, Ambassador, that it *isn't* open to a Security Council review and a change of policy.'

Ambassador Shaheen gave a strange smile and with a hostile tone, said, 'Is that so, Mr President? The thing is, Qatar has been a supporter of NATO, and as you know we're a very active partner of the Alliance. If you think back, we were – apart from the United Arab Emirates – the only Arab state to participate in the NATO-led military operation in Libya. So as you imagine it isn't NATO we have a problem with. Far from it. It's America. After all, this international rescue was led by the US, aided by NATO helicopters. Qatar spent billions and billions of dollars last year on buying advanced weapons from the US. We also accommodate the US's need to have an essential military base in our country. But I feel, under the circumstances, I'll have no alternative but to get *our* policies reviewed, and recommend to the Qatari military council that we instigate an extensive and overdue assessment of our weapons deals and imports from the United States, and perhaps look at alternative tenders.'

Annoyance shifted Woods in his chair. Hell, he didn't appreciate the underlying threat. But not appreciating it wasn't the same as having to accept it – though that's what he had to do. Suck it up. Swallow it hard. 'Ambassador, one thing I wish I could do as President is undo things. Reverse them. But as none of us have that gift, I can only apologize and hope that our countries *can* move on from here. And I give you my assurances as President that such a situation will never arise again. I hope we'll continue without prejudice to carve out deals and continue with the special relationship our countries have.'

Shaheen bowed his head. Twice. Woods wasn't sure if the man was looking down at the crumbs of ginger cookie he had on his lap, or he was doing it out of reverence. Deciding it was more likely to be the former, Woods, assuming the meeting was drawing to a close, reached across to the plate of oatmeal cookies, but stopped. Hand froze in mid-air when he heard the words.

'Abdul-Aziz bin Hamad.'

Woods said, 'Excuse me?'

'Abdul-Aziz bin Hamad. The United States are still holding him prisoner.'

'Ambassador, this wasn't on the schedule of discussion.'

'No, but we *have* discussed it before, both ourselves, and with Chuck Harrison, and we didn't come to a satisfactory conclusion. Though I have a feeling your head of CTC sees things in a slightly different light to the position your administration holds.'

'My acting head of CTC often has a different perspective, but it's important to be able to see things in other ways. He brings a fresh viewpoint. But ultimately Chuck Harrison, and this administration, have the United States' best interest at the forefront of their minds. And releasing a terrorist who plotted massive homeland attacks, and was the mastermind behind the bomb attack on an American passenger plane, *as well as* being affiliated with Al-Qaeda, is not in anyone's best interest.'

Shaheen sniffed with contempt. 'In the United States you have a presumption of innocence, so I'm puzzled as to why you're using the word *terrorist* when Bin Hamad hasn't stood trial. Correct me if I'm wrong, but America prides itself on the judicial process, and on democracy. Are you not constantly condemning my neighboring countries in the Middle East for what you see as violations of human rights? Yet to hold a prisoner without due process, and justify this by keeping them off United States soil, as the legal counsel advised the Bush administration they could do back in 2002, is not only hypocrisy, Mr President, and totally goes against international law – which you proclaim to hold in high regard – but it's also morally wrong. Qatar takes personally that you're holding one of our nationals without trial in one of your detention centers – which to us are a symbol of torture.'

Just as contemptuous, but with the right amount of politeness, Woods replied. 'This administration has worked hard to roll back any contentious and provocative interrogation and detention practices. We condemn the use of enhanced interrogation. And as you know, Ambassador, we use military commissions with improved rules to try the detainees. So to say they have no due process is wholly incorrect.'

Scoffing to the point of spraying tiny crumbs from his third cookie over his pristine blue suit, Shaheen said, 'Mr President, your military commissions do not meet fair trial standards, and I could count on my hand how many of the detainees who were once at Guantánamo, and the detainees where Abdul-Aziz bin Hamad is currently being held, have actually faced *any* kind of trial. Most are being kept indefinitely without any legal proceedings, which we both know is illegal under the Geneva Convention. And as you know, a lot of the others were recommended for release after a review by the detention center review task force, but are still waiting, many months, many years later, to obtain their freedom. And we, as a proud nation, won't have a Qatari citizen being held like this. These centers are emblematic of the flagrant abuse of human rights committed by the US government in the name of countering terrorism.'

Woods heard the volume of his voice go up. Brought it down by the diplomatic raise of Teddy's eyebrows. 'International laws do not apply to *unlawful enemy combatants* who are taken to the detention centers. We have *evidence* Abdul-Aziz bin Hamad is a key member of an offshoot of Al-Qaeda.'

'Then try him on US soil, Mr President. Qatar could accept that... Or couldn't you afford to execute such transparency? Are you worried that Bin Hamad would expose things the United States would rather keep away from the public domain? It seems your fight against terror has overridden the responsibility to respect human rights.'

The Ambassador locked eyes on Woods, inviting him to dispute his statement.

Woods said nothing.

Shaheen said, 'It's unfortunate you've decided that your administration won't contemplate the release of an innocent man, or even a *prisoner transfer*. So be it, Mr President. But one way or another, this situation with Bin Hamad will be resolved.'

58

Bc8 Ra4

With Ambassador Shaheen now gone, Woods turned to look at Teddy and Lyndon.

'Would it be appropriate to use the word *bastard* now?'

Lyndon answered, a semi-smile on his face. 'Mr President, that all depends on who you're talking about.'

Woods slumped in his chair. Not resisting the call of the cookie. Bit into it.

'Do I really need to do this? Seriously, is there no other way, because it strikes me that the United States shouldn't have to do this. Right now it feels like our integrity is being compromised by having to deal with the likes of Shaheen. It's a joke. Abdul-Aziz bin Hamad is as guilty as sin. Shaheen needs to take his head out of his ass and stop making Qatar out as the playground for nymphs from the fountain of the innocents.'

Teddy said, 'Run that again.'

'You know what I mean. He makes out that Qatar is naïve to terror groups. I mean two of Al-Qaeda's most senior financiers are living with impunity in Qatar *in spite* of being on a worldwide terrorism blacklist.'

'I guess that's why they call it the Club Med for Terrorists.'

Woods nodded contemplatively. 'But of course their stance is Qatar has never supported, and will never support, terrorist organizations. And publicly we've rebuked them multiple times over their refusal to take a tougher approach against terrorist financing. And our financial sanctions and embargos are ineffective. But then what do we do? Do we push towards tougher sanctions? No. Like hell we do. Instead what we do is to continue to sell them weapons, knowing what we know and knowing more than likely those arms will be channelled along with cash to violent organizations. And then there's the small matter of the base we have there. It's one of the most important, if not *the* key military base for the region. Like I say, it's a Goddamn joke. Don't you guys hate how we play this game? They serve a rogue ball and all we do is hit it back over the net. Over and over again.'

Teddy, who'd joined Woods in devouring the oatmeal cookies, but was having less luck with keeping the crumbs off the floor, said, 'I try not to think too hard about it, mainly because what other alternative is there? It's a country endowed with massive reserves of gas and oil, and has one of the world's biggest sovereign wealth funds, so they have the ability to exert enormous influence.'

Trying not to transfer his anger towards Shaheen onto Teddy, Woods rolled his tongue around his mouth before taking a stick of gum – which Jackson had given him earlier – out of his pants pocket. Bent it in two, then two again, before firmly pushing it into his mouth.

'But what the hell has that got to do with having to compromise integrity?'

'Jesus, John. It's got everything to do with it. And the last time integrity was synonymous with politics was when I was a freshman and you know that.'

Woods exploded. 'And you don't hate that?'

'Of course I do. But since we were in the Ivy League you've always been much more idealistic than I was.'

'You make out that's a bad thing.'

'Not bad. *Misguided*. And that's why it hits you so hard. There's nothing idealistic about this situation. Turning your back on a snake that strikes is never a good thing, so we align with the lesser evil, though that in itself comes with its own pitfalls. And there are dangers of not working with them, as well you know, Mr President. You've got to admit that their association with terrorist organizations like the Taliban and Hamas and, to a point, Al-Qaeda, have made them a valuable go-between in the region.'

'And a pretty capricious ally,' Woods said.

'It's a new dawn,' Teddy said.

Woods cut a hard stare. 'What's that supposed to mean?'

'They give us what we want and we give them what they want.'

'At a price. But let me tell you it certainly won't include Abdul-Aziz bin Hamad. Al-Qaeda has been comparatively quiet since Osama bin Laden was killed back in 2011. But just because the dragon sleeps, it doesn't mean it's stopped being a dragon. We know that Al-Qaeda is slowly regrouping itself, and actively recruiting, as well as trying to replenish their bank accounts in preparation for their next phase. So I *don't* trust the reasons why Qatar are so keen to have Bin Hamad released or transferred. I suspect, from the discussions I've

292

had with not only the Security Council but also central intelligence, that groups masquerading as Qatari Charities, similar to the ones who were Bin Laden's major source of funding, are pushing for it... God, it's a mess. I'm telling you guys, over the next couple of years this administration needs to really reassess our relationship with certain countries.'

'And in the meantime?' asked Lyndon.

Woods, looking like a defeated man, replied, 'In the meantime, Lyndon, we continue to listen to Qatar telling the world they do not fund terrorists, and we continue to sell weapons to them, knowing some of them will be shipped unchecked with our blessing to enemies of this nation, and our military will continue to fight to defend this country and for global stability, whilst being attacked with the same weapons we sold. And then as the cherry on the Goddamn cake, Lyndon, we'll watch and condemn the actions of the rest of the Middle East from our high tech military base ivory tower in Qatar, as they top up the Pentagon funds with their billions... Hey, and there's me thinking we're hypocrites.'

59

Kf3 Rc4

Ellie.

That's all Cooper could think of as he lay on his back, drunk and counting stars by one of the streams on his ranch, which looked across to the seemingly endless mountain range sitting under the Colorado night sky.

Without moving from his position, Cooper stretched his arm across to one of the bottles of beer lying in the grass next to him. Attempted to drink the remainder whilst still lying down.

'Shit!'

Spluttering, he sat up. Quickly. As the alcohol spilt and drained over and off his face, trickling into his ears and seemingly down his nose.

Hurling the bottle away, Cooper rested his head on his knees.

Dizzy.

Ill.

He fumbled to the side of him, feeling the cool of the earth and the grass on his hand. And then his fingers touched it. The steel. The cold metal of his gun. Smooth like silk. Inviting. Alluring. Urging him to soothe away his pain... His guilt.

Dragging it towards him like a heavy weight, his index finger hooked around the trigger, Cooper, with his head still down, neglected to look at the 44 S&W Special, almost as if he was trying to sneak the gun up on himself.

Pushed the barrel hard against his head, against his mop of thick hair, hearing his own muffled cry. 'Come back to me, Ellie. Don't leave me like this. *Please* don't leave me on my own, baby. I can't do it without you.'

Lifting his head up, his eyes closed, his face wet with beer and tears, he opened his mouth. Slowly he slid the gun in, hearing the steel clatter against and past his teeth as he pushed it towards the back of his throat. Tasting the steel on his tongue. Feeling the conflict of the hard steel against the soft palate of the roof of his mouth.

Pulling the chrome hammer back with his thumb, he was vaguely aware of his body juddering. Shuddering. Jerking with emotion. Anticipation... Fear.

Pull the trigger; that's all he had to do. That's all it'd take. One pull. One shot. Then it'd be over. Everything. Gone. No more pain... Well, not for him anyway... But it wasn't just him, was it? What about Cora? What about her? Would she spend her life wondering? Hating him? Hating herself? Questioning why he'd left her? Shit... No. He *wasn't* going to think like that. Couldn't. Wouldn't. He needed to finish this. End it. Period.

Determined, he pushed harder. Jammed the gun further back into his mouth, inadvertently instigating a pharyngeal reflex, causing the beer which sat at the bottom of his stomach like a well to be retched up and flood over and past the gun in his mouth and pour out either side of it and drip down onto his chin, covering his hands with sweet, sticky vomit.

His thumbs shook, hovering over the trigger. Why couldn't he do it?

Why?

God help him, why? *Just pull the trigger. Pull it. Pull it.*

The image of Cora – of Ellie – of Jackson – of Levi – of Dorothy – of Beau – of John – of Maddie – came into his mind. And right then, right there he ripped the gun out of his mouth, smashing his teeth on the way out. And then fired it into the air. Over and over and over. Into the darkness. Into the bright. Lighting up the starry sky.

60

Bd7 Kf6

'Remember that old boyfriend of mine, Tom?'

Cooper washed his face in the large, stone outdoor sink, part of the open-air kitchen which he'd built for, and in honor of, Levi's love of cook-outs.

The cold water refreshed his skin. His body. But not his mind. And if the water wouldn't work, a mouthful of beer might.

He reached over to finish off the Busch beer, which sat next to the loaded 44 S&W Special and his cell, resting on the whitewashed fence post with Maddie on speakerphone.

He felt rough. Dog tired. He'd slept outside all night and woken up to the Colorado morning sun and to the mother of all hangovers. And now most of all he was angry as hell with what seemed – what was – the entire world. 'Which one? Jesus, Maddie, I lose count. Good job they use abacuses in school to teach math to first graders, rather than the number of boyfriends you've had, otherwise, hell knows, poor babies would lose count.'

A pause. And Cooper could visualize Maddie chewing on

her lip. Contemplating whether or not to react. Part of him wanted her to. God knows he could do with a fight. Give him a good excuse, rather than just a regular one, to drown his sorrows… again.

Not biting, Maddie asked, 'Have you finished now? Feel better now you've been a jackass? Because I don't have to bother, you know? Down to you.'

A long sigh. A draw on his cigarette and a struggle to put the thoughts of Ellie and the events of last night away. Cooper, feeling genuinely ashamed of himself, meekly said, 'Sorry. I was completely out of line there. You didn't deserve that.'

'You okay, Tom? Has something happened?'

Oh, hell yeah. God, had it just. It had spun and turned and moved and blown and torn his world upside down. He felt as if the accident had just happened that very day, and he didn't know what to do, and he didn't know how to feel, and he didn't know how to breathe, and God how he wished he could share it with Maddie, but instead he mused, 'Just tired, that's all. Was up with one of the horses last night. I think there's something wrong with her front right tendon. I'm going to call Ace to come and look at it.'

'Do you want me to call him, I could…'

He cut her off. Briskly. 'It's fine, I can sort it. What is it you want anyway? Sorry, that came out wrong. I just…'

She cut in as fast and as briskly as Cooper had done. 'Don't bother, I don't want to hear it. I was just calling to let you know I'm off to see Joshua Bradley at fifteen hundred hours, which will give you enough time to fly over here. He's the guy who works for the NATO Allied Maritime Command. I thought it might be interesting to talk to him. Who knows, maybe he'll be able to tell us a little bit more about Ismet and his boats. I'll text you the address… If you turn up you turn up, and if you don't… whatever.'

The line went dead and Cooper stood staring for a good few moments at his cell. Letting the feeling of frustration and anger and pain and hurt rush right through him and over him. Then slowly, real carefully, he reached to put the gun away. Afraid to make any sudden movements, in case that sudden movement might trigger an urge to put a bullet right in his head.

61

Kg4 Rd4

In the Breckenridge, Colorado, Maddie stared at Cooper. 'Wasn't sure if you'd show, Tom.'

Dark shades on to protect his eyes from what felt like an apocalyptic sun, unshaven, a headache sent from hell itself, and Maddie waiting by the gate with her hands on her hips and a tight look on her face. This was going to be some afternoon. 'Hoping I wouldn't, so you guys can go over old times? Tell me, Maddison, how come I didn't know about this guy?'

'Seriously, Tom, you're really starting to annoy me. Whatever the hell it is you're talking about... don't.'

Not backing down, thinking about Rosedale, Cooper asked, 'Where's lover boy?'

Cutting her eye at him as she knocked on the door, Maddie said, 'Which one?'

Before Cooper could combust into a ball of fury, the door was flung open. Wide.

'Hey, Maddison! God it's been a while but damn you still looking good. What's your secret?'

Joshua Bradley – six-foot-tall and movie star looks – gave Maddie a hug. A squeeze. Real tight. Hands real low. Too low for Cooper's liking.

'Sorry, my manners.' Bradley reached out his hand to Cooper, who stared at it. Didn't bother taking it. Leaving Bradley hanging in the air until he wiped his hand self-consciously on his trousers.

'Well it's good to meet you, Thomas.'

A single begrudging nod. A single word. 'Cooper.'

'Cooper. Sorry...'

Relieved to have Maddie to bridge the awkwardness gap, Bradley led them both inside. Gestured towards the large, tan leather couch.

'So, I know you couldn't talk fully on the phone but I got your gist... Sorry, can I offer either of you a drink?'

'Yes.'

'No.'

Grinning, Bradley pushed warmly. 'Cooper, are you sure I can't get you anything?'

'What am I, a three year old?'

'Josh, can I apologize for Tom's rudeness? We really appreciate you giving up your time like this. And don't worry about my drink, I'm fine.'

Deciding it was probably best not to ask Maddie if she was sure, Joshua Bradley sat down opposite, trying his hardest to ignore Cooper's hostile stare.

'Can I ask why you're so interested in this ship? Or shouldn't I ask that?' Joshua said.

'Only because we want to tread very carefully, and to tell you the truth, Josh, we're not quite sure where we're heading with it really. It's nothing to do with trust though.'

Josh smiled warmly at Maddie. Winked. Left Cooper more pissed than he already was.

'I know you trust me, but I appreciate you saying that, and I'm sure *you'll* appreciate I can only divulge so much, and even that's too much… I shouldn't really be doing this, but I know you wouldn't ask if it wasn't really important to you. And hey, I've never been able to say no to you.'

Ruminating on the end seat of the couch, Cooper, knowing his behavior wasn't something he was proud of, and working out how he was going to make it up to Maddie later, said nothing. But the awkwardness sat, hung and loitered in the air until Maddie, simmering with fury, spoke. 'I know you're a busy man, Josh, so can I ask you a few questions then we'll leave you to get on?'

'Sure.'

'What we don't understand is why Ismet's ship wasn't on the marine traffic reports. Or on the shipping position data. Or even on the API or AIS. Nothing. There's no record of it. Not *when* it was sailing. Not the history of it doing so. I understand that it has stealth technology, but that's purely for being less visible on radar. There has to be some official record.'

'Nope.'

'But there does, maritime law states…'

Bradley cut in. 'Not when it comes to these particular ships.'

'Why?'

'It's a Qatari ship, right?'

'Yeah, so? That exempt it from having to follow maritime protocol,' Maddie said.

Bradley, rooting and staring into the family size Lay's spicy ketchup potato chip bag, in the hope of procuring the last remains from the bottom, shook his head, flicking off the bits of chips from his fingers before noisily sucking each one clean.

'Not usually, but then the people behind this aren't usual.'

Maddie looked puzzled. 'I'm not following you.'

'Now it's my turn to know if I can trust you. What I'm going to tell you can't go past these walls. And whatever happens, Maddie, you didn't hear this from me. Right?'

'Absolutely. And I can speak for Tom on this when I say you can trust us unequivocally.'

Josh's eyes flicked across to Cooper who nodded in agreement. 'Okay, well, the people behind those boats – and I don't exactly know who they are – but they have a deal with the US government to be able to sail around the Med and Africa unhindered. With their blessing. NATO and the Combined Task Force 150 have no choice but to go along with it.'

'And the reason?'

'It's to do with the American weapons they've bought from our government, which are sold to Qatar, who in turn sell or give them to their allies, who aren't always our allies, and there's nothing we can do to regulate or keep check on who and where these shipments of arms are going.'

Maddie pulled a face. One that spelt disbelief with a capital D. 'So you just let them ship arms about with no checks? And all off record? That is asking for trouble.'

'It's not quite *me* letting them but yes, it's part of an

arrangement between America and Qatar. You must know all about this, Maddie?'

'Of course, but when I was a serving naval officer there were slightly more regulations, plus an entirely different military and political climate.'

'I hear you on that one. And to go back to what you said about them being off record, yes they are, but we kind of track them anyway. Ironically, we know and are told about the ships, because for us to *not* stop or check them, and to pretend *not* to know about them, we have to be told about the ship's course in the first place. It's crazy. When they use stealth ships, it does make it harder to know where their heading, but not impossible. Of course, we're not supposed to be interested, but human nature being what it is, being told not to be interested in something only makes us more curious.'

Thoughtfully, Maddie wondered aloud, 'So you never stop them? Ever?'

'Well, here's the rub: we can't intercept them, and we can't check their cargo *even if* we suspect something's not right. Which on a side point, after you called me, Mads, I did some asking around and apparently the guys who came to rescue that young boy off the Qatari ship you were on, they got in a hell of a lot of trouble. Big time. If I said it'd caused somewhat of a diplomatic incident, I wouldn't be exaggerating.'

Cooper, who'd sat listening, trying real hard to put his instant dislike for Bradley to one side, and his hatred of John and his administration policies to the other side, eventually spoke. 'Christ, Bradley, are you telling me that the powers that be would rather you guys *hadn't* come to help the kid?'

'That's *exactly* what I'm saying. Strictly off limits. No matter what. Thank the President and the Pentagon for that one.'

Quietly, through gritted teeth and with tightened fists, Cooper uttered, 'Oh I will. Believe me, Bradley, I will.'

'It sticks in a lot of military guys' – and women's, sorry – throats that this is how it is. And I know for a fact that these weapons being shipped around, and given to different rogue states by Qatar and other Middle Eastern countries, have been used against the US Army out in the field, as well as innocent civilians. In actual fact, the shipping of arms is a huge problem and governments often turn a blind eye, as well as getting NATO to be discreet for the sake of international relations. And there's *no* repercussions. I've been a Democrat all my life, but I tell you I'm heading across to the other side the next time Presidential elections come around. Woods can kiss my South Dakota ass.'

Didn't he just want the words not to come out. Didn't he just want the feeling of protectiveness not to be present. Didn't he just want the thought of *who the hell does this Bradley think he is*, not to be there. But it was. Goddamn it, as usual it was. 'You can't put it all on Woods. If you knew anything about politics, and really understood about interparty ideology and the continuity of foreign policy, both on philosophical and practical levels since the end of the Cold War, you'd see that it doesn't start with John... Woods. He's in a corner. One that was already built for him. So before you go pointing that judgmental finger, know your facts, Bradley.'

The atmosphere was what Cooper might, diplomatically, have called tense.

'I'm sorry. I didn't mean to offend. I wouldn't have said

anything if I'd known you were such a staunch Woods supporter.'

Feeling – and not appreciating – the hard glare from Maddie, Cooper shrugged, muttering, 'I'm not.'

'It's just that you seem…'

Not wanting to talk about it anymore, Cooper cut in. 'Don't worry what I seem. What I seem is not all that I am… Look, can we just get back to what we were talking about? And hey, I appreciate you giving up your time for us.'

With more gratitude than he'd intended to show – and certainly more than Cooper deserved – Bradley exclaimed, 'Yes, please. Yes. Gosh, yes.'

Cooper raised an inward eyebrow but spoke as cordially to Bradley as he could. 'So, with what we know, I guess that's why Ismet was pretty ambivalent about the boy on the ship. Yes, he'd be pissed that you guys had come and assisted us, *especially* if he was trying to keep the fact that he may have lost the boat quiet from whoever owns it. Clearly, they're not people to be messed with, but ultimately no one was going to investigate what a boy was doing on the ship.'

'So you think they were shipping arms from Turkey to Libya?' Maddie said.

Bradley looked confused. 'Turkey to Libya? I don't think so. Let me show you something. Come on.'

Bradley got up and walked through to his study with Maddie and Cooper following a step behind. He sat at his computer. Looked at both of them earnestly. 'I shouldn't be showing you this, and I could lose my job for even having you in here, but if you look at these retrospective radar graphics… here, look. I can tell you for sure your stealth ship didn't go to Libya. We tracked it – unofficially of course – heading west out of Turkey, past Libya and then we lose it. It doesn't register on our system again until two days later. Then we pick it up again passing through the *Straits of Gibraltar* – the narrow channel between North Africa and Spain. The sea is only about nine miles wide at that point and there's a British military base right on the Rock of Gibraltar. On a clear day you can see North Africa even without binoculars. Nothing gets through that gap without being spotted. Look, you can see here that your ship went through the Straits and out into the Atlantic, then headed south down the Moroccan coast. And then, if you take a look at this, it then goes down to about Casablanca, and strangely, for some reason, turns right around. Does a great big U-turn out at sea, and sails back on itself, past Gibraltar, into the Mediterranean and then, as you said on the phone Maddie, you find it a few days later abandoned off the coast of Libya, south longitude to Crete.'

Maddie looked at Cooper. 'Morocco? What the hell was it doing right out there? And why go all that way, only to turn right around and come back?'

Bradley said, 'Out of interest what did this Ismet guy tell you they were carrying?'

Maddie gave a wry smile. 'Amongst other things, olives.'

To which Joshua Bradley grinned and replied, 'Is that what they're calling it now?'

62

Bc6 Rd8

'Hey John, I'm glad I saw you. I didn't realize you were going to be about. I brought those books on China's power plants Jackson wanted to read. Didn't he tell you I was coming by?'

Listlessly, John said, 'No.'

'You don't look so great. You coming down with something?'

'No.'

Beau frowned, looked down the hall by the entrance of the Executive Residence.

'Well, if you're sure. But anyway, listen, good news… Is it okay to talk? Is there a blackout along here?'

With a heavy-lidded gaze, John nodded. 'It's fine, Beau, there's no ears here but I've only got a couple of minutes.'

'No problem. I'll make it quick. Just wanted to say we were right not to go charging in about the letters with Coop, because guess what…? I was sorting out my room in the monastery and I found one of Cora's crayons in my drawer.

Then it came to me. I don't know why I didn't remember before, but then I guess that's old age for you... The last time Coop came to see me, Cora had wanted to do some drawing, some kind of bug or something. Anyway, my sciatica was acting up so I stayed out playing in the gardens with Cora... when I say playing, I was sitting down with one of those cigars you gave me, and she was chasing the cat. Point is, I sent Coop into my room to get some sheets of paper from my top drawer. That's where the letter was, with other kinds of correspondence. He must have thumbed through the pile of paperwork to find a plain sheet of paper for Cora. That's how the print must have got on it. I must say, John, it's a damn relief it wasn't him, but more of a relief that we didn't accuse him. I think us not trusting him might've sent him spinning, and he's already on the edge. Anyway, you're not the only one who's got a busy life. I got to run... But John, I'm glad it's turned out okay.'

John Woods said nothing.

63

Kh4 Rg8

Chuck Harrison crinkled up his face as the chocolate marsh-mallow ice-cream hit his tooth, sending his nerve-endings into overdrive and a metachronal wave of pain through his body like it was a Mexican wave at a soccer match.

With his cell on the dash, Chuck smiled to himself, still grimacing slightly from the pain. The US could do worse than use a tub of Ben and Jerry's Utter Peanut Butter Clutter for enhanced interrogation. It'd have the terrorists talking like they were telling bedtime stories. He laughed out loud at the image in his head. And then pressed fast dial.

Three rings followed by a quiet, 'Hello.'

Chuck said, 'It's me.'

'I know. Who else calls me?'

'It's on. But you've got less than forty-eight hours.'

'There's no way. It's impossible.'

'That's where you're wrong. There's every way because, Harry, failure isn't an option.'

64

Be4 Rg1

Peering down the corridor for any sign of Granger, Maddie stepped into the main office, where the AC was on full blast and Rosedale, Levi and Cooper were sitting. Not speaking. Feigning busyness by means of studying paperwork which didn't need to be studied.

'What are you doing, guys?'

Levi: 'Work.'

Rosedale: 'Work.'

Cooper: 'Work.'

Maddie nodded and said, 'Looks important.'

To which Cooper replied, 'It is.'

'Then just a quick heads-up, Tom. It'd probably help if you held the document the right way up.'

Cooper slammed down the paperwork. 'What is it you want, Maddie?'

She walked across to sit on Rosedale's desk which caused Cooper to fight the urge to get up, grab him by the lapels of his white, sharp, linen shirt and throw a hard, well cantered right hook.

But instead he cricked the tension out of his neck. Out of his fingers. Knew he needed to be on his best behavior. Sat watching Maddie give Rosedale a smile, who accepted it like a hungry kid in a candy shop.

'I'm actually glad you're all here. Because our conversation with Joshua, it got me thinking. But I needed to check something out first before I said anything... I've just come off the phone to Gap clothing. After we'd had the discussion with Bradley the other day I called Gap, and they've just got back to me. And I *think* now I've got my head around some of what's going on... You'll remember of course the kids who were washed up on the beach of Algeria wearing the *same* yellow T-shirts with the purple logo across the front. And as Tom rightly identified it was the same top our boy, Andreas, was wearing when we found him on the ship... Because all the kids were wearing them, I suspected they might've been donated by some organization. Turns out that's *exactly* it. Those particular T-shirts never actually got on the open market, because after a quality control check – which they do after every five hundred prints – Gap realized that because of the script they'd used, one of the letters on the logo looked more like a letter D than an A. So they stopped the print, fixed the problem, but also changed the color of the logo for the next run. So there are literally *only* five hundred of those tops in that particular color with *that* particular design fault. Obviously they couldn't sell them, so they organized for a couple of charities to have them. One's in Yemen, but the other one is the one I'm interested in. It's called *Syrian Relief Clothing*. Gap told me this charity is located in the north-west of Syria... Right here…Look…'–Maddie pointed to the large map on the wall before adding. 'And as you can see it's just under thirty miles from Ismet's shipping company.'

Rosedale whistled. 'So what are you saying? You think those kids were originally on the ship after all?'

Maddie shrugged. 'I don't know, but it's looking more and more likely.'

'Jesus. That's some kind of statement… What is he up to?' Cooper said.

'There are still so many dots which need to be joined up. They told me the refugee camp is for orphans, as well as kids who've been separated from their families. The average age of them are between eight and twelve.'

Rosedale threw his cowboy hat to the side. Stood up. Walked across to the map. Stared at it intensely, as if somehow looking closer would give him the answers he needed. 'I'm guessing the levels of security in a place like that is next to nothing.'

'Yep. Every possible resource is stretched to the absolute limit, and there just isn't the manpower to have the luxury of anything near a safe haven.'

Rosedale took a deep draw on his Graycliff cigar, his voice becoming angry. 'Which makes it a great place for anybody who wants to find kids to exploit.'

Maddie glanced at Cooper, who'd managed to spill his coffee all over his highly polished desk. 'Exactly. And the tragic thing is they aren't missed. On occasion there's some kind of head count, but mainly it's about having somewhere to go to get away from the conflicts. The most basic kind of sanctuary.'

'And it seems not even that, in this case,' Rosedale added.

'No, exactly, and worse still, when I contacted someone from the charity they said they were so overwhelmed they wouldn't know if eighty kids were missing or not. Many of the kids are so traumatized, even basic information like names isn't taken. The guy from the charity said he's worked in a lot of places, but this one, and others set up specifically for younger refugees, can end up becoming really dangerous places for the children.'

'And there's nothing that can be done?' Cooper asked hopefully.

'There's no-one to complain to, is there? And no-one high up in authority will do anything either. The country is in chaos. No authority is going to spend time looking into it, and we've got no hard evidence to prove those poor kids were on this ship. Even if we had the power to push someone to look at it, they'd say that the kids could've been on any trafficker's boat.'

'You think they're trafficking, Maddie?'

She nodded at Cooper. 'I guess that's the obvious thing, isn't it?'

'But who's paying?' asked Rosedale. 'Usually people traffickers like to get paid, and it's hardly as if these kids have money to pay to be smuggled into Europe.'

Levi, finishing off the last can of Mountain Dew, that he professed not to enjoy nor drink, nodded. 'What about sex trafficking? Using the kids for that?'

Maddie felt sick. 'Christ, I hope not. That's another thing the charity guy said. There's been lots of reports of sexual abuse, and violence towards the kids. It's the worst kind of situation.'

'And the obvious place to be trafficked is mainland Europe, and from there they're free to travel, mainly unchecked.'

Maddie shook her head. 'That's not where they went though, Levi. The ship passed Europe. We *know* it went out into the Atlantic but we don't know exactly why... But I've got a theory. Let's say for argument's sake the kids were definitely on the ship, okay? Well, I don't think there's any chance they drowned. They didn't fall off that ship. And it's not as if it's one of those tragic accidents we see on the news where a boat carrying migrants overturned. This is different.'

Levi sat up in his chair, which faced out towards Granite Mountain. 'You think they were thrown off?'

'I do. But I think they were dead first. I think like Andreas, who died of dehydration and heat exposure, those other kids had an awful death too. Slow and agonizing. Cooped up below deck with no oxygen.'

'And obviously eighty dead kids are no use to anyone,' Rosedale said.

'Right. And if we supposed the crew panicked when they realized, then what do they do?'

'Dump the kids overboard, but out into the Atlantic,' Cooper said.

Rosedale asked. 'Do you think dumping the kids was the only reason they went out to the Atlantic? Do you think, like Levi says, they usually take them to mainland Europe?'

Shaking her head, Maddie said, 'No, because Josh told us *even though* they're not supposed to track the ships, which are allowed to sail unchecked, they still do, and often Ismet's ships sail around and down the coast of Africa.'

Levi frowned. 'Okay, but if they went out into the Atlantic *before* they turned back so they could dump the bodies, they wouldn't have washed up in the Mediterranean.'

Maddie, not enjoying the subject matter, but enjoying being in her element when it came to talking maritime matters and anything nautical, said, 'No, you're wrong. The kids would still be washed up somewhere in the Mediterranean, and in this case on the beach of Algeria, because of the special way the tides work. The Atlantic Ocean is huge and, as you know, water levels rise and fall with the gravitational pull of the moon as it orbits the earth, which in turn causes the *tides* to rise and fall at the shore.'

'I'm still not following how the kids ended up there,' Levi said.

'My point about the Mediterranean is that it's not tidal. The only natural outlet is through the Straits of Gibraltar to the Atlantic. Not only are the Straits only about nine miles wide, but there's an underwater shelf which inhibits the flow of tides too. But here's the really interesting thing. As a result of this restricted flow, the Mediterranean acts a bit like a huge lake – geographically, it's hot and the sun evaporates more water than gets replaced by the rivers that run into it. The water level in the Med is always slightly lower than the Atlantic and so water constantly pours through the Straits of Gibraltar to fill it back up. Coupled with that, all that evaporation makes the Mediterranean water much saltier, much warmer and slightly heavier than the Atlantic water, so even when Atlantic tides are pulling water out through the Straits of Gibraltar, the water moves out through massive deep warm water current flows, but at surface level, the top 50 meters or so are constantly moving eastwards from the Atlantic into the Mediterranean, which means...'

With a grin of real pride in his voice, Cooper said, 'Which means apart from you being brilliant, it means that anything, or in this case *anyone* thrown into the sea around that part of the Atlantic, around Morocco, will get sucked straight back into the Mediterranean via the Straits of Gibraltar and could easily have been washed up on the coast of Algeria.'

Maddie smiled back. 'You got it, Tom.'

With love and tenderness, Cooper winked. 'No baby, you're the one who's got it.'

A sudden bang made Cooper and Maddie turn around to look at Rosedale. He smiled innocently. 'Sorry. Hand slipped... What were you saying, Maddison?'

Cooper seethed. Didn't want to give Rosedale the satisfaction of an argument, nor did he think it was appropriate to deflect from what they were saying. He turned his attention back to Maddie. 'We have to do something, Maddie.'

'But this is the problem, Tom. What? Are you suggesting we try to turn around the way refugee camps are run? Because we'll be in for a losing battle. And it isn't a question of not wanting to try. Or are you talking about Ismet?'

'Everything. The kids. What Ismet is doing. And why he can use those ships? I mean we keep saying *the Qataris*, but that's pretty general.'

Rosedale had tried to make a point of not speaking to Cooper, but couldn't help but question him. 'You're talking about taking them on? That's not a good idea.'

'And what, leaving kids vulnerable to whatever the hell it is that Ismet's doing is?'

'No, I'm not saying that, Thomas, of course it's not okay. So far from okay it's unreal, but if Ismet's using Qatari ships, which have the go ahead from the powers that be to go unchecked, well that means the people behind them have some pretty big influence. We can't forget the threats and break in. You're not in the SEALs anymore, sugar.'

Frustrated, Cooper lit a cigarette. 'You know, what I can't forget is the eighty dead kids. Anything else, I don't give a damn about.'

'But that's exactly what you have to do. These aren't your regular guys. I don't know exactly what's happening, but we can't go storming in,' Rosedale said.

Levi had been deep in thought but now chipped into the conversation. 'I'm sorry to go back on this, but why would they keep the same clothes on the kids though? It's like a red flag.'

Maddie shrugged. 'You gotta think, that T-shirt may be all those kids had. The charity said that particular refugee camp was certainly overlooked by the bigger charities, and they struggled to get any form of relief aid, whether it be clothing or food. And Ismet wasn't to know that the crew were going to do this. And sometimes, the most obvious thing is overlooked. Obviously this is conjecture, because nothing we have proves unequivocally that the children were on the boat.'

'And that's exactly why I'm going to go back to Turkey,' Cooper said.

'Tom, no.'

'Come on, Maddie, what do you expect me to do?'

'You're crazy.'

'Am I, Rosedale? Or do I just want to see what's going on and do what I can to help?'

Rosedale, having mopped up the spilled coffee with Levi's sweat top, leant back on Cooper's desk. 'Oh, I don't think you're understanding me. When I say you're crazy, I'm not talking about whether or not you go and investigate this Ismet guy. I'm talking about you, Thomas. You're a liability. You're in no fit state.'

'I need to do this, Rosedale, and I need you to come with me.'

'You're cookin' up a pot of crazy in that head of yours. There's no way.'

'Why?'

Rosedale looked at Cooper incredulously. 'Why? Have you lost all sense? Apart from the fact we don't really know who we're taking on, there's the small matter of you being hook-assed on those pills you like to take. You're not safe to be around. Unreliable. If you were the Thomas from years gone by, then maybe. But it'd still only be a maybe. I can't believe, after everything, you want me to risk my life for you.'

'Not for me, Rosedale. For those kids. For Andreas.'

'Have you forgotten the last time you asked us to do something? It turned out that you were working for Ismet.'

Angry, both at himself, and at Rosedale, Cooper dragged hard on his cigarette. 'I wasn't working for him. I... I... Goddamn it, you know what happened. It was a mistake. I was desperate, and I am sorry, *really* sorry that I compromised myself and *us* in that way.'

'And what if this is the same? You and Ismet have something lined up.'

'You're talking crap now.'

'Am I?'

'Yeah and you know it. There's no way this has got anything to do with Ismet and I.'

'Actually, Thomas, I do know that, but what I'm trying to show you is that no-one can trust you anymore. You can't even trust yourself to guarantee it won't happen again... Tell me what happens if you get desperate again?'

Cooper's reply was faint. 'I won't.'

'How do you know?'

'I'll make sure I take enough.'

Maddie put her head down. Levi put his in his hands. And Rosedale shook his and said, 'Have you heard yourself? You're now going to go all Scarface on our ass, and risk getting busted by customs?'

Cooper walked towards the wall-to-ceiling window. Running his hand through his strawberry blonde hair, he turned to Rosedale. 'I'm just saying it like it is. I'm sorry. I really am, but I can't just stop and I can't just leave those kids. Don't look at me like that, Rosedale, I have tried to give up, but it's so Goddamn hard, and right now with everything that's going on, and to be one hundred percent honest with you, I can't even begin to imagine life without the pills... It's screwed up, I know, but I have to be straight with you if I'm asking for your help.'

'And you're seriously wanting us to come with you with your head so messed up?'

'Yes I am because...' Cooper stopped. Tried to regain his

composure, which he could feel was breaking. Giving way to a flood gate of emotions. Sniffed. Put hands on hips. Looked up. Looked down. Stalled for time. Unsure whether or not to give them anything but the full, unedited version. Inhaled. Exhaled. 'I don't want to die.'

Shocked, hit by a curve ball, Maddie said, 'What?'

Cooper ran his hand again through his thick hair, which just flopped back into the same position. Falling over his eyes. Concealing the pain. 'I don't want to die, but death sure as hell seems to keep calling my name.'

'What are you talking about, Tom?'

'I'm just saying I'm tired. Real tired of this battle. So I need to do something which takes my sorry ass out of where I seem to have landed. I can't help myself, but perhaps, just perhaps, I can help these kids.'

Rosedale shook his head. 'You're living in a dream world, Thomas.'

Maddie shot a stare. 'Let him finish.'

Cooper smiled gratefully at Maddie. 'I'm begging you. Levi. Rosedale. Maddie. You're always saying you want to help me, so now you can. I *need* a reason to live, because God knows I feel like I can't find one. So please. Help me so I can help them.'

A pause.

A silence.

A stillness.

Then with her voice cracking, Maddie said, 'I'm in. And not just for me, for those kids.'

Levi stood up. Gave a big, firm, loving hug to Cooper and with a smile full of pain he spoke quietly, 'I'm in too because there's no way I'm going to lose you on my watch. And besides, if anything did happen to you, I couldn't take Dorothy's nagging.'

Rosedale picked up his cowboy hat. Placed it firmly on his head. Walked towards the door. Stopped. Turned. 'I'm in, but Thomas, you do anything which jeopardizes our safety and you won't have to worry about finding a reason to live, because I'll kill you myself.'

65

Nh5 Ke6

'Any luck, Mads?'

Cooper, wired and tired and on edge, felt the blister packet of OxyContin in the front pocket of his faded jeans. He pushed away the thought of making Maddie, Rosedale and Levi complicit in his struggle. Intentionally handing them the sign which read in bold, bright letters, *Enabler*.

Yes, it was true that he couldn't do without the daily, unregulated dose of OxyContin. But it was also true that medicating himself would now be a lot easier. Not hiding. Not lying. And maybe now not even trying to give it up.

With that thought making him feel even worse than he did already, and wanting but struggling to concentrate on what Maddie was saying, Cooper said, 'Can you repeat that please.'

Maddie was looking at several computer displays in front of her, all with black screens and thousands of green text codes running down at blinks per second. She smiled. 'Sure... On the USB key you took from the ship, they haven't used a standard commercial encryption software. I hoped they would, but didn't really hold out much hope. Anyway, this makes it slightly precarious to work on. My worry is if they may've programmed a set number of tries before the information is deleted and the device wipes itself. Neither can I download the information to our computer and then decrypt it. When it's encrypted like this you can't touch any of the information.'

'I'm guessing you don't want to try to take it to a lab. I know a few guys who are really trustworthy. And fantastic at this stuff. Supreme ninja badasses.'

Maddie turned to look at Cooper for the first time. Her heart melted for the pain screwed up and tightly set on his face. She knew he was fighting an unseen battle, but she also knew she could only get so close, otherwise she'd start drowning too, pulled in while reaching out her hand to help him. 'I really want to say yes, because this has been driving me nuts, but I think the sensitivity on this whole case is something we have to be careful with. What do you reckon? Think I'm being over cautious?'

Squeezing the bridge of his nose, stopping the burn from his headache, Cooper replied, 'No. I'm with you on that. Trust nobody... But now what?'

'Well, I've done some coding, as well as ported and complied, and I'm trying to exploit a vulnerability. I'm hoping that it's just the password which is locked in an encrypted vault rather than the whole information on the USB.'

'Is that what you're doing now?'

'Yep. Trying to. If you look at this computer, I'm running

a program I made to try to undo the cipher text. Now it's just a question of waiting... And waiting.' She stopped and smiled. Gave a small laugh. Then said, quietly, 'I know we're not together, Tom, but if anything happened to you, I don't know what I'd do. You hear me?'

'I hear you, baby, and maybe I don't say it enough, or didn't say it enough, but you know I love you –'

Before Cooper could say anything else, his face lit up. A grin. A wink as he watched the computer over Maddie's shoulder go from black screen and green text, to flash an access denied bypass screen, before loading up into the USB's folder option.

He grabbed Maddie. Hugged her tight. Planted a big kiss. 'Have I ever told you how brilliant you are?'

At which point, Rosedale walked in. Walked straight back out. Maddie looked at Cooper, then at the empty entrance to the office. She unlocked herself from Cooper's embrace and said, 'Sorry.'

Cooper shrugged. Flat tone. Flat look. 'There's nothing to be sorry about. Hey, we're all adults. We've all got our lives to live.'

With a nod, Maddie ran out. Called down the corridor. 'Rosedale... Stop. Wait!'

Rosedale, not one for showing sentiment, nor one used to feeling anything like tender emotions, after so long in the clandestine unit of the CIA, tipped his cowboy hat.

'Sugar, it's okay. I get it.'

She walked up to him. Looked up at him. Shook her head. 'No, you don't. We were just happy because I managed to get into the USB file.'

Rosedale turned his head, a look of relief creeping over his face. 'No kidding?'

She reached out her hand and smiled. 'No kidding... Come on. Let's go and see what's on there.'

66

Ng3 Kf6

'Is Granger going to be a problem?'

Standing by the computers, Maddie answered absent-mindedly as she stared at the screen.

'I don't think we have to worry about Granger, Tom. He's locked himself away in his office for the rest of the day... Have you got any clues what it might be? It's the only file on the flash drive. It doesn't make any sense to me.'

Cooper walked up to the extra-large computer screen. He looked at the seemingly random abstract shapes. There were no words, just outlines of what reminded him of a geometry math class back in middle school. 'If I didn't know better I'd say this was encrypted too.'

'You know, I can't help but feel disappointed. I was hoping that we'd find something solid. Confirming our suspicions. Or at least pointing us in the right direction.'

Lighting a cigar, Rosedale continued to study the screen in silence. Memorising the pattern of shapes and outlines. Looking to see if there was a mirroring theme. Looking to see if he could work out any mathematical formula behind it. 'You're not the only one, honey. I can't even begin to guess. So now I suppose there's nothing else for it. We go to Turkey... along with Billy Hayes here.'

67

Kg4 Ra1

Inside the air was as thick as it had been before, and the smoke and the aroma of alcohol, mixed with the sizzling meats on the grill mangal cooking over a charcoal fire, smelt just the same. And the chattering voices rose up just as high. Serenading the night just as loud. And in the corner, a dark-haired, black-bearded man with a wind-leathered face, sat just as hunched as he had before. Only this time the fear in his eyes was much greater than it had been.

'I told you I'd be back. Now it's down to you. We can do this the hard way, where I drag you out like before, or we can do it the easy way where you walk out yourself. And as you can see, this time I brought my friends along. You remember them, don't you?'

Rosedale tipped his hat.

'Well? Which is it going to be? And don't bother saying *please*, you know how much I hate that.'

Without bothering to open his mouth, the fishing captain scraped back his chair. Stood up. Following the Onyx team into the night.

68

Bd5 Ra5

The lapping waves hit the side of the anchored fishing boat with a rhythmic sound. And the moonlit Turkish night only served to emphasize the serenity of the dark. An explosion of stars decorated the sky, and the warmth of the night gave a false sense of ease.

'Tom, come here.'

Standing on deck at the stern, Maddie gestured to Cooper. Spoke in a whisper as she looked at the distant land lights. Bringing her hand out of her pocket she stretched it out. 'There you go. Just one.'

Cooper's face crumpled up. Part humiliation. Part annoyance. And taking the pill from Maddie's hand, he said, 'You don't have to do this. I could sort it myself.'

'That was the deal, Tom.'

'You're not my nursemaid. I'm a grown man,' Cooper said, not unkindly.

'No I'm not and yes you are, but you're also an addict and we're here to do a job and there's no way I'm going to make this harder than it should be. This is about all of us and what's best.'

'Are you sure this way is the best way?'

'Listen to me. In less than ten minutes we're going to jump into that sea and swim to shore. The same shore where Ismet and his men are based. And what that might entail, none of us knows. So I may not be a doctor, but I know that each one of us has to be as vigilant and as sharp as we can. Which means you self-medicating isn't even an option.'

Cooper rubbed his face. He hissed a whisper. 'This is not okay, Maddie.'

'You're right it isn't. None of it is. Not you taking them. Not us taking them through customs with you.'

'Have you ever seen that movie, *One Flew Over the Cuckoo's Nest*?'

'You know I have.'

'Well, right now you remind me of Nurse Ratched.'

Maddie stepped forward. Looked up into Cooper's handsome face. 'Stop feeling sorry for yourself. This, right now, is not going to work.'

'What are you talking about?'

'I'm talking about you trying to make me back down by saying all this stuff so eventually it becomes too much for me, and then because I've thrown in the towel you can do what you like and take as many OxyContin as you want. But I've got news for you, Tom, you've picked the wrong person if you think your behavior is going to affect what's best for us and for you. I've been married to you for a good while now, so I know all your ways. I also know how an addict behaves. So it basically comes down to this: it's this way. My way. Or we turn back home. Right now. It's your call.'

'Look, Maddie, I'm not trying to be a jerk, all I'm saying is one pill isn't always enough.'

'I said it's your call. But just so you know, I'm going on the correct dosage, not what *you* want it to be.'

'You can't just drop the amount like that. It's an opioid, for God's sake. I've developed a tolerance to it and if I don't get enough I'll start withdrawing. Is that what you want?'

A blink of hesitation. Uncertainty. Then Maddie said, 'I don't want any of this. And as for the dose, I'm sure it'll be fine. You've got Xanax as well. You can take four of those a day and we can reassess. And besides, we're not planning to be here longer than forty-eight hours... So come on, Tom. What's it going to be?'

Pushing his face to touch noses, Cooper said, 'I love you, but you are going to be the death of me, woman... And as for what's it going to be, you haven't really given me a choice have you, Maddison?'

'Glad you understand that. That's exactly what I wanted to hear... Hey, Rosedale.'

Cooper swallowed the pill.

Raged inside.

Rosedale asked, 'How's the patient?'

Raged outside. 'I'd be a hell of a lot better without your comments. We're here to do a job. Anything else, I don't want to know.'

'Well, Rosedale can only apologize if he's offended you in some way.'

Cooper gritted his teeth. Spoke through them. 'What is it

with you, Turkey and speaking in the third person? What's the connection? Actually, no. No, I don't want to know. I don't care. Just leave me alone.'

Wanting to get back to some form of reason, Maddie, still talking in a whisper – aware how voices travelled across the silence of the water – turned to Rosedale. 'Do you think we can trust the captain not to sail off? Taking into account the last time.'

Rosedale shook his head. 'Nope. No way. The minute we swim for shore he'll be gone.' He held up a rope. 'So that's why I've just tied him up. Can't say he was taken with the idea. But he won't be going anywhere… You okay, Maddie?'

'Yeah, you?'

'You can stay here, you know?'

'I was about to say the same thing to you.'

Rosedale shrugged. 'Touché.'

'I'm being serious, Rosedale, when was the last time you swam more than fifty meters?'

'Maddison, you and Thomas here may be the water babies but that doesn't mean I'm staying on this boat whilst you two go and get yourselves into trouble. We stick together. The whole thing's crazy but for better…' He paused, looked at Cooper and went on, '…or for worse, we're a team. No matter what, we stick together… Are you really sure about this, Thomas?'

'No, but it's the only way I can think of. And at least this way, swimming to and around the shoreline, we'll be unseen.' Cooper said.

Rosedale looked out towards the shoreline. 'It's a hell of a swim. What do you estimate?'

'Three miles, maybe. Could be less. And it'll be relatively easy because there isn't a pull tide in the Med.'

'Three miles. You kidding?'

Cooper couldn't help but smile. 'Come on, Rosedale, that's half what he'd swim in basic training in the SEALs.'

'And when we get there, Thomas. Don't forget Ismet and his guys are heavily armed. American military grade weapons. So we know we're not playing games here. Fully automatic. Not semi. And all we've got are Turkish combat knives.'

'That's not our objective. We're not taking them on, Rosedale.'

'Sure we're not. Until we have to take them on, that is.'

Cooper tried to sound reassuring. 'Even if we were armed, we'd be outnumbered. We wouldn't stand a chance. Let's just do a reconnaissance and get out of there. See if we can find anything which is linked to the kids. It's three in the morning, so I doubt there'll be too many people about.'

Rosedale looked at Cooper ruefully. 'Thomas, it doesn't take many people. It takes one man, one gun, and a bullet.'

69

Bf3 Ra1

Heavy. So heavy. The weight of the water pushing him down as the cold hit. Striking hard into his muscles. The goose fat they'd slathered on didn't help. Didn't work. As the bracing temperatures of the water began to cramp his body.

And the salt sea lapped and ebbed and flowed and rushed in and out of his mouth. Ahead he could see Maddie and Rosedale looking like they'd never left the Navy. Expertly executing the SEAL combat side stroke. Efficient. Low energy. Performing without tiring. Without faltering. Reducing the body profile in the water, making the swimmer less visible to the enemy.

Top arm pull.

Bottom arm pull.

Breathe.

Kick.

Glide.

And repeat. But it wasn't any use to him. Not now. The pain was already burning through his legs. The water already dragging him down, wanting him to go under. Pushing through each stroke was like pushing through a quagmire.

And he could hear the sound of his own breathing.

Panting.

Struggling.

Fighting to keep going.

And the dark sea below like a void. As if he was walking on air and any minute now he was going to fall. Nothing underneath to stop him going under. Going down… Like Ellie.

Diving underneath the surface to fill his ears with the sound of the rushing water, with *anything* other than the sound of his own thoughts.

Holding his breath, he opened his eyes. Wide. Seeing nothing but nothingness. A dark isolation of space. Like looking into a black hole. And cold. So cold. Then, he saw something.

Coming towards him.

Floating towards him.

Nearer.

Nearer.

Until he realized what it was. And in the deep he opened his mouth and cried out, filling his lungs with ocean and expelling his breath as he flailed and lashed and splashed, trying to get away from the horror of what it was… From the horror of Ellie. Her body. Floating. Deformed. Grotesque. Twisted. Taunting features. Whispering. Calling his name. Louder and louder through the chamber of the waters. Passing underneath him. Staring up at him.

Looking up at him with eyes as black as the pit of hell.

Upwards. Rotating his hands. Kicking his legs to get back up to the surface to the silence of the night... Cooper trod water. Whipping his head around. Whipping his body around in a three sixty to look into the abyss of the night... Nothing. Only the darkness. Only his breathing. In. And out. In. And out. His head playing tricks. Playing games. The kind of games he wanted to stop. To stop and leave him alone. *Just leave him alone.*

It wasn't real. None of it. That's what he had to keep saying. *It wasn't real.* This was. The here and now. This was what was real. Here, in the cold Mediterranean Sea. But he couldn't feel it. He couldn't feel now. All he could feel was her. Haunting him. His guilt haunting him.

Sliding the combat knife out of his ankle strap as he trod water, he held the leather-bound handle. His hands shaking from the cold. Trembling. And turning the knife towards himself, he plunged the sharp blade in and quickly out of his hip. Feeling the shock of the pain. The burn. Finally feeling the here. The now.

And then the ease. Spreading over his thoughts. Spreading over his body. A relief. A respite from feeling something other than nothing. Nothing other than her.

Spreading open his arms, Cooper put his head in the water. Let his legs fall heavy. Stopped treading water. And let the ocean begin to pull him down.

Down.

Down.

Down.

Down.

Rushing. Bubbling water sped down past him as he passed

up and out, being brought, being dragged up. High above the surface.

'What the hell are you doing? Thomas, what are you doing?'

A hand on each arm. Maddie and Rosedale on each side of him. Treading water as they stared at him. And getting his breath. Spitting out the sea, Cooper stared back. Feeling the warmth of his blood trickling out of the wound in his hip, in stark contrast to the icy cold of the sea.

Breathing. Panting. His words staggered. 'I got cramp... Jesus... Sorry...I don't know what happened. One minute I'm swimming. The next my legs just spasmed up on me.'

In the moonlight, Cooper could see Maddie's face. Concern. Doubt. 'Tom, are you sure you can do this? Rosedale and I can handle it.'

'Of course I can. It was only cramp. Look, we haven't got far to go. I'll be fine. The cold must've just gotten into my muscles. Come on. It's not good to be here, the moon's bright and we could be seen.'

With a nod to both of them, Cooper glided his body, streaming it through the water. Heading towards the craggy shore.

*

Squatting down low on the large, aslant rocks of the shore, Maddie looked at Cooper, trying to put the thought *this was a bad mistake*, out of her mind.

'Okay, look, I actually think rather than trekking around the shoreline, it'll probably be best to get back in the water

338

and swim round. It'll be quicker for a start. We could get to the private harbor in less than five minutes. Rosedale, what do you think? Jesus, Tom, you're bleeding.'

Cooper gave a tight smile. Touching his hip where the blood showed through his lightweight khaki pants. 'Oh, it's nothing. When we were coming up to these rocks, I caught myself on a sharp corner. Just a nick.'

Maddie nodded, then turned back to Rosedale. 'Any thoughts?'

Rosedale looked at Cooper. 'Oh I've got plenty, but none you probably want to hear right now. But as for what the best thing to do is, I think you're right. If we were to hike round this cape there's a higher likelihood of being seen. And as much as I like to keep my feet on dry land, hell, honey, now they're wet, what's another five minutes?'

Maddie smiled as she spoke, relieved to have Rosedale countering the intensity of Cooper.

'I could see the stealth ship docked in the harbor, so if we head for there and swim wide, if you remember there's that steep hillside on portside we could climb up, and hopefully be hidden by the ship. It's risky but I think it's doable. And like you say, Rosedale, it shouldn't take us more than five minutes to get there. But I think vigilance is key.'

Wiping off the dripping, trickling water which ran down his face from his soaking hair, Rosedale said, 'I don't suppose now is the best time to say this, but I've got a bad feeling… A really bad one.'

70

Kf4 Ke6

Wet and cold, the three of them lay on their stomachs, high on the hillside in the coarse sandy earth, looking down towards the bay and the stealth ship. The aroma of the olive and lemon trees drifted down from above them.

Taking off her head-mounted night vision binoculars, Maddie passed them to Cooper.

'That's not the same ship as we went on. That must be the other one Ismet was talking about.'

Rosedale spoke in a hushed voice. 'In a couple of hours the sun will begin to rise, so I vote we go across the top to directly opposite Ismet's office. Then from there, as long as we get a clear visual we'll head down. Have a look about. What do you say?'

Cooper nodded.

Maddie nodded. 'You're on. Let's go and see what that bastard's up to.'

Running. Ducking. Hiding behind trees. The three of them worked in sync in the darkness of the night. Keeping down. Keeping watch. Keeping each other in their eye line.

Maddie nodded to Rosedale and ran and crouched. Lying low. Pausing. Waiting to get a clear visual with Cooper a few feet in front holding up his fingers. Counting them down. Pointing to the next spot they'd run to. Stop at. Vigilant and precise. With Rosedale at the back, heading forward but running backwards, making sure no-one could come up from behind. Jumping across dry branches and bracken and brushwood. Avoiding any sound. Communicating with silent signals. Reading each other's movements.

Behind the twisted, gnarled olive tree, hearts beating, adrenalin rushing, Cooper said, 'Okay, I got a clear visual of Ismet's office. An all clear. You second that, Rosedale?'

'Second that… Maddie?'

She took in the short slope leading down to the white building which jutted out over the sea. It couldn't be more than one hundred and fifty meters but it was a hundred and fifty meters of nowhere-to-hide hillside. No trees. No bushes. Just them exposed. 'Yeah, clear visual… So now we head down. Agreed?'

Rosedale nodded. 'Okay. Five…' His voice trailed off as his fingers took over. Counting down until he got to: '*Go! Go! Go!*'

Bounding down the hillside with speed. The three of them chased their legs as the slope of the hill ran them faster. Quicker. Heading them downward to Ismet's office.

'Get down!' Rosedale bellowed as he heard the undisputable whiz and thud of a passing bullet as it hit the soft earth.

Within a blink of a second, all three of them had dropped to the ground. Breathing hard, pushing and flattening their bodies as low as possible, and with eyes darting round, Maddie shouted over the sounds of the bullets.

'We got to get out of here, where's it coming from?'

Not wanting to put his head higher than it was already, Rosedale rolled over on his back and tipped up his chin, surveying the landscape upside down and using the back of his heels to rotate himself to get a full three-sixty view.

'Shit! Shit! Over there. Look on top of the hill. There's an autonomous gun turret. Wherever the radar is, it must've detected us and sent across its signal to make it start firing. It'll be locked on to us now, and won't stop tracking until somebody... Holy shit!' A bullet grazed past Rosedale's fingers. 'Move it! Go! Go!'

Assuming the military low crawl, they began to speed backwards using their arms and elbows hoping to get back up onto the hillside.

Cooper gave a quick glance round. 'Jesus, no, stop. Behind you, Rosedale!'

More bullets began to blaze down, firing from a different but identical robot sentry gun, preventing them from heading for cover. 'We can't go back. Go forward... To the side. Maddie, move it. Rosedale... '

Cooper continued to shout but stopped as stadium-size floodlights on the surrounding hills switched on, lighting up the area. Lighting up them.

Maddie, with her cheek pressed into the sandy earth, yelled out orders.

'Roll. Roll. That's our only chance, and we gotta get out of here before Ismet's men come. Head for his office, that'll probably be the safest place, the guns are probably programmed not to fire in that area. Now let's go! Go!'

Following the others, and through the automatic gun fire,

Cooper pushed forward. Threw himself at speed into a log roll. Chin tucked and arms clutched and wrapped around his chest, momentum sending his body spinning and tumbling and turning down and down the dry shingle incline, taking with him a cloud of dust.

They thudded.

They pounded.

They came to an abrupt halt as they crashed into the six feet high white wall which acted as a barrier and ran around the outer edge of the compound. Quickly they scrambled over and ducking down and catching his breath, Cooper smiled and panted and whispered at Maddie and Rosedale. 'Everyone OK?'

They nodded. Gave a thumbs up, saving their breath and restoring their energy.

Across from where they were, roughly forty meters away and shrouded in the looming shadow of the stealth ship, was Ismet's office. Two storey. Flat roofed. Whitewashed building which stretched towards and hung out over the water's edge, with a set of outside stairs leading up to a door, which Cooper remembered opened into the main office area.

Maddie, crouching opposite Rosedale, noticed shadows moving across his face. She whipped round. Braved a glance over the wall to see what was coming. And right then, right there, her worst fears were realized.

On the surrounding hill tops she could see the headlights of four... maybe five SUVs, appearing over the headland. 'Time to get out of here.'

Cooper said, 'How long have we got?'

Maddie glanced at Rosedale, then back to Cooper. 'Five

minutes, maybe… *maybe*. Those guys will be responding to their defense security system being triggered. Right now they'll be getting the data from the linked computer system, trying to find out if it was something like wild animals, or something like us, which set it off. They don't know we're down here, *yet*, but it won't take them long to work it out.'

The SUVs sat on the top of the hill, like a pack of lions waiting to race down on their prey. 'So what's the plan?' Cooper said.

Quickly noting the time on his watch, Rosedale caught hold of Maddie's arm. Held his grip. Leaned in close to her ear. 'We need go now, then. There's no way round the East side of the building. West side negative. And the roof is so exposed we'd be like target practice once those guys come down. The only way out is to try to get through Ismet's office somehow.'

Maddie nodded. Turned towards Cooper. 'Did you copy that?'

Cooper nodded. 'Affirmative.'

'Ready?' he asked Maddie.

'Ready.'

Rosedale followed the headlights of the SUVs as they swung round from their vantage point on the hilltop before disappearing from view. Which could only mean one thing.

'They're coming. Go! Go! Go!'

Running along the shadow of the wall they made their way to and up the steps of the building to the door.

Maddie pointed. 'Shit, Tom, look. We've got no chance.'

A steel door stood between them and Ismet's office. And Cooper's gaze searched. Looking. Hoping for a solution.

His eyes rested near the top edge of the building. He spoke hurriedly. 'Rosedale's right, we can't go onto the roof. It's too lit up, but you see that cable running along the edge of the roof? We can climb up. Shimmy along it and once we get to the window over there, we can all drop our weight through the frame at the same time and that way, when the window breaks, it'll shatter evenly, which means there'll be less chance of one of us getting badly hurt. And at the other side of Ismet's office there's another window which hangs out over the water. We can dive into the sea from there.'

'Then hell, Thomas, what are we waiting for?' Rosedale said.

Leaning against the security door and holding out his clasped hands as a step, Rosedale expertly lifted as Cooper expertly walked up him like a ladder. Standing on his shoulders. Stretched up. Hands gripping the edge of the flat roof, to hands gripping the large electricity cable bolted to the wall. And hanging his weight from it he moved along. Slid along. Edging himself towards the window.

With Maddie quickly following Cooper, Rosedale jumped onto the stair's wrought iron hand rail. Precariously balancing on tiptoes to stretch and reach his six-foot-five frame towards the wire, all too aware of the thirty-foot drop below him.

As the three of them hung precariously from the cable, knowing time was their enemy, Cooper shouted his orders. 'On a count of three, we drop all together and kick this son-of-a-bitch in.'

Heaving themselves up by their hands. Arching, their backs, they inched their feet upwards. Placed them firmly between their shoulder-width-apart arms, until they looked like three swimmers poised for the start of a backstroke race. Cooper counted down. 'Three. Two...' And as the SUVs flooded the compound with dipping and bobbing headlights, Cooper said, 'One!'

The three of them crashed through the window, pushing the whole frame off its mountings, landing it and themselves in the stairwell that Ismet had led Cooper to on their first visit.

Scrabbling up, and checking no-one was hurt save a few cuts, Cooper spoke hurriedly.

'Come on, it's this way.'

Two flights of stairs.

One hallway.

A half-landing.

And a hell of a lot of panting led them into Ismet's open-plan office.

Rosedale's eyes darted around as they headed for the large window.

'Help me pick this up,' said Cooper. 'We can run at the window with it, throw the whole thing through. That way it'll be easier to dive through.'

Rosedale took hold of his side of the wooden desk. Looked up at Cooper. Saw the beads of sweat running down his temples. Waited for the nod.

'Ready, Rosedale?' Cooper whispered.

'Always.'

Making it look effortless, the men picked up and swung high and threw hard and crashed the desk through the window and out into the sea.

'Maddie, you go first. Then I'll follow. Rosedale you go last.'

Without a word, Maddie stepped up. Looked around. Checked down. Then dived out expertly into the darkness, followed immediately by Cooper.

And as Rosedale began to step up onto the ledge, he stopped. Suddenly. Stepped down quickly. Walked towards the shadowy picture on the office wall. He stared at the familiar shapes. Recognizing the jutting irregular lines. The number of corners. The vertex. The acute and obtuse angles, precisely as it was in his memory. Precisely what'd been on the USB key Maddie had decrypted. The only difference with this image were the new added details. New lines filled in. And new digital overlay. But there was no mistake. No mistake what he was looking at... A map. That's what it was on the file. *A map*. The only question now, was *where?* Where the hell was this place?

A moment later, Rosedale dived in, hitting the sea without a sound.

71

Nc5 Kd6

Out in the bay the three of them bobbed. Slowly treading water in the cold sea. Needing to move so the chill didn't begin to take over, but needing to stay as quiet as they could. They kept low. Submerging as much of their bodies as possible in the dark of the water. Their nostrils skimming the surface and their faces painted with two color camo paint, and the only thing that shone bright was the whites of their eyes.

Catching a few moments rest, and as Cooper's muscles began to give out the warning signs of cramp, he knew there was a hell of a swim back until they could do anything like relax. He was tense. And not just because of the cold. But hell, that didn't help. He was tense because of the wait. The watching. Assessing. Wondering whether anyone had realized yet the windows of the office had been smashed out. And waiting for Ismet's men to come after them, hunting them down like rats in a river.

The darkness was soon going to give way to daylight, and they had to decide when it was the right time to head back to the fishing boat. By Cooper's calculations, they probably had no more than an hour before the Turkish sun began to rise. The problem was there was suddenly so much activity in the small private port. There were the SUVs. Ismet's men. And now a large truck had just arrived, parking carefully up by the stealth ship.

In the quietness, with only the sound of the lapping sea, Maddie whispered, 'Oh my God, Rosedale, Tom, look!'

Stepping down off the back of the truck, thirty, forty, perhaps fifty small, bewildered and dirty-looking children were herded into the floodlit area. Their faces held fear. And to her horror, Maddie realized that none of them looked over twelve years old. So thin. So skinny. So gaunt... So lost.

'What are we going to do?' she said.

Rosedale spoke more to himself. His words full of pain. 'Jesus, I don't think there is anything we can do... Look.'

They watched the children being shunted and pushed and shoved and thrust towards the stealth ship. A little boy fell over and burst into tears, before he was roughly dragged back up. Maddie turned away. 'I can't watch this.'

But almost immediately she heard Rosedale say, 'Maddie, *this* you have to see.'

She turned and watched a tall man with a familiar-looking face. Bearded. Dressed in a simple long shirt over simple white pants and a black and white ghutra tied loosely. He walked towards the edge of the harbor. Feet away. Almost looked at right them. Causing the trio to sink even lower in the sea. Breathing small bubbles onto the surface as their noses immersed into the water.

The man turned his head. Giving them a clear profile view

of his face. Giving them the confirmation. Giving them no doubt as to who it was.

But a sudden shout had the man at the harbor's edge turning round to watch one of Ismet's men come hurtling down the stairs from the office block. Signaling and gesturing and waving and beckoning.

Cooper spoke urgently. 'They must've seen the broken window. Come on, we gotta take our chances... Move it.'

And to the sounds of shouts and cries and running feet, and the skidding and screeching of tires, Maddie, Rosedale and Cooper sunk silently into the deep.

72

Nge4 Ke7

Back on the fishing boat, with the pink of the sun above the Turkish mountains, the three of them sat on the deck getting their breath and energy back, trying to get some clarity on the events of the night.

'I know what it is. On the USB file,' Rosedale said.

With a mix of intrigue and tiredness, Maddie looked at him quizzically. 'How? But more importantly, what is it?'

'The shapes we were looking at were actually the first overlay of a map. Or rather, an image of a particular area.'

'When did you find this out?'

'On Ismet's wall there was exactly the same image, no doubt in my mind. Only difference was, on his image there were other digital layers stacked on top, which of course helped because it made it pretty damn obvious what it was. There wasn't any labeling on it to say where the place is, but I reckon once we get back we could take it to a cartographer. There's a great guy I've worked with many times over the years, when I was in the CIA. When documents came into our possession which looked anything like an area of land

and we couldn't work it out, he'd be the guy to tell us. He'd do his thing, and before you knew it you'd have everything from the coordinates to the population density of the area. He's retired now, but I'm sure that won't be a problem. I'll get on to it the moment we get back.'

Trying to be discreet in passing Cooper one of his pills, but aware it was a pretty pointless exercise, Maddie stared intently at Rosedale. 'And now the big question is about who we saw. Or who we thought we saw. Maybe we got it wrong.'

Rosedale, trying to be just as discreet in giving Cooper a disapproving look, pulled a face whilst massaging the muscle in his calf. 'Got it wrong, how?'

'Maybe just a massive similarity.'

'Come on, Maddie, we all know we're not wrong.'

'I know it looks that way, and I'm not naïve, I get what goes on, but I can't imagine...'

His words laced with acrimony, Cooper cut in. 'That our President would allow it?'

Maddie nodded. 'Exactly.'

Contempt was scrawled all over Rosedale's face. 'Well as we know only too well, what they tell the people and what really goes on are two different things entirely. And who we just saw, sugar, is a case in point... There's no doubt about it, that man was Abdul-Aziz Bin Hamad.'

73

Ke5 Rf1

Sitting with her legs dangling in the pool outside her sprawling single family home, north-east of Desert Mountain, Maddie sat next to Rosedale, who seemed to be enjoying drinking the pretend iced tea out of the invisible teacup which Cora had given him a few minutes ago.

Maddie said, 'She's gone now, so you don't have to do that anymore.'

'But I haven't finished.'

'Sometimes I wonder about you, Rosedale.'

He shrugged. 'Why? Because I was thirsty?'

'Shut up, Rosedale, and tell me what happened.'

Carefully putting his cup down, Rosedale wiped his mouth. 'Firstly, I've spoken to the cartographer about the USB. He says he'll have a look at it but he can't make any promises. I also made the calls to the people that I needed to, and what came back is *not* what I thought. None of the guys I spoke to in central intelligence know anything. In actual fact, the resounding response was Abdul-Aziz bin Hamad is *still* locked up at a secret intelligence base. And, get this, one of them I spoke to actually saw Bin Hamad two weeks ago.'

'Where?'

'At the intelligence detention center. Locked up as he should be. He flew there from the military base just outside Tampa to question another detainee.'

'So is Bin Hamad being kept in south-eastern Cuba?'

'Yeah, though it's a place they try not to talk about.'

'Okay, so let me get this straight. Within the last two weeks Bin Hamad's been released, and you're saying the guys you know don't seem to know anything about it?'

'Right.'

'But would they know otherwise?'

Picking up and drinking the iced-tea again, to Maddie's distraction and befuddlement, Rosedale nodded. 'Absolutely. Not only can I trust them, but they're also on the front line so these people, above anybody else, should and would know.'

'But that doesn't make sense. Because obviously they *don't* know what they *should* know, because we saw him.'

'Exactly.'

'Did you tell them why you were asking?'

'No, but I did get a bit more information. Apparently, beyond the usual tight security for suspected terrorists, Bin Hamad had HS – heightened security. Which means he's locked – or *was* locked – in a cell where he has no human contact. His food gets pushed through a hatch. And so does the bowl of water he has to wash in, which also doubles up as a john. And that's it, any communication is done via video call. No-one can let him out. It's a coded lock. And it takes two people to release him.'

'Is that usual?'

'For prisoners like him it is. Back when I was in the CIA, there were so many deals and so much swapping of prisoners, nobody knew if a particular detainee from a black site had been shipped to another site, or had been freed in some kind of deal. No-one questioned it when a high-ranking central intelligence officer came to speak to a prisoner, or transfer him out with them. Top secret was and is top secret. Period. Deals were always being made. No deals means no moving forward on human intel and no preventing of terrorism. That's just how it works in the clandestine and CTC division.'

'And how does that fit in with having the high security?'

'With guys like Khalid Sheikh Mohammed, the principal architect for 9/11, or Abdul-Aziz bin Hamad, then you have HS because they're the ones who've been privy to the planning, and have given the orders to execute massive terror attacks. Therefore these guys can supply vital information, so they can't be accessible to anybody and everybody... Only the real select few.'

Maddie trailed her hand into the water. 'And the public never knew what was going on.'

'Everything was so covert, which often reflected the government administration at the time, with some being more covert than others. But a lot of stuff was off record.'

'Which it still is now?'

'Yeah, a hell of a lot, from drone strikes to weapons deals, even proxy wars. But all this makes it difficult for the field agent, who's putting their life on the line but doesn't actually know what's going on either. You couldn't trust anybody, and you couldn't tell anybody that you didn't trust anybody, in case *they* ended up not trusting you. Paranoia was something you had for breakfast. Everything was top secret and no-one knew what was supposed to be and what wasn't.'

'So where does that leave us?'

'It leaves us with the bit I haven't told you. Like I say, to get Bin Hamad out of there, well, it needs two people, because they have two different parts of the code. One of the people is always the head of the CTC, or in this case the acting head, Chuck Harrison. A low-down bastard if there ever was one. I knew him when he was station head in Khartoum. I was only there for three months but, Miss Maddison, believe me when I say that was long enough. The other person who holds the code is never known to anybody, apart from the head of CTC, as well as the Commander-in-Chief and a couple of other people in office.'

Maddie looked at Rosedale with her warm, big brown eyes. 'So how does any of this help?'

'Because, as someone once said, there are always the *known unknowns.*'

Not wanting to sound irritated, but sounding irritated nonetheless, Maddie said, 'Rosedale, please, just tell me.'

'I know who the other person is. His name is Senator Michael Rubins. And tomorrow we're going to pay him a visit.'

74

Bg4 Rg1

'Sorry I'm late, guys. It took longer than I thought.' Cooper hurried towards Rosedale and Maddie, both standing by the rental car, both looking like they were on the moderate side of pissed with him.

Rosedale asked, 'Where the hell have you been?'

On the extreme side of pissed.

Cooper replied, 'I had to get these.' He held up a white envelope in front of him.

'Problem?'

Pushing up the brim of his cowboy hat and wiping the sweat which trickled and zigzagged down the back of his neck, right to the base of his spine, Rosedale stared intensely, squinting his eyes in the Alabama sun. 'As long as that's the only reason why you're late.'

'I'm not hiding anything, alright? You know everything there is to know.'

Rosedale continued to stare at Cooper. 'You see, whenever a man says those words, I can bet my Goddamn life on the fact there's a hell of a lot more to know... Shall we?' He gestured his hand towards the senator's imposing home security gates.

Maddie gave a small smile to Cooper as they walked behind Rosedale. 'I can't help thinking about those kids we saw. I haven't slept properly since. I can't make any sense of it. Have you had any thoughts?'

Cricking the tension out of his neck, and not wanting to tell her that so much of his thoughts were taken up by Ellie, he could barely function, he said, 'Not ones which are going to help anybody, which is the worst thing about this damn thing. Right from the beginning there's been nobody to tell. Nobody to turn to for help because we just don't know enough, so the pressure's on us to find all the answers when we don't know what *questions* we should even be asking. It just feels so overwhelming, honey. And I feel so tired. I'm the same as you. Keep seeing those kids washed up on the shore in their yellow tops... Who were they, Maddie? How can they have no one? Dying at such a young age but having no-one to care. And then the other kids being marched onto the ship like they were soldiers. They reminded me of those pictures taken in the war of the Jewish children on a death march, walking towards the gas chambers. Jesus, I thought I'd seen a lot, but their eyes were so sunken, full of nothing but fear, and all we did was watch.'

Maddie stopped suddenly. 'What did you just say?'

'When?'

'Just now. Repeat what you said.'

'All we did was watch.'

'No, before that.'

Cooper quickly thought and frowned. 'About the kids being marched on the ships like they were soldiers?'

Maddie's eyes lit up. 'Yes! I think that's it. It's gotta be.'

Joining them, Rosedale said, 'What am I missing out on?'

'The fact that Tom's a genius.'

Finishing off his cigar, Rosedale nodded slowly. Felt the hot laze of the Alabama day. Glanced at the Senator's white, Georgian colonial mansion, festooned with a multitude of pale, yellow roses climbing and exploding up the front of the building. 'Yep, I sure as hell missed the memo on that one.'

'But he is,' Maddie said.

Cooper winked. 'An unintentional one, and I hate to admit it, but how, exactly?'

Maddie grinned at him.

'You said soldiers. The kids. That's what they must be for. They're using the kids for child soldiers... No, don't look like that. Think about it. That's what Bin Hamad was known for. His training camps... Remember? He had all those training camps in Afghanistan. They were full of refugee children... If we hadn't seen him on the dock, I would've kept thinking that the kids were something to do with trafficking. But Bin Hamad isn't interested in that. That's not his style. He's all about war. About terror. And what better way than to train up kids who are vulnerable, but also dispensable... He's obviously taking them to a training camp somewhere.'

'I think you might be onto something, Maddison. It makes sense to me. What doesn't is why they've let him out to become active again,' Rosedale said.

Determination threaded through Cooper. 'Well, let's go and find out.'

As they headed for the Senator's house, Cooper pulled

on Rosedale's arm. Pulling him back. Allowing Maddie to walk ahead. Quietly he said, 'Rosedale, when this is all over, you and I need to have a conversation about you sleeping with my wife.'

75

Be6 Rel

Senator Michael Rubins drawled each word out. Nasalizing vowel sounds and protracting each word so much, and so slowly, that Cooper wondered if he was trying to stall for time somehow. Agitated by this unnecessary affectation, which had already stretched out the niceties of formality by an extra few minutes, he chewed on his lip and listened as Rubins spoke directly to Rosedale.

'When Jerry asked me to see you, I was more than happy to oblige. He tells me you two worked together in Islamabad. Though what he didn't tell me was *what* brings you here, Mr Young.' Rubins' smile, which was framed in his rotund face, was frozen and cloying.

'Call me Rosedale, Senator. But to answer your question, the simple fact is he didn't tell you because *I* didn't tell him.'

Pointing to the leather armchairs which were already facing his locally-sourced rosewood desk, Rubins said, 'Please, take a seat, this sounds intriguing.'

'I could call it many things, Senator, but *intriguing* wouldn't be the first word which came to mind,' Rosedale said.

'Excuse me? Have we got some kind of problem here?'

'I think, to use a cliché, we should cut to the chase, don't you, Senator?'

Rubins' coldness was in stark contrast to the heat of the Alabama day. 'I don't know who you think you are, *Mr Young*, nor what your difficulty is, but this isn't what I expected when Jerry asked me to open up not only my time, but also my house to you. I'm not sure how alienating me serves any purpose. But as you're here now, let's hear it. Let's cut to the chase.'

'I want to know about Abdul-Aziz Bin Hamad.'

Rubins shuffled the papers in front of him which didn't need shuffling. 'Okay folks, well, this meeting's over. Show yourselves out.'

Rosedale didn't move. 'Not until we have some answers.'

'You can have your answers, but down at the precinct, unless of course you leave now.'

'I'd put that phone down if I were you, Senator, unless of course you want the whole world knowing Bin Hamad's been released.'

In slow motion Rubins frowned at Rosedale, held the phone in mid-air and put it down gently on the cradle. 'What the hell are you talking about?'

'About the fact a well-known terrorist has been allowed to walk free and now it looks like he's active again,' said Maddie.

The Senator leant forward on his elbows and rested his chin on his hand and stared at Maddie with as much hostility as he could muster. 'I don't know what crazy idea you have in your heads, nor who put that crazy idea there.

But even if I could talk about Bin Hamad, it would be clear to any sane and rational citizen of this great country that the notion he's been released is beyond absurd. Y'all have lost your minds.'

Rosedale said, 'Don't play games with us. The problem you have, Senator, is I know different. *We* know different. I also know that you're the number two, along with Chuck Harrison – the person with the other part of the HS code.'

The Senator replayed picking up the phone. 'This is an outrage. I want you to get the hell out of here by the time I count to nine-one-one.'

Rosedale's long arm reached across and clicked off the call. 'Where were you on the seventeenth and eighteenth of this month?'

Rubins' face flushed. Affronted and incensed by this intrusion, and wiping the sweat from the back of his neck with his pink spotted handkerchief, Rubins retorted, 'I don't have to answer any of your Goddamn questions! Though I will tell you something, y'all are in a whole kind of trouble.'

With his deep Texan drawl matching that of the Senator's, Rosedale shook his head. 'Now, what happened to good ole fashioned Southern hospitality? But if you want us to get out of here, Senator, I'd just answer the question… Where were you?'

From left to right and right to left the Senator looked at the Onyx trio. Deciding he was defeated, he conceded and glanced at the digital calendar on his desk, before pointing at them.

'I want to put on record that the only reason I'm answering this is so you guys will head on out, but trust me when I say, I'll be speaking to Jerry about this, Rosedale.'

'Whatever you need to do Senator, just roll with it.'

Rubins cleared his throat, along with his attitude. 'Well, those days were a Friday and Saturday which means I was here... In fact, I know I was. So now I've answered your question... *get the hell out*!'

It was Cooper's turn to lean forward. 'That's what I thought you'd say and that's why I brought these.'

He waved the white envelope he'd been carrying in the air which annoyed and perplexed Rubins in the same measure, as he sat back on his extra wide leather chair. 'What are *these*?'

Cooper opened the envelope and threw the contents on the desk.

'*These*, Senator, prove you're lying.'

Glancing at Cooper, then down at the documents, Rubins began to flick through the three page print out. 'Where the hell did you get these?'

'Does it matter?' Cooper said.

'Oh it matters alright, and I don't know what game you're playing, but you'd better start talking.'

'That's our line, Senator... So how about you start again, and tell us exactly where you were on the seventeenth and eighteenth?'

'I've already told you.'

Cooper pulled a face. 'You did, but these bank statements say different. According to them, on the seventeenth, you withdrew five thousand dollars from the Bank of America in Citrus Park, Florida, and again on the eighteenth in Port Charlotte. That's hardly here in Cottonwood, is it?'

The Senator stretched his weighty body across the desk, his stomach knocking over a pen pot as he grabbed the print out from Cooper. 'Show me that.'

'It's right there in black and white. Look. I even high-lighted it for you.'

Rubins glared at Cooper. 'That's impossible.'

'Not according to your bank it isn't.'

'Bullshit. I haven't been to Florida. Well, not for a while anyway. And I know I haven't gone through my financial particulars for some time with my accountant, but this is clearly wrong. So wherever you managed to acquire my statement from – and God knows where it was and what you had to do to get it – it's obvious my details have been mixed up with somebody else's.'

'You'll have to do better than that, Senator. There's no mistake on our side. I'd say the mistake is all yours by not admitting to being in Florida when the evidence is right there on the page,' Maddie said.

'Listen to me, lady, and listen good. I don't like your insinu-ation that somehow *I'm* deceitful. when *you* were the one who walked into my house under false pretenses. I can't believe that you think this is okay, or that you're going to get away with marching in here and as good as holding me hostage.'

Rosedale smirked. 'You invited us in, and eventually we'll all walk on out of here, but when, and how long that will take, is down to you.'

Rubins looked at the trio. 'Fine. I'll prove it. Though this goes against my better judgment…'

The Senator stopped talking to grab the phone roughly and angrily out the cradle, and with a ferocity which made Maddie raise her eyebrows, he punched in a number. After a few moments he said, 'This is Senator Rubin, I'd like you to put me through to my personal bank manager... Well, put me through to anybody then.'

Another pause before the Senator gave the details to get through banking security.

'Okay? Good... Right, well, I need to check transactions on certain dates... seventeenth and eighteenth of this month... Yes... Okay... On a couple of withdrawals which shouldn't be there... Florida... Okay... Yeah... okay... No... Five thousand dollars... What? Are you sure?... No... Positive... Thanks, that would be good. How long will that take? Alright. Appreciate that. Y'all take care.'

Rubins put the phone down and stared at Cooper with a look of shock on his face. 'I don't know what to say, but apparently you're right. However not only are you right, but she said...'

The senator stopped.

'She said what, senator?' Cooper asked.

'Their ATM machines are linked to their CCTV system to prevent fraud. So basically you're taped, and then within a few seconds of the transaction finishing the footage is uploaded onto your personal bank files, for exactly this kind of reason... What's so disturbing is when she logged into the computer system on her end, according to the computer not only did the money get withdrawn as you said it did...' Rubins paused again and took a deep breath, stared at Cooper as if searching for answers before continuing. 'But apparently

I was the one who withdrew it. She crossed matched my bank photo ID with the recorded footage...But I have no recollection of it. None whatsoever... They're sending a copy of the CCTV over now.'

76

Bc8 Rc1

'You've done well.'

Abdul-Aziz Bin Hamad gazed past Ismet as they stood in the middle of a barren stretch of land. The African skies, like blue wash paint, held burning rays of sun which beat down on the tops of the sand colored canvas tents dotted around as far as the eye could see.

'Where's the Commandant?' he asked.

'Down at the training camp,' Ismet said.

'And how are we getting on? Are we ready?'

'Perhaps, though I'm worried some of them may not be capable. Their credence to our cause is held not by their hearts but by their fear. And our vision of a state, a longed for caliphate, is not theirs.'

Bin Hamad turned to stare at Ismet, his dark, tired eyes intense. 'It is not for us to worry, my brother, it is for us to trust and know that we've been guided and will wage war on the unbelievers, and that the tools we have acquired will be adequate. Remember, we do not question. Our job is to continue on the journey that has been set out for us. We need to finish it. Our group has been decimated by the Kafirs. But the jihad will expand once more, and in the following of Bin Laden, and one of our founding leaders, Sheikh Abdullah Azzam, as they planned to destroy us we now we plan to destroy them. It is our turn to rise up and wage a holy war without borders. *Allah will not be merciful to those who are not merciful. Fight them as they fight you.'*

77

Kd4 Rd1

Four coffees and three bottles of water and two biscuits and one trip to the bathroom later, Senator Rubins clicked the wireless mouse. 'I think this must be it.'

'May we?' Maddie gestured, getting permission to come round and look at the screen. They watched the grainy CCTV image the bank had sent through. Watching the Senator getting out of a small car and walking up to the ATM to withdraw money, and then walking back and getting into the car, before it drove away.

'Are you still trying to tell us that you didn't go down to Florida, Senator?' Cooper said.

Looking genuinely shocked, Rubins replayed the few seconds of footage. Then looked up, visibly upset, and stared at Cooper. At Rosedale. At Maddie. Hoping they'd give him answers. 'I don't understand. Like I say, I have no recollection at all. None... I don't know what to say. That's me. I mean of course it is, but...' He trailed off whilst Rosedale gently took the mouse from him. Re-clicked. Restarted the recording.

Three seconds in, he paused it. Zoomed in. 'Senator, do you recognize him?'

Rubins leant and stared and glared intently at the screen, looking at the man sitting in the driver's seat. Light blond hair. Stubble to match. 'No. I haven't ever seen him in my life. Though obviously I *have* because I'm driven to the bank by him and driven away, but I have no idea who he is, Rosedale.'

'You said you went to a bar that night.'

Rubins nodded at Rosedale. 'I take it I did because every Friday when I'm at home that's where I go, but I have no recollection of it… Oh my God…I don't know why I didn't think of it when you were talking before. I know exactly the Saturday it was.'

Cooper looked at Rubins questioningly, not knowing whether to trust the Senator or not.

'How?'

'When I woke on the Saturday it was late. Really late. And usually I get up and go for a run about eight but it was after three in the afternoon.'

'Didn't your staff wonder where you were?' Maddie asked.

Rubins took the tiniest sip of water, to wet his lips rather than to quench his thirst.

'No, because that's their day off. It's the one day I'm alone and can get on with paperwork undisturbed. Myself and a lot of people around these parts go to church on Sunday, so that's always a busy day. Speaking to people or attending lunches takes up most of the day and obviously during the week I could be over in DC, so Saturday is a day of quiet when I do nothing.'

'And everyone would know that?'

Frowning at Maddie, Rubins said, 'It's hardly a secret.'

'Can I ask you something about when you woke up, Senator? And I apologize for being personal... but were you alone?'

'I'm an openly single gay man, Maddie, and the bar in question I go to is also a gay bar, quite a rarity as you can imagine in these parts. I go there not because it's the *nicest* bar in the area, but to show my support for the LGBT community and to continue the fight for openness and acceptance. There's been a few petitions to get it closed, but it makes it harder to do that if I'm a regular. But I make it my business *not* to do the whole pick up thing, because whether it's right or wrong I would surely get judged, and I don't want anyone to have an excuse to try to close it down more than they do already.'

'So you can't think of anything that happened which was slightly out of the ordinary?'

'I suppose...' the Senator had a habit of trailing off...

'You suppose what?' asked Maddie.

'Ok, look, I'd appreciate it if this didn't go any further, Maddie.'

'You have our word.'

'Well, I was worried I'd been drinking again.'

Maddie, sounded surprised. 'Again?'

'I used to have a problem with alcohol. It got so bad I was at the stage where I was having blackouts. Couldn't remember from one end of the day to another. What I'd done. Where I'd gone. Nothing.'

Cooper asked, 'And is that common knowledge?'

'Yes it is. But it's a long time ago and I take my sobriety very seriously. I've been fifteen years sober, but on that Saturday, I woke up with an empty bottle of vodka next to me.' The Senator paused, his lips pursed. Took a few breaths. Composed himself. 'It was always my poison of choice. And to my shame it was obvious that I'd taken a drink and, like always, one drink led to another. I must've had a blackout. As I say, I can't remember picking up the bottle of vodka or buying it, or wherever it was I got it from. But that's how it always went. My last memory of the seventeenth is having a meeting about solar paneling, and then there's nothing until the eighteenth when I woke up with the bottle of vodka next to me...' The Senator trailed off again, staring into the distance. 'I'm hoping to have got it in check... I've been to some AA meetings since, you see.'

Studying the tape once more, Rosedale shook his head. 'There's no sign that you're drunk here, Senator, you take that straight line like a pro.'

The Senator leaned forward and studied the tape, and Maddie heard the tiniest hint of relief in his voice. 'You're right. Oh God, look. When I'm standing at the ATM I'm not dancing.'

'Dancing?'

Rubins gave a half smile to Maddie. 'Yeah, you know one of those guys who sway on the spot going backwards then forwards, a bit to the left and a bit to the right, as if they're listening to music, and you wonder how they don't fall over. Well that was me. The dancer. And on that footage I'm solid on the spot.'

Rosedale smiled, 'Yes you are, sir.'

Rubins looked at Rosedale, his face lit up with hopeful alacrity, his voice almost childlike. 'So you really think I wasn't drunk?'

'That's right.'

The trio were taken aback as Senator Rubins suddenly slumped in his big wide chair and put his head in his hands and filled the air with loud sobs, and struggled and just about managed to get out the words. 'I'm sorry... Oh my God, I'm sorry, but you have no idea what a relief that is... I thought I was heading to hell again. I was so scared and so angry with myself for allowing it to happen, after nearly destroying my family and all those around me before... Sorry, give me a minute... Addiction is a terrible disease.'

Cooper said nothing.

Maddie said. 'It's okay, Senator, take your time. But what we have to figure out now is what exactly happened to you, and why you don't remember.'

'At least we have the car's license plate number,' said Rosedale. 'It's something to work with, I guess. Try to find out who that other guy was if we can.'

Cooper agreed. 'I could give my friend Jeb a call. He's a license plate recognition investigator. He'd be the perfect guy. And he's discreet. What do you think, Maddie?

Seeing the Senator had begun to regain his composure, Maddie kept her attention firmly on Rubins. 'I realize you're in a difficult position, Senator, and I want to try to respect the fact you can't talk about Bin Hamad, but if you would, could you nod your head to confirm to me that you have no knowledge of the fact that he's been released.'

A pause.

A look.

A glance.

And then Senator Rubins nodded.

'And would you make sure you don't discuss this with anybody else until we get back to you?'

The Senator nodded.

78

Nd3Kf7

Two days later, on the outskirts of Storm Lake, Iowa, Cooper, Rosedale and Maddie stepped inside what'd once been a craft supplies warehouse, but had now been transformed into a state of the art living and workspace, spread over two floors.

'Hey Jeb, thanks so much for turning this around so quickly… And you've done a great job here. Last time I saw it, all there was was a hell of a lot of dust!'

Jeb Anderson, a one-time off Broadway actor who'd spent most of his glory years *resting*, whilst working as a glass collector in various downtown bars, grinned and gave Cooper a hug. 'I know, thought I'd never finish it off… Anyway, I'm glad you like it. It's a great place to live, and I can run this business out of here.'

'I'm forgetting my manners, Jeb. This is Maddie.'

'Hey, Maddie. I've heard a lot about you.'

'And you've met Rosedale before.'

Jeb gave a warm smile and a nod to them both. 'Come on upstairs. I managed to track your car on the date you gave me. Pretty detailed actually… Take a seat, guys.'

Whilst the Onyx trio sat down on the purple velvet couch, Jeb sat in front of the computer monitors.

He glanced at his notes. 'Okay, so the car you wanted information on, I first pick it up on the cameras leaving Cottonwood, Alabama, heading South on Route 53. It then went down through Grangeburg and over the state line into Florida. I lost the trail for a while but it must have headed East on Route 69, because I traced it again on interstate 10. Again, traveling east... Coop, I forgot to tell you I've got a casting for an infomercial. I've got a good feeling about this one.'

Cooper reached over and slapped Jeb on his back. 'Good for you. I'm pleased for you, buddy. What's it about?'

'It's for hair dye, but it's the principal part. If I get it, my face will be everywhere.'

Cooper's grin may have been slightly too wide. 'Well, that's swell. Real swell. And like I always say, if it doesn't work out for you this time, at least you've got this business to fall back on.'

Absentmindedly, touching his fine, receding comb-over, Jeb smiled back at Cooper. 'Oh it'll work out alright, Coop. This time I know it. The Hollywood dream's right there for my taking. It's in touching distance. I can smell it.'

Maddie, having never met Jeb before, raised her eyebrows at Rosedale, who nodded thoughtfully. He spoke in a serious tone. 'And I wish you the best with that, Jeb, but let me give you some advice – when you're out there, just don't go around lending Spielberg any money. You'll never get it back. Guy still owes me fifty bucks, and now he thinks offering me a part in one of his movies will make it alright.'

Whereupon it was Cooper's turn to raise his eyebrows, as he mouthed to Rosedale, *What is wrong with you?* Then, wanting to bring the subject back to something relevant, he turned his attention back to Jeb. 'I really appreciate what you've done here, Jeb. Big Brother's certainly watching your every move with all those cameras, isn't he?'

'He absolutely is. And luckily for me, our government has continued to let the industry and technology evolve beyond what even I imagined. It's big business. And there's no escaping, and there's definitely no hiding, whether you're driving or just walking about. They make millions of dollars in toll road journeys, and from speed cameras. Even big gas stations have got on the bandwagon, scanning cars before the pump will even turn on. And now it's all linked up to police computers, which trawl for stolen cars, known felons, even terrorists. And all that data is bundled, analyzed, and sold on. Though there are still some people who think we're back in the nineties, and they can beat the system by spraying hair spray on the license plate to cause a glare, thinking that the camera can't read it. It used to work, but not anymore.'

Picking up a previous point, Maddie asked, 'Sold on? What's the point of that?'

Turning his slim, five-foot-three frame towards her, Jeb crossed his legs. 'Money, of course. Specialized companies call it *mining the data*. You know, to predict their customers' behavior. From tracking where folk live, where they work, where they shop. And from that they learn where to place advertising. It's market research and crime prevention all in one.'

Cooper said, 'I know the hair spray trick doesn't work

anymore, but if people wanted to hide, couldn't they just change the font on the plate? Move the spacing around, splatter mud on it? Or even put a false plate on that's the same as an identical model car?'

'It's difficult because what the police are doing is crunching the data from all the public and private camera systems almost in real time. Taking readings from all over America. If there are two identical plates in two different places it shows up. The text recognition software can accommodate all state license plate fonts, and foreign ones too. If there are any plates it can't read, it sends a photo to a police officer or a guy like me who looks at it to try and interpret the picture. One of the best things I love about the technology is it helps with child abductions, especially when they try to cross state lines with the kid.'

'That's what you specialize in, isn't it?' Maddie said.

'Yes I do. Parents come to me as well as going to the police. In particular, when the kid's older. Often the cops may not act straight away if the child's older, but often time is of the essence. The technology really makes it difficult to go anywhere without, as Coop says, *Big Brother* watching. So, unfortunately for the guy you're looking for, but fortunately for you, there was little he could do to stop me following his journey... So what he does is keep heading east on I-10, then turns onto the I-75 southbound, almost as far as Port Charlotte, where I lose him. Or rather he stops there for about seven hours to do whatever it is he's doing, because the next day at around 0500 hours the National Data Computer picks him up again, travelling the same route but in reverse. Heading back north, then northeast, back through

Cottonwood, Alabama. Again the car drops off the radar for a couple of hours.'

'And this place in Cottonwood he went back to, is that roughly the place where this whole journey started?' Cooper asked.

'I'd say so. He was probably in that area for a couple of hours as we don't have anything till later. But what he was doing is anybody's guess.'

Cooper looked at Maddie. 'That would give whoever it was plenty of time to take the Senator back to his house before he left the area... What were his next movements, Jeb?'

'Well, after the time spent back in Cottonwood, he cuts across country. Must have taken all kinds of back roads through the east part of Alabama, because it's only later when I pick him up, but just in a few places which are big enough to have the ALPR cameras. The time signal on these sightings show he's making good time. Driving quite fast, and not likely to have stopped anywhere for long, maybe only just long enough to buy gas and eat. He makes it to route I-65, because then he shows up on every camera through Nashville and Louisville, before driving along the I-64 into West Virginia, until he comes off the interstate at Sissonville, a small town with one gas station... And this is where your guy stops. Probably running real low after that long drive. And now here's the really good news. We lose the trail completely.'

'How is that good news?' Cooper said.

'Well, he's driven non-stop through three states to get there. Gone cross country to mask his route, then buys gas at a small station which did – but maybe looked like it wouldn't – have cameras. You know, old school: guy comes out to fill up the car for you, checks the oil, chews his tobacco, says have a nice day and you drive off in a dust cloud out the other side of the classic one horse town... Except he doesn't.'

'Doesn't what?'

'Doesn't leave town. Never even makes it into the center of town. The ALPR camera on the main street is a modern camera but it doesn't register him. Nor does he go back to the interstate, where he would be picked up at the junction he came off at.'

'Maybe the camera missed him?'

'Maybe Coop, but he isn't picked up *anywhere* else on the network at all, not even the interstate routes, not that day, nor any day since.'

'So what are you saying? He's parked up at the gas station and caught the bus home?'

Jeb smiled. 'That's a possibility, though he'd have to walk quite a way. There's no bus stations or stops in that area. But of course he could've hitched a ride, or been picked up by somebody else. But even if he did get a ride out of there, my point is the car's still somewhere in that area. I did a check, and there aren't any reports of abandoned cars in that town. The place is so small it was real easy to find out.'

'I'm still waiting for the good news,' Maddie said.

Jeb Anderson chuckled. Span his monitor around so they could all see it clearly.

'Here, look at this...' He traced his finger along the circuitous route, all the way from Port Charlotte in Florida, back though Alabama, Tennessee, Kentucky and into West

Virginia. 'Your guy's driven all this way. No real stops. No sleep...' Then zooming the map in to show interstate 77, along with the small gas station just off the intersection, Jeb tapped his finger on the glass screen. 'He comes off right here. And like I say, he buys gas but doesn't get back on the interstate, otherwise he'd be picked up by the cameras, and like I also said, he never makes into the town, otherwise he'd be picked up by the camera there. The area is surrounded by just countryside. Only a few little roads with small shacks and houses set back into the trees and a river runs through. It's real private. Real quiet. The only way to drive cross-country, avoiding cameras, would be going east to a place called Aarons, but that road has been closed for years due to landslides from aggressive forestry back in the nineties. Apparently, it's too expensive to fix an unstable mud road, that was only built for forestry vehicles, which ironically caused it to wash away the hillside in the first place.'

'But what does all that mean for us?'

'It means, Coop, your guy either drove 1500 miles just to dump his car in some random wood in Virginia, or he and his car are *still* hiding out there. Somewhere off... ' Jeb paused. Leant forward to read the tiny text on the zoomed-in map. '... Grape Vine Road. I think that's where your car is. Somewhere in that square mile. In fact, I'm one hundred percent sure it is.'

'You're a star,' Cooper said.

'Well, I'm hoping to be.'

79

Ke3 Ra1

Virginia had always held a place in Cooper's heart. A place he often escaped to when he wanted to lie low. A place of beauty and warmth but as his foot fell down into another grass-covered hole, twisting and biting at his ankle, he wondered whether a review was needed.

The long rushes of dry yellow grass hit and twisted around Cooper's middle. To the right of him he could see Maddie and to the left of him, where the undergrowth was even higher, all that could be seen was Rosedale's cowboy hat, looking like it was just floating along.

'Hey, Rosedale, see anything?'

'No, and I think we better head north up towards those trees. We've already found a whole lot of nothing. We've nearly covered the whole square mile.'

Cooper was tired and grateful that one side of the long straight road was a large wide river. Bridgeless. Which was good because it meant the only real place the car could've been dumped was the south side. The side they were on. Though Maddie had put forward the idea of the car having been dumped in the river. And it sure as hell looked deep enough. But the way he felt at the moment, there was no way he was buckling and dressing down and diving in anywhere. Least of all some muddy-ass river. If Maddie wanted to go swimming, she could be his guest.

'Hey, Maddie, Rosedale and I are going to head up to the trees.'

'Good idea. If anybody gets lost the signal here seems surprisingly good, but maybe it'd be wise to try to keep in shouting distance... See you on the other side.'

Dark and deep and far into the woods they ventured, which made Cora pop into Cooper's mind. He knew she'd love it here. Imaging herself entering a world of fairy tale, where elves and goblins lived and played. As usual, the thought of his daughter began to have a tightening effect on his chest. Made it hurt to breathe and slowed his pace, so he pushed her out of his head and instead let the heavy silence engulf him, which was only broken on occasion by the call of Maddie or Rosedale.

A few minutes later, not being able to see anybody, Cooper hoped nobody could see him, and as such he quickly popped a pill before shouting out to Maddie, 'Hey, Maddie? Are you okay? Maddie?'

'I think I see something.'

'Okay, stay where you are. I'll come... Rosedale! Rosedale!'

'I'm right here, sugar.'

Cooper – not one to jump – jumped.

He turned to see Rosedale leaning on the tree, an unlit cigar in his mouth.

'Jesus, Rosedale, do you have to creep up on people like that? You gave me a fright.'

'I bet I did… Want some water with that? Help it go down better?'

Cooper rolled his tongue to the right. To the left. Clenched his teeth. Clenched his jaw. 'Why don't we just go and see what Maddie's found?'

'I thought she was supposed to be handing those out to you? Does she know you've got another supply?'

'What are you talking about?'

'I'm talking about how once again you're not to be trusted.'

'Just leave it, okay?'

'You haven't answered my question. Does she know? She trusted you.'

Cooper came to an abrupt halt. He turned. Hurt and angry. 'And I trusted her not to sleep with the first cowboy she came across. But hey, we live and learn, Rosedale, we live and learn.'

'Tom! Rosedale! Over there… ' Maddie stood in a small clearing fifty meters away, pointing.

Cooper looked around and shrugged. He spoke warmly. 'You have to help me out here. What am I supposed to be looking at? The scrub?'

'It's not a scrub… Look.' Purposefully, Maddie walked up to the large, dark-leafed bush in question, and with ease began to pull away large branches, to reveal a mound of green tarpaulin. She lifted up an edge of the fabric.

'Gentleman, this here is our car.'

Rosedale walked across to Maddie, pulling off the rest of the tarpaulin to uncover the car. Taking out his handkerchief he opened the driver's door, looked in and opened up the glove compartment. He then carefully examined the side door pockets, as well as checking to see if there were any hidden compartments in any of the panels.

'Nothing here, not that I expected there to be anything.'

'Down that path there's a wooden shack,' said Maddie. 'We should go and have a look at it.'

Automatically, Rosedale drew his 38 S&W special, followed by Maddie and Cooper who each drew their weapons with a silence and a matter-of-factness that only mavens could have.

'Come on, I'll lead. Maddie, I think it'd be a good idea for you to take the rear if you don't mind. Thomas here isn't feeling his best, and I'd rather have someone more on the ball watching my back, if that's all the same with you.'

Not waiting for a reply, Rosedale crouched down and crept along through the dry undergrowth, carefully moving in a zigzag direction he crept along just off the path, heading down towards the shack.

With brambles and thorns and spikes and bristles dragging at his clothes, he stopped and leant on a tree. He turned to Maddie and mouthed to her to go round the other side of the cabin, then in a whisper he said, 'No you don't, Thomas, you stay here. Maddie and I have got this.'

'I'm fine.'

Rosedale hard-stared Cooper. 'Then you can be fine here… I mean it.'

Whereupon Rosedale took the safety off his gun, and the hat from his head, and began to run.

He kept low.

Moved and weaved until he sidled up to the end of the shack.

Leant forward.

Craned his head around the corner.

Saw nothing. Moved closer. Moved down and under the shack's broken window.

And hunkering his body he darted along the front of the shack. Edging now. Real slow. Breathing. Keeping his gun tight against his chest. And standing motionless for a moment, he listened. Nothing apart from the silence. Then deliberately, cautiously, Rosedale reached out his hand and with the tips of his fingers touched and pushed the door of the shack, which creaked and moaned on hinges as it swung open.

Moving his lips he counted down...

Three.

Two.

One...

...then ran and spun round into the well of the door, his gun ready and pointed. Finger hovering and twitching over the trigger...

But he stared ahead and almost immediately began to lower his gun, slipping it back into his shoulder holster, and in the doorway of the wooden shack, in the darkness of the woods, Rosedale pulled his shirt up and over his nose. 'Maddie! Maddie!'

Within a few seconds, Maddie appeared from round the back, gun held in both hands, and like Rosedale a few moments before had it pointed and ready to go.

'I think I've found our guy. Problem is, somebody found him before we did.'

Maddie walked up to where Rosedale was standing, her eyes following his stare.

'Jesus,' she said. 'He's been shot.'

80

Kf4 Ke7

The smell was overpowering, but she'd smelt worse. A hell of a lot worse. But it still took concentration, along with deep, hard swallows, to not hurl up this morning's strawberry smoothie and pancakes. The dead she could cope with, but the rotting, putrid aroma of a corpse in the Virginia heat on a full stomach pushed the hardiest of limits.

The shack was simple. One living-cum-kitchen-cum-dining room, with a fold-out sofa bed taking center space, which held the rigor-mortised body.

'How do we know this is even our guy? I know everything points to it, but we did only manage to get the briefest of looks at him from the bank's CCTV footage, and we need to be really sure. Granted, his hair looks the same color, but then so does half of America's.'

Rosedale, who'd been meticulously looking, but being careful not to touch anything, nodded.

'I say circumstance says it is, but I reckon if I can find the keys for that car, then likelihood is this is definitely our man. Place is pretty sparse, and I've looked everywhere apart from that cupboard, which is locked, but I really don't want to start smashing it open... Have you got a manicure file?'

'Are you kidding?'

'No. I don't think it'd be sensible to bust the lock. We want to leave the place as untouched as we can. Not a good idea to have any trace of us here.'

Maddie tilted her head. 'I don't mean the cupboard. I mean the manicure. What episode of *Charlie's Angels* have you stepped out of, Rosedale? Do I look like I carry around a manicure?'

'Just thought you might have one in your purse in your back pack.'

'Not now. Not never.'

Rosedale shrugged. 'Maybe you should.'

Maddie blinked and gave a crooked smile. 'Maybe I should carry a manicure? Seriously, Rosedale... You know what, maybe you should.'

He looked at Maddie incredulously. 'I do. Usually. But it was a strange thing that happened. I was...'

Maddie cut in. 'Stop. Save me the details... Here, try this instead...'

Expertly and swiftly Maddie began to dismantle her Smith &Wesson M&P. First removing the magazine. Checked there was nothing in the chamber. Gave the grip frame tool a quarter turn and twisted and pulled to remove a thin, two-inch-long pin spike of metal. She said, 'Will this do you?'

He shrugged, unimpressed. 'I guess so, but I'd rather have the file.'

*

With Rosedale now attempting to open the cupboard with as little damage as possible, Maddie turned to Cooper, who'd now joined them. 'What puzzles me, Tom, is the fact that there's nothing here. No photos. No letters. No keepsakes. There's nothing personal.'

'Guy obviously likes to keep it simple.'

'I don't know. There's simple and then there's secretive.'

'And Thomas would know all about that,' Rosedale said.

Maddie turned her back, preferring the sight of the corpse to having to deal with the ongoing hostilities. She carefully picked up and pulled up the bed sheet which was covering the body.

The waft from the sheets exaggerated the smell and this time the deep breath and the swallows almost didn't make a difference. Almost. But she bent over with her hands on her knees, trying to compose herself. As she did, she closed her eyes, but immediately opened them as a thought came to her. 'You know what I think? I think that body and perhaps this whole place has been washed down with bleach. I can smell it.'

Cooper glanced down at the corpse. 'I can't smell anything apart from him. I'll have to scrub that dead stench off me tonight.'

'I know it's overpowering, but smell again. Go on, Tom… Underneath it all, can't you smell the bleach?'

Cooper sniffed, managed not to vomit, and shook his head. 'Nope. All I have is him in my nose.'

'Then look around you. What do you see?'

'A whole heap of nothing,' Cooper said.

'Exactly, but a whole heap nothing with no specks of dust

whatsoever. It's spotless. Look on the shelves. No dust. There or in the corners. Along the skirting boards. Nothing. You'd have thought there'd be something, especially out here. The floor's pristine.'

Kneeling down to the floor, Maddie put her nose close to the wooden floorboards.

'Bleach. Everything's been bleached, Tom.'

'Are you sure?'

'Absolutely. And whoever's done it has done a pretty good job.'

'Bullseye!'

Maddie and Cooper turned to Rosedale who'd managed to open the small wooden cupboard. He held up a white plastic bottle. 'Well it would be if there was anything in it apart from, get this, bottles of bleach... Why the hell lock them up though?'

As she walked over to Rosedale, Maddie quietly said, 'Exactly. Why would you? It's not like the killer would've cleaned up and then locked bottles of bleach in a cupboard. It doesn't make sense.'

Pulling out a pair of disposable surgical gloves from her rucksack, she put them on. 'Pass them to me, will you please, Rosedale.'

One at a time she took the bottles from him and proceeded to shake them, before unscrewing the red lids and pouring the bleach down the sink.

Coming to the sixth bottle, she shook it. Then shook it again. Turned it upside down and banged the bottom of it before pushing and hooking her finger inside it. 'There's something in there...' With her tongue sticking out in concentration, Maddie began to grapple with the object, which was now just inside the small opening of the bleach bottle and, managing to grip it, she eased it out gently.

It was a small wrap of foil, sealed and taped up in a transparent grip-seal plastic bag. She shook it gently and watched as flecks of white powder began to spill out into the sealed bag. 'I won't open it, but what do you guys say we take this with us? We could get it analyzed by Eddie. Tom, would you take it to him?'

'Yeah, of course, I could fly across to DC the day after tomorrow. Drop it off. I'm sure he'd turn it round as quickly as possible.'

'You don't want to leave it for the cops, Maddie?' Rosedale asked.

'We can call them anonymously once we've left here, but it's not like it's this stuff that killed him. I'm curious to know what it is.'

Rosedale peered closely at the white powder. 'You don't think it's coke?'

'No, do you? I mean it's such a tiny wrap, perhaps a gram or so, if that. There's no way you're going to bother hiding such a small amount of coke, *especially* if you're way out in the middle of nowhere. And then of course there's all these bleach bottles. Makes me think… So, what do you say?'

Rosedale said, 'I say, whatever we need to do, we do.'

81

Nb4 Rc1

'Eddie! Come here, buddy. It's good to see you.' Cooper ran up the stairs of the private Forensic Laboratory of Entomology and Archaeology in DC which Eddie ran and owned, two at a time. He gave his old friend a big hug. 'Thanks for sorting this out so quickly. Eighteen hours, I'd say that's almost your record… I'm sorry I missed you yesterday when I dropped it off, it would've been nice to go for a beer. It's been too long.'

'It's been too long, Coop, because you keep ignoring my calls. The girls are really upset. They think they've done something wrong.'

Trying to take Eddie seriously as he stood in a beaver costume, complete with giant buck teeth, Cooper said, 'Why would they think that?'

'Because they're little girls and those little girls adore their Uncle Coop. So when you keep on promising to come over and see them and you don't, well, what are they supposed to think? What are any of us supposed to think?'

'Not that. Jesus, Eddie, you should've told me.'

Eddie, a second generation Burmese, smiled sadly. 'I did and so did Jennifer and so did Maddie. Jennifer thought you'd at least have come to see the new baby, seeing as you're Godfather.'

Cooper felt like he wanted to run, like he was being carpet-bombed with emotion. 'Look, Ed, I'm on a bit of a clock here. I need to get back to Scottsdale, but how about...'

Eddie put up his hand, which happened at that moment to be a huge beaver paw, and cut in. 'How about you don't make any more promises to me, and I don't ask you anything as a friend, then nobody can disappoint.'

'Eddie...'

'No, Coop. You want my help to analyze any of your stuff, I'm right here. Anytime, dude. But anything else, I'm not available until it's a two-way road.'

The awkward silence certainly wasn't helped by the giant teeth which hung down from the two-foot-high beaver's head perched squarely on Eddie's own head.

Trying to break the tension, Cooper remarked, 'Nice outfit by the way.'

'Thanks. Jennifer and I are booked for a birthday party for a five-year-old later. He's been in hospital for the past eight months. The parents got in touch with our charity, told us he loves all things wildlife.'

'I think it's great what you two do with the Wish Kids' Party Foundation.'

'Well, you have to pay it forward sometimes, don't you? Some of us just aren't born as lucky as others... Anyway, sadly I can only give you fifteen minutes, but I've got the results you wanted. I'll show you.'

Cooper followed Eddie into the small lab.

'Did you have any ideas yourself what it might be?'

Cooper shook his head. 'No, not really, though obviously the first thing which comes to mind is coke or speed.'

'Wrong on both counts. Not even close. It's hyoscine hydrobromide, also known as scopolamine hydrobromide. They use it for motion sickness and postoperative nausea.'

'So why would anyone try to hide it?'

'Because there's a darker side to it. You must've heard about it. They sometimes call it the truth drug, which is basically a colloquial name for a whole heap of psychoactive medications used to gain information from people. Maybe you'll recognize the other name scopolamine goes by. The one they use in Latin America... *Devil's breath*. The most dangerous drug in the world... Yeah, now you know what I'm talking about.'

'I know a bit about it but not enough for it to make sense.'

Eddie glanced up to the large red clock on the wall. 'You want me to give you a little history of it, Coop?'

'If you've got time.'

'I'm okay for ten minutes... '

Cooper jumped up onto one of the work surfaces, listening to Eddie get into his stride.

'It's derived from a particular type of tree common to South America, but the main place it's grown is Colombia. The most dangerous part of the tree are the seeds which, via a chemical process using bleach...'

Cooper cut in. 'Bleach?'

'Yeah, there are a lot of similarities to how you go about making the drug, to that of how you make cocaine. But you need a hell of a lot of bleach because unlike coke, the smallest amount of scopolamine can do some real damage. Bleach will not only help the chemical process to make the scopolamine powder, but it'll also help clean the whole place up. With this stuff you need to wash everything down. The guys that make this stuff illegally often do so naked, then wash themselves down in a solution of bleach to make sure they get rid of any trace... Anyway, once you've done all the processing, it's pounded out and you're left with a hell of a drug which basically puts the victim in a hypnotic trance.'

'How's it administrated?'

'The perpetrator could blow it in somebody's face, or put it in their drink or food. In a lot of the cases in Colombia the incident occurs in night clubs or bars, and what's really disturbing, Coop, is that anyone could be a victim in a matter of moments, and put under the *power*, shall we say, of scopolamine. Happens within seconds. You then spend the next few hours, or however long it is, being a slave to the drug and the offender. Scopolamine basically robs a person of free will. Like a genie in a bottle under a person's control. Doing anything they ask. Telling them anything they ask.'

'And can you tell they're under the influence of it? Do they look like they're drunk or anything?'

'No, you wouldn't know. Which is scary, right? People who've ingested this drug lose their rational thinking, and are under the total command of whoever's given it to them, but they don't lose control over their bodies. It's the mind only, and it's a real problem in Colombia. Gangs are using it more and more to rob people, and prostitutes use it on their clients, so they can rob them. The victims really are acquiescent to any demands. Everything from being raped, emptying bank accounts… '

'How do they do that?'

'It's literally just a case of saying to the person, get some money out of the ATM, or what's the pin number of your bank card? Hard to believe, but absolutely true. No question. There are even incidents of people donating, or rather being forced to provide, their own kidney. Coerced into giving up an organ. International organ trafficking is a big business of course, especially in Latin America.'

'So could someone potentially take the victim somewhere, and get them to do something like give up their ATM number, or give up a special secret code even? Before taking them back to where they came from, without the person objecting, or anyone else around suspecting they're under the drug's control?'

Eddie nodded his head vehemently. 'Totally. Scopolamine is odorless and tasteless and the recipient becomes like a child, but after it wears off, the victims have no recollection of anything. Nothing. What they did or where they went or what they said. People can't even identify the criminals responsible for administering it. The drug, basically, and put simply, blocks memories from forming. It's like the blackout some people have when they've been drunk. They can't remember anything.'

Cooper spoke, half to himself. 'That's exactly what he said.'

'Who?'

'Oh, just this guy we've been speaking to.'

Eddie talked as he collected up his things. 'You know, interestingly, the CIA used it in the Cold War.'

'The CIA?'

'Yeah, and the Soviets... You okay, Coop?'

'Sorry, yeah. I'm just thinking.'

'You know, from a forensic point of view, I'd say it's the perfect substance to commit criminal acts, because the victim won't realize what's happening and won't remember anything either. It's a hell of a drug if you're a criminal. Plus, there's the added bonus that it's not detected in your blood stream. Only a special kind of hair strand test can do that. So if you're not looking, or don't know you should be looking for scopolamine, you sure as hell won't find it.'

'Could you?'

'Find it?'

'No, do the hair strand test? Could you do it here?' Cooper said.

'Yeah, sure.'

'Once I've got the strand, I'll courier it over. But I'll call you direct for the results, I don't want Granger knowing anything about this.'

Eddie said, 'When do you? That man really isn't the one running the show, is he?'

Cooper smiled. 'As long as he thinks he is, that's all that matters. Thanks for everything. You've been brilliant... And Eddie, I know I'm not a good friend, and I'm truly sorry. Sorrier than you'll ever know.'

82

Nd5 Kf7

Sitting in the rental car outside Senator Rubins' house, Maddie watched Rosedale talk on his cell a few meters away, whilst the AC blew out and Cora played with three curious looking worms she'd found in the forecourt of the diner they'd been too thirty miles back, whilst Cooper covered his face with Rosedale's hat, lightly falling in and out of sleep.

Clicking off his cell, Rosedale walked up to the car. Leant his arm against it and immediately regretted it as the hot metal of the car roof burnt his arm.

Wiping the sweat from his forehead with the blue hand-kerchief which had been tied round his neck only moments earlier, he said, 'So I managed to get an ID on who our guy is. Rather who he *was*. Turns out his name was Harry Gibson. Ex-CIA.'

'Seriously?' Maddie said.

'Yeah and this is where it begins to get stranger. I knew him. Or rather I knew *of* him. He was a fantastic agent, great reputation and he had his head straight – which, let me tell you, isn't easy when you spend your life working clandestine. Anyhow, next thing everyone knows the guy's in the slammer in Saudi. Turns out he had a thing for young boys. *Really* young boys.'

Maddie glanced at Cora who was quietly chattering away to the worms.

'Rosedale, watch what you're saying.'

'Big mouth. Sorry. Anyway, he was given a long-ass sentence.'

'No more than he deserved.'

'Right. But here's the thing, Maddison – and of course I haven't seen any evidence and the guy could be as guilty as sins in southern hell – but I do remember at around the same time there was a rumor going round about how Gibson wanted to whistle-blow. Apparently he was unhappy about what was going on in one of the black sites. You know, enhanced interrogation ,and the use of illegal substances on the prisoners. But his main beef was with one person in particular. The guy in charge. A certain Mr Chuck Harrison.'

'No kidding?'

'No, honey, none whatsoever.'

Hearing the word, *honey,* Cooper stirred and took off the hat covering his face and and turned to stare at Rosedal,e as Maddie continued to talk.

'So when was he released from Saudi?'

'He wasn't. Or he wasn't supposed to have been.'

'You think our government brought him back on the quiet?'

'No. No way. But somebody else did. Someone with influence.'

'You're not thinking Senator Rubins, are you?' Maddie said.

'No,' said Rosedale. 'I think he's an innocent party in this. Rather that's how it looks, but how it looks isn't always as it seems.'

'But the upshot is,' said Cooper, 'Gibson ends up hiding out in the woods and most likely making scopolamine.'

'Yep.'

Maddie pulled a face. 'Not exactly a life, is it?'

'It's a life away from a Saudi prison. Those woods were paradise in comparison.'

'But of course all this needed somebody else behind it, because he needed money. Clothes, food. Everyday essentials to live.'

Rosedale lit his cigar and took a deep drag and snatched back his hat from Cooper. 'Give me that… Sorry, Maddie… And you're right, because I'm betting Gibson was both desperate and grateful, but also completely reliant on whoever had got him out of prison. Because let's face it, it's not like the guy could go and get a job and be out and about much; he'd have to work some big favors and do stuff in return.'

'Like finding out about the Senator's movements and then setting about drugging him.'

Blowing out the cigar smoke, Rosedale said, 'Baby, you got it.'

83

Bd7 Rf1

Pleased to be away from Maddie and Rosedale, Cooper leant his head on the Senator's front door. Dreams of Ellie had come thick and fast through the night and he was struggling. Tired. Everything felt too much. Cora. Maddie. Even the trip to Eddie had taken what little energy he had. And the only thing which was keeping him standing, keeping him going, were the pills. The Goddamn pills he hated and despised and reviled and couldn't wait to be rid of and couldn't live without. 'Goddamn it! Goddamn it!'

Senator Rubins flung open the door, which in turn flung Cooper forward, straight into the Senator's large round body. Rubins looked shocked. 'I thought I heard somebody. You okay?'

Straightening himself up but not looking Rubins in the eye, Cooper shrugged. 'Yeah, sorry, I was doing my lace. Lost my balance. Must be getting old.'

'Come on through…'

Cooper followed the Senator into his office as the Senator continued to talk.

'... You want a drink of water, Cooper? Iced tea? The Alabama heat still gets to me sometimes.'

'No thanks, the others are waiting in the car, but I appreciate you putting time aside to see us again. As I said on the phone I won't keep you long... I need to take a small sample of your hair, Senator, so we can get it analyzed.'

A combination of shock and concern passed over Rubins' face. 'What! Why? You need to tell me what the hell is going on. I haven't mentioned the incident to anybody yet, but I will do if I don't start getting answers because when you start asking me for hair samples, then I begin to worry there's a whole lot more that you're not telling me.' Rubins stopped and then as an afterthought added, 'I've just got back from a security briefing with the head of CTC. It was about other matters of course, but it was very tempting to speak to him about what happened to me.'

Cooper kept his voice even. 'I take it we're talking about Chuck Harrison.'

Rubins nodded. 'Yes.'

'Then I'd say it's doubly important not to voice anything. Just act as if you don't know what's going on.'

Leaning his large behind on the rosewood desk, Rubins narrowed his eyes. 'Well, that won't be difficult, seeing as I *don't* know anything. You do realize this is a very difficult position I'm in. I don't want to be compromising myself in any way, and now you're asking for a hair sample from me... How do I know I can trust you, Cooper? You've got to understand what happened to me is *very* troubling, especially given my position.'

'Senator, we realize this is a big ask, but it's vital at this point to keep it to yourself. Once we know more, then it'll be down to you to decide what you want to do with the information.'

Suspiciously, Rubins asked, 'And why can't I do that now?'

'Because it'll probably do more harm than it'll do good.'

'Harm to who?'

'The country.'

'Christ almighty, what is going on?'

Trying to placate the Senator, Cooper said, 'Just give us a bit more time, that's all we're asking.'

'But what I don't understand is why I can't just go to people I know in the FBI, or even in the CIA. Chuck, even. I've suddenly become part of something I don't even understand… I'm sorry, Cooper, this isn't the way things should be done.'

'We're this close to having answers.'

'No, I'm sorry. I wasn't comfortable before, not calling in the appropriate authorities, and even more so now.'

'Senator, please, there's lives at risk. The safety of the American people. We've already had a recent spate of terror attacks on homeland, so we need to do all we can to keep this country as safe as possible.'

Rubins wagged his large finger and said, 'You see that's what I'm talking about. You want me to keep quiet about compromising safety? You want me to leave the lives of US citizens in your hands… No. Sorry.'

Curbing his temper, Cooper spoke with authority. 'You don't know what you're doing, Senator. We *know* Bin Hamad is out there somewhere, whether you believe that or not. We saw him. And whatever it is he's doing, we know he'll be active right now. Planning God knows what.'

Rubin's anger was lit up. 'This is madness. I have no idea why I agreed to any of this nonsense in the first place. If you think the imprisonment of Bin Hamad has been compromised, then we need to act fast and inform the appropriate people.'

'Can't you hear yourself?'

'What are you talking about?'

'We're trying to help you, Senator,' Cooper said.

'How do you work that one out?'

'You're talking about the appropriate people, but one or more of those *appropriate* people are behind this. And once they know you're onto them, they'll make it look like it's *you* who compromised security. After all, there are only two people with the code to Bin Hamad's jail cell.'

'You're not implying that Chuck Harrison has something to do with this, are you? That's absurd.'

'All I'm saying is they'll make it look like you, especially as we haven't got all the evidence we need yet to make anything stick. So I'm telling you, Senator – *warning* you – that if you open your mouth now it'll be you who's going down.'

Confused and troubled at what he was hearing, Rubins sat heavily back in his chair. 'Y'all aren't making sense. How could that even be?'

'You say you've no recollection of going down to Florida, but that was you on the CCTV footage by the ATM. And as you say, there's no dancing, no swaying, nothing. You look as sober as the morning sun. Yet there you are sitting in the car with an ex-CIA agent who's now dead and shouldn't have even been in this country in the first place.'

'What? What do you mean he's dead?'

Cooper walked up close to Rubins, and with his tone lowered to a quiet firmness he said, 'Oh yes, didn't I mention that? That guy's dead. Been shot. A bullet straight through his head. And you, Senator, were probably the last person to see him alive.'

Nervously, Rubins retorted, 'I don't like your tone.'

'You don't have to like it. I'm just laying it out how it is. Who's going to believe you? Think about it, Senator. You're driving around in a car with a guy who's supposed to be in a Saudi prison, but instead you and he are taking the scenic routes around the country. Taking money out of the ATM, having a nice jaunt to Florida...'

Rubins cut in. 'How dare you! It wasn't like that.'

'Well, no it wasn't, because I haven't finished yet... The next thing which happens is the guy's lying dead with a bullet in his head and Bin Hamad is winging his way to God knows where.'

Rubins slammed his hand down on his desk, inadvertently causing his palm to sting. 'I had nothing to do with that. I didn't even know the guy and as for...'

It was Cooper's turn to cut in. 'Try explaining that to the authorities. Your prints will be all over Harry Gibson's car, you're on the CCTV footage with him, and that's just for starters, Senator... Doesn't look good, does it?'

'I trusted you to...'

Stepping away from the Senator, his voice warmer this time, Cooper said, 'Stop, Senator. I'm not actually accusing you.'

'I thought...'

'I know you're innocent, but what I am doing is showing

you how it'll look without our help. You're a man of influence and a man who holds a huge deal of responsibility. You are just the sort of person who'd be able to get Harry Gibson out of prison. And you hold the code for Bin Hamad.'

'But I didn't and I certainly didn't have anything to do with Bin Hamad.'

'I know. But someone did, and this someone doesn't know you know anything. But you know. It's all about the *known unknowns*… So let's keep it between ourselves as long as we can, because the person behind this has got a huge amount of influence. Much more than either of us. We don't want them to be able to go and hide, and cover what tracks it is they're making. This goes beyond just you and me… I promise we'll have all the answers soon.'

With the tension slightly easing from his face, Rubins stayed quiet for a moment, then he stared at Cooper. 'Forty-eight hours. And that's it. After that, Cooper, I call in who needs to be called. You understand me? I'll give you forty-eight hours.'

84

Ke5 Ra1

'Forty-eight hours? You're kidding, Thomas! There's no way.'

'It's fine, trust me.'

Rosedale raised his eyebrows and finished off the bottle of water he was hungrily consuming. Threw the bottle in the bin in a perfect overhead shot. 'Thomas, trusting you is like taking your chances in a pool of piranhas.'

'Look, Rosedale, Eddie is going to get me the results through and then we'll know for certain what's happening on that front.'

Rosedale's laugh felt like a swarm of ants crawling under Cooper's skin. 'No, what we'll know is just what we now suspect. The Senator was given scopolamine, probably or undoubtedly by Harry Gibson, who now happens to be dead. Anything else is just supposition and bits of ideas. There's no way we're going to give anything concrete to Rubins in that short space of time. I don't know why you even agreed to it.'

Irritated, yet relaxed in the knowledge that Granger was

away for a few day and wouldn't suddenly appear in the doorway, Cooper sat down in the Onyx kitchen. Dusted off the piece of broken biscuit left on the table, probably by Levi. 'I *agreed* to it, Rosedale, because that's the only thing I could do. He gave me no other choice.'

Maddie said, 'It's not ideal but at least we've got forty-eight hours. Rosedale, what's happening with your cartography guy? It feels like he's had that USB key for ages. Do you think it's not going to come to anything? Because we really need to find somebody to tell us if it *is* the basis for a map, like you thought it was, and if so, where is it?'

Pulling off his brown suede cowboy boots to massage his feet, Rosedale pulled an apologetic face. 'Greg has always liked to work on Greg time, and now he's retired seems like Greg time's got even slower. But if anybody can work it out, he can. He was the number one location and navigation person at the CIA. When I was in the clandestine unit, at certain times something would come into your possession, you know like some small imaging or a drawing or even a sketch that you might've found at a suspect's house, which didn't look like anything at all. But then we'd take it to Greg and he'd would work out exactly what and where it was. It was like a jigsaw puzzle to him. And I mean you give him one piece of the jigsaw and he'll work out what the whole picture for you. He was a legend. Still is. And even though he's retired now he does the odd bit of stuff for the CIA when they're desperate. There's nobody better. I was thinking of taking a trip over there, he doesn't really do phones.'

To which Maddie said, 'Well, there's no time like the present.'

85

Ng5 Kg6

By the time Rosedale and Cooper had travelled from Scottsdale to Wapiti, Wyoming – a state defined by its canyons and
mountains and vast plains where the buffalo had once roamed
freely – apart from the occasional cuss word neither man was
speaking, and each had come a hair's breadth from a fight.

Standing on the doorstep of the ranch, which sat on the
river front of the north fork of the Shoshone River, set in
25 acres of horse pasture and mountain springs, Rosedale
knocked hard. Couldn't deny he was imagining it was
Cooper's head.

The sound of shuffling came first, and a barking of dogs,
and then the door was opened wide by a man with wild
white wiry hair, a large moustache and a face which looked
like it'd lived several lives over. A pipe hooked and crooked
in the corner of his mouth and the baggy, creased shirt and
shorts shadowed over the socks with sandals.

With an awkward gait, he shuffled towards Rosedale, his
smile beaming. 'It's so good to see you. But you didn't have
to come all this way, you could've called.'

Rosedale grinned. 'I did. Several times.'

'Did you? Damn answering machine, always forget I got it. Though don't get me wrong, it's nice to have an old face come by especially out here. There are days when I don't see anybody.'

'Sounds ideal,' Cooper said.

'It is actually. Suits me just fine, and I got the dogs to keep me company... Here, boys, come on! Come and see who's here.'

From seemingly out of nowhere, six dogs sped and scampered and barked and yapped and jumped and licked and nipped the visitors with excitement.

'Get down, Boo, get down! Bailey, Buddy, Charlie, down! Sorry, they're a bit excitable... I said, get down! Obama, down! Biden, down!'

Rosedale chuckled. 'Obama? Biden? You're a Republican though.'

Greg said, 'Yeah, just my little joke. I can tell them to sit, roll over, get down, get out, and on occasion, when they're being a pain, I can smack their ass – something I would've liked to have done when I worked under them, believe me. But now I get to do all that. It's me who's calling the shots and they have to listen... Don't you, Biden? You have to listen to what I say... Hold on a minute, guys, you'll like this... Woods...! Woods! Come here, boy. Come here! There's a good boy.'

Round the corner of the small ranch a three legged mongrel dog appeared, wagging its tail and looking slightly boss-eyed.

Greg, patted Woods. 'I found him up by Yellowstone.

Didn't think he'd make it through the night. But he came through and I nursed him back to health. He's simple as sin though, can only grasp the fewest of commands and hardly ever listens to anything you tell him. Likes to do his own thing... Thought the name was perfect. What do you think?'

Rosedale laughed loud and hard. 'I think you should ask Thomas here that.'

'Why, are you a Republican, Thomas?' Greg said.

Cooper gave a half smile. 'To tell you the truth, I don't know what I am, but I think you've got Woods down to a T there.'

With a rush of energy and a big wide grin, Greg suddenly became very animated. 'What am I thinking, making you stand on the doorstep? Come in, guys, my office is through here.'

Throwing Biden, Obama and Woods a dried pig's ear from his pocket, Greg led the men through the wooden living room and up a flight of stairs to his large but sparsely furnished office.

In the middle, two computers, along with several messy piles of papers, sat on a desk which faced a worn, brown leather sofa. 'Have a seat, gentlemen.'

Rosedale and Cooper both sat down on the two-seater sofa, and both felt themselves sink a little too more deeply than expected. They both masked their surprise as they sat awkwardly low, tilted in, shoulder to shoulder.

Managing to reach forward enough to place his cowboy hat on the floor, Rosedale adjusted his position, aiming for comfort. Failed. Caused Cooper to slide and slope further in, their bodies looked conjoined.

Ignoring his own discomfort, Rosedale asked, 'So how did you get on with the data from the USB? Like I say all we saw were crazy shapes, senseless patterns layered on top of one another. It was like some modern day hieroglyphics. It wasn't until I saw a drawing on the wall down in Turkey that I realized it was a map.'

Greg smiled sympathetically. 'I know what you mean, it does look meaningless if you don't know what you're looking at.'

Rosedale winked. 'But you know what you're looking at, right?'

'Of course. That's why you always used to come to me, back in the day. He used to call me up in the middle of the night sometimes, didn't you?'

'It was only the middle of the night, Greg, because usually I was on the other side of the world. That, and it was often the safest time to call. You were never in bed anyway. You sleep like a cat.'

Greg, about to answer, saw Cooper looking at his watch. 'Sorry, am I keeping you? That's what happens when you have no human company – when guests come, you talk enough for ten men.'

Rosedale was now sitting too close to Cooper to even turn his head towards him and glare. 'Oh no, it's not that, Greg, Thomas here has to keep an eye on the time because of his medication. He can't afford to miss it. Hey, Thomas.'

Cooper said nothing but gave a tight, polite smile to Greg.

'I'm sorry, I didn't realize. I hope I wasn't being insensitive. Another consequence of being on your own. Good manners go out of the window. Let me just get on with this for you. And if you need a drink of water, Thomas, please ask... Okay, what you have on your USB key are a whole series of digital elevation models and geospatial scans processed from satellite images. In other words, you've got the framework, the basics of a map, but all the labels and key information are missing. Your USB stick, as you know, had encrypted data on it, some of which I couldn't access. It's high-grade, military-style coding.'

'Yeah, Maddie was only able to get into certain files as well,' Cooper said.

'Right. It was obvious to me what the images were, but of course in such a basic format they were no use to anybody. There could of course be other maps on the key in different files, perhaps more detailed, but at the moment they're inaccessible so if we concentrate on what we *have* got, that's probably the best way to go.'

Greg logged into the computer. Stood up and hobbled across to the window and rolled down the blinds, which plunged the room into semi-darkness. He pressed a remote control button and projected images lit up the white wall next to the door.

'These images here I'm showing you aren't yours, but it's just to give you an idea. They're made up by analyzing satellite data. The software program uses pixel pattern, as well as lines and shape recognition, to differentiate various surfaces such as land, water, vegetation, people, etc. That's why if you know what you're doing you can program in something like your images, something which looks to most people like strange, multi-sided shapes and squiggles; I basically input the set of existing geometric data, such as the shape of your

415

map, with all its unlabeled subdivisions and contours, and the computer scans existing data for a match. It'll bring up all the areas in the world which have that geographical or border area and formation. And then it's a question of filtering in or out the details required. Building up the area. It is complicated, but essentially it's an interactive mapping system which saves on thousands of man hours at the click of a mouse.'

'So nobody uses an old school map or satellite navigation system anymore?'

'Amateurs and hobbyists do of course, but not if you're serious in my field. You'd be left behind. This technology, Thomas, is so different to what we used to have. So much more advanced. It creates very high resolution images and lots of detail from the most basic of frameworks, like what you guys brought me. The software these days can even work out what type of rocks form the landscape in an area, or if you want it to it can calculate the size and material of objects, such as buildings and cars. It can instantly map, not just the road network, but fine detail like what kinds of houses, and what shape trees are in the back yard. It can show how many people are driving down those roads, and can calculate the size of a crowd of people during a humanitarian crisis, for example. These data breakdowns are being used corporately and politically, to help with disaster response, risk management in environment, and in military defense and intelligence, as well as monitoring changes in land cover and usage. And the image can be refreshed constantly, and tracked every time a satellite passes overhead. These are maps that can constantly update themselves and track changes. It really is brilliant.'

Rosedale nodded. 'So what about our images on the USB?'

'Well, I've built them up because, as you said, they were just hieroglyphics. Just a lot of shapes and lines. But I managed to layer in the details, and now you can see clearly for yourselves it's a map.'

Greg clicked the remote button again.

Cooper stared at the image projected on the wall. 'That's amazing. I can't believe it's the same thing.'

'It is amazing, isn't it? From the size of the trees I can tell that we're looking at an area of about five square miles. You can make out a river on the top right, but mostly it's dry ground, and you can also see rocky hills to the north if you look at the craggy representation there.'

'And that's a road, presumably? Though it looks more like a dirt track.'

'Yes, and if you see the next image…' Greg paused to press the remote again and then continued. 'You can see it's the only road in that particular area. It's basically a pretty dry, rural place. But you can see several villages; simple, hut-like structures. An area of people and life. Though here's the thing, gentlemen. This map was created by the images from the USB key, but once I'd created it, I then uploaded it into another software program and the metadata showed me something else.'

Cooper looked puzzled. 'Now you've lost me.'

'Okay, basically the map was built using the information on the USB, but remember when I said the maps update themselves? Well it turns out the information was old, though I didn't know that when I created it. If you program in old data it will produce a map of that period of time, because it thinks that's what you want. For example, New York. You could either feed data in from pre-9/11, and the computer would give you a map with the Twin Towers on it, or you could feed data from post-9/11 and you'd get a post-Twin Towers map. If, for any reason, you had created a pre-9/11 map, the metadata would then give you the latest version of that area as well… And that's what happened with your map. The computer gave me an updated version of your area. Look here… The villages and huts and buildings which were once there, aren't… Everything's gone. All the huts, the agriculture. The entire area of land has been cleared. Like it's Ground Zero. Nothing left. Like an Armageddon has occurred.'

Cooper pointed to the new version of the map. 'What are those, though?'

'I couldn't tell you for sure but they look like tents. Odds are, that's some kind of camp.'

'Do you know where it is?'

Greg nodded. 'I do. It's West Africa. Burkina Faso. Gorom-Gorom.'

*

Once outside, Cooper turned to Rosedale and smiled. 'There's been something I've wanted to do all day.'

He clenched his fist and bent his knees and kept his hips down low and rotated his body and released a perfectly timed uppercut with maximum impact, sending Rosedale hurtling to the craggy ground where Biden, Woods and Obama licked his face better.

86

Nf3 Kg7

With boots on the table, and ignoring the angry swelling of Rosedale's lip, Cooper lit a cigarette in the Onyx kitchen.

He said, 'We got to get over there.'

'No, Thomas, we don't.'

'Then what the hell was all this about?'

'It was about getting people to listen. Those in authority. The people that can make a difference. And that's not us. It was *never* about us rushing off to wherever it is you think Bin Hamad is hiding out.'

'I don't think. I know. He's just outside Gorom-Gorom. Greg basically spelt it out for us.'

'That's the location of the map, anything else we don't know for sure.'

Angrily, Cooper said, 'Oh come on, Rosedale, it's all beginning to make sense. We see Bin Hamad getting on a boat in Turkey, a *Qatari* owned ship, which goes completely unchecked because of the Goddamn agreement this country has with Qatar, allowing them to ship weapons around, but

419

like we've seen for ourselves, it's not just weapons, is it? It's people, Rosedale. Kids. And then there's Maddie's friend, the one who works for a branch of NATO, he tells us that Ismet's ships go around the top of Africa then down the coast. Plus, the USB key was found on Ismet's other stealth ship. Everything's pointing to Bin Hamad being there and setting up camp.'

Conceding, Rosedale spoke thoughtfully. 'It does seem that way... So okay, Thomas, let's say Ismet's ship sails around and down to Dakar, or even stops off along the Western Sahara, and from there they either cross by air or land to Gorom-Gorom And it *is* the perfect place for Bin Hamad to go and set up a camp. Away from anywhere, with no-one watching.'

'Exactly. Taking the kids with him. God almighty, Rosedale...' Cooper paused. Punched the wall. Took a deep breath to calm himself. Didn't work. 'Jesus Christ! Jesus Christ! I can't even begin to think about what's happening to them.'

'So that's why we need to get all the evidence we have together. Pass it over to the people who can.'

'What? Monkey can, monkey do? Seriously, Rosedale, how long do you think it'll take the military to take action based on our word? It just won't happen.'

Rosedale's eyes flickered down to the blood trickling off Cooper's knuckles. Calmly he said, 'That's why we're doing this. The hard proof is our key, because at least you and I agree on the fact that no-one in their right mind is going to listen to us, no matter who we are and what at our background is, unless we have some hard-ass facts to give them. Once we have that, Thomas, we'll give it to the Senator. Rubins can take it from there. Okay?'

Agitated and pacing, with sweat dripping and trickling and seeping, Cooper shook his head furiously. 'But if evidence is our key, like you say, surely that means we need to do a reconnaissance and go to Burkina Faso.'

'Come on, Thomas… '

'Don't *Thomas* me! Listen! Just listen and think about it. The tents that Greg pointed out on the map *must* be a terrorist training camp. Agreed?'

'Most likely.'

'So Bin Hamad's preparing fighters as we speak, teaching them not only survival skills but the art of combat. Training them to become suicide bombers… Training them to wage war on US soil. There isn't time for the usual red tape. We have to act now!'

'You need to calm down, Thomas… Are you wired? Are you?'

Stopping to stare at Rosedale, Cooper tilted his head. Looked at him curiously, like it was the first time he was seeing him. He spoke slowly, disappointment coating his tongue. 'Is that all you care about? Whether I'm high or not? Is it? Don't you get it, Rosedale? Don't you see how insignificant it is? This. Me. My problems fade into nothing when you look at the big picture. There are kids out there who need our help. They're the ones who you need to be worrying about. Them. Not me. So if I want to kill myself then let it be my choice, but until I do, until that day, we can't turn our backs and wait for other people to do what we should be doing. We need to act now. We can't pretend, and we can't say we didn't know what was happening. I will not have any more blood on my hands.'

The silence of the men felt like another presence in the room, until Rosedale lit a cigar and said, 'Tell me more. What are you thinking?'

'How much do you know about Burkina Faso?'

'Let me guess… you're about to tell me everything.'

'Well, we know there's been an upsurge in terrorist activity, especially in the north of the country, which happens to border Mali – not good news for us, as that's where Gorom-Gorom is located. And since the coup which toppled the long-serving leader Blaise Compaore, there's been a whole heap of chaos to add to the unrest already bubbling under the surface. A perfect breeding ground, with all the necessary ingredients to cultivate terrorists.

'The other thing we know is that Bin Hamad has affiliations with Al-Qaeda. He's been marked as one of the main leaders of an off-shoot. Only a little while ago AQIM, Al-Qaeda in the Islamic Maghreb, attacked a hotel in the capital, Ouagadougou, killing over thirty people. Turns out Bin Hamad's right hand man, *the Commandant*, as they call him – who's also a Qatari national, and was based in Pakistan – is now based in Burkina Faso. That's according to security advisors. Has been there, apparently, for the past eighteen months. It's obvious he's continuing with the branch Bin Hamad set up, as well as trying to re-establish Al-Qaeda as the number one terror group. As we know, they certainly took a hit after Osama Bin Laden's death.

'Before Bin Hamad was captured, his off-shoot were one of the wealthiest, best-armed militant groups in Pakistan, mainly because of the huge amount of donations they got from wealthy Qatari sympathizers, and even Qatari royalty. And the sympathy's certainly still there. After all, the stealth ship was at Bin Hamad's disposal, and of course the access to American weapons.'

'Thomas, I'm trying to hear you, and I want to help, but you're in a fantasy world if you think it's possible to just go in like that. Or rather, we'll have no problem getting in, but getting out is another matter, especially if you need to get out fast. It's a hell of a place to escape from. The country's landlocked. And you can take your pick of troubled countries bordering it.'

'We've been in worse,' said Cooper. ' Besides, the place is only slightly larger than Colorado.'

Rosedale stubbed out his cigar in one of the unwashed coffee cups in the sink. 'Listen to me, sugar. That area in the north of the country is desolate. It's in the Sahel belt of Africa. Hot, dry and barren. It's unsafe for many reasons, least of all the deteriorating security situation of Mali. The place is vulnerable, which would make *us* vulnerable. There's no hiding. And we saw from what was on the USB key, and Greg's imaging, that that particular area's been cleared, which means there's no going in there without being seen. It's not even a starter. So whatever it is in your head, let it go.'

87

Bg4 Kg6

An hour later, Cooper, still agitated, let the smoke rise up and over his face from his tenth cigarette in an hour. 'I've just spoken to Eddie, and it's like we thought. Senator Rubins' hair strand has come back positive for scopolamine.'

'Shit. I know we were expecting that, but it's not good,' Rosedale said.

'When are we going to tell him?'

'We're not.'

Cooper looked surprised. 'He needs to know.'

'I know he does, but not yet. We have less than twenty-four hours until Rubins picks up the phone to the person whose name keeps popping up over and over again in this whole picture.'

'Chuck Harrison?'

Not bothering to offer Cooper a drink from the Onyx fridge, Rosedale broke open a can of Red Bull. 'Yeah. His name's crawling all over this like bugs on a bed. He had the access to Bin Hamad, the knowledge of who held the other part of the code, and he was also Gibson's station boss out in Khartoum. They are the facts. Period. Also my hunch is, and go with me on this one, Chuck was behind bringing Gibson back from Saudi.'

'You think there was some kind of deal made?'

'Absolutely. Maybe he arranged to give the family of the abused boys blood money, which is pretty common. And then once he does that, what Chuck has is a brilliant ex-CIA agent, who not only has to live in secret but is completely reliant on him. All the dirty jobs Chuck needs doing, including giving the scopolamine to Rubins, he gets Gibson to do. Probably not giving him any other choice. And all under the radar of the agency. By using Gibson, he can get jobs done which even in his position he'd struggle to get authorized.'

Cooper walked over to the fridge and took out the only drink which was left – a battered can of Pepsi. 'Go on.'

'Chuck got Gibson to drug Rubins, and knowing his movements on that Friday, it was a pretty easy job – we now know how quick and easy it is to administer the stuff. He then takes him to Florida where Chuck probably meets him, then flies him out to the black site in Cuba and brings him back and Rubins is none the wiser. They obviously did their homework on Rubins. Gibson must've planted the vodka in Rubins' house, knowing it was his poison, and knowing the blackouts from scopolamine gave similar effects to that of alcohol. So he wouldn't suspect anything and he also wouldn't be shouting about it to anybody thinking he's had another relapse. But Gibson's mistake was stopping off at the ATM. There's no way I can believe Chuck knew about that or authorized it. Though Gibson probably didn't realize that the ATM machine had a linked in camera, or he didn't think about it. Desperation has a way of doing that to you.'

Maddie who'd been sitting quietly, contemplating how and where and when Rosedale's lip had been busted, said, 'Desperation?'

Rosedale nodded. 'If, like I suspect, Chuck is behind this, then it's him who Harry Gibson was reliant on. Like you said, for food, clothes, money. The whole thing. So perhaps what Harry Gibson did was make the most of an opportunistic moment.'

With neither of the men offering her a drink, Maddie walked over to the fridge to find it empty. Making a mental note to chase up the ordering, she drew a glass of tap water. 'It was hardly tens of thousands. Why risk it?'

'Because what else did he have left in life apart from risk, Maddie? He was hiding out in the woods, and although it's certainly better than a Saudi prison cell, like you said, it's hardly a life. It's a prison in itself. He probably hated what he was doing. So maybe knowing how hypnotic scopolamine is, Gibson took the risk by getting Rubins to withdraw money for him. I suspect he was then going to take his chances and head off somewhere far away from Chuck… Lie low until he can figure out what to do, or even just keep moving. Anywhere but here. That was until he got a bullet through his skull.'

'You think Chuck was behind that?' Cooper said.

'Don't you? Who knows, maybe Gibson was surplus to demands.'

'But why did Chuck get him to do it?'

Offhandedly, Rosedale touched and licked and sucked his

lip. 'Are you kidding? What's wrong with you? You need me to paint it by numbers? Bin Hamad of course. He got Rubins to release Bin Hamad with him, because Chuck and Rubins arriving at the black site to take Bin Hamad somewhere, well nobody would've questioned it. Or talked about it. Or followed it up. Nothing. And if we hadn't seen Bin Hamad, nobody *would* know because the setup of HS around him made the guy only accessible to the very few, and those very few would only be answerable to those who were right at the very top, *if* those at the very top ever found out.'

Maddie nodded in agreement. 'Yeah because why would they find out? And *how* could they find out, because nobody's talking or saying anything. And it's not like there are spot checks. And besides, the checks would go through Chuck. So really, to all intents and purposes, Chuck is his own master, unless something goes wrong. But he's smart enough to make sure something doesn't.'

Rosedale winked at Maddie, making Cooper ruminate further. 'But something did go wrong, because *we know*. What Chuck had on his side was the fact Bin Hamad has been sitting in a cell for a long time now – or he was, prior to this. So nobody's thinking about him. Not the US government, and not the American people. They've moved onto the next thing. Therefore, as far as everybody is concerned, Bin Hamad is living out his days in whatever black site they put him in. Untroubled and troubling no-one. Like so many of the other prisoners held at black sites without trial.'

Cooper stubbed out his cigarette angrily. 'It's you who needs the color by numbers. I get all that, what I don't get – and clearly *you* don't even get my question – is why.

Why would Chuck Harrison release Bin Hamad? From what you tell me, and from what I know of him already, Chuck Harrison is a lot of things but he isn't a double agent. This country means everything to him. His methods and his integrity might be as twisted as a coiled spring, but helping the other side is not on his agenda.'

'I agree, Thomas, but I think that's what we've got to properly find out... Which is why I want to go back to Virginia.'

'What for?' Maddie asked.

'Harry Gibson was a CIA agent. And therefore he must have had a plan B. There's always a plan B. Without question. Everyone in the CIA has one. So if we need to get out, we can. It's what you're trained to do. I've got one now. It's a habit which stays with you long after you walk away from Langley. Working undercover and out in the field, you don't know who to trust, so it's part of the job to have an emergency escape plan. Money, details, weapons, false passport, even an L-pill, a lot of us who work in certain places and countries have that stored away somewhere.'

'You're talking about a suicide pill, right?'

'Sure am. There are some places you just don't want to spend a day in. Death has got its freedom... So what I'm saying is I reckon Gibson will have his plan B tucked away somewhere. If he does, then maybe there's something in it to give us more answers than we have now.'

'You think he had one, even though he was hiding out in the woods?' Maddie said.

'More of a reason for him to have one.'

Cooper drank back the last drops of Pepsi. 'For all the good it did him.'

'Right, but that doesn't mean he didn't have one. It just means he was taken by surprise. Or, more likely, he'd done what no CIA agent should do. He'd come to trust whoever it was who shot him. And in this case I think that was Chuck.'

'But Chuck would know everyone has a plan B.'

'You're right, Thomas, and for all we know he found it and took it, if there was anything worth taking. But what if he didn't? After all, he didn't bother going in the cupboards and looking in those bleach bottles. Maybe Chuck's arrogance has made him not be so vigilant. After all he doesn't know we're onto him. There's a possibility he didn't think Gibson would have one, or maybe he couldn't find it. But I think it's worth going to look and see.'

Maddie raised her eyebrows. 'A needle in a haystack comes to mind.'

'Not really, because his plan B would've been hidden far enough away from the shack to make it covert, but *near* enough to get it if necessary. That's why I think it was Chuck himself who pulled the trigger. Gibson would've been alert to anyone coming near that place, and there wasn't any sign of a forced entry. The only thing was the broken window but that was too small to get through. I think he didn't feel the need to be on high alert when Chuck was around. Like I say, I think to a certain point he trusted him. Then, bang... So we really need to go and find it if it's there.'

'Find what? And get your Goddamn feet off that table.' Granger stood in the doorway, giving the three highly trained, highly skilled, ex-military a fright.

Under his breath, Cooper muttered, 'I thought you said he was away.'

'What was that, Cooper? Surprise you, did I? Well, I'm glad I did, because now I want to know what you jokers are up to. It's like walking in on a bunch of hyenas. Cackling and plotting away. Come on, let's hear it. After all, in case you've forgotten, this is *my* business and you're in *my* building and you're sitting in *my* staff kitchen. So I think I deserve to know.'

Cooper said, 'We're doing nothing.'

Granger growled. 'Which translates to *you're up to no good*. Maddison? Rosedale?'

'Really, Granger, it's no big deal, we only dropped in to see if any jobs had come in,' Maddie said.

'You've never heard of a phone?'

'Yes, but we haven't seen Levi for a while.'

Granger eyed her suspiciously. 'But he's not here.'

Maddie shrugged. 'That's why we haven't seen him in a while.'

'Are you being funny, Maddison?'

'No.'

He wagged his finger furiously. 'Sometimes, Maddison, I think you're the ringleader of this so-called gang.'

Maddie tried not to smile, failed. 'Granger, we're not in high school and there is no gang.'

Granger narrowed his stare at her, his bushy eyebrows – which his wife was always trying to get him to trim – pinched over his eyes. 'The three of you together means you're up to something. So I'll ask you again: find what, Maddison?'

'Find Levi… We really need to go and find Levi. Maybe we should see if he's at home. In fact, come on, guys, why don't we go now?'

Maddie got up and gestured for the others to follow, which they hurriedly did. Granger grabbed hold of Cooper's arm as he was heading out of the door. 'Not you. I want a word with you.'

'Not now, Granger.'

'No. *Right* now... Some man came on by looking for you.'

Cooper's stance shifted. 'Who?'

'That's exactly what I want to know. He wouldn't tell me his name or why he was looking for you. But he looked official. You don't think that's strange?'

'I don't think anything.'

Granger poked Cooper hard in the chest. 'Let me tell you something now. Don't bring trouble to my door. This is my business. My reputation. And whatever you think you can get away with, let me tell you right here, right now, you can't.'

'I'm not trying to get away with anything. I don't know what he wanted or who he was. It's probably nothing.'

Granger gave Cooper a scornful look. 'When do people ever come looking for someone because of nothing?'

'I don't know. You probably know more than I do.'

'Is it to do with your court case? Your supervised sessions?'

Looking down. Looking up. Cooper sighed. Real heavy. 'No, I'm on top of that... Look, Granger, I have no idea what he wanted, or who he is for that matter. I've done nothing.'

Granger let go of Cooper's arm. '*Nothing*, hey? That word keeps on being bandied about this afternoon. But you better hope for your sake that it really is nothing. If I find out there's anything on you, even a Goddamn fly, I'll revoke your investigation license and make sure you don't work in this business again. You hear me?'

Cooper stared at Granger, his head beginning to throb. His jaw beginning to ache.

'Who couldn't hear you, Granger, when you're standing right there? Now get the hell out of my way.'

*

Walking down the hallway, Maddie turned round. 'What did Granger want with you?'

Cooper said, 'Nothing. Nothing at all.'

88

Nf4 Kg7

'Get off me.'

'I'm not on *you*. It's *you* who's on *me*, Rosedale.'

In the dark of the storm-filled, moonless night, Cooper couldn't see more than a few feet in front of him or a few feet behind him. He tried to position himself where he wouldn't be squashed and cramped by a twisted tree root, or by Rosedale's body as they lay on the wet ground, with the Virginian rain crashing through the woods around them.

With drenched and mud-clogged clothes, and his hand trembling with cold, Cooper held his gun tight, tapping Rosedale on the shoulder. 'Come on, let's risk it. I doubt anyone is out in this weather. We might as well head nearer the shack.'

Stumbling over tree roots, running low and following the path down to Harry Gibson's cabin, the rain and wind battering their faces, Rosedale and Cooper darted and moved and rushed and tore through the scratching of bushes, twigs and trees.

By the front of the shack, Cooper crouched down,

searching and looking as his knees sank into the mud, squelching up and soaking into his khaki pants. The rain poured down on his face, running into his mouth. 'Where now? This is crazy, Rosedale. Where the hell are we supposed to look now?'

'I don't know, just keep looking.'

'Where though? Look around you, it could be anywhere. We've been looking for over two hours now and we don't even know if it's actually here.'

Down on his haunches, his saturated clothes black from the Virginian earth and and sticking to him, Rosedale tried to wipe away the deposit of water on his face. Gave up.

'Then the only way to find out is to keep looking. Gibson was a clever guy, trapped in this mosquito infested place. I know he'd be working on getting out of here. Planning. Like I said before it'll be well-hidden but with easy enough access to get at it in a hurry. Far enough away not be found, near enough to retrieve in a rush. Look, Thomas, if you want to go, be my guest but I'm not going anywhere until we've either found something or until I'm sure there's nothing here.'

'We're in this together. However long it takes, I'll stay, but I feel like we've dug up half of Virginia and we're not getting anywhere. This, here. This isn't where he would've hidden anything. We gotta think... What about the river? The one just behind the shack? That's a good way to travel if you're trying to get away quickly, silently. You could get away, moving along the bank, and disappear before anyone realizes you've gone. It's also somewhere you could hide some stuff. Hide your plan B.'

Standing up and no longer bothering to brush any water off his clothes, Rosedale nodded. 'You could be onto something. Come on...'

Rushing and hurrying, the men ran past the side of the shack, along the short path to the river with their weapons drawn, pausing only to check and be sure no-one was coming through the curtain of rain. With an all-clear nod, Rosedale pulled at the dense brush, which tore into his fingers and ripped and shredded his skin as he slipped through onto the river bank.

They had to shout to be heard above the rushing river which hungrily swelled and swept along broken branches and leaves, as the heavy, torrential rains filled it with angry abundance.

'What about that?' Cooper pointed to a tree in the middle of the angry water, which had lifted and twisted and grown out of the river revealing a wide barrel trunk. 'I reckon that's a good place to start. Tree's pretty dead but see on the left side of it, there's a cavity. A hollow's formed. We could try there. I'd say it was a perfect hiding spot.'

Rosedale shook his head. 'There's no way we'll get to it. Look at the river. It's too fast.'

Beginning to take off his blue jean jacket, Cooper shouted, 'I'll go.'

'No you won't.'

'I said, I'll go.'

'Damn, Thomas, don't you ever listen?'

The rain beat down. 'What's your problem? Let me just go.'

Rosedale grabbed hold of Cooper's arm. 'If you're really

determined to do this, it's me who should go. Those pills you like to take, and that river, well, that ain't a real good combination… Go get the rope out of the rucksack, we're going to need it.'

*

Five minutes later, and with the rope tied round a small stump by the river bank, Rosedale held onto the other end. He edged into the water. And the water river rushed over.

He waded out carefully, as Cooper yelled out directions. 'Try to keep to the left… That's it. You're nearly there.'

Cooper watched as Rosedale fought to get to the gnarled tree, whilst his opponent flowed with torrential ferocity. And getting to the hollowed trunk, Rosedale, gripping and clinging onto the rope, rooted and rummaged in the hollowed out tree. 'Shit, there's nothing in there… Shit!'

'Look out, Rosedale!'

Before he could turn, a bouncing, bobbing log, carried by the current, hit with savagery, smashing and crashing into Rosedale's head, taking him under the water. Cooper ran along the bank, slipping and tripping and wading in. The river gushed over his face as Cooper fought to keep his head above the water level, clinging onto the bank at the highest point as it gave way.

And the river ran red, whilst Cooper swam towards Rosedale, who turned and twisted underwater, his hands floundering, battling against the current, being thrown backward and forward, moving towards unconsciousness.

Cooper reached for him, dragging him back towards the bank. 'Rosedale, hold on… Stay awake, try to stay awake.'

He heaved and pulled Rosedale's body up, slipping and struggling and grasping and breathing, tugging and ripping Rosedale's clothes whilst trying to get a grip, trying to get a foothold onto the soft bank.

Dragging him up to the wooden porch, Cooper turned Rosedale on his back. Pumped his chest. 'Come on, Rosedale, breathe! Breathe... Come on...'

One.

Two.

Three.

'Come on, man, come on, dude. Breathe... Breathe.'

A splutter. A cough. Then Cooper turned Rosedale back on his side and, banged him hard between the shoulder blades. Rosedale began to choke and gasp, fluttering his eyes open and laying his hand on his chest, taking deep breaths as the rain fell hard on the corrugated tin roof of the shack.

'Can you hear me? Rosedale? Can you hear me?'

In a strained, whispered voice, Rosedale said, 'I got a lung full of river, I didn't lose my hearing... Help me up.'

'We need to get you to the hospital.'

'I'm okay. Same can't be said for you though. You look terrible.'

Cooper snapped. 'I'm okay. Just... I'm glad you're okay...'

He trailed off and both men stared at each other, both looking at the other's face, both etched with shock.

Then Rosedale said, 'Just help me up.'

'Just stay where you are. Rest.'

'Fine, I don't need your help.'

At which point Rosedale struggled up on his side, having to pause to cough as he pushed himself into a sitting position.

'You're as stubborn as I am. I'll get you something to lean on… And don't move.'

'Anyone tell you you were bossy?'

Cooper walked along the covered porch, but he stopped short of walking inside Gibson's cabin. He walked back to where Rosedale was. Then turned and moved back down towards the door.

'Thomas, what the hell are you doing?' croaked Rosedale. 'Have you lost your mind?'

Again, Cooper walked to the door and stopped, he turned to Rosedale. 'Do you hear that?'

'What?'

'The rain, can you hear the rain on the roof?'

'Like I said, sugar, it wasn't my hearing I nearly lost.'

Cooper ran the few short paces back towards Rosedale. 'Right here, at this part of the roof, the rain's tapping down. There's a tip-tap. Tip-tap. But over there it's heavier, more like a thump. A bam. Listen. Bam. Bam. Bam.'

'Jesus, Thomas, what is this? You suddenly turned into Gene Kelly?'

'Shut up, Rosedale. I'm being serious. The sound pattern's different. Listen again, this area's quieter. The rain sounds less heavy. Over there sounds like we're sitting in a drum, but this part, here… It sounds tinny.'

Cooper looked up and stared, then running from under the cover of the corrugated, pitched roof, which sloped down and out, he studied the tin sheets bolted to a ridge beam as the rain pelted down, blinding his vision.

Leaping up, he jumped onto the rickety, wooden porch railing, holding onto the low roof for support, whilst the water rushed down in rivulets between the waves of the corrugated metal.

'Rosedale, there's a false panel. A second one's screwed on top!'

Quickly, Cooper hurdled off the railings, going into his rucksack and pulling out a thin crowbar and torch, before bounding back up and forcing it between the two corrugated sheets, pulling the false panel off the roof.

Throwing it onto the ground, Cooper vaulted down next to it. He flicked on the small torch before turning the false panel over and there, carefully tucked and taped into the waves of the corrugated sheets, were several transparent bags which held various things.

A bag of rolled up hundred dollar bills.

A bag with a small recording device.

A bag which held a roll of what looked like seismograph readings.

And Cooper nodded, and in the dark of the moonless night, with the rain thundering down, he said, 'Rosedale, I think we've just found our plan B.'

89

Nd4 Re1

'Jesus.'

Senator Rubins sat in shock in his office, staring across his rosewood desk at Maddie and Rosedale. He switched off the small voice recorder, not knowing quite what to say next. And he rubbed his face and his chin, and he took off his blue glasses and wiped them with his blue tie and put them back on, and opened his mouth but closed it again, and fiddled with the seismograph readouts in front of him, and Rosedale said, 'Are you okay, Senator?'

'To tell y'all the truth, I'm not. What you've just told me and what I've just heard, well, to put it mildly, I'm in shock. And I certainly don't know what I'm supposed to do with all this.'

'We thought perhaps you could give them to Brent Miller.'

'He's only just come out of hospital after his stroke,' Rubins said.

'Think about it. Until recently he was the chief of CTC. Chuck only took over because Miller was *literally* incapacitated. And okay, Miller may not be ready to come back to work yet, or even ever, but right now, Senator, he's our best bet. Our *only* bet.'

'I don't know, Rosedale.'

'Look, a long time ago I worked under Miller. I think we can trust him.'

'You only *think*?'

'Senator, that's as good as it gets when it comes to me trusting anyone… Take it to him and everything we've told you. He'll do what's needed. I'm sure of it.'

'And what about your involvement in this, Rosedale? All of your involvement in this?'

Earnestly, Rosedale looked at the Senator. 'Sir, I'd appreciate it if you'd keep us out of it.'

'That might be difficult.'

'Everything we know, you know, sir. There's no need for us to have our names put in the ring.'

Rubins frowned in concern. 'I don't know. I think at this stage transparency is vital.'

Rosedale stood up and tipped his hat. 'Senator, although I'm no longer in the CIA, I have a duty and I continue to do all I can for this country. I will go to the redline to serve and honor my promise to the flag. I will give my life if that's what it takes, but what I won't do is put those I care for in danger. There's no doubt about the people we're dealing with, and what they're capable of, so I ask you to give me your word as a soldier, and as a member of the Senate, that we remain anonymous.'

Rubins stood up and faced Rosedale. He blinked and thought and finally said, 'Okay, if that's what it takes.'

Maddie also stood up. 'Senator, can you keep us informed?

This is important to us all. Those children are real to us. We care what happens.'

Rubins raised his right hand and brought it up to his brow, saluting Maddie.

'Lieutenant, you have my word, and thank you.'

90

Kf5 Rc1

President Woods sat between Teddy Adleman and Lyndon Clarke, and opposite Senator Rubins, who sat next to Brent Miller, who sat on the cream couch hooked up to a portable O_2 cylinder, taking the occasional deep, noisy inhalation of oxygen, putting Woods in mind of Dennis Hopper's character in *Blue Velvet*. 'Jeez, Brent, are you sure you're okay? We could've done this without you.'

Brent's reply was as straightforward as he was. 'And miss speaking to that son-of-a-bitch? I don't think so, Mr President. I need to hear what he has to say.' Whereupon he took another large gulp of air.

Woods, feeling slightly surreal, looked around the Oval Office. 'Okay, so let's do this… Rubins, if you could do the honors.'

Rubins got up and started handing out a multi-page document. 'So these are the transcripts of the recordings. These were taken pre-David Thorpe – or, as the press named him, the coffee shop bomber. Some of the audio is a bit muffled.

Sounds like it was recorded next to water, maybe a fountain or something. But hopefully the type-out will help. You'll also find that some of Harry Gibson's questions sound leading. I guess that's because he needed to make sure that Chuck would hang himself.'

Rubins sat down and reached across to the device on the table and pressed play.

Top Secret.
Transcript 1.

Transcription of recording between Harry Gibson and Charles (Chuck) Harrison. Unintelligible phrases are marked with a question mark in brackets [?], followed by dashes signifying the estimated number of words that are unintelligible. [?——] means that approximately four words plus are unintelligible in the phrase.

Participants: **Harry Gibson**
                 Chuck Harrison
Recording time: 2 minutes, 45 seconds

Gibson Who is this guy anyway? Or rather what
        has this [?]---you.
Chuck   What's with all the questions?
Gibson Curious to know who I'm dealing with
        that's all.
Chuck   Being curious isn't something I'm asking
        you to do.

Gibson   Then how about you do it yourself.
         Because God only knows at this point I
         don'treally feel like there's much more I
         could lose anyway. It's [?]-- Chuck. This
         is some game [?—]
Chuck   I wouldn't say that, but what I would
         say, Harry, is be very careful. Threats
         are something I take real seriously…
         Here, take this.
Break in recording.

Gibson   What difference [?—] let's say that's
         what it is.
Chuck   You need to let that go, Harry. And my
         advice to you is to ease up on that
         temper of yours, it'll get you in a lot
         of trouble.
Gibson   How do you live with yourself?
Chuck   Just fine, Harry, real fine. What about
         you? Maybe you should be asking yourself
         the same question, after all it's not
         me who was found with my pants down in
         Saudi.
Gibson   [?—] Bastard! You son-of-a-bitch. You
         know that's not what happened.
Chuck   There's that temper again. Besides, I
         saw the photos the Saudi police took.
         Remember? You and those boys. Not a nice
         thing to see.

Gibson   I'll kill you, Chuck, one way or another
         I'll kill you.

Chuck   And then what? What will you do then?
         How long can you hide out in those woods
         without me? Face it, Harry, I'm your meal
         ticket. I'm your butcher, tinker and
         tailor. I'm your Momma. I'm your every-
         thing.

Gibson   Go to hell, Chuck.

Chuck   It won't be me going to hell, it'll be
         you. Back to that prison cell... How long
         do you think it'll take them until they
         send you back once they find out you're
         here? But this time there won't be any
         getting out. You'll rot in there for
         life.

Gibson   And why will I? Don't pretend you didn't
         set me up. I know what you did.

Chuck   I have no idea what you're talking about.

Gibson   Bullshit. That night, you *laced* my drink
         with scopolamine, why don't you just
         admit it?

Chuck   Because I don't have to.

Gibson   Just tell me why then? I was a damn good
         agent and I had a good life. A wife.
         Kids. And you took it all away from me.

Chuck   No, Harry, you did that yourself. You
         threatened to bring me down. Whistle-
         blow, like the dog you are. What was

446

I supposed to do? Just let you destroy
everything that I'd worked hard for?

Gibson What you weren't supposed to do is torture prisoners and question people under
such extreme circumstances. People died
because of the things you did. It was
inhuman.

Chuck Bullshit! They were Goddamn terrorists.
They deserve everything that happened to
them. Everything. I was protecting this
country and I needed to make sure those
scum bags opened their mouths and talked.
Whatever it took and whatever it takes, I
will do. And you, Harry, you were either
with me or against me. With me or with
them. And the minute I heard you wanted
to [?] — then I knew you were with them.

Gibson I was not with them! I was with my country, protecting and serving, but you,
Chuck, you went too far.

Chuck Going too far is what those bastards did
on 9/11, what they did in Florida, in San
Bernardino, Paris, Turkey, Belgium, in
Washington, Denver and what they're about
to do in Chatham, Illinois.

Gibson What are you talking about?

Chuck There's going to be a bomb, in a government building in Chatham.

Gibson How the hell do you know that?

Chuck Because they told me, that's how.

Gibson	Wait. What?
Chuck	The terror group behind Bin Hamad.
Gibson	What? You're talking to them?
Chuck	Negotiating.
Gibson	Now that's crazy.
Chuck	No, it's not, Harry. What it is, is a deal.
Gibson	A deal? [?—]
Chuck	Prisoner exchange.
Gibson	I thought President Woods ruled those out especially when it came to major terrorists.
Chuck	He did, but then that's what happens when you have a jack-ass for a President. This is a global war on terror, not a Goddamn contest to see who can be the biggest schmuck and biggest liberal sympathizer. My job is to protect this country, and I've got to do that as I see fit… With negotiations, I've managed to do deals and exchanges with Bin Hamad's group, that have not only seen some of our own men freed, but also helped prevent terror attacks on US soil. Do you know what it's like to have to work out which is the right move? Which move will be the lesser of two evils? No you don't, because that's my burden, Harry. So whatever it is President Woods has got to say to me about what I can or can't do, well I'm

not interested until he gets his head out
of his ass. There are a lot of powerful people who aren't best pleased with
the fact Bin Hamad is being imprisoned
without trial or charge. This is a game
of chess, Harry. Sometimes hands get tied
when you don't want them to be. But that
doesn't mean you don't see it for what
it is. If Bin Hamad's released, then the
attacks are called off. I had no choice.
I was doing it for the American people
because Woods wouldn't.

Gibson   You really believe that don't you? That
you're some kind of anti-hero. Well, let
me tell you, that's not a deal you made,
Chuck, that's blackmail.

Chuck   Don't be an asshole. If you want to be
precious about words, be my guest, but in
the meantime, I'll carry on saving this
country from unnecessary terror attacks.
There are enough home-grown terrorists in
this country, without bringing Satan to
our doors.

Gibson   But Bin Hamad? You're crazy.

Chuck   So I release him? So what? That will save
hundreds of American lives.

Gibson   You've played this one wrong, Chuck. Bin
Hamad will never stop. Once released
he'll be more powerful than ever. Come

	back with a vengeance that America has never seen before.
Chuck	Look, I know what I'm doing. There's been too many warnings already. That's why I need you. I'm going to get some of the roads closed down in Chatham, along with the government building where they've hidden the bomb.
Gibson	I don't understand. Why not just get the bomb squad in and defuse it?
Chuck	Because then I can't keep this whole thing quiet. It'll come out. There'll be investigations and before we know it, it'll become obvious who's behind it. And then it'll be impossible to go through with this deal, which translates to me not being able to protect this country from Bin Hamad's group.
Gibson	So you're going risk lives by not calling in the FBI? I thought you loved this country?
Chuck	Nobody's life will be at risk, the area will be closed down under the premise of a chemical spill.
Gibson	You got this all worked out, haven't you?
Chuck	That's why I'm the best. They'll think it's a home-grown terrorist. David Thorpe. He's known to the FBI, been on the No-Fly List. He's had strong affiliations with Boko Haram; he's done hate

preaching, and at one point tried to recruit online for a group he was running. I want you to give him the scopolamine you've been making. And then I want you to get him to drive a truck to the government building. It'll have explosives inside. After that I want him to go to a coffee shop, or somewhere obvious where he's caught on camera. Then I want him to go back home. The explosives will detonate and then once they do, the blast will be big enough to trigger the bomb planted in the government building. So all it'll look like is one big bomb blast. David Thorpe will then be picked up by the FBI, but then I'll have him taken into CIA custody, and from there fly him to the black site in Turkmenistan and go through the motions. I can blame the bomb and the suicide bombs on Thorpe and Boko Haram, and that way the Qataris and Bin Hamad are kept out of it... I reckon if we play hard enough, I might even get a confession out of Thorpe.

Gibson You're pure evil, you know that, Chuck?

Chuck   If it makes you feel better to think so, be my guest. I'm just part of the whole process. Just a link in the chain. And I'm also a realist, and David Thorpe's no innocent.

```
Gibson   He is when it comes to this.
Chuck    Technically, he won't be. He'll be on
         that CCTV for all to see. Driving that
         bomb to that building. Then boom.
Gibson   [?——] Funny? [?——]
Chuck    [?——] And everything stays quiet that way and
         nobody's focusing on Bin Hamad's group and
         then I'll have time to do what I have to do.
Gibson   How are you going to do that? How are you
         going to release Bin Hamad?
Chuck    You ask too many questions, Harry. Always
         makes me nervous when a man starts to ask
         so many questions.
```

End of recording

President Woods looked at Lyndon, then at Teddy, who had his head in his hands and then at Brent Miller who sat taking large gulps of oxygen. And the only thing Woods could think of to say was, 'Jesus Christ.'

Rubins said, 'There's one more recording which I think is really important to listen to at this point, if that's alright with you, Mr President? It's much shorter.'

Woods nodded.

Rubins said, 'Again, I've got a transcript here for y'all. The recording's exceptionally bad on this one. But I'm sure you'll get the gist of it.'

Rubins pressed play.

Transcription of recording between Harry Gibson
and Charles (Chuck) Harrison. Unintelligible
phrases are marked with a question mark in brackets [?], followed by dashes signifying the estimated number of words that are unintelligible:
[?—] means that approximately four words plus
are unintelligible in the phrase.

Participants: **Harry Gibson**
               Chuck Harrison
Recording time 45 seconds

Chuck   [?—] gun. I want a clean shot. Don't
         even leave the bullet.
Gibson   Will he be a problem?
Chuck   No, he's just some jerk off kid.
Gibson   Jesus. Then why kill him?
Chuck   Because he's got a big mouth, and he
         seems to want trouble.
Gibson   Why? What's he done?
Chuck   The kid's got a hobby. Does amateur seis-
         mology. Apparently he's got a recording
         of the bomb blast in Chatham and he's
         going around shouting about it. How there
         were two bomb blasts that day. At the
         moment nobody's listening to him, he's
         some kind of simpleton, but eventually,

	imbecile or not, if he makes enough noise for enough time, someone will start listening. So before that happens, I want you to get rid of him and the seismograph read outs he's got. Just go in, then out. Make it quick and make it fast… Oh, and Harry, you did well with the Senator.
Gibson	Yeah well, he was like putty in my hands. I have to give it to you on that one.
Chuck	It helps that the man's an idiot.
Gibson	You make it sound like it's personal.
Chuck	Harry, I've known the Senator for a long time, I've also had a few run-ins with him in the past. The man wouldn't know loyalty to this country if the Stars and Stripes fell down from heaven on him. But everything that goes around comes around. He's just a vain, greedy, power-hungry fool. And God forbid it comes out, well then what's he going to say? Because he won't remember anything, but then neither can he deny it – after all, he's the number two. So it'll either be blamed on his drinking blackouts or they'll think he was a willing participant. Either way, he'll be finished, Harry. Mark my words, he'll be finished.

End of recording

Without looking at him, President Woods spoke to Teddy. 'So the kid was right all along. Two bomb blasts. Two recordings.'

Teddy nodded. 'Poor kid... I take it we all agree it was probably Chuck who killed Gibson?'

Lyndon said, 'I have no doubt about it. Maybe Gibson was asking too many questions, or maybe it was the old adage, *he knew too much*... Senator, you really can't say where you got these recordings from?'

Rubins, with only the slightest hesitation, shook his head. 'They came into my possession from a source who's extremely reliable, and he was given them anonymously, anything other than that I don't know.'

Woods asked, 'Senator, would you be willing to do a polygraph test in regards to your involvement in the release of Bin Hamad?'

'Of course.'

Woods turned to Brent, who looked pale beyond his already pallid complexion. 'Miller, can you set that up for this afternoon?'

'No problem, Mr President, but if it's okay with you I'd like to ask the Senator a few more questions.'

'Fine by me.'

In the comfort of the Oval Office, Brent turned to the Senator, taking a gulp of air before speaking. 'So, there's nothing else?'

'No, I've told you everything I know.'

'But you haven't told us who you got them from.'

Rubins sighed in exasperation. 'Like I said it came from an anonymous source.'

'Pretty convenient, wouldn't you say? How do we know you're not hiding a whole lot more?'

'And why would I do that?'

Brent leant forward to tipping point. 'I don't know Senator, you tell me.'

'Look, I'm not the enemy here.'

Brent took another guzzle of air and aggressively said, 'No?'

'No.'

'And you're categorically telling me there really aren't any other recordings.'

'Absolutely. That's what I'm telling you. And that's the truth.'

Brent pushed harder. 'So we've heard everything there is?'

Getting annoyed by the barrage and accusations and tone, Senator Rubins' temper snapped.

'For God's sake this isn't one of your CIA interrogations. How many times do I have to tell y'all, that's it? I do *not* know any more.'

'If I find out, Senator, that...'

Woods cut in. 'Brent, that's enough. It won't help turning on ourselves. This is hard enough already.'

Cordially, Brent replied, 'Sorry, Mr President, I just feel very strongly about this, and the implications of what it means to our country. I need to make sure there aren't any other recordings, or any other evidence we haven't seen or heard.'

'I know, and I appreciate your input on this matter, as well as overseeing the imminent process.'

'It's my honor, Mr President, and the least I could do.'

Woods took a deep breath. 'Okay, well let's hear what Chuck has to say... Teddy, can you get Janice to show him in? And Senator Rubins, would you mind leaving the Oval Office by the other door? I'd rather Chuck not know you're here... And Senator? Thank you.'

91

Be2 Rel

Chuck nodded his head in greeting. 'Mr President... Hello, Brent, I must say this is a surprise. A *really* big surprise. You didn't mention anything about a meeting when I spoke to you the other day.'

Tightly, Brent said, 'No, I didn't.'

'But hey, here you are sitting on the couch looking... well, how should I put it? Looking all Brent-like...' He turned to look at the others and, with a greeting brimming with hostility, he added, 'Lyndon. Teddy... Well, well. This will be fun.'

Lyndon P Clarke knitted his brow. Furrowed it deeper until large, waved creases spread across the length of his forehead.

Woods spoke. 'I'd appreciate it if you could address me and me alone during this meeting, Chuck.'

Chuck gave a wry smile. 'Whatever you say. Where do you want me to sit?'

'Anywhere will be fine.'

Chuck squeezed himself next to Brent and using his elbows to dig out some space he grinned. 'Why, this is cozy.'

Woods craned forward in his chair, irritated by Chuck's blatant arrogance. 'I have a sense that you find all this amusing.'

'All what, Mr President?'

'Let me put it a different way. I always get a sense that you're just humoring us. Tolerating us mere mortals. You'll nod in all the right places and you'll make all the right noises, but the truth of the matter is you really don't have any respect. Not only for myself and this administration, but also for the integrity and ethical code of conduct for an employee of the CIA. You continue to mark out a circle around you, and within that circle you just do your own thing in your own way. It's almost like you don't even work for the CIA. You've created a divide. An intentional one, separating you from the rule of law.'

Chuck's eyes flicked round the Oval Office, his gaze settling on Lyndon. 'You paint a pretty picture, Mr President. Sounds very inviting. But that's not how it is.'

Woods' face was splashed with fury and over the sound of Brent Miller taking loud gulps of oxygen, he raised his voice. 'Oh, that's exactly how it is. We both know that, so why don't you cut the crap? The way you work is directly at odds with this government.'

Chuck answered calmly, his hostile stare firmly on Lyndon. 'I wouldn't say that.'

'No? So come on, Chuck, what would you say? What would you call your method of working?'

Chuck's supercilious and disdainful smirk, mixed in with a touch of feigned thoughtfulness, had Woods sitting on his hands so as not to get up and grab the acting chief of CTC by his immaculately starched white shirt collar.

'Unorthodox...? Sometimes my methods are a little bit unorthodox. But then the results are there to see.'

Woods snapped. 'It's not unorthodox, it's blatantly going against everything the CIA is supposed to be. Transparent...'

Chuck butted in. 'Transparent? That's a Goddamn joke. How can you expect to have an intelligence agency which is transparent? That's like inviting the terrorists to come and work in the mail room.'

Woods' anger filled the room, and this time he did stand up, and he paced and turned and pointed. 'You went against everything I said. You *knew* Bin Hamad was untouchable where prisoner exchange was concerned. I didn't sign any special orders. I didn't give you any permission, yet you released him. I'd call that treason.'

Chuck gave nothing away. Didn't flinch. No sign of stress. No discomfort or look of surprise. But Woods knew that came from years of being in the CIA.

Chuck just smiled pleasantly and glanced down at his manicured nails. 'Treason? Seriously? Mr President, what I did was negotiate a deal which was vital for making this country safe. That's why you gave me the job, and I did what I saw fit and what had to be done. To call it anything else just wouldn't be true.'

'I'd call it section 110 of Article III of the Constitution of the United States.'

Chuck said, 'You're really serious, aren't you?'

'Yes, I am.'

'Less than thirty people in the history of the US have had treason charges brought against them.'

'Then we can add you to that list. The legalities around

section 110 might seem arcane but I know treason when I see it,' Woods said.

'If I remember rightly, Section 110 of Article III says *treason against the United States shall consist only in levying war against them*... That's not even close to who I am and what I do.'

Woods gave a bemused smile. 'But it also says, *or in adhering to their enemies, giving them aid and comfort*... I think that's exactly what you've done, Chuck, by releasing a high value terrorist who was never on the table. By that action, you have given Bin Hamad's group *aid and comfort*.'

'Mr President, I reiterate what I said before, I was just doing my job. We have to win this war on terror, and we can't do that by just killing our way to victory. We have to be cleverer than that, which means covert operations and doing deals with people we'd maybe rather not do deals with. The CIA have always run covert operations.'

'Which the executive branch and select members of Congress should know about.'

Disdain carved Chuck's words. 'Then it wouldn't really be covert, would it?'

'Damn it, Chuck, you are *not* a one-man army.'

'Sometimes I feel I am. With respect, Mr President, you have continually undermined what the CTC has to do. If anybody *aids and comforts* the terrorist, I'd say that was you.'

Coldly, Woods said, 'You're not helping yourself here.'

'You're right, I'm not, but then I'm not here to do that. I'm not looking out for number one. So whatever it is you want to throw at me, go ahead. Whatever it is you want to accuse me of, I'm listening, and I'll also take whatever consequences come with that, but what I won't accept is you and those around you thinking that I was doing anything but serve this country. Five years ago there was an order signed by the office of Legal Counsel that legally authorized the CIA to do and strike as they saw fit.'

Woods pointed, his hand shaking with anger. 'And since I came into office that's been revised! As is how we go about collecting intelligence and dealing with terrorism. You have manipulated and interpreted extensions of the old laws to authorize new operations and deals with enemies of the United States.'

Chuck yawned. 'Oh please, the hypocrisy is painful to hear. In one hand you're carrying the liberalism torch and in the other hand there are the flames of an Orwellian government.'

'That's absurd.'

'Correct me if I'm wrong, Mr President, but every Tuesday you and I attend, along with a dozen security officials, a counterterrorism meeting, something your aides jokingly call *Terror Tuesday*. And there, along with the CIA, you go through photographs of terrorists like we're all playing a game of baseball cards. And then you decide which name is going to be on the kill list that week. In that meeting, Mr President, you not only have the power of the accuser, judge and jury, but also the executioner. Now tell me that isn't Orwellian.'

Woods managed to regain his composure, as cool and as calm as Chuck had been earlier. 'None of what you've just said changes anything. And you do realize that after this meeting, the CIA will be officially suspending you from all your duties, which Brent Miller will oversee?'

Chuck shook his head. Looked at Brent. 'Will he now? That is interesting.' Then with a contemptuous smile, added, 'Then throw the book at me. Hell, I'm willing to catch it. Do what you have to do… By the way, have you spoken to Senator Rubins?'

Woods feigned innocence. 'We wanted to see what you had to say first.'

'Okay, well I've said what I've said, and now you know. But I will say it all just feels like red tape to me.'

'Red tape? The only way this country sets itself apart from countries which are led by dictators is by the rule of law, not by the rule of man… Tell me, Chuck, where is he?'

'Who?'

The composure went straight back out. 'Who? Why, SpongeBob of course… For God's sake, Chuck, who the hell do you think I mean?'

He smiled as he answered. 'I take it you're talking about Bin Hamad?'

'Too Goddamn right I am. So come on. Where is he?'

'I have no idea.'

'Jesus Christ, Chuck, the man could be anywhere, planning any kind of attacks. How the hell can you have no idea where a major terrorist is?'

'I just don't,' Chuck said.

'You're lying.'

'I'm not. He was released and picked up by a speedboat, anything further I don't know… You want me to take a polygraph test, I will. Not a problem.'

'Chuck, you and I both understand very clearly that in your position you know how to pass a polygraph test with flying colors.'

'Then it's a bit of a stalemate isn't it? But that's what happens sometimes when you play chess, isn't it?'

*

With the meeting finished and Chuck gone, Brent Miller managed to say, 'Mr President, I'm curious, why you didn't tell him about the evidence we've got against him?'

Watching one of the White House cats stalking a bird on the lawn, Woods slowly said, 'We don't know how and if we might need him yet. I have to think... But Chuck's right on one thing: this is one hell of a game of chess.'

92

Bh5 Ra1

'I haven't heard anything back. The last time I spoke to him he said things were still under negotiation, and he couldn't say anything more but he'd be in touch. That was over a week ago, and now he's not even answering his Goddamn calls. I've a mind to go down there. If it wasn't for us, they wouldn't know anything about it, but now he's shutting me out. The man's got a Goddamn nerve.'

'Pass me that will you, Tom?' Maddie calmly gestured to the lead rein as she saddled up Cora's new pony in the outdoor horse arena, under the Arizona sun.

'She still need that?'

'No, but I do.'

'She'll be fine, she's a born horsewoman… So, what do you think?'

'I think she thinks she can ride just like her Daddy, and she's not interested in taking it easy or listening to me.'

Cooper gave a small smile. 'I'm talking about the Senator.'

'Well, maybe things aren't sorted out yet.'

Cooper raised his voice. Kept it up there. 'What things? Jesus Christ, Maddie, there isn't anything *to* sort out. They don't give a damn about those kids, and probably they're making some Goddamn deal with the Qataris as we speak.'

'Then maybe you should've told the Senator, or even *given* the Senator, that USB key. At least that way if we're right, they'd know where Bin Hamad was… Maybe that's what's slowing them down. Ever thought about that?'

'Chuck probably knows where Bin Hamad is.'

Maddie looked up. 'Yeah, he may do, but he may not. And even if he does, who knows what the guy will say? He'll be doing everything he can to save himself. You just need to tell them about Burkina Faso.'

'No.'

'Why not?'

'Because I don't trust them.'

Maddie looked at Cooper curiously. 'Tom, what are you talking about?'

'Nothing, just… Look, I'm going to go over there. Try to get the evidence we need.'

'No you're not! It ends here. We did what we had to and we handed what we knew over to the Senator, who's taken it to the appropriate people. We can't do any more.'

Cooper stepped in inches away from Maddie. Bent down to her face. 'Honey, there's always more.'

Barging past Cooper, and tying Narnia's reins to the fence, Maddie shook her head.

'Burkina Faso. Hear those words, Tom? Don't they ring a bell to you?'

'The only thing that rings a bell is the fact those kids have no one else but us. Jesus, Maddie, I'm not stupid, I'm going to try to get the evidence we need, and once we've got that then we, this country, will have to do something about it.'

'No they won't. And they don't. Not always. Everything is so politically weighed up and balanced.'

'I love you Maddie, but please don't lecture me.'

'Well, somebody has to. You're idealistic, Tom. And in one way that's a beautiful thing, but I'm a realist and I know even when kids are dying, if it doesn't suit their purposes to go in, governments don't.'

'So we just sit back and watch the horrors unfold?'

'Tragically, yes. Think most recently. Syria. Aleppo… Don't you see, Tom?'

Passionately, Cooper said, 'What I see is those kids *need us* to do something.'

'Tom, come on, don't be…'

'Dramatic? Is that what you were going to say?'

'No, it wasn't actually. But Tom, why do you do this?'

'Why do I do this? Me? What am I doing, Maddison? I know I've been a jack-ass recently but this is different. Because when did wanting to save those kids all of a sudden become a crime?'

'Of course it's not.'

'What is though is the whole world looking on. Tragedy after tragedy and all anybody does is say *what a real shame that is*, before they forget all about it and get on with their lives. But I can't forget it. Neither can I save the whole world. But I can do something about it. Like getting more evidence.'

'No, like telling the Senator where Bin Hamad is.'

'You just don't understand, do you? Oh brilliant, here

comes lover-boy… Count me out of here… I'll be leaving on Wednesday.'

'No! Tom! Wait! Just come back.'

Rosedale lifted his hat in greeting. 'Good to see you, Thomas.'

Cooper stomped past him. 'Go to hell.'

*

Leaning her body against Rosedale's, Maddie watched the cloud of dust from Cooper's car disappear over the cactus-lined horizon.

'He's going, Rosedale.'

'I guess that means so are you.'

She turned to look up at him. 'Are you crazy?'

'No. But he is. And I know you.'

'Not this time. We're talking about Burkina Faso.'

Lighting his cigar, Rosedale drew deeply then looked at the burning tip.

'We are honey, but we're also talking about you. Do you really think that you're just going to stay here while Thomas jumps on a plane to Africa?'

'I do. This time I do.'

'Baby, how I wish that were true. Because then it'd mean I didn't have to go either. *Unus pro omnibus, omnes pro uno.*'

'Portuguese?'

'Latin. And in some crazy-ass way it's exactly what you, me and Thomas seem to be, sugar, whether I like it or not… One for all, all for one.'

93

Nfe6 Kh6

'Hey, dude!'

'Coop!'

Jackson jumped up as Cooper put his head round the bedroom door, pulling him into the room for a big embrace.

'It's so good to see you. I've missed you.'

'I've missed you too, Coop. You've been off the radar.'

'You got my messages though?'

'I did, but it's not the same as seeing you in person.'

'Your Dad's not about, is he?' Cooper said.

'He's down in the West Wing, but he's coming up soon. We're going to shoot some pool and watch a movie later. You want me to see if he can come up now?'

'No,' said Cooper, too quickly.

Jackson looked hurt as he sat down on the large, wooden, French-style bed. 'What's going on with you two? Since that day you stormed out of here, you haven't been around. Has he done something to upset you?'

Cooper didn't really want to get into it with Jackson.

Realized he shouldn't even have mentioned John. 'Why don't we just leave it now?'

'Just tell me, Coop. What can be so bad that you don't want to see or speak to him? He keeps asking about you.'

'Jackson, listen to me. I love you very much, you know that, right?'

Sitting crossed legged on the bed, Jackson looked at Cooper warmly. 'Yeah, and I love you, man.'

'Okay, that's all that matters then. So just leave it… For me. *Please.*'

Jackson's mouth opened at the same time the door did. 'Great,' said Cooper. 'That's all I need.'

Beau's smile dropped and he tilted his head to one side. 'What are you talking about?'

Cooper turned to Jackson. 'Excuse me for a minute, I just need a word with *Uncle Beau.*'

In the hallway of the Executive Residence, Cooper leant towards Beau. He was angry, and hell he was going to let Beau know it. He hissed a whisper. 'Didn't John tell you?'

'Tell me what?'

'You really don't know? Jesus, that guy loves to keep a secret.'

'Coop, pull yourself together, you're starting to sound hysterical.'

'Thanks, Beau, always can depend on you for a bit of TLC.'

'You're a grown man, not a child.' Beau said.

'Even when I was, I still didn't get it, did I? Five a.m. runs when I was barely thirteen through the Missouri snows. Or how about the cold river swims, or the night treks without food or water, when all my school buddies where tucked up asleep in bed. That was your idea of TLC, was it?'

'I would say it'd made a man out of you, but clearly it didn't.'

Cooper went to grab his Uncle but restrained himself and instead hit the wall. Hurt like hell. 'I shouldn't expect different from you, should I?'

'Is this why you wanted a word with me so you could rake up the past?'

'I know,' said Cooper, with zero expression.

'What are you talking about?'

'I know you thought it was me who wrote those letters, and I know that you hid the fact there were three skiffs. How could you do that to me, Beau?'

'Jesus, Cooper, you really need to let that one go. It makes no difference how many damn skiffs there were.'

Cooper looked at his uncle, wide-eyed. 'No difference? To who, Beau? I always knew I saw three skiffs that day, but everyone said I was crazy. And you know what? Over the years I've questioned my own sanity, done things I shouldn't have done, and either pushed people away I shouldn't or taken them down the black hole with me. But now I know I was right and instead of it giving me peace, my sanity's being eaten away by guilt. I should've never stopped searching for her, and I blame you and John for that. Your lies helped me abandon her.'

'For God's sake, get a grip. That's not how it was.'

'Save it, Beau. I don't want to hear it. I don't want to hear any Goddamn thing you've got to say... I don't trust you as far as I could spit you. So now you need to stay out of my life. You and John. From now on, Beau, you and I are no longer... Now excuse me, I need to go and speak to Jackson.'

'Sorry about that.'

Jackson looked up from the book he was reading. 'Are you alright, Coop?'

'Not really, but I will be... Look, I'm going to head off.'

'But you've only just got here.'

'I know, and I'm sorry.'

'When will you be coming back?' Jackson said.

'I don't know. I got to go away.'

Jackson touched the angry scar on his forehead. 'Coop, you're frightening me now.'

'I need you to look after this.' Cooper handed Jackson the USB key. 'It's where I'm going.'

'Coop...?'

'If anything happens, then you give it to your Dad. But not before.'

'Happens, how?'

'To me.'

'Coop, whatever it is you're doing, please don't.'

'Just tell me you'll do that,' Cooper said.

'You know I will, I'll do anything for you but please, Coop, don't go. Look, man, I can't lose you.'

Cooper gave Jackson another hug but this time longer. Harder. He kissed him on his cheek. 'I love you but I got to go. If I don't, I won't be able to live with myself.'

94

Be8 Ra8

'No way, Maddison. Not this time, honey.'

'Daddy, please. I've got to do this. We won't be gone long. Cora loves being with you and Mom. It'll be fine.'

Marvin stood in his white cotton toweling robe, his Afro neatly tucked under a night time wave cap. 'That baby girl in there, she needs you. She needs her Momma but for some reason her Momma just can't see that.'

Maddie tucked her mop of curls underneath her baseball cap. 'Of course I can see that.'

'Then stay.'

'If I were a man, you wouldn't be saying this to me.'

'That's right. I'd be knocking some sense into you instead.'

Maddie sighed. 'Please don't make this harder for me. Why do you always think it's easy for me to leave Cora? Because it's *not* easy. Not one bit. I love her but I also need to do this. I wouldn't be going if I didn't have to. Trust me, I would far rather be staying and watching her ride Narnia. Anything but this... Look, I promise this will be the last time, Daddy. Something's got to give, I know that, but for now, just let me go with your blessing.'

Angrily, Marvin snapped, 'Don't give me that, Maddison, you just sound like that man.'

'He's got a name.'

'Yeah, one I wouldn't want to say in front of my daughter… It's always the same, isn't it? Always the last time with you. *This will be the last time, Daddy, I promise*… You know you've got some kind of sickness when it comes to him. Can't let him go. You don't need him any more, Maddison, you got Rosedale now. He'll take care of you.'

Putting her rucksack on her back, Maddie stared at her father. 'For God's sake Daddy, we're not in the nineteenth century, I don't need anyone to look after me.'

'You're so wrong, Maddison, everybody needs somebody. And I need you to be here and be safe… *Please*, just put your bag down and let Cooper do what crazy thing he has to do. Let him go.'

Maddie kissed her father on the cheek and headed for the door. 'The thing is Daddy, it's not about letting him go, I wish it was… It's about keeping him alive.'

95

Bc6 Ra1

In a cloud of red dust, under the Burkina Faso sky, the beaten up 1970s Ashok Leyland bus, crammed and packed and heaving full of people, came to an abrupt stop by a herd of long-horned cattle nibbling the last bits of grass stubble along the edges of the sandbank.

The electric folding doors on the bus were broken. They wouldn't close and they wouldn't open, instead they continued to bang in annoying repetition every few seconds against the scorching metal frame. Maddie and Rosedale stepped down off the bus, which proceeded to speed off before Cooper's feet had properly touched the sandy, hot desert ground.

Several dozen donkeys, carts and a caravan of camels, along with heavily-laden motorcycles went by, all kicking up dust. Rosedale bent and arched out his back and wiped away the dripping sweat from every possible part of his body.

'Jesus, they don't make buses like that anymore... So what's the plan, guys?'

'I think we should maybe look around a bit,' said Maddie. 'The fact that it seems to be market day couldn't be better. There'll be plenty of people we can talk to and get a feel for the area. Obviously we have to be discreet, but the people of Gorom-Gorom are known for their welcome, so I don't think we'll have a problem. We just want to get what evidence we can and get home.'

Cooper nodded. 'I agree. The wind is getting up, though, which will take away any kind of visibility. We'll only be able to see a few feet in front of us, if that. A pain in the ass if we want to go and find somewhere to pitch our tent. But hey, I guess that's the southern edge of the Sahara for you. Come on, let's go...'

The market was an imposing riot of colors and bustle, an assault of sounds and smells hidden in the remote, wild, beautiful landscape. And between the livestock being traded, the rainbow of hand-printed batiks, colored beads, crafted leatherwork and earthen jars, there was food laid out majestically in high piles on the floor. Dates and sweet-tasting fruit, fresh peanuts, millet seeds, beans and cassava, alongside a garden of herbs and spices.

'What's that? Qu'est-ce que c'est?' Maddie pointed and smiled at a velvet-skinned old woman, who sat hunched and cross legged on the floor, smoking a long, thin wooden pipe.

A toothless grin and a cackle of a laugh from the lady. 'Il est poisson séché.'

'Dried fish?'

'Oui.'

'You know, I think they're lungfish,' said Rosedale. 'You want a little fact?'

Cooper sighed. 'Do we have to?'

'Funny thing is, Thomas, those fish remind me of you. You see they bury themselves in the mud, hide away from the world, and can sleep out of water for years without moving or having any kind of sustenance at all. Like they're in a state of suspended animation. And you'd think they'd die, wouldn't you? Rot away. But just as you think it's all over, some rain comes by and fills up the river and damn it, there they are, flapping and fluttering and spluttering to get to that water. A one track mind, and nothing but nothing else matters.'

Cooper threw down the butt end of his cigarette. 'Oh my God!'

'Hey, lighten up, Thomas, I was...'

'Shut up, Rosedale. Look, over there... By the milk churn stall. There's a kid, you see him? He's wearing one of the yellow T-shirts...The same T-shirts the kids were wearing on the boat.'

With the wind getting up, and whipping red dust in their faces to hinder their vision, Maddie squinted and tried to protect her eyes. 'Are you sure?'

'Absolutely. Come on... '

The trio rushed, leaping over the mounds of food, swerving the stalls, and sprinted past the men holding the camels, waving their hands in apology as they barged past people. Then, speeding round the corner and stumbling over a pile of yams, Cooper caught a blur of yellow T-shirt through a cloud of red dust. 'There he is... quick!'

But without warning, a white flash of light and flames exploded, filling the air. Screams and shouts and torn limbs and flesh showered down, sending the trio scrambling back for cover as large plumes of smoke billowed up, mixing with the Saharan dust whilst blood rained biblically down over the stalls and the locals, who ran in all directions in a chaotic, mass panic.

'Oh Jesus!' Maddie yelled to Cooper. 'Look… Jesus Christ, the kid was wearing a suicide vest.'

They walked over to the small, smoking crater, where the shredded torso of the child displayed the remnants of the ragged yellow T-shirt, the device strapped to what remained of his tiny chest.

To the left of her, Maddie could make out a man who was scooping up a pregnant woman, whose legs had been blown off and instantly, instinctively, Maddie pushed herself from under the wooden stalls and ran over. 'Que pouvons-nous faire pour aider? What can we do to help?'

Speaking English, the man said, 'Across the road is the school house, bring the injured there.'

*

And for the next few hours the community of Gorom-Gorom, along with Maddie, Rosedale and Cooper, battled their way through the dust and the whistling whirling winds, carrying the injured and mutilated, covering the dead and laying them by the side of the road.

By the end of the evening the body count was forty-five dead.

Thirty women.

Ten children.

Five men.

Sixty injured.

*

Exhausted, covered from head to toe in thick red dust, Maddie, Rosedale and Cooper sat by the dead in silence, the wind howling around them, the sting of the dust barely registering as the horror sunk in.

The man from the market walked towards them with a tired smile.

'Thank you for your help... welcome to our country.'

96

Kf6 Kh7

The tea was prepared desert-style. Water boiled over hot, glowing embers, before being poured back and forth between a small black pot and an even smaller cup. Bittersweet and strong. But it was good, and exactly what the trio needed as they sat in the small hut with the Harmattan night winds raging outside.

Swallowing the OxyContin that Maddie had just secretively given him, Cooper listened to the man from the market – whose name was Moussa, and who'd once spent ten years living in Fort Greene, Brooklyn – talk.

'There are refugee camps everywhere because of the situation in Mali. They accommodate thousands of refugees, but it's put such strain on the area. Both politically and economically.'

Rosedale, on his third cup of tea, asked, 'Is there a lot of tension between the community and the refugees because of it?'

Moussa said, 'Thankfully not too much. The World Food

480

Program do what they can to help, but of course in a country like this, it isn't enough. Burkina Faso is already one of the poorest countries in the world. And tens of thousands of refugees fleeing the fighting in Mali, of course has generated further challenges. How to feed them as well as ourselves? It's created a huge problem, but it's the Fulani tribe who've suffered the most. For centuries they've travelled with their cattle, from one grazing ground to another in a seasonal cycle. But now their herds have dwindled to virtually nothing. The cattle are either dead from hunger, or livestock disease, or sold for next to nothing to raise money for millet. The grazing grounds have shrunk away to nothing because of drought, or been taken over by the refugee camps. It's all putting pressure on their way of life, and of course there's also...'

He stopped suddenly.

'Please, go on,' Maddie said.

Looking around as if someone was standing behind him, Moussa cautiously continued. 'Because of the training camp. The soldiers from there, they cleared a massive area. Smashing down villages, burning churches and houses. Killing whole communities.'

'And nobody did anything?'

'There was nothing anybody could do! This country doesn't have the ability to fight groups like that, and no other country is coming to our help. We've got no oil to make it worth their while, no minerals, nothing. All we have is ourselves and lots of sand. So with no-one rushing to our aid this place becomes a perfect breeding and training ground for terror groups.'

Rosedale scooped up the ground millet dumplings from the communal bowl which Moussa had put in front of them. 'But are the Fulani tribe *wanting* AQIM and Bin Hamad's group to take over? After all, the Fulani once established one of the largest Caliphates.'

Moussa laughed. 'You're going back a long time, Rosedale. But you're right; the Fulani Jihad was in 1804, and led to the Sokoto Caliphate. And then like so many things when the British came, it was abolished when they defeated the Caliph. Obviously there are a number of Fulani men who've joined AQIM or Bin Hamad's group, because of history, because of economic pressure or just because they believe in the ideology. But most just want to get on with their traditional way of life.'

Cooper rolled his tongue round in his mouth and tried not to sound slurred.

'What else can you tell us about the training camp?'

'It's run by a soldier who goes by the name of *the Commandant*. Another name I've heard him go by is Jihadi Al Begum. They say he's from Belgium. But I don't know for sure. Occasionally you'll see him around here, surrounded by soldiers.'

Cooper nodded. 'We've heard of the Commandant, but what about the other soldiers? Where are they from?

'I don't know exactly, some look like they're from Western Africa, some look more Middle Eastern. But what I do know is the training camp is for children. They're training them to become jihadists. The child who blew himself up today was the third in less than a month... The children are definitely are not from here. They're foreign.

We sometimes see them taken through here in lorries, herded like cattle... Look, why don't you get some rest now and, in the morning, I want to show you something which might interest you.'

97

Ng5 Kh8

'What have you got for me, Teddy? Something to make me smile? And if you can't make me smile, how about giving me a large, neat bourbon.'

Teddy Adelman sat down by the Roosevelt Desk, staring at his long-time friend and boss. 'I don't think I'm going to make you smile, and as for bourbon, no can do either. But I do come bearing gifts, Mr President... How about a sugared donut with cream and jam?'

'Are they the ones from the district doughnut shop on Eighth Street?'

'The very same.'

'And did you make sure they double coated the sugar?'

'Yes, I did.'

'Then what are you waiting for, give them here.'

*

Five minutes later, Teddy said, 'You got some sugar on the side of your mouth... Yeah, there... It's gone now.'

'Is it my imagination, Teddy, or have you Jheri curled your hair?'

'Yeah, but I'm not keen though. I'm seeing Shalamar and I should be seeing Vandross.'

'Maybe it's the moustache, have you ever…'

The knock, followed by Janice putting her head around the door, stopped Woods from finishing his sentence. 'Mr President, Lyndon Clarke is here for your sixteen hundred.'

'Great. Show him in… '

A moment later Lyndon P Clarke, walked in.

'Mr President, how are you? Teddy, how are you doing…? I like the hair by the way… Very Shalamar.'

Woods smiled. 'Take a seat, Lyndon… We'll just get straight to it. As you know I thought it was important to have another meeting as quickly as we could after speaking to Chuck. Basically, so we can decide what to do. And just to bring you up to date, as requested Brent Miller did a polygraph test on Senator Rubin. It was really just a formality, because as we thought it would, it came back inconclusive. Which, as we know, is what happens when a person has been exposed to scopolamine. On the one hand, the subconscious knows it carried out whatever action it was, and on the other hand the conscious part of the brain really does have no idea, which causes a conflict and an inconclusive reading. So we can just put that to the side. The main thing was David Thorpe. Teddy, do you want to update Lyndon?'

'Sure… We sent instructions to our site in Turkmenistan to send over samples of hair from our coffee shop bomber. We ran the tests, and it's positive for scopolamine. Not that we doubted that, after hearing those recordings, but it proves he's innocent.'

'So what are we going to do?' Lyndon said.

Woods rubbed his chin and gave out a long sigh. 'Nothing for now. We can't. And we don't really have to move on Thorpe until we've decided how we're going to proceed with Chuck.'

Teddy frowned at the President. 'I realize that to do anything with him now would be showing our hand, but, Mr President, Thorpe shouldn't be in there. He's innocent.'

Guilt turned into anger for Woods. 'For God's sake Teddy, you don't have to tell me that. I know what he is. He's another pawn in Chuck's game... Look, I'm setting up a meeting with Ambassador Majdi Shaheen, hopefully by then intel will have some idea where Bin Hamad is, and then we can do a deal, see what they want, because there's no way the Qataris will let us just go in and kill Bin Hamad. We don't want, and can't afford, a diplomatic incident. Then after that, well, we can relook at Thorpe... Have you got a problem with that, Teddy?'

'You know I have. Bin Hamad's a terrorist. Period. We should be able to do what we see fit. *In* the way we see fit.'

'He's not a terrorist in their eyes. As Shaheen says, Qatar takes personally that we're holding one of their nationals without trial. To them no trail equates to Bin Hamad being innocent... Though I don't think it would matter to Shaheen if Bin Hamad was caught with a ticking bomb in his hand. He's a sympathizer, but what can I do? He's the Ambassador to Qatar, who buy our weapons and host our military base. And the fact is they're probably still not happy with us descending on their stealth ship like we did, so we have to go in with baby steps.'

'Goddamn baby steps! It's a joke, Mr President!'

'Look, Teddy, I don't like it myself and believe me it's tough to even talk to Shaheen. There are just times I have to roll over like a dog. But that's the way it has to be. Irony is, it's situations like these when I think maybe Chuck just might have a point.'

98

Nde6 Ra6

The morning brought a river of dust, with the hot dry Harmattan winds blowing and bringing in the Saharan sand. Wearing head scarves to protect their faces from the whip and sting, the trio followed Moussa. Bent double, with minimum visibility, no-one spoke, preserving their energies as they battled through the extreme elements, not knowing when their journey would end, concentrating instead on not losing sight of the person in front.

By the time Moussa signaled to head down a craggy dune towards three shanty mud huts, they'd been walking for well over three hours. Mile upon mile through the wilderness of sand dunes, rough, sand-baked soil, and stone terrain.

At the door of the largest of huts, Moussa gestured for the trio to step inside. His words were only just audible above the wind.

'Welcome to America.'

Slowly unwrapping the dark blue scarf on his head, Cooper stared in amazement.

'Jesus.'

The whole hut was crammed with an arsenal of weapons and ammunitions, row upon row of grenades, MANPADS, M16s, M4A1s, M26s, submachine guns, anti-tank assault weapons.

Just as quietly as Cooper had spoken, Maddie asked, 'Are they all American made?'

Moving large hessian covers to expose more weapons, Moussa nodded. 'All of them. When the dust storms aren't up, it's easy to drive out here. And when the Commandant's men were raiding and clearing the land, their lorries came through Gorom-Gorom, full of weapons. What you see here is only a small part of the cache. There are a few more huts to the north where they're also storing arms, but those huts are guarded. According to some of the Fulani herdsmen, it's the training camp where most of the weaponry is. This is just surplus stock. Probably why there's no guard.'

Cooper whistled. 'It's like an Aladdin's cave. Even what's here is enough to equip a small army. This must be part of what Ismet's shipping. Goddamn unregulated arms trade. It's given advanced, American-made weapons to exactly the people we don't want to have them.'

Moussa nodded. 'Just last week some women were blown up on the road from Gorom-Gorom by children from the training camp with shoulder-fired missile launchers. People are really only travelling about now if they have to.'

'Which must be difficult given the fact a lot of people round here earn their living by trading at markets,' Maddie noted.

Moussa looked at Maddie, his face lined with torment. 'And nobody knows when and *how* it's going to end.'

Angrily, Cooper pulled back another large piece of hessian, uncovering dozens of tactical multi-purpose hand grenades. 'The people of Washington who've signed off billion-dollar military contracts to equip Qatar need to come and see this.'

'I doubt they'd be interested. This has always been the case, my friend,' Moussa said sadly.

'Man, it's a bitter irony that one day the US will have to fight against what they sold. American guns versus American guns,' Cooper said.

Rosedale, who'd been quiet until now, spoke to Moussa. 'Do you think it's possible to get near the camp? We need photos, evidence. Anything that we can take back and shake up the US government so they have to act.'

'Usually I'd say no, because the approach to the camp is totally exposed, but you've got the weather on your side. At this time of year, the dust storms feel as if they'll never end. The visibility will be too bad for anyone in the camp to see you approaching, but that will also be a problem for you. If the dust keeps up, to get your evidence, you'll probably need to get closer to the camp than you'd really want to.'

Cooper said, 'If that's what it takes, then that's what it takes.'

Moussa smiled. 'Some people might say that's the talk of a crazy man.'

'They might, and God knows, Moussa, in the past they have. But I say, never take on a crazy man who's got nothing left to lose.'

'Then, my friend, let us all be filled with crazy together. Let us dance on fear and dance with courage.'

'It's too much of a risk, Moussa, you don't need to do that,' said Cooper. 'You've been helpful enough.'

'It was written that our lives should cross. So now we travel as one. Your risk is my risk.'

'I don't know, Moussa.'

'Well I do, Cooper. Let us shake on it.'

Moussa reached out his hand and after a moment's hesitation, Cooper took it. 'Are you absolutely sure? It'll be dangerous.'

To which Moussa said, 'A ship is always safe at the shore but that is not what it is built for.'

'Okay, then… And welcome on board… Now all we have to do is figure out the plan.'

Moussa walked towards the entrance of the hut. 'With the weather as it is I think we should try to head towards the camp as soon as possible. It'll be the best way. If we wait, the winds might've dropped, which means so will the sandstorms. It'll take us a couple of days to get there in these conditions but then, hopefully, you'll get your evidence. And, God willing, the weather stays our friend.'

99

Be8 Ra8

Ambassador Shaheen sat at the large conference table in steely silence opposite Woods and Lyndon P Clarke. Sipped the sweet, black coffee which matched his immaculate, polished hair. As ever his presence filled the windowless Roosevelt Room with contemptuous disapproval.

The false skylight gave off a dismal hue, which only served to create an even more uncomfortable atmosphere.

'This seems to be becoming somewhat of a habit, Mr President.'

Woods gestured with his arms. Pulled a face. 'Humor me, Ambassador, I'm not quite sure if I understand.'

The rigidity of Shaheen's face was equaled by the stiffness of his manner as he pushed an envelope across the table to Woods. 'Mr President, once again, I find myself in a state of compromise, but more to the point as do the Emir's advisors. This situation we find ourselves in is regrettable to say the least, especially as you understand our position on Abdul-Aziz bin Hamad, as a Qatari national.'

'Ambassador, you have my sympathies when it comes to

difficult decisions. As men of the world and men who have families, often what we come across tests all our limits, our inadequacies, our integrity. The core of who we are. And sometimes we succeed, but often we don't. However, when it comes to this, this situation with Bin Hamad, well, I can't see what's difficult... He's a terrorist, Ambassador, and as of now, he's become a wanted one again. Thankfully intel seems to have information on his whereabouts. Though that still needs to be corroborated.'

Sucking out the fleck of macadamia nut from his front teeth, Shaheen sighed. Looked at Lyndon. Looked right back at the President and said, 'In that envelope is what we require. See it as a gesture of goodwill from our country. If you agree, then you have our blessing to take what you feel is the appropriate action against Bin Hamad. However, as is always the case, goodwill comes with clauses... We need your answer by tomorrow morning.'

100

Bh5 Ra1

In the early hours of the morning, Woods, tired, stressed and longing for sleep, looked around the table at those now present.

A dozen national security advisors.

His chief military advisor, Josh Hawking.

Lyndon P Clarke.

Senator Rubins.

Brent Miller.

Oxygen tank.

Holding the envelope Shaheen had given to him, Woods said, 'Before this meeting comes to a close, gentlemen, I'd like first to take a minute to thank Brent Miller for the integrity and commitment he's shown over this matter. *Especially* as he's been so unwell. He showed an extraordinary amount of determination to put his own health and convalescence to one side in order to put the safety of this country first.'

A round of applause followed and Brent put up his hand. Took a slug of air. 'I'm sure any one of us would do the same but thank you for your kind words, Mr President.'

Woods nodded.

'And now, as we're all in agreement with the Ambassador's request, I just want to check the timings with you, Brent.'

'I imagine as long as there are no unforeseen circumstances, Mr President, which I can't imagine there will be, I suspect the request can be achieved by... Maybe sixteen hundred hours? Hopefully before,' Brent said.

Woods turned to the General on his left. 'And what about the time aspect on the action we're going to have to take?'

General Hawking cleared his throat. Cleared it again. Took a sip of water and then decided whatever it was tickling the back of his throat wouldn't clear and, with a croaky voice, he said, 'I've discussed the intel we have with the Joint Special Operations Command and, just before the meeting, I had a quick briefing with Brent. The consensus is as far as we're all concerned it seems straight forward... I'd say we could be up and running within thirty-six hours.'

'Then let's do this, gentlemen,' said Woods. 'And let's make it good.'

101

Bg6 Rf1

'Hey Coop, it's Jackson... Come on, man, pick up the phone, dude. I'm worried about you.'

Beau sat on the end of Jackson's bed. 'Nothing?'

'Not a thing.'

'And he didn't say where he was going?'

Jackson's eyes flicked across to the USB key on his desk. He shrugged. 'No.'

'Are you not telling me something? Come on, Jackson, unlike the rest of us, you've never been good at keeping secrets.'

'There's nothing to tell.'

'Then why the concern about getting in contact with him? You know what he's like. He licks his wounds, turns off his phone, but as sure as day follows night, you'll hear from him... Unless of course you know something I don't.'

To which Jackson said, 'Like I say, there's nothing to tell.'

102

Ke7 Ra1

Chuck Harrison walked to his car in the secluded driveway of his house. Looked at his watch.

15.30.

Took a bite from the roast ham, mustard and fried egg baguette his housekeeper had made him. Thought about Harry Gibson. Decided he needed to go and speak to Brent Miller. God, did he just. Then, once he'd done that, he'd speak to Woods. Whether he believed or not. It all began to make sense now.

And satisfied he knew exactly what it was that had been bugging him these last couple of days, Chuck Harrison put the key in the ignition, sending the car up in a ball of orange and yellow flames.

103

Nf7 Kg8

Watching Chuck's car engulfed in smoke and flames on the screen at the CIA headquarters in Langley, Lyndon P Clarke, standing next to Brent Miller, picked up the phone to President Woods. He simply said, 'It's done.'

There was a silence before Woods asked, 'You think we've done the right thing, Lyndon?'

'I think we've done the only thing we could've done, Mr President. It was the only way the Qataris would've let us go after Bin Hamad. Plus, he was a liability. What else could we have done with him? We couldn't really lock him away, and we couldn't really have him walking about freely. Mr President, this really is the best outcome.'

'What? That we assassinated one of our own?'

'But that's not how the official line is going to be, is it? We're going to blame it on a lone wolf with affiliations with Boko Haram. Nobody will know different, and it'll sitwell with the story Chuck gave out about the coffee shop bomber, as well as the suicide bombs in Washington and Denver.'

'And just like that we leave David Thorpe to rot in a cell

in Turkmenistan? The man's innocent. It makes us as bad as Chuck, which is something he said all along.'

'Mr President, I understand your feelings about this, but for all intents and purposes David Thorpe is *not* innocent. He was seen on CCTV by the whole of the world. Driving that truck, then leaving it to explode.'

'Come on, Lyndon, the guy was doped.'

'What are we going to do? Suddenly tell everyone in fact he's innocent? That he was set up by the acting head of CTC, so that he could release Bin Hamad because it was the right thing to do for this country?'

Woods sighed with frustration. 'I'm not saying that.'

'With respect sir, that's exactly what you are saying. If anyone found out what Chuck has done, they'll want to rip the CIA wide open, and God knows what else they'll find there. I don't even want to think about the deals, the operations, the interrogations which go way beyond any red line.'

Woods said nothing.

'Look, we'll make sure that he's comfortable and who knows, in a few years it might be possible to release him and give him a new identity so he can live happily ever after in another country.'

'Jesus Christ.'

'Mr President, he isn't the first person to take a hit like this and he certainly won't be the last.'

Wryly, the President said, 'And that's meant to make it feel better *how*?'

'It isn't and it won't. David Thorpe is collateral damage and if we blame what happened on Boko Haram then we can stop a bad situation becoming your worst nightmare…

They're an easy group to blame, *especially* when we say it was a lone wolf who just slipped back into the shadows... The irony is, Chuck would probably approve. He'd undoubtedly see the joke himself.'

'Goddamnit, Lyndon, I wouldn't call it a joke.'

'Mr President, these are things we have to do to keep our country safe. It's a game of chess and it was our move... As Malcom X and – oddly, given his feelings towards Afro-Americans – as Chuck once also said... *by any means necessary.*'

104

Nh6 Kh8

'Are you okay, Mr President?'

Teddy Adleman stood in the 'sit' room down in the basement of the West Wing, looking with concern at his friend, as the milling presence of the National Security Council team surrounded them, and the six flat-screen televisions booted up, preparing for a secure video link. Staff busied themselves coming in and out of the NSC watch room, where officers sat behind two tiers of curved computer terminals, monitoring both classified and unclassified data from around the world.

With dark bags under his eyes, Woods said, 'I don't think a couple of hours sleep in thirty-six hours agrees with me. Hey, what can I say? I'm getting old, Teddy. And to tell you the truth, none of this sits comfortably. For me, it's the worst part of the job... Look, I'm going upstairs to see Jackson. Try to relax for thirty minutes before I'm needed here.'

'I think that's a good idea... And John, what you're doing, no matter how it feels, it's the right thing to do.'

105

Nf5 Ra7

'Who you on the phone to?'

Woods put his head round Jackson's bedroom door.

'No-one.'

'That didn't sound like no-one. Plus, you look suspicious. The same kind of look you had on your face when you'd done something wrong as a kid.'

Jackson got up from the bed and sat in the leather chair in front of his computer. 'Dad, please, I love you, but I'm not a kid, so if you wouldn't mind, some kind of privacy would be nice.'

'Okay.'

'No, Dad, can you close the door?'

Woods looked at his son warmly. 'You don't fancy a chat? I don't know about you, but I could do with one.'

'Give me five minutes and I'll be out.'

'Okay, I'll be in my room, but I have to go back downstairs in twenty minutes… You sure you're okay?'

'*Dad!*'

Laughing, Woods put up his hands in surrender. 'Alright, alright. I'm going.'

*

With the door closed, Jackson stared at the USB key.

Picked up the phone.

Dialled Cooper's number again.

'Coop, it's me... Why aren't you picking up the phone? What's happening? I'm worried, okay... Call me when you can.'

Then, with a quick outbreath of nervous energy, knowing he was doing something he shouldn't, Jackson reached for the USB key, quickly placing it in the side of his computer.

106

Kf6 Ra1

'Hey Jackson, what's with the knocking?' Woods wearily got up from his bed, opening the door for his son. 'Manners all of a sudden become important to you?'

'Mr President.'

Woods stopped. Stared at the two secret servicemen, clothed in black and carrying semiautomatic pistols under their jackets.

He frowned. 'Sorry, I thought it was my son... What's going on?' He looked at his watch. 'I've still got fifteen minutes.'

'Mr President, we have a problem.'

Woods looked from one to another. 'Which is?'

'There's been an alert down in the intelligence management center in the watch room. We've just detected activity of concern on the unclassified EOP network. We identified it coming from computer 2316/3. Mr President, we really need to check it to make sure there's no nefarious activity going on. We've shut down that part of the network.'

Woods began to walk down the Executive Residence

hallway, followed by one of the secret servicemen. 'What kind of activity are we talking about?'

'Sir, that's classified.'

Woods swiveled round, looking bemused. 'You're kidding me?'

'No sir, until we establish the security threat we aren't at liberty to say.'

'For God's sake Bob, not to put too fine a point on it, you came up into the Executive Residence unannounced, and want to discuss a computer which we use here in our home, and you won't tell me why?'

Looking as uncomfortable as he felt, Bob Wray said, 'That's the point. The activity of concern is coming from a computer which is used *exclusively* in the residence... It's just protocol, nothing else.'

'It's a good job I can be thick skinned then, isn't it? Otherwise I might take it personally... How's the family, anyway?'

'They're good, sir.'

'I'm glad, and I'm looking forward to seeing them all again when we have the next staff barbecue... Come on, it's down here.'

'Sir?'

'Yeah?'

Bob Wray glanced down the hall to make sure Jack Jones, the other secret serviceman, was out of earshot. He spoke quietly to the President. 'I shouldn't say this but the data activity we detected is a match for one of our code red targets. It's highly classified, sir.'

Woods opened Jackson's door.

'Jesus, Dad, couldn't you knock? I said, I'd be out in a minute.'

Without glancing at his son, Woods said, 'Wait a minute, Jackson... What?'

Bob Wray continued. 'It's an exact target match, but this data has come from an outside file. It's not one of ours, sir.'

Woods turned to look at Jackson who was hurriedly trying to take the USB out of the computer. Then he looked at the screen, and looked back at his son. 'What the hell are you doing, Jackson? What is it that?'

'Nothing.'

Woods' angry voice filled the room as he snatched the USB key out of the computer. 'Don't give me *nothing*. You better start talking. And fast.'

Jackson looked at Bob Wray. 'There's nothing to say.'

Woods' temper exploded. 'Bullshit! You're looking at highly classified information. Where did you get it?'

'I found it.'

This time Woods banged both his fists on the desk. Hard. 'For God's sake, Jackson. I need you to give me some answers right now. Do you understand? You're my son, sitting in the White House, and you're looking at a highly classified map of where Goddamn terrorists are. What am I supposed to think, hey?'

'That I found it.'

'Sir? Sir?'

'Not now, Goddamnit!'

Wood's Assistant Chief of Staff, Chris Maple, stood in the bedroom doorway. 'Sir, I'm sorry, you're wanted in the sit room. We're approaching target. ETA, fifteen minutes.'

Bob Wray said, 'Sir, I'm afraid we'll have to confiscate the computer as well as the USB.'

Woods was enraged. 'Just take the Goddamn thing, do I look like I care? Jackson, this is not over. You hear me? You have a hell of a lot of questions to answer.'

'Dad, you can ask me whatever you want, my answer's the same: *I found it.*'

'Sir, we really need to go.'

Woods continued to bellow. 'I'm coming! Whether it's the same answer or not, Jackson, that doesn't make it the truth. Seriously, you need to come up with something better than you *found* it. Jesus Christ, you're looking at an operational target match for a terrorist camp for God's sake.'

Bob Wray put up his hand. 'Mr President, I'm sorry but I have to stop this conversation, it's classified information.'

Maple said, 'Sir, we have to go.'

'Jesus Christ, I'm coming!... Jackson, I *will* be back.'

107

Ne3 Re1

Half way down the stairs which led from the Executive Residence to the ground floor of the White House, Jackson caught up with his Dad. 'I need to talk to you.'

'Not now you don't, but believe me, we *will* talk.'

As Woods continued to quickly run down the marble stairs towards the sit room with his Assistant Chief of Staff, along with the two secret servicemen, Jackson grabbed his arm. 'No, now! It's got to be *now*.'

Seeing the fear in his son's eyes, Woods nodded and turned to Maple, Wray and Jones. 'You go down, I'll be with you in a minute.'

Turning back to Jackson, Woods stared at him hard. 'This better be good.'

'The target you were talking about. Is the map on the USB key your target?'

'Jackson, I can't tell you that. Now I have to go.'

'You have to listen to me, Dad. You said it was an operational target match. And Chris said something about approaching the target. Please tell me you're not about to do some kind of strike there. Tell me anything but that.'

Woods looked at his son in a mix of confusion and exasperation. 'I can't tell you anything, Jackson, and you *know* that.'

Jackson dropped his Dad's arm in shock, backing away, a look of horror crossing his face.

'Oh my God! You are, aren't you? You're about to do an air strike. Dad, you have to call it off right now. It was Cooper who gave me the USB key. He's there, Dad. That's where he is. He's there, right in the middle of your target.'

108

Nd5 Rg1

'You got to stop the strike! Stop it!'

'Sir?'

General Hawking stood up as Woods, red-faced, eyes wide, charged into the sit room. 'I said *stop it*! Call it off!'

Lyndon P Clarke stared at Woods, 'Mr President, I'm not quite sure what you're saying.'

Everybody in the room looked at Woods, unable to process quite what was going on. He knocked the chair over, leant across the table and glared at Lyndon. He took a deep breath, wiped the sweat away and glanced at the screens. 'What part of *stop the Goddamn strike*, don't you fucking *understand*, Lyndon?'

'Mr President, what I *don't* understand is what has happened?'

'You don't need to understand, Lyndon, the General just needs to stop the strike.'

General Hawking walked around the table and spoke in a quiet voice. 'Mr President, perhaps we should talk outside. Perhaps you need a bit of air.'

Woods pushed past and ran to the screens, which showed real time aerial shots. Banged his fist against the wall. 'General, we don't need to talk outside, we just need to stop this.'

'Mr President, I can't do that.'

'You can and you will, General, Goddamnit! As your Commander-in-Chief, I am ordering you to stop the drone strike. Abort mission, now!'

'Sir, I can't, because it's no longer a drone strike, we've sent targeted missiles.'

'What? Why wasn't I informed of that? Who the hell gave the okay for that?'

Brent Miller coughed and gasped for air. 'The weather's too bad for the drones… so we programmed the coordinates. They'll strike in about two minutes.'

Woods pointed accusingly, his hand shaking. 'You don't think I know about Goddamn missiles? You can redirect them with seconds to spare.'

'To where, sir? Where do you want us to redirect them to? There is nowhere. We *can't* redirect hundred pound bombs to the surrounding areas. You got refugee camps and villages sir, that target's happening and it's happening right now.'

Woods spun round. 'Give me your cell. Anyone, just give me your cell.'

Teddy Adleman, who'd been absent for most of Woods' showdown, stepped into the sit room holding a can of Coke. 'Mr President?'

With his voice breaking and his heart racing and his chest tightening, Woods yelled, 'Give me your fucking phone, Teddy.'

'Okay… okay… Here, what's going on? John, talk to me.'

Woods ran out of the sit room, punching in a number from memory.

'John, what the hell is going on?'

Ignoring Teddy, Woods spoke into the phone, 'Coop… Cooper… Shit!'

'John!' Teddy said.

Still ignoring him, Woods pressed redial. 'Come on… Come on… Coop!… Oh thank God. Coop! Can you hear me? Coop?'

A faint voice was heard on the other end of the line. 'John? Is that you?'

'Listen to me, Coop, you got to get out of there.'

Teddy gestured to Woods. 'What the hell are you doing, John? You're breaking every security rule there is… John!'

'Coop, can you hear me? Coop?'

'… Just.'

'I haven't got time to explain, Coop, but there's going to be an airstrike. In thirty seconds we're going to hit with vengeance… We are sending hellfire.'

Cooper's voice screamed down the phone. 'You got to stop it, John! There are kids here. Do you hear me? There are kids here… Send a plane, anything, but do something.'

'I can't, Coop.'

'Then damnit, I can't just leave them here.'

Woods gripped the phone with fury and fear and love and pain. 'You're breaking up… Coop, are you there?'

'I'm not leaving them here, I can't do that.'

'Listen to me you stubborn son-of-a-bitch, I love you and… Coop!… Coop!… Shit!'

And as the phone cut off, Woods ran back into the sit room and looked at the screens, then he dropped to his knees as he watched the missiles carpet bomb the targeted area with screaming accuracy.

*

And on the other side of the world the missiles began to drop. Cooper, Maddie, Rosedale and Moussa scrambled back but there was no place to hide, only the barren lands which were being hit mercilessly and unforgivingly, as red and orange flames mushroomed and black smoke plumed, as they darted and ran blindly, unable to see through the sandstorm.

'Get the kids! The kids!' Cooper towards the tents in front of him whilst Maddie called to Rosedale and Moussa.

'I'll take these tents with Tom, you guys stick together. Search the tents over there. Okay?'

And without another word Cooper and Maddie ran.

Cooper charged ahead, he could hear the sounds of trucks speeding past and hear the sounds of the soldiers running and shouting, mixed in with the tormented cries of children, but he couldn't see them through the curtain of sand.

As he ran he tripped over the countless dead. Bodies of soldiers. Bodies of kids. The young and innocent who lay burnt on the ground.

He felt the heat of the crackling fire and faster and faster he ran as another missile impacted, picking him and Maddie off their feet, sending them twisting and turning on the ground. And they scrambled back up, battling against the maelstroms of emotions and chaos, whilst darkness descended from the skies, thick and black and choking.

'I can't see anyone!' shouted Cooper. 'Maddie, can you see anyone? Is anyone alive?'

She shook her head as she stared at the dust-covered dead. Children whose bodies were veiled in sand, looking like they lay in ancient graves, stretched out in front of her.

'Keep looking, Maddie, we've got to keep searching.'

Tent after torn and twisted tent.

Dead body after dead body.

Children burnt alive by the oceans of flames.

An atmosphere of panic sat in the air along with the smells and screams as torn body parts were scattered around like raindrops in the desert of the dying.

'What are we going to do? Maddie, what are we going to do? Oh my God, did you hear that?'

Maddie swirled towards the noise and immediately the two of them set off running in the direction of the sound of coughing.

On the ground lay a little boy no older than eight. Quickly Cooper knelt down, holding the boy's head up and feeding him the bottle of water Maddie had hurriedly given him.

Cooper spoke softly, gently to the boy. 'Don't move, sweetie. Try not to move.' And he watched the tears run down the boy's face and the fear fill up in the child's eyes. His flesh hung off, ripped away from his tiny body, and the wounds were so deep Cooper could see the bone. His life, slowly ebbing away.

Cooper held him, and Maddie knelt by him, and Rosedale, who'd just appeared, crouched next to him and watched as he shook as shock set in.

Maddie looked up at Cooper. 'He's in so much pain, Tom.'

'My tablets. Give him my tablets. Quick!'

'They're too strong, Tom!'

'He's dying, Maddie, let him at least die without pain.'

Nodding her head, frantically, Maddie rummaged into her rucksack, pulling out a blister pack of pills. She passed it to Cooper and, his hands red from blood, he broke one out. Gently he placed it into the boy's mouth, then gave him water.

'I'll go and see if there's anyone else,' Cooper said.

Moussa shook his head. 'No, you stay here, I'll go.'

Cooper handed the rest of the pills to Moussa. 'Here take them, you might need to give them to the others.'

Moussa looked at Cooper doubtfully. 'If there *are* any others.'

With that, Moussa left. Cooper continued to hold the boy's head in his lap. He held him closer. Rocking him as the boy shook with pain. 'My daughter's name is Cora. She's five years old, and when she gets scared, she likes me to tell her about the man in the moon and how the man in the moon came tumbling down too soon and…'

A gurgling sound from the boy stopped Cooper's next words, and he watched as the child's eyes rolled and went back into his head, as blood filled his mouth and his face turned white. Knowing that this was the end, Maddie leant across and kissed the boy's cheek before she looked up at Cooper. 'He's dead, Tom.'

Placing the boy gently on the ground, Cooper refused to feel what he was drowning in.

'I'm going to see if there are any more.'

Rosedale kept the emotion away from his voice. 'I think Bin Hamad's men have rounded most of the kids up and driven off in the lorries… They're either gone or dead.'

'Then I have to know that for certain, and for myself.'

Speeding off, Cooper charged back through the burning camp, stumbling and tumbling over tent ropes, banging into objects he didn't know were there, whilst waves of heat and sand hit his face.

He was hurting now and his body tiring, but he kept pushing forward, trapped in a sea of sand with no escape.

Pulling back the flap on another tent, Cooper froze.

A little girl stood at the back, her eyes wide with fear.

Slowly moving towards her, Cooper's voice was soft and warm. 'I'm not going to hurt you… I promise… Please, take my hand.'

The girl said nothing and Cooper edged slightly closer, which made her stand further back, pushing herself into the walls of the tent. Cooper knelt down and put out his hand, urging her to trust him. '*Please.* Come with me.'

Trembling she shook her head and pointed, but Cooper turned around too late.

The Commandant came in, holding a machete, and he lunged at Cooper. With the benefit of surprise, the Commandant was able to wrap his arm round Cooper's neck. Pulling him backwards in a tight choke hold. Forcing and pushing the blade towards his face.

Struggling, the men continued to fight. Cooper tried to break free but as he gasped and fought for air the chokehold was getting tighter. The whites of his eyes becoming red.

Cooper fought hard, trying to push off twenty stone of

weight, but he was held down. Pressed down. His strength giving way as the blade came ever nearer to Cooper's face.

In the corner of his eye, Cooper spotted something.

Urgently, he slid his hand towards the knife to the side of him, stretching and straining his fingers, but it was too far away. Too far out of his reach to get it. And then... then like magic, he felt the round leather handle of the knife placed gently into his hand. Quickly he looked up to see the girl crouching, gently pushing the knife towards him as fear engulfed her eyes.

Cooper exchanged the briefest of glances with her. He held the knife tightly before driving the blade hard into the Commandant's neck. Thrusting it in. Forcing it into the thickness of muscle. Tearing the flesh as he gouged the blade in. Round and round. Blood oozing and pouring as the Commandant let out a gruesome scream, his body falling hard on top of Cooper.

Rolling from underneath the Commandant, red with blood, Cooper looked at the girl and smiled. 'Thank you... You saved my life... My name's Cooper.'

In a hushed voice the girl whispered, 'My name's Amira.'

He crouched down and the warmth of his gaze held in his voice. 'Hello, Amira. It's good to meet you.'

She held out her small hand which Cooper took. 'I want you to trust me. Do you think you can?'

She nodded her head.

'Okay, great, well, let's get you out of here.'

*

They ran together holding hands to where Rosedale and Maddie and Moussa were standing with ten other children. Cooper smiled at them but spoke to Moussa. 'Is this it?'

He nodded. 'That we can find. The others are all dead or loaded up onto the trucks already. They must have used the trucks we heard to take them out of here. Part of me hopes the lorry carrying them wasn't blown up by the airstrikes, but the other half of me thinks maybe death for those children was the kindest option. Their only chance of freedom.'

Cooper put his head down at the enormity of Moussa's words. 'Jesus Christ.'

'It's tragic, but if we want to get out of here alive we need to go ourselves. Once the sand storm drops we'll be seen. We *have* to go.'

'Back to Gorom-Gorom? That would be too dangerous *and* too far for the kids,' Cooper said.

'I know… but if we can manage to get them to walk a bit, we might have a way out… I've got a plane. A small one. I haven't used it for a while but it's about an hour's walk from here. Maybe more in this weather. We could fly it across the border to Nigeria. There's Embassies in Abuja, and good hospitals. I think it's the best place for these children…'

One of the children wailed. Cooper turned to see blood pouring out from the shoulder of a small boy, who collapsed in pain. He ran to him. Scooping him up into his arms as Maddie encouraged the other kids to follow her.

To keep on going.

To keep on running.

Faster and faster.

Rosedale turned to Cooper as he ran, looking at the child in his arms, screaming with pain.

'Thomas, give him the pills for God's sake! Give him some of your pills!'

'I haven't got any left.'

'What?'

'Moussa gave them all out.'

'What about your spare ones? The ones Maddie doesn't know about. Have you still got them?'

Cooper shook his head as he stumbled through the sand, trying to ignore the weight of the boy in his arms. 'No.'

'Well, where the hell are they?'

'They're finished. I took the last ones ten –' Cooper stopped suddenly. Without words he gave Rosedale the boy to hold. Quickly he ran a few paces away from them, before turning his back and crouching and thrusting his fingers hard down his throat to retch and vomit up the pills.

His stomach lurched up its contents and Cooper hurriedly searched through the watery vomit.

A few seconds passed then jubilantly Cooper was able to recover three, still-whole green capsules from the yellow bile. Quickly pouring some bottled water from his rucksack over the tablets, to clean them of vomit, Cooper ran back to where Rosedale was standing, and gently gave them to the boy. 'They should help him with the pain, at least for now.'

Satisfied, Rosedale nodded. 'Come on, Thomas. We have to keep going… Come on, kids.'

But they were young and little and traumatized and tired, and the sand and the wind blew, and Rosedale looked down at the child who ran by his side. And in that moment he threw his rucksack down and leant his six-foot-five frame towards the boy and smiled the biggest smile.

'Here, kid. Get on my back. Jump up. I'll give you a ride.'

With the injured boy in his arms and the other little boy on his back, Rosedale, along with Cooper and Moussa and Maddie, carried the children, stopping every so often to change and swap, to let another child take a rest from the relentless desert storm.

They gave encouraging words to the children as they battled through the rough terrain and the heat of the desert, whilst their vision was nothing but sand. They sang and talked and hoped somehow their journey would soon be at an end.

Finally, exhausted and having travelled for over two hours, Moussa shouted to the others.

'The plane, it's over there by the hut.'

Squinting through the storm, Rosedale stared in dismay at the old plane, which stood covered in sand, looking like it hadn't been flown for years. 'Jesus, Moussa, I thought you said you had a plane.'

Running up to it with one of the children on her back, Maddie quickly scanned the plane.

'It's fine. It's a way out of here. We'll have to instrument fly, the vision's non-existent. It'll be dangerous to take off, and in a plane like this the sand will seriously affect the flight, but what other choice have we got? For all we know there'll be another air strike, and we've no idea if Bin Hamad's men are still in the surrounding area. Plus, some of these children need urgent medical attention. So, given what we're up against, it's our best chance of getting out of here alive.'

'That's if we can even get the plane off the ground. It's only meant to carry four, maybe six people at the most. There are fourteen of us,' Rosedale said.

'Yeah, but it's our chance.'

'I don't think it'll even be that. Seriously, Maddie, the engine will be totally damaged by ingesting all the sand, once we're up in the air.'

'Let's at least try.'

'And what if we crash, Maddison? What then?'

Maddie stared at Rosedale. Behind them they heard the plaintive wails of the wounded children. 'Better to crash than be killed here... Come on, Rosedale, will you go with me on this? It's a chance, however slim to get those kids out of here.'

Rosedale looked at Maddie. He closed his eyes then slowly nodded.

'Okay. Let's do this.'

Hurrying into the small cockpit, with Rosedale helping the children onto the plane, Maddie called to Moussa, 'Throw me the keys.'

A pause. A cough. Then Moussa spoke. 'I... I haven't got them.'

'What?'

'I didn't bring them, Maddie.'

'What are you talking about?'

'We were only supposed to gather evidence, so...'

'So you left them and you didn't think to tell us when you suggested the plane? Jesus, Moussa.'

'I'm sorry...Maddison, I'm so sorry.'

Realizing she shouldn't take out her frustration on

Moussa, Maddie backed down, speaking warmly to this man she barely knew, but who had risked his life for them. 'Look, it's fine... never mind. You don't need to apologize. You have done so much for us. It's an old plane, so it should be alright. I should be able to get it started... Rosedale, can you see Tom yet?'

'No, but he'll be here. He was only a few meters behind. Best thing we can do is get this plane up and running.'

Not bothering to say anything, Maddie knelt on the floor of the cockpit, feeling the shake of the plane as the desert winds blew. Knowing old planes were easier to hot-wire than any car, she pulled and dragged at the dash, which gave way easily in her hands, exposing the wires she needed. Then, skilfully bypassing the ignition switch, she called to Moussa.

'You have to hand crank the propellers. This thing won't work otherwise, because of the way I've had to override it... You okay with that?'

He gave a thumbs up then gripped one of the propellers, gathering momentum before he swung his body down whilst Maddie opened the throttle and closed the cowl, and the engine spluttered and shook to a start.

Maddie looked around. Was it her imagination, or was visibility getting better?

As she began to turn the plane she could see Cooper appearing through the diminishing clouds of sand.

'Tom! Tom! Hurry! Come on!'

With the sandstorm beginning to die down, Cooper stumbled forwards until he saw the plane. He tried to go faster but his body craved for the pills. It shivered and trembled and his legs and muscles became heavy. Cramps and pains tore through him, as he staggered along with the children on his back. Harder and heavier they felt. Cold sweat dripped down, washing his face of the sand as his head began to swim.

'Thomas, run! Behind you! Run!'

He quickly turned round and there on the horizon, running down over the hill like buffalo, were Bin Hamad's soldiers. Charging and shouting as the plane began to slowly move along the rubbled earth.

'Thomas, run! Run!'

Putting down the two children, Cooper shouted instructions. 'Go! Go! Go, Amira. Run! Run for the plane.'

As the children ran for the plane, Cooper pulled his gun from its holster and pointed it at the approaching soldiers. His hand shook and his vision was blurred, but then... then he saw what was in front of him...

Calling from the plane, Rosedale cried out. 'Thomas, shoot! Shoot for God's sake! What the hell are you doing?'

'I can't! I can't, Rosedale. Look, they're only kids! I can't...'

'Just shoot, Goddamnit!'

'No!'

He dropped his gun and watched as the children approached, and he put up his hands, ready to die... And then he felt someone else. Standing in front of him was Amira, holding the gun he'd dropped and, as if time had slowed down, he watched as she expertly took off the latch and aimed then fired...

'Amira, no! No!'

The bullets flew and struck the young soldiers. And one by one the child soldiers dropped to the floor and then, suddenly, slowly, Amira began to slump to the ground. Cooper caught her as her head lolled back and her tongue lolled out and blood seeped and flowed, her eyes staring right at him.

He cradled her in his arms and rocked her gently. 'Amira... Don't you die on me... Amira. You hear me? You need to stay alive so you can meet my little girl... You'd like her, and I know she'd just love you... Amira, you gotta stay awake, *please*... Amira! Amira!'

And the little girl for a moment held his stare, and a tiny smile appeared on her face, before the wind blew and her eyes closed as her life ebbed away.

'Thomas, come on! Come on! For God's sake, come on!'

In the distance, Cooper heard Rosedale's voice and for a moment he didn't move.

'Thomas, damn it, come on!'

He glanced around at the plane, then turned back to Amira, and gently laid the little girl's head down on the sand as more of Bin Hamad's soldiers appeared on the horizon. Cooper began to run.

He followed the plane but his legs began to give up underneath him as his body shook and cramped. He held his stomach as he tried to run, and Rosedale gestured and shouted, leaning out of the open plane door. 'Come on, Thomas! Come on! Run!'

'Go... Just go!'

And without a moment's hesitation, Rosedale jumped out of the plane and stumbled and fell to the ground. But he got back up, slipping and sliding in the sand, running across to Cooper, aware of the soldiers approaching, and conscious that Maddie was trying to slow down the plane as much as she could.

'I got you, Thomas, I got you.'

Rosedale scooped Cooper up, throwing his body over his shoulder then sprinting with all his might towards the airplane.

With Moussa now leaning out to help, Rosedale pushed forward, running harder and leveling himself with the plane's open side door, and with one almighty effort he managed to heave Cooper's battered body off his shoulder and into the taxiing plane. Straight away, Rosedale threw himself at the open door, as Maddie began to accelerate for take off, and he scrambled and cycled his legs in the air whilst Moussa pulled and heaved him inside.

The plane flew up. Shuddering and shaking and flying through the sandstorm as bullets fired up from below and Maddie battled with the controls, trying to steady the plane. And Rosedale looked at Cooper, who sat shivering amongst the few remaining children.

He passed him a drink, and with sweat dripping from him, Rosedale gave a warm, genuine smile.

'Thomas J Cooper, you will be the death of me. But what can you do? Unus pro omnibus, omnes pro uno. One for all. All for one.'

109

Bf5 Rf1

'Jackson, it's me.'

Jackson Woods gripped onto his cell phone. Closed his eyes and silently mouthed *thank you* before he said, 'Are you okay?'

'If you mean *am I alive*, yeah.'

'Where are you?'

'Emerald Isle.'

'North Carolina?' Jackson said.

And as Cooper stood, bare feet on the cold white Carolina sands, the place he'd once come to scatter his Momma's ashes, the wind blew and he looked out across the sea.

'Yeah. I haven't been here for a long time. Too long. Perhaps I'll bring you here one day... Look, I'll see you real soon, and Jackson... always know I love you.'

110

Ndf4 Ra1

'Oh God, Coop! It's so damn good to see you. Jesus, you had me worried for a moment back there. I can't even begin to tell you how good it is to see your face. When I heard you were okay, well… What I mean is… Christ, I'm not good at this. Just come here and let me give you a hug.' John Woods stretched out his arms as Cooper walked up the quiet hallway of the Executive Residence.

He stood in front of John.

Face to face.

Man to man.

Son to Father.

Then he clenched his fist and punched Woods right in the mouth. Sent him stumbling to the floor.

'That, John, is for all those kids you left out there. Abandoned. Bombed. It's about the handshake you made with the devil… You know in that camp alone there were three, four hundred kids? And you know how many we were able to save, John? Do you?'

Woods touched his bust lip. Shook his head.

'Ten. That's all. Ten kids, who we took to the Turkish Embassy in Abuja. The rest, John, we were too late. Either taken by Bin Hamad's men to God knows where, or bombed by you in your off-record strike. Because it was, wasn't it? Off record.'

Still sitting on the floor, John mumbled, 'I can't tell you that.'

'You can't tell me? You Goddamn bastard, I was there! I know what you did. But of course you wouldn't and couldn't let the world know that you were bombing kids.'

'Jesus, Coop, what do you take me for? I was after Bin Hamad. And we got him. He's dead. Which means our country will be a safer place for it.'

'What? Are you trying to tell me you didn't know there were kids there? I even told you.'

'No, I… intel said… Look, we weren't certain.'

'You weren't certain? But you thought there might have been a possibility, right? But you still went ahead with the operation.'

'I don't know, Coop… Look, like I say, we weren't certain.'

'Shall I show you certain? You want to see certain?' Cooper opened his jacket. His khaki shirt red with dried blood. 'See this… This is certain. This was from a kid. No older than nine. Her blood, John. She died in my arms, and you know why? She was trying to save me! You hear that? A kid trying to save *me*. Which is more than you did for them.'

'You don't know what you're talking about. When I realized you were there, I tried to stop it… I tried to stop that Goddamn strike. I did that for you.'

'I don't need you to save me, John. Never have done, never

will do. It was those kids you needed to save. They were the ones who paid the price. And this blood on my shirt, is blood on your hands... I hope you can live with that, John, because I can't...I'll see you around.'

111

Ng6 Kg8

'Teddy, tell me you haven't come to make my bad day even worse.' Woods sat behind his desk with his feet up, looking out across the White House lawn from the Oval Office window.

'What have you done to your lip? Looks nasty.'

'Don't even ask... So, come on then. Tell me. Tell me what today is going to bring.'

'Okay, are you ready for this? They're looking to impeach.'

'What?'

'Some key Republicans heard about what happened in the situation room. They're going after you, John. But look, they're never going to succeed. Even if they get it through the House of Representatives, the Senate will never find you guilty.'

'Are you kidding me? They hate me up there... Is it just talk? I mean, how far have they got with it?'

'It's such a long process to impeach, you know that, but the Republican Party are ready to form a select committee to draft the articles for impeachment.'

'Based on what?'

'A whole bunch of nothing,' Teddy said.

'I said, based on what?'

'On Section 110 of Article III.'

Woods looked mystified. 'For treason?'

'Yeah, but like Chuck said, nobody *really* gets charged with treason.'

'Oh my God, you're quoting Chuck at me? The irony. That man will be looking down from whatever heaven or hell there is and laughing hard.'

'Look, they're grasping at straws, John, it's more about embarrassing you.'

Woods sucked on his lip and quickly regretted it as a sharp pain went through it. 'I think it's more than that, don't you? Come on, I broke every rule in the book, calling someone and telling them about a mission which was just about to happen. The watch room will have heard everything. You know that there are sensors installed in the ceilings to detect cellular signals and record them. It doesn't look good, does it? First there's Jackson looking at highly classified information from an outside source. Then there's me, giving out America's secrets. Jesus, Teddy, even I can see their point. The mail man could see their point. I was talking to somebody, on an unsecured line. I could've compromised the mission, helped our enemies, put people in danger. The list goes on.'

Woods stopped. Slid his feet off the desk. Sent the bowl of M&Ms shooting through the air.

'Goddamn it, Teddy. If I was them, I would impeach me too.'

'Which brings me to another point, John. They want to know who exactly who this Cooper is.'

112

Ne7 Kh8

Maddie, Rosedale and Levi stood opposite Granger in his office. Lined up like school kids as he pointed his finger along the row. 'I don't know what it is you guys have been up to, and to tell you the truth, I don't want to know. But I will tell you this: I am just about ready to get rid of you all. You're more trouble than you're worth. If I find out you've done *anything*, and that's *anything* to put this firm, my business in disrepute, then God help you all. You understand me?'

Rosedale pulled on his cigar. 'Easily.'

'You being funny, Rosedale? Because you'll be the first to go, right along with the foot print of my boot on your ass... Anyway, why I wanted to see you all is there's a job which has just come in for you. A fleet of planes unpaid for. It's a guy who works for the Nigerian government. You interested? Though it's probably best you just take it. I don't think spare time and you lot bode well. The devil makes work for idle hands.'

Rosedale smiled. 'Don't be too hard on yourself, Granger.'

'Right, that's it! I am sick... Oh, I wondered when you'd show your face.'

Cooper stood in the doorway. Leant against the side. Cigarette in his mouth.

'Have you ever just tried just being nice, Granger?'

'And have you ever tried just being sober, Cooper? You're high, aren't you? Popping those Goddamn pills... Look at the state of you.'

Cooper swayed and stumbled and staggered across to where Maddie, Rosedale and Levi were.

'Tom, why don't I get you home? Why don't you come to the house to see Cora, she'd love that,' Maddie said.

Slurring, Cooper smiled at Maddie as he spoke to her. 'I don't need to go home, Maddie. I need to know why he finds it so hard to be nice. There are so many bad things and bad people in the world and all you do, Granger, is make it a whole lot harder.'

Standing up from behind his desk, Granger walked around to Cooper. 'Get out! Get out of my office. Out of my sight. You're through.'

'Well, isn't that funny? Because the thing is, that's what I was coming here to tell you. I'm through. I quit.'

'He doesn't mean it,' Maddie said.

'Shut up, Maddison.'

Rosedale's eyes narrowed as he looked at Granger. 'Careful, Granger. I don't appreciate you talking to her like that... And Thomas, you need to take Maddie's advice, just go the hell home and sleep it off. We can all talk in the morning.'

Ignoring Rosedale, Granger growled out his words. 'You

are nothing but a mess, and a whole lot of trouble. Everywhere you go, trouble follows you... I even had that man looking for you again. The official looking one. Wouldn't say what he wanted. Wouldn't say where he was from, but I do know if it's anything to do with you, it's gotta be a whole heap of bad. You're a mess, Cooper... I don't know what my daughter ever saw in you.'

A flash of hurt pooled into Cooper's intoxicated eyes. And a moment later, Thomas J Cooper left the room.

'I'll drive him home,' said Levi. 'Don't worry, he'll be okay.'

'I hope so, Levi. I really do.'

113

Ng5 Ra6

'Look, why don't I come inside? I could rustle up some food or just watch some TV with you.'

'Go home, Levi. Go home to Dorothy. I'm fine.'

'But… '

'I said, go home!'

Cooper got out of the car and, holding a half empty bottle of whiskey, staggered to the front door of his ranch.

*

'Levi, didn't I tell you to go home! And if you have to knock, knock quietly!'

Cooper pushed himself up from the couch. Kicked the bottle of pills out of the way. Bleary eyed and wired and bare chested, he pushed open the door of his ranch. A new bottle of whiskey in hand. 'Levi, for Christ…'

He stopped.

'Lieutenant Cooper?'

'Yes.'

'I've been looking for you, Lieutenant. You're difficult to find. I went to your work place a couple of times but nobody knew where you were. I spoke to a man called Granger. I didn't want to leave a message... I've been trying to track you down for some time now.'

'Well, now you've found me.'

'I wanted to see you before I left...I'm going to live in Italy with my fiancée.'

Cooper took a swing of whiskey. 'Swell.'

The man put out his hand. 'Sorry, I haven't introduced myself. I'm Officer Rowling. I was a helicopter pilot serving on the USS *Abraham*... I served on there for six months. I was there on the day of the incident involving the yacht and the pirate skiffs... Can I come in? I think what I have to say may be of interest to you.'

114

Kf7 Rf6

Ambassador Shaheen smiled. A big wide smile that failed to reach his eyes.

'Brent. This is a pleasure, and also something of a celebration for you, I think.'

Brent Miller nodded. 'It worked out well and I appreciate your assistance in this matter. It could've become very difficult.'

'For you, perhaps, but we were happy to help nonetheless.'

'And I'm grateful. Chuck had become a liability to me. He stopped wanting to play the game by my rules. He took too many risks. Made too many mistakes. Harry recording him being one of the biggest. It was only luck that I wasn't mentioned on those tapes, but I knew the minute Senator Rubins brought me them, I had to do something... So my gratitude goes a long way.'

The Ambassador smiled cloyingly. 'I always think that gratitude is an overused and somewhat pointless sentiment. Thanks is what we do in our *actions*, not in our words. But I have no doubt you're sincere, and therefore I'm quite certain that when the time comes we can rely on your assistance as a way of showing your *gratitude*.'

Tightly, Brent said, 'I thought we were good now.'

'So we're good, rather than grateful?'

'What I mean, Ambassador, is we're even. Chuck and I helped to coordinate the release of Bin Hamad. Of course it was unfortunate how events turned out, but I did as requested. Then you *in turn* helped me get rid of Chuck by asking Woods to get rid of him. And as we both knew, the US government would have no choice but to agree to the request. After all, once they'd discovered Bin Hamad was released they were desperate to take action, but they couldn't afford a diplomatic incident or your country pulling out of multi-billion dollar deals… That, Ambassador, is what I call *even*.'

Ambassador Shaheen stayed silent for a moment. 'Do you know what stalemate is, Brent?'

'Yes.'

'Well, that's where we all find ourselves. The whole world is at an impasse. Where no progress can be made and no advancement is possible. One minute it's your turn, the next it's mine…'

Brent turned to walk out of the room but the Ambassador stood and blocked his way. 'I think Chuck underestimated you. He let down his guard. He let you take a turn when it was his move.'

Before answering, Miller took a gulp of his oxygen. 'I just needed to get rid of him before he brought me down with him.'

'That's right. Always get rid of the people who know too much... Don't you think, Brent?'

Brent's manner spelt unease. He muttered and shuffled and strained. 'I do.'

'You know what Chuck's real mistake was? He really did believe he was doing what was right for the country. You, however, are much more straightforward...Power and greed. The eternal flames of desire.'

'I take offense to that. I love my country, Ambassador.'

'Don't fool yourself. Never do that. We're all the same. You don't need to apologize for it... But Brent, don't make the same mistake as Chuck... Never let down your guard.'

115

$\frac{1}{2} - \frac{1}{2}$

'What the hell? Are you kidding me? You better be God-damn kidding me. Get out of here. I don't want to see you.' The wind blew and the rain fell and Cooper stood, wet and swaying with the effects of the pills and booze. 'Do you know what time it is, Cooper?'

'I know and I'm sorry but I really need to speak to you. You got to listen to me.'

'Where you're concerned, I don't have to do anything. Now get the hell off my porch. You hear me? I said, go! You want me to get my gun?'

'Granger, hear me out.'

'And why would I want to do that?'

'I promise I'll go. I'll leave you the hell alone once I've told you what I came here to say… I saw that man.'

'What man?'

'I saw Officer Rowling.'

Granger growled. 'You're talking gibberish. Now go on, get! I haven't got time for any of this.'

From inside the house, Granger heard his wife calling him. 'It's no-one, honey... Go back to bed.'

Wrapping his robe tightly round his grey pajamas, he stepped down the porch stairs. Poked Cooper hard in the chest. 'I already told you, you're finished, and you turning up here has just put the seal on it.'

Wide eyed and still high and desperate to say what he needed to, Cooper stood his ground. *'Please*, hear me out... Officer Rowling. He was a helicopter pilot on the day of the accident. Served on board the ship. He told me that a few days after it happened, Beau ordered a secret search and rescue operation to Mogadishu. Officer Rowling said the reason he ordered it was because Beau knew there were three skiffs, not two, but he kept it quiet due to mistakes made during and immediately after the accident. So he tried to make it right by getting a small team to follow up some intel reports. By all accounts, a woman had been seen in Mogadishu with a group of known pirates. She fitted the description. Blonde. Blue eyes... Beautiful...

'But when they got there and were ready to execute the rescue, the situation quickly became too dangerous because of a counterterrorism mission operating at the same time in the same area. So they were ordered to pull out, even though they had visuals... They left her there. Never went back. Beau told them to bury the report, he never wanted anyone to find out he'd ordered a search... But what he didn't bank on was Woods digging out the report years later, so he pretended he didn't know anything. I don't know, maybe over time he felt guilty, and wanted to tell me, so I'd stop torturing myself... But he just didn't know how to.

'But that's why Officer Rowling came to find me. He couldn't live with it. He says that day of the operation, and leaving her there, still haunts him. The look in her eyes gives him sleepless nights... But he was certain it was Ellie. I showed him a photo of her... Granger, it was Ellie... She's *alive*. Your daughter's alive.'

ONE PLACE. MANY STORIES

Bold, innovative and
empowering publishing.

FOLLOW US ON:

@HQStories